LUCY'S LAST HONEYMOON IN HAVANA

SCOTT JAROL

Copyright © 2018 by Scott Jarol

All rights reserved.

No part of this book may be reproduced in any form or by any electronic or mechanical means, including information storage and retrieval systems, without written permission from the author, except for the use of brief quotations in a book review.

❀ Created with Vellum

For Nancy

A WORKING VACATION

After six hours in the air, Lucy wasn't about to leave their chartered plane until she'd refreshed her makeup and hair, which left Desi plenty of time to smoke a couple of cigarettes and flirt some more with the starstruck stewardess. It also gave their ersatz camera crew time to get out and size up the security situation.

They could have flown to Havana in three hours, Lucy thought grumpily as she fluffed the flat spot in her hair where she'd napped with it crushed against the window. But Allen Dulles, the CIA director, had given orders to bring them in from the west, as if they were traveling directly from Los Angeles. He must have assumed, or at least hoped, that Castro wasn't smart enough to guess that US intelligence had invited themselves into his scheme. Made no sense, but it was Dulles's show.

Desi looked out the window. "I thought he said he would keep things quiet. There must be three hundred people out there."

"Maybe that's quiet to him," Lucy said, peering past him. "You've seen the crowds that turn up for his speeches."

"I hope he's not planning a meet and greet with all those people."

She had tried to dream up every conceivable excuse to wriggle out of this government junket. She'd been looking forward to the time off for herself and the kids. It had been a grueling season. Their own show was enough work, but now that Desilu had nine shows in production, Desi was also dealing with contracts, actors, tradesman, and every kind of equipment breakdown imaginable. Up until a couple of months before, he'd been drinking more than ever. To calm his nerves, he said. She'd nag him about it. He'd drink more. Divorce or no divorce, if Desi didn't get back on his feet, the studio was heading for disaster. Thankfully, he'd been sober for a couple of months. Time would tell.

Maybe this Cuba contract was what they both needed. Despite her objections, which she'd expressed so relentlessly over the past few weeks that even she was getting tired of her own whining, she'd begun to look forward to working with Desi on a little project again. So what if it was a propaganda film for an emerging communist dictator? You couldn't have everything. The subject matter wasn't so important as the chance to work side by side on a scrappy little film without the stress of managing a union crew, dealing with wardrobe, hair, makeup, and pleasing a live audience. No bright lights. No network executives. No sponsors, even, unless you counted their host. Just a travelogue, really. Maybe Desi's natural surroundings would bring him some peace, help him stay on the wagon. And there was always a chance they'd find a fresh creative spark, like the one that had ignited their romance.

Desi turned to look her over. He peeled back his lips. She rubbed away a lipstick smear from her own teeth and pressed her scarlet lips together once more to even them out. He gave her a curt nod. They stepped through the hatch onto the landing of the aircraft stairs.

HOME ALONE

Same story. Darlene, Lucy's personal assistant, said Desi had gone to the club. Oh, well. At least he still had the courtesy to let her know. Sometimes she thought it was better when he passed out on his couch and she didn't have to wonder what, or whom, he was getting into. Sobriety had unintended consequences. Not that it mattered much—not for her, anyway. Better for the kids, though.

Lucy finished removing her stage makeup. She tried to resist putting on a fresh face, but she couldn't bear the thought of being out in public with no makeup at all, no matter how briefly. She asked Darlene whether her driver was waiting, then put on her street clothes and hurried out to the car. Another episode in the can.

The moment she walked into the house, she could hear the kids giggling. She found little Lucie, Desi Jr., and her mother, DeDe, on the sofa watching Jack Paar.

"You let them stay up too late again," she scolded. She sent the kids to bed and told them she'd be up in a few minutes to tuck them in.

DeDe looked back with not one ounce of defensiveness. Lucy marveled at her mother's aplomb. She hadn't said one word, yet she'd already changed the subject.

"Why are you looking at me like that?" Lucy asked.

DeDe crossed her arms. "Where is he?"

It was a rhetorical question. Always the same point.

DeDe shook her head and went back to watching Jack Paar.

After saying good night to the kids and changing into comfortable men's-style pajamas, Lucy went to the kitchen to make herself a sandwich. As on most final shooting days, she'd skipped food altogether. DeDe came in and took over, so Lucy sat down at the kitchen table and began reading the evening *LA Times*. Her mother finished making the grilled cheese and slid it in front of Lucy with a cup of tea.

Lucy set the tea aside. "Do we have any orange juice? I want to sleep tonight."

"It's only tea." She poured a glass of juice for Lucy and took the tea for herself.

"It keeps me awake."

"You have plenty of time to rest."

"I've never looked so forward to a hiatus. I'm beat."

"The kids miss their mommy."

She wondered whether that was true anymore. She brushed some bread crumbs from the pages of the folded paper and took a big bite.

"Three weeks now without a drink?" her mother asked.

"Mmm-hmm, unless he's found a druggist to cook up some antidote. I'd smell it on his breath."

"You should give him the benefit of the doubt. He's never tried before. Albert'll keep an eye on him at the club."

She finished her sandwich in silence, and her mother cleared the plate and mostly empty glass. Lucy brought the paper with her to the living room, arranged herself among the deep ruffled cushions of the settee, and continued reading.

Her mother followed her, drying the freshly washed glass with a dish towel. "It's not the end of the world, you know."

Lucy looked at her quizzically.

"It's written all over your face. Those worry wrinkles make you look a dozen years older."

"Very comforting."

"You're assuming the worst."

"You're not being realistic."

It was an impossible choice. Together, she and Desi were a household name. The studio was booming—nine shows in production. He needed her creative instincts as much as she needed his razor-sharp business sense. If they split up, that would be the end of it. He'd be happy banging his bongos and every broad on both coasts, while she'd haunt Hollywood, another washed-up Sunset Boulevard maven, rich and forgotten. At least she'd have time to be a real mother.

"You spend too much time feeling sorry for yourself." DeDe wasn't one to pull punches. "He's got more to lose than you do. He's been riding your coattails for years. It's a wonder he's still alive. The booze should have killed him years ago."

She flopped the paper into her lap. "That's an awful thing to say."

"Only because you still love him. If you weren't so blind, you would have walked away a long time ago."

"The only reason we're here in this house, on this street, in this town is because I didn't."

"You don't know that. You've worked hard since you were a kid. Don't give him more credit than he deserves."

It wasn't as if she hadn't replayed her life over and over again in her mind. Like a game of backgammon, she'd considered all the alternatives. A different throw of the dice could have changed everything, but somehow she and Desi had always beaten the odds. Together, they were a force to be reckoned with. Separately, they might just fade into obscurity like every other Hollywood has-been. But she was too young to throw in the towel. And maybe she didn't need to. If he could give up booze, they might just find a way to make it all work again.

"You've got plenty of bookings," DeDe said.

She grimaced. "Let's hope it's not a farewell tour."

Her mother held up the glass to the light to inspect it and nodded, finally satisfied. "Something'll break—that is, unless you're determined to give up."

NO PROMISES

Desi stepped out into the street and raised the wide collar of his suit jacket, not so much for warmth but for disguise. Celebrity was intoxicating but inconvenient when you preferred to avoid detection. George Burns had told him once, with vaudevillian wisdom, that it was all about misdirection, like a card trick. Distract the audience with flash and you could pull off just about any deception.

He walked the wrong way for a couple of blocks, partly to throw off any paparazzi but just as much to get a little air after filming. He needed a leisurely smoke in the cool night air to get the buzz out of his head. For the past couple of weeks since he'd knocked off the booze, he'd been finishing off a couple of packs a day. Every season felt eternal, with little time for himself, and when he did have a few hours off the set, the attention was always on Lucy and the kids. Not that he was complaining about success. Who knew he'd end up running a studio? He just couldn't always suffer the grind.

Before he could turn the corner onto Sunset, two men approached him from directly ahead. He ducked under the brim of his hat and started across the street, but it was useless.

"Mr. Arnaz?"

He could pretend he was someone else, but that never worked anyway, and these two clearly weren't tourists or autograph hounds.

"We need a word, sir."

He had expected this moment. Lucy was still keeping an eye on him.

"Boys," he said in his most charming Latin accent. "What can I do for you?"

"It's an important matter," said the shorter man.

He had no desire to waste another minute with a couple of private dicks. "Listen fellas, whatever my wife asked you to do, it's a waste of time—yours and mine. I'm heading for the club to relax."

"You think we're PIs?" asked the shorter man.

"What else?"

"We'd have to be pretty poor excuses for detectives. You think we'd show ourselves if we were trying to catch you chasing tail?"

He bristled at the man's crass accusation, no matter it was true. "Then we have no business."

"Are you familiar with the House Un-American Activities Committee?"

Desi didn't bother to protest or declare his innocence. This wasn't about him, not directly. Once you got the commie stink on you, it was almost impossible to scrub it off. "Yeah, sure. You do know this is Hollywood, right? Congressman Walter is well known in this neighborhood. Remember, my wife was cleared six years ago. Besides, I thought the committee was on its way out."

"The congressman has taken a renewed interest in Ms. Ball and her family."

"My wife's grandfather was a kook with some unpopular opinions, none of which are shared by my wife or me. Tell the congressman we'll send him some autographed photos and tickets to the show." He was only half joking. Lucy's past would haunt him for good, with or without a divorce. "You two work for Walter's anticommunist crusade?"

"We're independent."

"So you're PIs?"

"Not that independent," said the taller man. The shorter man produced a leather wallet containing an ID card and a badge. CIA. These fellas were a tougher breed than they'd faced last go-around.

"You think we're Russian spies or something like that?" Desi asked.

"We're here to call in a favor."

"You could have fooled me. Didn't you just threaten my wife?"

"Not a threat," said the shorter man.

"Just a reminder," said the tall one.

"Funny," Desi said. "You two don't say much of substance. Seems like I've done most of the talking. No wonder they call you guys spooks. Very tricky."

"It's our specialty," said the shorter man. "A craft, really."

The taller man stepped closer. "Mrs. Ball—"

"Arnaz." Desi tapped his wedding ring. "Mrs. Arnaz."

"Yeah, Mrs. Arnaz… She got the easy treatment. Now Walter wants a little reciprocity."

"One scratch deserves another, so to speak," the shorter man said.

"What's the payback? An anti-Red PSA? We don't make propaganda films. Strictly entertainment. Make people laugh, you know, to take their minds off Russian A-bombs."

"Close," the taller man said.

"We've intercepted a message from an old friend of yours," the shorter man said. The taller man handed Desi an open letter-sized envelope. "He sent you an invitation."

Desi unfolded the letter and tilted it to catch more light from the streetlamp. "This is who you're calling 'an old friend'? Fidel Castro?" Just because they'd grown up in the same town and attended the same school didn't make them friends. They weren't even the same age. "Let me guess again. He wants to send us a screenplay."

"Close again," the shorter man said.

"Not exactly," the taller man said. "More complicated. He wants to make a film—in Cuba."

"And what would that have to do with me? Of course, maybe I'd know if you hadn't stolen my mail. By the way, isn't that a federal crime?"

"Federal crime." The two men shared a grin. "Castro knows how popular you are. He figures if you tell the story, Americans will understand what a big favor he's gone and done for his people."

Mierda! Desi threw his unfinished cigarette to the ground and spat at it before crushing it to shreds with the tip of his shiny wingtip. "How could that bastard think I would have any interest in promoting his lies? He's scum. A low-life, power-hungry son of a bitch."

The shorter man looked up at his companion, and the two nodded in agreement. "No question."

"Then why are you wasting my time?"

"Opportunity," the taller man said.

The shorter man continued. "He wants you to make a film. It's the perfect chance to get inside. Suss him out. Point your cameras maybe in places not in the script. Collect some info."

Desi looked them up and down. "I'm not the spy here, and even I know that's exactly what he'd expect."

"Exactly. You're not a spy, and neither is the missus, so he'll think he can control everything you see, hear, and smell—even what you think. It'll make him cocky. Let his guard down."

"And then what?"

"Who knows? All you have to do is get some footage. Our people will comb through it. He's bound to show you things he thinks are unimportant."

Desi crossed his arms, pursed his lips, and pretended to give it serious thought. "My wife won't agree."

"We hear you're the businessman in the family, a negotiator. Convince her."

Just what he needed—another reason for Lucy to get her claws out. She wasn't in much of a mood lately to listen to anything he had to say. "You think anyone can talk my wife into doing something she don't like?"

"I wouldn't know," the taller man said, "but if anyone can, you'd be the one."

"My wife's not like that," said the shorter man, shaking his head.

Desi narrowed his eyes. "Like what? What are you saying about my wife?"

"No offense," the shorter man said. "I mean, my wife, she's no big movie star. She's a housewife, a mother. She leaves the big stuff to me. I imagine Mrs. Arnaz is not like most wives."

"You bet your ass."

The men laughed uncomfortably.

Desi offered them a smoke, which the taller man declined. He snapped open his lighter and lit the other man's cigarette first. "It's a bluff."

"It's a favor. None of us want the Reds in our own back yard. The president would appreciate it."

"The president. You didn't say nothing about the president." He took a dramatic drag on the cigarette and blew the smoke up into the shaft of lamp light. "Like Sinatra."

The men nodded and smiled at his theatrics.

It was getting later by the minute. Anything to end this little chat. "I'll talk to her." He smiled wryly. *Funny story, sweetheart. You'll never guess who I ran into tonight. How about we kick off our new lives with a tropical getaway—on Uncle Sam's dime?*

The taller man handed him a card. "Enjoy your evening, Mr. Arnaz."

He pocketed the card without a look and continued on his way. "No promises," he added over his shoulder.

PAYING THE PIPER

The front door lock turned slowly until it clicked. Desi came in with one hand on the knob while holding a business card in the other hand at arm's length.

Lucy glanced at the mantel clock: ten past three. She wasn't surprised. "Try your glasses. No one's going to see you in the middle of the night." She had tried to go to bed earlier, but couldn't sleep, so she'd come back downstairs and fallen asleep reading.

"That crazy grandfather of yours," he said.

She rubbed her neck, stiff from the awkward position in which she'd been sleeping.

"Aren't you a little curious?" he asked.

"About what?"

"Why I'm worked up."

"You're always worked up." She stood and straightened her robe. "I'm going to bed."

"This is serious."

"And that's what you always say. Armando leaves the band—you're upset. The studio needs a new roof—you're upset. The network wants to change the contract—you're upset. Berle has a better deal than you —you're upset."

"This is different."

"Okay, it's different." She wasn't sure whether to be happy he'd come home before dawn or annoyed that he was still keeping her awake. "What on earth are you babbling about?" He was probably just dreaming up another news flash to preempt the regularly scheduled argument.

He waved the business card. "We're going to Cuba."

"Who's 'we?'"

"Us. You and me."

She stood and faced off with him toe to toe, sniffing.

"I'm not drunk."

That might be true. She could smell no booze on his breath. She should be appreciative, she supposed, if only he could make it home without monkey-wrenching his absence with crazy talk.

"First of all, I'm not going to Cuba," she said. "Second, we couldn't go if we wanted to. We have to start preproduction on the variety show." She tilted her head. Desi had little contact with his extended Cuban family or childhood friends, but once in a while a bit of news would reach him. "Did somebody die?"

"That's cold." He sank into the sofa and kicked off his shoes.

"That's the only reason you could possibly want to go down there."

"I turned down the variety show. And as far as I know, it's because of your grandfather."

He might have been on the wagon, but the damage was already done. "You're making no sense. What does Grandpa Fred have to do with the show?"

"There's no deal. They wanted us to eat all the production costs. I said we wouldn't. That was it."

So the Cuba story was a stomp on the foot to distract her from the piano he'd just dropped on her head. "You turned it down without telling me? That was my project." There was more to it than Desi was saying, and she knew it. With their divorce pending, CBS must have gotten cold feet. Jim Aubrey had been looking for a way to weasel out of the deal.

"It was a bad deal. Too risky. Grandpa Fred put us in this predicament."

"Grandpa Fred passed sixteen years ago." She shivered and pulled her dressing gown closely around her.

"It's because of that membership card of his." He held a cigarette between his lips and patted his pockets until he found his lighter. "It's the government. We have to go, or they'll subpoena you again."

"For what?" She burped quietly behind one hand. It wasn't just the orange juice giving her heartburn.

"They found more things." He sank into the sofa, slouching with his legs stretched out in front of him and his head resting on the back, eyes to the ceiling.

"Things? What kind of things?"

"How should I know? Someone says something. This one talks to that one. That one wants to make a name for himself—reel in a big fish."

"I'm no communist."

It didn't matter. She had dreaded this day. Once they got hold of how Grandpa Fred had talked her into registering socialist, they'd hold it over her head until they could put it to some sort of use. She and Desi had talked about it. What would happen to their careers now? TV was all they had. If she ended up on the list, that would be the end of them for sure, divorced or not.

"Yeah, well," Desi was saying, "that makes no difference to the feds."

"So what do they want?"

"CIA says we go to Cuba. Make a movie. Get some good pictures. No more investigation. No hearing. No nothing."

This would be a PR nightmare. She slumped back on the divan and lit a cigarette. "What makes the feds think Castro will let us show up with our cameras and start shooting a picture?"

"It's his idea. He asked for us." He slipped the envelope from his inside coat pocket and handed to her.

She put on her glasses. The two-page letter was too long to read every word, but she got the gist of it: Their names at the top. An invitation to make a picture. Signed by Castro with a fountain pen.

"What will people think?" she asked, more to herself than to Desi. "How are we supposed to explain why we're making a movie in Cuba? No matter what we do, we lose."

"It's a secret."

"We're supposed to take the whole family to Cuba, and no one will know?"

"Not the family. Just you and me."

She'd promised the kids Mommy and Daddy would be home more during the hiatus. The kids deserved more attention before they broke the news to them. "What about the kids?"

"They'll stay with your mother. It's just for a couple of weeks. No one will know where we're going. The spooks'll spread a rumor that we're trying to patch things up—a second honeymoon. Isn't that what you want, anyway?"

Second honeymoon? Maybe third. Or fourth. She'd lost count. This had become a regular routine—another last straw, more calls to her lawyer, a getaway to patch things up. "Did the CIA script the whole story for you?"

"Yeah. It's their show." He mashed his cigarette out in the ashtray on the coffee table. "We go in January, right after little Desi's birthday. Two weeks."

"And what kind of movie are we supposed to be making in two weeks? Is there a script?"

"Who knows? We'll call it *Cuba, Jewel of the Caribbean*, by Fidel Castro."

She looked him in the eyes. "We're making a propaganda film for Castro? That's the government's way of helping me clear my name? I'm supposed to make a hero out of that Cuban Napoleon? Why would you sign us up for a suicide mission?"

"We're not gonna die."

"Career suicide, Cuban style." Congressman Walter had them over a barrel. "What's the point of going down there and making a picture for Castro? How is that supposed to help the situation?"

"CIA says any information is good information. Keep a wide angle, catch whatever we can."

She noticed a smudge on the coffee table and used the corner of her dressing gown to polish it out. "I've got an idea. You go. I'll stay with the kids. It'll be your perfect vacation."

"You have to go."

Desi Jr. had parked a fire truck under the table. She reached down for it. Cleaning always took the edge off. "Why me? I'm no director. What difference does it make which of us goes down there as long as Eisenhower gets his footage?"

"He asked for you."

"Who, the president?"

"Castro." He poked toward the letter still in Lucy's hand. "He specifically said he wants to invite Mrs. Lucille Ball and her husband, Desiderio Alberto Arnaz y de Acha III, to be his guests in Cuba and to see firsthand the paradise the people of Cuba are building for themselves."

"You sound like a PR man." She set the fire truck down and reread the letter more thoroughly. "In writing, his English is perfect. Better than yours. You think he wrote it himself?"

"That's my cue." Desi always exited after a tease or insult.

She set the letter down and drifted to the mantel, tidying the family photos there. When her father had died when she was four, her mother had taken her and Freddy to live with their grandparents. Her grandmother had always called her grandfather Daddy, and that's what Lucy and her brother had learned to call him too.

Daddy had preached the gospel of the working man since she before she could understand the words. He'd been a hard worker who'd come to the States from the Ukraine to make a living, but he'd never liked the way the rich made their money on the backs of the workers. He hadn't lived long enough to see her make her own fame and fortune, but she liked to think he would have approved. She didn't run a sweatshop, and he would have seen that the crew at the studio loved her. While he hadn't managed to turn her into a socialist, something must have rubbed off on her, because she and Desi took care of people. She had found the American dream without crushing anyone to get there.

But that hardly mattered in this country anymore. Once a communist, always a communist—at least according to the McCarthy doctrine, and he had plenty of followers, including Nixon. The first time they'd dredged up this oddity from her past, she and Desi had been at the peak of their popularity. Frank Walter had made it easy on them, and her name had been cleared publicly. So they'd thought.

Maybe this time, she could buy a little credibility for her own patriotism. Besides, Cuba was still a tropical island. No one would know them there, and she could use a few days on a sunny beach. They could enjoy a little time alone without photographers, reporters, or autograph hounds.

She straightened the last photo and turned away, ready for bed. Work had brought them together in the first place. Maybe it could do it again.

FOGGY BOTTOM

When they arrived at CIA headquarters, a dull building located on E Street in Washington, DC's Foggy Bottom district, Lucy and Desi were escorted directly to the office of CIA Director Allen Dulles—VIP treatment except for the god-awful coffee, which could have stripped the varnish off the director's walnut desk. A fellow who introduced himself only as Officer Bradley did most of the talking while Dulles leaned back, tending and smoking his pipe.

"You'll be well protected," Bradley said. "We're sending you with a trained undercover film crew: two cameramen, a sound technician, and a couple of roustabouts."

"Roustabouts are circus hands," Lucy said. "We call them grips."

"Grips," he repeated with a wink. "They'll be with you every step of the way."

"What do they know about making pictures?" Desi asked.

"These skills are also valuable in our line of work. They have no experience in the movie business, but they do know how to operate their equipment. I'm sure with your knowledge, you'll be able to get what you need from them."

Lucy sat back in her chair. "What difference does it make, anyway? Who's going to see it?"

True or not, they were just the kind of questions that would rub Desi the wrong way. When it came to his work, he was a perfectionist, a trait they usually shared and that had paid off handsomely. In this case, however, it hardly seemed worth the bother.

True to form, Desi glowered at the officer. "It's not going to look very convincing if we're running around with the Keystone Cops."

"I wouldn't worry about that," Bradley said. "These men are top performers in the agency. They could convince the Kremlin they were rocket scientists if they had to."

"We're not trying to win an Oscar," she said. "I feel much better having the protection."

Bradley nodded and then waited until Desi conceded. "The most important things you're liable to notice won't likely end up on film. Keep your eyes and ears open. Nothing is insignificant. And that goes two ways. Be careful what you say, even in private. Assume Castro will always have someone listening."

"Twenty-four hours," Dulles added, "in public or private."

Lucy examined her manicure on one hand. Good thing they had nothing private to worry about.

"If it helps, keep a diary," Bradley said, "but make sure it's safely hidden, preferably on your person at all times. No detail—just hints to jog your memory when you return."

Dulles's desk phone buzzed, and he picked up the receiver. He said only "yes." A couple of seconds later, his secretary poked her head in as if popping out of the shower. "Mrs. Arnaz, you have a call."

Lucy touched her throat and looked wide-eyed at Desi. No one knew where they were except her mother. What could have happened already?

"You can take it in the conference room," the secretary said.

* * *

AFTER LUCY LEFT THE OFFICE, Dulles and Bradley glanced at each other, clearly figuring out how to broach the next subject. Desi crossed his legs and brushed some lint from the cuff of his slacks. The other shoe was about to drop.

"What do we need all this security for?" he asked, angling in. Clearly, Lucy had been called away for a reason.

"The Castro regime is unpredictable," Dulles said.

"What kind of thing is that to say to me when we're about to fly to Havana? A week ago, you told us we were going on a busman's holiday. Now all of a sudden you want us to be a couple of spies. We could end up in prison—or worse."

"You won't be in any danger," Bradley said. "The only risk is that he'll paint you a pretty picture and we won't get any useful intelligence. We're sending experts along who know where and how to look. They have the skills to mingle with the locals, pick up the scent of the Reds, read between the lines. The extra benefit is that they'll give your wife some peace of mind."

Dulles set down his carved pipe in its matching cradle, sat upright in his high-backed leather chair, and rested his hands, fingertips to fingertips, on the desk blotter. "At some point, we expect Castro may take you back to your hometown in Oriente."

"Santiago de Cuba," Desi said. "Why would I want to go all the way out there? There ain't nothing there he can show us we can't see in Havana."

"Nevertheless, he may—not with certainty—but he may want to impress you by taking you to the heartland of his revolution."

"Maybe reintroduce you to common allies," Bradley added.

These fellas were beating around the bush. "And if he does?"

"Many Cubans are dissatisfied with Fidel, even those who supported the revolution. They want to know when he's going to reinstate the constitution."

"Imagine. A politician who doesn't keep his promises."

"Mr. Arnaz, we've planned an operation."

If drama was what Dulles wanted, drama Desi could deliver. He stood and removed his coat and hat from the rack in the corner. "No one said nothing about an operation. Take some pictures. That was the deal."

"You yourself have been supporting the counterrevolutionaries."

Of course they knew he'd been writing checks to some old family friends in Cuba. He just wondered how they were going to leverage this fact to blackmail him into an even more ridiculous commitment. "Isn't that what Uncle Sam wants? Americans doing their part to fight the commies?"

"We don't have it on authority that Castro is a communist," Bradley said. "We know he's courting the Russians for oil, but that's about as far as their relationship has progressed. The VP believes he's a Red, but Nixon believes everyone's a Red until proven otherwise."

"Even then," Dulles added. He and Bradley found this funny. Dulles sobered. "You may not be aware that it's illegal for American citizens to interfere in the political process of foreign nations."

Asinine bureaucrats could throw up a smokescreen with their nonsense and then land a sucker punch. He'd been outplayed. He re-racked his coat and hat and sank back into the chair. "First you tell us we gotta go to Cuba to prove my wife is not a communist—again—and then you tell me anything we do to help the anti-commies is illegal. You better figure out what the fuck you want."

Dulles came around to the front of his desk. "We're a complicated agency. We don't mean to sound like we're threatening you. It's a bad habit. We could have run this operation without your awareness, but as a courtesy, we wanted you to know that everything may not be as it seems. You can take comfort from knowing that there will be friendly faces all around you. If things get complicated—"

"Complicated?"

"It's not a risk for you and your wife," Dulles continued. "In fact, you don't have to do anything other than what we've already discussed. You may pick up some signals from the folks out there in the sticks. If Castro suspects anything, he may get nervous. At the first hint that he's picked up the scent, we'll back off. You'll finish your film and then hop on a plane straight back to Los Angeles."

"And if he doesn't suspect anything?"

"Same outcome, only Castro will be in US custody, awaiting prosecution by the constitutional government of Cuba."

"He's not going to take any chances," Bradley said. "Once you arrive at the eastern end of the island, we'll set him up."

"How are you planning to do that?"

"You'll need to trust us."

This was looking more and more like a setup. They already knew he'd been feeding cash to the resistance. It was the perfect cover. He could see the headline: CUBAN ACTOR DESI ARNAZ TAKES DOWN FIDEL CASTRO IN THE NAME OF DEMOCRACY.

"You're going to shoot him," he said flatly.

Dulles punctuated his words with the stem of his pipe. "There are people in Congress who've been raising hell about political assassination. Better to make a show of it: capture, trial, conviction. That way, we make him into a criminal instead of a political martyr. If he's dead, we can't discredit him."

"As soon as he believes you're at risk," Bradely added, "he's going to find a safe way to get you out of the country, and we'll be able to pick him up."

Once Lucy heard about this, she was going to turn around and catch the first plane, train, or bus back to LA—and he'd be right behind her. "Risk? What do you mean, risk? My wife isn't going to go along with this caper."

Dulles frowned. "She can't know about it. Too dangerous. It's too easy to let things slip, especially when you're not trained. There's no sense in putting you both in that position. And in the extremely unlikely event that Castro catches on to the plan, the less she knows, the better for her."

And what about him? He supposed he'd already set himself up by backing the resistance. He'd make the perfect sacrificial lamb. Still, despite his best efforts, Lucy had always seen right through him. "How the hell am I supposed to hide something like this from her?"

Dulles nodded and smiled. "All you need to do is play along with Castro. You'll be nothing but a bystander, so there'll be nothing to explain to Mrs. Arnaz."

"Do you know how to use a pistol?" Bradley asked.

Desi scooted forward to the edge of his chair again. After the draft had tagged him in 1943, he'd been through army boot camp, although a bad knee had kept him out of combat. Other than that, he'd never fired a weapon. Not even a prop. "I thought you said there wasn't gonna be no shooting."

"We would never ask you to use a weapon," Bradley said. "It's up to you, but you might want to carry a gun for defense."

He slid back dubiously. "You see? You had me convinced, almost, that this was going to be a safe trip."

"Some people get a sense of security, confidence, if they know they have personal protection," Bradley said. "I can assure you the gun is absolutely unnecessary. However, if you wish to carry the extra insurance, as a courtesy, we can provide you with a weapon that can be fully concealed within your luggage."

If he knew anything, he knew that guns had a tendency to get fired, which led to a tendency for getting shot. "No gun."

Lucy returned and arranged herself back into the leather armchair.

"Everything is okay?" Dulles asked.

"Some painters showed up wanting to paint our house beachhouse blue. Good thing my mother was there to stop them." She turned to Desi. "You wouldn't know anything about that, would you?"

He played along with the ruse. "Don't be ridiculous. Why would I want to ruin our house?" Still, this was exactly why he'd had enough. Everything was always his fault. Even after they'd agreed they were finished, she couldn't get off his back. "I just hope they didn't do any damage, or I'm going to sue someone."

She smiled at Dulles. "I took care of it. What did I miss?" She gave Desi the evil eye. "I hope you haven't planned any surprises."

He held her gaze. She was sure she could see right through him. Not always. Not this time. "The fellas were just asking me if I planned to visit my hometown."

"Fellas, huh? All of a sudden you three are thick as thieves."

Bradley pulled up a chair. "We were alerting your husband that you should be prepared for the possibility that Castro may take you on an excursion or two. Santiago de Cuba seems like a logical choice, given that Desi has roots there."

He could have visited Santiago de Cuba many times over the past few years. He hadn't. He had no happy memories there, and one broken promise. He rubbed his chin thoughtfully.

"Keep an eye on the folks you see," Bradley was saying. "Size them up. Castro claims popular support. If the people scurry away like cockroaches every time he shows his face, that's good information."

Dulles returned to his chair. "We don't want to make this any more complicated than necessary. This should be a quick trip, in and out. You just do what comes naturally. Make Castro's movie and come home. As far as you're concerned, our men are working for you."

"A regular honeymoon," Lucy said.

"It's actually not a bad story," Bradley said.

"Fairy tale, you mean," Desi groused.

Bradley handed Desi a pair of airline tickets. He looked them over. "We're flying commercial?"

"Commercial charter. It would be a dead giveaway to fly you over on a government plane. We're routing you through Houston, as if you were traveling from LA."

"That'll really fool 'em," Lucy said. "Must be a good seven hours on a plane."

"First class," Dulles said. "I hope that at least makes it more comfortable."

"Allen, I don't mean to sound unappreciative, but we always fly first class," she said with her most ingratiating smile.

"Then I'm glad we are able to accommodate you in the manner to which you're accustomed."

"We're awfully spoiled, but we'll make do."

She was never this snitty with strangers unless she was nervous. Desi slapped his palm with the tickets. "These say we're leaving in two hours."

"Your luggage is on its way to Washington National. A driver is waiting for you downstairs. We'll be within reach twenty-four hours a day. The more casually you treat this, the easier it will be for you, and the more successful. If your guard is down, then Castro will follow your lead. Relax and let us manage the details."

Lucy arched her eyebrows, a practiced expression. "You make him sound like a dog."

"Soldiers and canines have a lot in common," Dulles said, rising to usher them out. "Keen instincts keep them both alive."

WELCOMING COMMITTEE

When they finally emerged from the plane in Havana, hundreds of people on the ground shuffled into position on the tarmac below. The January air was not too hot, not too cold—a little humid, not much different than LA. Fidel Castro, whose face had become familiar to Americans from his multiple television appearances, looked up at them with a neutral expression. A line of men in green fatigues, most of them bearded, waited a few feet from the foot of the stairs. Other men and women in uniform flanked Castro and his closest officials. Their utilitarian uniforms completed their revolutionary personas. One man, standing farthest to Castro's right, wore a gray pinstriped suit. There was no red carpet.

Lucy and Desi waited in the unsettling silence as a couple of movie cameras and a roving photographer captured their arrival. She smoothed her dress and tucked most of her red curls more neatly under her broad hat, leaving a few loose wisps to frame her delicate features, then leaned close to Desi, a picture-perfect smile plastered across her face. "Is this part of the film? *Desi and Lucy Go to Cuba?*"

She held the railing and eased herself down the steep, narrow stairs, taking care not to catch a heel. Desi followed two steps behind her.

"La bienvenida a Cuba—welcome to Cuba," Castro said, at last, as they reached the tarmac. "Thank you for accepting my invitation."

Castro first took Lucy's hand in both of his, then firmly shook Desi's. He didn't smile, and he spoke softly and avoided eye contact. He was tall, several inches taller than Desi, and under his rough beard she detected hints of a youthful face. She'd been expecting more bravado from this triumphant revolutionary.

"Señor Desiderio Alberto Arnaz y de Acha III, welcome back to your homeland of Cuba. And Mrs. Arnaz, welcome to our country."

Castro had recited Desi's name in the elaborate Cuban tradition of combining the names of their parents' families—in this case, Arnaz for his father and de Acha for his mother. No one at home ever addressed Desi by his full name, and he noticeably winced at the mention of his Cuban roots. It wasn't that he rejected his heritage, per se, but he hadn't exactly left the country on his own terms, and his family had paid a hefty price for Cuba's political turmoil. Despite his incurable—and bankable—accent, Desi was a dyed-in-the-wool American.

"I wish to introduce my staff," Castro continued.

He didn't use the word "compañeros" as he had in the filmed speeches she'd been shown at the CIA, apparently wise enough at the tender age of thirty-three to understand the associations Americans made with certain words. Americans already equated "compañeros" with "comrades," the familiar villainous moniker of the Reds. They had just met, and already Castro's whitewashing agenda was surfacing.

They shook hands with a dozen officials, including a couple of young women wearing the same olive green uniforms as their male colleagues. They spoke their names in rapid Cuban Spanish, using the same lengthy form with which Castro had greeted Desi. The effect was musical but difficult to remember, and Lucy caught only those names she'd learned during their orientation in DC.

Castro paused the introductions as their film crew filed down from the plane, lining the stairs behind them, and the ground crew began unloading equipment crates. "You bring with you so much, and all these people."

Desi tried to put him at ease. "We're here to make a picture. This is our crew. I'll introduce you."

"No need." Castro instructed the ground crew to take the film crew and their crates to customs. Apparently, he liked to do things by the book.

He resumed introductions with his brother Raúl, then Huber Matos Benítez, Juan Almeida Bosque, Celia Sánchez, and then finally the man in the suit, President Osvaldo Dorticós Torrado, who smiled but said only sí and deferred entirely to Castro.

Castro's wave to the remainder of those assembled elicited a round of applause. A microphone stand was brought out, placed before him, and raised to his considerable height.

Castro invited Lucy and Desi to stand with him. "We welcome our guests today, two of the finest entertainers in North America, Señor and Señora Desiderio Alberto Arnaz y de Acha III, known by millions as Desi Arnaz and Lucille Ball."

The crowd applauded. An unseen interpreter repeated Castro's words in Spanish over the crackling PA system, and the crowd reprised their applause. Castro rambled on about their show, their popularity, and Desi's Cuban roots, somehow managing to drag out their introduction to at least half an hour, although it seemed like twice that. Lucy enjoyed making public appearances—especially when she could stand out, which she certainly did on this tropical Latin island—but her feet were killing her. They had dressed appropriately for a meeting with a head of state but not at all appropriately for a prolonged ceremony in the middle of an oversized parking lot. The lingering fumes of jet fuel didn't help, either.

Castro asked Desi to say a few words, which he did in Spanish. Lucy smiled and put on her best Hollywood charm, as if posing for the press at a premiere. Desi kept it short. He loved an audience, so he must have been holding back intentionally. Although she understood only bits and pieces, she recognized by his tone that he wanted to project more of a businesslike attitude than his usual charisma.

When it came her turn to take the microphone, she refrained from embarrassing herself by attempting to speak Spanish. She said a few brief words thanking Prime Minister Castro and President Torrado for their hospitality and saying how much she and Desi looked forward to their stay in the country and the opportunity to share their accomplishments with their fellow citizens at home. The crowd applauded with much less enthusiasm when she was done.

Castro must have noticed her dismay at the tepid response, because he leaned in and asked her what concerns she had.

"It's nothing." She rummaged around in her handbag for her sunglasses. "You know how arrogant actors can be. We get so accustomed to attention that it seems odd when the crowd doesn't respond."

"I think they expected you to be funny," he said.

She pursed her lips, intentionally suggesting both dismay and apology.

"This is how you are known," he said.

"Thanks to good writing. I'm not so good at winging it."

Castro raised his arms in a broad, embracing salute to the crowd, who took his meaning and began to disperse. A black Lincoln that had been waiting nearby pulled up, and a soldier stepped forward to open the doors for each of them. Castro invited Desi to take the passenger seat, while he folded his long legs in behind the driver next to Lucy.

It soon became clear that they were not going directly to their hotel. Castro invited them to join him and a few other guests for dinner that evening and then proceeded to narrate their circuitous drive through Havana, pointing out landmarks and adding historical color, mostly having to do with revolutionary heroics.

"You've visited Havana before, Mrs. Arnaz?" he asked.

"Once or twice." She looked directly at him, hoping to coax him into eye contact. "You needn't call me Mrs. Arnaz. Lucy is fine."

He only nodded. So strange that this man who had sent the world into a tizzy was so timid. Could he have been shell-shocked?

"If you prefer something more formal, then please call me Lucille. Everything else makes me feel old."

"Ah, so you do have a humorous nature." He glanced briefly in her direction.

"She can be funny when she needs to be," Desi said.

"It is best to be yourself."

They arrived at the Hotel Habana Libre with no further fanfare. The modern high-rise was heavily guarded by Castro's soldiers, patrolling both the outside and inside, while the hotel staff performed their duties as if nothing had changed. Prime Minister Castro explained that he and his staff had made the hotel their new headquarters, eschewing the opulence of the Presidential Palace as well as its sullied history as a "citadel for tyrants." The once-grand hotel, a place she and Desi had stayed before, had been transformed into a new type of citadel, Lucy felt for sure. What exactly that was remained to be discovered.

DINNER WITH SPIES

*L*ucy adored attention but disliked making entrances. It had been difficult enough to be taken seriously as a so-called starlet in Hollywood. She tried to make it a point now to let everyone around her know that she and Desi were partners, equal partners. He might have been the business brains of their partnership, but she was better at reading people.

Still, she wasn't prepared for the dinner guests Castro had invited to join them on their first night. Besides Castro, ten people milled around the long, ornate inlaid table set with silver, Waterford crystal, and Wedgwood china. It seemed a little over the top for a socialist state, especially with Castro still dressed in green fatigues. She could only imagine his closet, probably no different than any military officer's.

Two uniformed women sat at the table having a private conversation in Spanish, while the rest had all remained standing until Lucy and Desi's arrival.

One woman, standing alone, wore a severe gray women's suit and a starched white blouse. Two of the men wore woolen suits far too heavy for the tropical climate, even in January. Another man wore an embroidered guayabera shirt with linen slacks, the customary dress for Cuban men. Desi had chosen a button-down sport shirt, beige with wide black stripes and cut similarly to a guayabera, which inspired the American style. Lucy felt a little overdressed despite wearing slacks, as she preferred, with a matching blouse and a scarf tied loosely around her neck. Her matching pearl stud earrings and necklace, in particular, seemed out of place among the odd assortment of outfits.

She counted thirteen chairs and only eleven guests present.

Along one side of the second-story room, a row of wood shutters opened to the street below. Distant brassy music drifted up, along with the sounds of people calling to each other in Spanish. A few vehicles roared and puttered past.

Castro invited Desi and Lucy to take the two chairs flanking him, apparently reserved for the guests of honor.

"I hope you don't mind that I invited a few friends to help welcome you to Cuba," he said privately before rising from his seat, holding a glass of red wine. "Welcome. Despite your ulterior motives, the Cuban people are humbled by your interest in our well-being."

Lucy and Desi glanced at each other. No one protested Castro's bluntness. Lucy might have spoken up, but it would have been a waste of breath. This man was no idiot, and he knew they hadn't come simply as celebrity emissaries. He understood their purpose. It was as if he'd issued them a challenge.

Castro continued by introducing Philip Bonsal, the American ambassador, and the man more casually attired in a white-on-white embroidered guayabera, a Mr. Allen Joffrey from the US.

"You're also with the embassy?" Lucy asked.

The other guests chuckled politely.

Joffrey was about to speak when Castro interrupted. "Mr. Joffrey is not a diplomat. He's a CIA operative, a spy."

Joffrey winked and nodded.

She looked at Desi, who only leaned back in his chair and crossed his arms, waiting for the other shoe to drop. She withheld any further questions. She could hardly wait to meet the other mystery guests.

Castro continued the introductions with a couple of familiar faces, including his brother Raúl and a woman soldier, Celia Sánchez, whom they'd met at the airport. Sitting between Raúl and Sánchez was Vilma Espín, Raúl's cherub-faced wife, who looked adorable in her soldier's uniform, as if she were dressed for a costume party. The next uniformed man looked out of place to Lucy in a Cuban military uniform, but he had sandy hair and blue eyes. He must have been a big shot, because Castro skipped him, maybe saving him for last.

The only person in the room older than Lucy was Ambassador Bonsal. The revolutionaries' youth made her feel downright matronly.

"And finally," Castro concluded, "we have two guests from the Soviet Union, Oleg Savenko and Tatiana Tatarenko."

"And you are with the Soviet embassy?" Lucy asked.

Savenko nodded. "I am on a diplomatic mission. Like Mr. Joffrey, Miss Tatarenko is an intelligence operative."

Lucy crossed her legs, snagging the tablecloth and knocking her array of silver utensils into the china plates with a clatter.

"I see you are surprised," Castro said.

Desi beat her to the punch. "What kind of spies are you?"

"We're all friends here," Castro said.

Odd that a bunch of double agents would be so willing to reveal themselves to a couple of TV celebrities. Seemed a little foolish.

"Whose sides are you on?" Lucy asked.

"We are loyal to our country," said Tatarenko, a stiff yet attractive woman who spoke in an accent only slightly less impenetrable than Desi's. "When cultivating friendship, it is most efficient for us to work out in the open."

Lucy inspected her dishes for damage and straightened out her place setting. "Is this how spying really works? No disguises? Everyone just shows up and announces who they are?"

"No," Joffrey said. "I would say not. This is a first for me."

Glad she wasn't alone. Their enigmatic host had already begun to turn things topsy-turvy. She placed her hand on the back of her neck just under her hair. "I still don't understand. How can you collect information for your governments if you don't hide your identities?"

"It's simple," Castro said. "The people of Cuba have nothing to hide. We wish to make friends with our comrades around the world—Russian, American, our Latin brethren. What would be the purpose of a worker's paradise if we kept it a secret?"

It made no sense for the CIA to send them on this junket if they already had their people running around down here in the open. What could she and Desi possibly find out that the professionals could not? This, of course, had nothing to do with Castro's motives.

"And that's why you've invited us," she said.

"This is precisely what I wish. Your government will collect all the information they need, but they will not share it with the people of your country. We hope you will show your fellow citizens what we are achieving in Cuba, so they will understand that we are no threat. We only wish to live free, just as they do."

"With all due respect, isn't that just propaganda?"

"Propaganda?" repeated the Russian man.

Although Savenko and Tatarenko were no more sober than you'd expect of any government official, including Bonsal, they both fulfilled Lucy's cartoon-influenced expectations. Here were Boris and Natasha in the flesh. If little Lucie had been there, they would have both broken out in giggles. Lucy hoped her smile would be interpreted as warm acknowledgment. Desi was drumming his fingers on the table, a habit that had become more pronounced since he'd cut back on his drinking.

"In the US," Castro was saying, "and especially in your business, I believe you call it 'advertising.' We call it information."

"And you will show us everything, so we can tell the truth," she said.

Bonsal stiffened, apparently stunned by her lack of diplomacy. Joffrey displayed genuine amusement, in contrast to Tatarenko, whose smile was sardonic to the point that Lucy wished she could reach out and slap it off her. But the other Russian displayed his outrage overtly, with his fist firmly planted on the table.

While Bonsal and the Russians sat stone-faced, awaiting Castro's response, two waiters began placing bowls of soup before them. After a long, silent eye-to-eye exchange with Desi, Lucy dipped her spoon into her bowl and startled herself with a taste of soup that wasn't just cool, but chilled.

Savenko finally erupted, banging his knee on the underside of the table, rattling the dishes and nearly tipping several crystal goblets of wine and water. The shock of the pain must have curbed his agitation, because he settled back down before launching into his invective. "Dr. Castro, I don't understand what you hope to accomplish by inviting these people to represent the achievements of your glorious revolution. Do they not represent the excess and hypocrisy for which so many Cubans sacrificed their lives, and the lives of their children? Who is this woman to question your integrity?"

"I don't think that was Mrs. Arnaz's intention," said the sandy-haired man. "We Yankees are an inquisitive folk. It's in our nature, leads to our ingenuity."

Castro introduced the previously silent guest. "This is Comandante William Alexander Morgan, a former citizen of your country."

Once she heard his name, she recognized the expat. "You've had some press at home."

"You're American?" Desi asked.

"Born and bred," Morgan said.

"What are you doing down here?"

Castro spoke for Morgan. "Comandante Morgan fought bravely beside us in our struggle and subsequent victory."

"Is that legal?" Lucy asked. "Are Americans permitted to fight for other countries?"

"So long as it's not on behalf of an enemy of the United States," Bonsal said. "That would be treason."

"Assuming your loyalties are as they seem," Tatarenko said to Morgan, "your contribution to the struggle is admirable, a suggestion that the people of our nations have much in common."

Morgan graciously let the loyalty crack slide. "I might not go that far. I think we still have plenty of differences."

Vilma Espín chimed in. "Gazpacho. Very refreshing."

After savoring a spoonful, Castro returned to Lucy's challenge. "We have nothing to hide and everything to share." Apparently in response to Savenko, he added, "Mr. and Mrs. Arnaz are here because they are widely respected and adored in their country."

Desi was studying the men sitting across the table. At last he could no longer resist asking Joffrey, "Why are you here? I mean, we understand that the prime minister and the Russians have their own agendas, but what's in it for you—the CIA, I mean?"

Castro merely looked up from his dish and acknowledged Desi's question with a flick of his spoon. As they all awaited Joffrey's reply, Lucy dipped in for another taste of her soup. It was rich in tomato and other fresh vegetables. Not quite as thick as the tension in the room.

Joffrey leaned in on his elbows as if about to tell a most interesting tale. "It's a very small country, and if you'll forgive me, Señor Primer Ministro…"—Castro nodded his acquiescence—"…uncomplicated. Covert operations aren't likely to accomplish any more than we can do out in the open, and this way, at least we can enjoy the visit. It's a beautiful island."

"Enjoy the visit," Desi repeated. "Now our taxes pay for your vacations."

Lucy asked the Russian man to pass the salt and pepper.

"I mean to say," Joffrey said, "things are calm here. Peaceful."

"Sure. Very peaceful."

"I understand your skepticism," Castro said to Desi. "It is well known that you've given considerable sums of money to the resistance."

A chill prickled Lucy's arms. Castro was serious about laying all cards on the table.

But Desi didn't skip a beat. "Then why did you bring us here?"

"If you come to accept the truth, that our purpose is noble and entirely compatible with values of the North American people, then you will be our best possible spokesman. Both you and Mrs. Arnaz. Your skepticism is our opportunity."

Nothing nefarious about that sentiment. Lucy smiled. "At home, we'd just say you are trying to win us over."

Castro saluted his guests with his spoon, as if to share his pleasure and urge them to enjoy. "Why any of you? Why now?"

The guests looked around at each other with polite smiles. Some even wiped the corners of their mouths as if preparing to answer, though none seemed anxious to respond first. The Russians must have believed they were already in Castro's good graces. Maybe they were, but it looked as though Castro was smart enough to keep them guessing. He was trying to get something from all sides, and he had surprising leverage for a kid who'd crowned himself king of a little Caribbean island. This picture she and Desi were about to make for him was all part of some kind of plan.

Finally, Bonsal spoke. "Not all of us are new to Cuba."

Lucy paused with the spoon before her lips. This looked like it might be the start of the evening's entertainment. She kept eating as if no elephant had just plodded into the room. Castro invited the ambassador to elaborate with a tip of his goblet—more subtle and stoic than a nod. She couldn't yet tell whether this was his natural demeanor or an affectation to compensate for some insecurity, like his age. Despite his scruffy beard and weatherworn features, he was clearly younger than most of his guests.

"In fact, we have always been interested in this island," Bonsal said. "We do, as you well know, have a naval base here."

"I'm sure you are interested in your naval base," Castro said. "It makes a fine outpost."

"We've also carried on economic activities, trade, tourism. Hundreds of millions of dollars enter the Cuban economy each year."

"And most of it returns through the companies who operate on Cuban soil. It is true that the US is our largest trading partner. It's also a fact that almost the entirety of our sugar, coffee, and tobacco crops, as well as our oil production, are owned by US companies. The money they make from these enterprises makes their *Yanqui* shareholders wealthier but brings no economic growth to Cuba. Cubans receive no more than the meager wages they're paid to pick and pack crops. Geographically, the distance between our two countries is small, but economically, we are separated by vast oceans."

If he continued to prod everyone at the table into giving him a launchpad for his next diatribe, this was bound to be a long evening. Lucy blotted the corners of her mouth with her napkin and then returned it to her lap, fussing with it to lie squarely. No one else at the table was smoking yet, so she resisted the temptation.

Bonsal tried another angle. "But you must understand, Prime Minister Castro, these companies have invested extensively in Cuban agriculture. They've imported thousands of machines and other essential farming implements, and they've built roads and installed electrical systems. These are expensive outlays, yet they enable Cuban crops to reach foreign markets. Jobs are created by these investments."

Castro settled back into his chair while the staff cleared the soup bowls. "In your country, laborers have organized into powerful unions to demand fair wages and working conditions."

"Yes, we've seen a rise of socialistic tendencies in the US."

The Russians perked up.

"You use the word 'socialism' with distaste," Tatarenko said. "This is what you call it when workers expect their employers to treat them with dignity."

"Unfortunately, these organizations not only threaten the viability of US enterprises, they are also corrupted by organized crime. What dignity is there in submitting to the exploitation of murderous gangsters?" Bonsal said.

"Gangsters are the product of the corrupting capitalistic forces of greed and profiteering," Savenko said.

Bonsal showed his cool diplomatic colors, continuing with no feathers ruffled. "Without profit, what incentive would they have to operate their businesses? Incentive motivates progress and economic growth. It's the lifeblood of our capitalist society. The people of the United States hope to continue a mutually beneficial trade relationship with the people of Cuba. Our people's wish for the Cuban people is that they may enjoy the same freedom and prosperity with which we are blessed."

Castro raised his wine glass to the light and peered one-eyed through the red liquid as if assessing a gemstone. "Here is the question you all bring to the table. I will ask it for you. 'Will Fidel Castro bring Soviet socialism to America's front door?' Is this not what you are to determine?"

Despite their stony expressions, the Russians managed to exchange smug looks.

"Okay," Joffrey said. "No punches pulled. Seems like a reasonable concern, given present company."

Bonsal tilted an eye at Joffrey like a disapproving matron. Apparently, spies weren't trained in diplomacy.

"I would agree," Lucy said, joining in the game. Desi subtly shook his head at her, as if they were in a negotiation and he wanted her to dummy up. "It looks like you're setting things up to play us against each other, Russians and Americans. See who'll give you a better deal. Not that I'm saying anything against that. Just an observation." She took a forkful of the baked snapper they'd just been served.

"My wife likes to stir things up—redhead," Desi said.

Vilma smiled deeply at Lucy. Not so much, the other two ladies.

Lucy made direct eye contact with Desi. She didn't like when he belittled her, especially in front of strangers. Desi speared his fish.

In intimate conversation, Castro was a soft-spoken young man. She was beginning to see how he used this technique to draw his audience's attention. He was no timid, awkward leader.

"We are very much in favor of a friendly relationship with the US and with the people of the Soviet Union, as long as it serves the interests of Cubans," he said. "We have certain resources and other benefits. Why should only foreign interests continue to benefit from our national riches? And whether Cubans prefer to eschew the corruptive and corrosive effects of capitalism in favor of cooperation and collectivism, this should not affect this relationship. The internal affairs of Cuba are of no economic consequence to the North Americans."

"And the Russians?" she asked.

"Soviets," Tatarenko corrected her.

"Mr. Arnaz," Castro asked, "as a Cuban and a businessman, would you not agree?"

Despite how often he tried to put words in her mouth, Desi

disliked when anyone pulled it on him. In an apparent attempt to avoid falling deeper into the political rat hole he himself had helped open up, he parroted Bonsal. "I believe every Cuban should enjoy the same freedom and opportunity I've found in the United States of America."

"The opportunity," Tatarenko said, "to do the bidding of the oppressors."

"Oh yes," Lucy said brightly. "We do so much adore crushing hopes and dreams."

Desi pushed his plate a few inches away. It was one of his tells, a sign of resignation, so well known among their friends that he'd started using it as a bluff—which had also become well known and was now usually good for a laugh. Not this time. There had been a time when his sense of humor was fine without booze. Not lately. Tonight, she was a solo act.

"You agree that the working people in your country suffer exploitation," Tatarenko said, clearly taken off guard.

"Sure," Lucy said. "And you know what makes it worse? They don't even know it."

"They are brainwashed."

She directed her full attention at the Russians, as if they were the only other people in the room. "Can you imagine? They're so absorbed raising their children, eating their three square meals, driving their Buicks to church, mowing their lawns, watching baseball on TV. With all those distractions, it's easy to see how they could be blind to their own suffering."

Desi closed his eyes and rubbed his forehead.

Castro placed his hand on Desi's forearm. "Everyone is free to speak their minds."

The Russians each had their own way of showing their disdain every time Castro addressed either Lucy or Desi. Savenko pursed his lips and trembled slightly. He looked like a kettle about to blow. Tatarenko, she was a cool cucumber, stone-faced. Once she had finished her dish, she sat nearly motionless with perfect posture, her back not touching the chair. If it weren't for the fact that they represented the Big Red Threat, they'd have made an entertaining pair of dinner companions.

"The ice is broken," Castro was saying. "Now we shall have a debate. Would you agree, Mr. Savenko?"

Lucy had delivered her punch line. She braced herself for Savenko's reaction.

Savenko's ears turned bright red. "We would agree that Cubans must have their freedom. However, we would disagree with Mrs. Arnaz that her country's sort of freedom would serve the people's best interests. The imperialistic actions of your country led to the degenerative conditions in Cuba."

"I'm afraid this is true." Castro had been waiting for the right moment to take sides. "However, the victim is almost always a willing accomplice—until he is not. Then we have revolution."

Savenko finally got so hot under the collar that he popped up and stood behind his own chair. With a white-knuckled grip on the chair's high back, he looked as if he were ready to hurl it across the table at Lucy. "Are the victims willing, or do the oppressors indoctrinate them into their social roles?"

Tatarenko touched Savenko's elbow and spoke with measured condescension. "Mrs. Arnaz, what of those who don't enjoy regular meals or watch televisions? What of those starving in the streets? Are they to be ignored, cast off as irrelevant failures?"

Desi intercepted the question. "We take care of our poor. The United States is a country of compassion."

"Compassion?" Savenko spit the word. "You American imperialists take whatever you want from the rest of the world, as long as you get what you need to watch your baseball games and drive your shiny automobiles. You pretend to spread freedom and prosperity while enslaving the children of other nations to pick bananas for your own."

Desi's patriotic zeal didn't surface often, but when it did, it was like the Fourth of July. After he and his family had been stripped of their property and exiled to Florida during the previous Cuban Revolution, he had taken advantage of all the freedoms the States had to offer. He'd pulled himself up by his own bootstraps to make a name for himself as a musician and entertainer, fueling the Latin music craze up and down the East Coast. Then he'd started a second career and built a television empire with Lucy from the ground up.

He was about to lay into Savenko when two men were shown into the room by a couple of Castro's guards. Lucy recognized one of them immediately—and judging from how Desi's eyes narrowed, so did he.

THE USUAL BUSINESS

*T*he last person she'd have expected to run into in Havana was Meyer Lansky.

"You got a funny way of making your guests welcome," said the man accompanying Lansky, in a Brooklyn accent. "We was practically apprehended at the airport and drug over here before we even had a chance to take a piss. But don't worry, we're good now."

"Except one thing," Lansky said. "We were expecting a private meeting."

The unnamed man smiled at Lucy, took a good long look, and raised his thick eyebrows. "I'll be damned."

"Sorry we're late," Lansky said. "The plane was delayed for weather."

"It's raining cats and dogs in Miami," said the other man.

Lansky paid his respects to Castro with a handshake and presented him with a bottle of Chivas Regal. He wore a fine suit, probably Italian, and smelled of cologne, an unfamiliar brand.

He turned to Lucy and bowed slightly. "Meyer Lansky."

"I'm familiar," she said. Lansky was the Mafia boss whose gambling empire had made Batista filthy rich, among the first to be run out of town when Castro rolled in to proclaim victory for the revolution.

"Pleasure to meet you... Do I say 'Miss Ball' or 'Mrs. Arnaz'?"

"Mrs. Arnaz," Desi said. "Ball is her professional name."

"Mrs. Arnaz, then," he replied smoothly. "I hope you'll reserve judgment until you get to know me better."

"Pleased," the first man chimed in. "Name's Marino. Frank. Call me Frank." He lifted his ass out of the chair a few inches and waved his hand over his head as a greeting to all the other guests, adding a wink for Lucy and Tatarenko. Apparently, he hadn't yet noticed or didn't much care for the women in green fatigues.

If Castro was trying to make a case for social justice, he'd picked the wrong guests for this party. Lansky was the worst kind of mobster, notoriously known as the Mafia's Accountant, and an accomplished criminal in his own right. Everyone in the business knew that Lansky had been in bed with Batista, and it appeared Castro had every intention of getting his share of the action now that Batista was out of the way. So all this talk about *la revolución* was beginning to look like smoke and mirrors.

Desi had crossed his arms as if Lansky's entrance confirmed his own suspicions about Castro's true motives. Since he'd stopped drinking, his dark eyes had become deep and clear again. Lucy remembered when that intensity had communicated something entirely different.

"Mr. Lansky," Bonsal said, "we were told you had returned to the States." Bonsal may have been a diplomat, but his narrowed eyes and flaring nostrils betrayed his distaste for Lansky.

"Yes," Lansky said. "Had some business back home."

"Mr. Lansky contacted me regarding his business interests in Havana," Castro said.

The waiter served Lansky and Marino their soup. Marino sniffed at a spoonful, touched his tongue to it, and snapped his head back as if it had bitten him. "Cold. I guess we was pretty late."

"It's a cold soup," Lucy said. "It's a Latin thing."

"Hmm." Marino laid down his spoon. "Come to think of it, I'm not much of a soup man. Drove my ma crazy. Everyone raved on her minestrone. I never touched the stuff. Beans. They give me the troubles."

Lansky hardly acknowledged Marino's chatter.

"The revolution forced us to shut down Mr. Lansky's business establishment," Castro said. "He's come back to discuss the possibility of reopening his hotels and casinos."

"Outrageous," Savenko said.

Castro introduced them. "Mr. Lansky, Mr. Savenko."

Lansky put on his surprised look. "Mr. Savenko, a Russian name?" Savenko affirmed this heritage by raising his chin in his revolutionary pose. "You object to entertainment?"

"Gambling is no entertainment," Savenko said. "It is theft."

Lucy propped her elbow on the table, tilted her head, and rested her cheek in her palm, hoping to mask her amusement with the Russian's trained party-line patter. Castro had arranged quite the floor show, pitting the Mob's best man against a full-blooded commie.

"I don't see what's so terrible about a little blackjack or some dice," countered Desi.

What made Desi side up with the mobster, she had no idea, except that he hated the Reds, and this was his first chance to take a couple of shots.

After Lansky finished his gazpacho, the server removed the soup bowls and brought Marino and Lansky their fish course, which Marino seemed to find more appealing. Lucy found Lansky surprisingly small for a prominent underworld figure—physically, that is, especially in contrast to his husky associate. He stood no more than five feet. He looked fit, with a chiseled but not attractive face. He had good manners, chose the correct fork, kept his elbows off the table, and thanked the servers with sincerity, yet his demeanor didn't fit. Not that it was a put-on. It might have been his voice or his way of speaking, but really, he just had the wrong occupation. Lucy couldn't quite put him all together—a real-life character.

"We've run legitimate businesses here in Havana," Lansky was saying. "Employed hundreds of people. Provided a good living."

"A good living cannot be made by preying on the weaknesses of your comrades," said Tatarenko.

Castro and his brother Raúl observed the exchange as if watching which way their wager would pay out, only Lucy couldn't read which way they'd placed their bets. The only motion Castro made was to signal for the next course.

"The fine folks who visit this beautiful country come here to enjoy themselves," Lansky said, "and they leave behind plenty of cash."

Savenko wouldn't let up. "Which you then deliver to your personal account."

"As I said," Lansky continued, unfazed by the Russian's antagonistic tone, "we bankroll a hefty payroll. It's not cheap to operate high-quality establishments."

"Gentlemen," Castro finally interrupted. "This is a fine discussion. You both make good points."

"Let's hear your deal," Lansky said to Savenko. "I'm guessing that your visit is a little more than a simple 'how do you do.'"

"This is a matter for statesmen," Savenko said.

"That's disrespectful," Marino said, leaning forward and wagging his fork in the air. "Disrespectful."

"We are here on a diplomatic mission," the Russian said. "It is customary to conduct these discussions with privacy."

"I get it," Marino said, mockingly tossing his head from side to side, "top secret. That's what Mr. Lansky was expecting. A private face-to-face with *el presidente* here."

"Prime minister," said Haydée, who'd remained entirely silent until now.

"Beggin' your pardon, your honor." Marino held up his glass as if toasting Castro, slopping a little wine over the rim in the process. "No disrespect intended." He caught the drip from the glass with his finger and transferred it to his tongue. "No sense in wasting good booze. I'm usually more of a beer and whisky man, but this stuff is pretty good. Reminds me of when I was a kid."

Ideas for scripts were popping in her brain, and Lucy reached for the notepad she always carried in her purse before thinking better of it. She tried to connect the dots. Why had Castro invited them to this party? Obviously, he was trying to demonstrate something, but for the life her, she couldn't understand what.

She checked in silently with Desi, but his narrowed eyes only reflected anxiety. The wine was flowing, and his willpower was under assault. She tried not to act like a shrew, monitoring his every move, but he was becoming restless and impatient. She declined a refill for her own wine glass.

Fidel was listening to the heated discussion politely but made no attempt to intervene. Like any talented host, he'd orchestrated this evening.

"Mr. Savenko," the ambassador said, "the timing of your visit is very interesting."

"Why so?" Savenko asked.

The servers delivered a plate to each diner. Savenko lifted his eyeglasses and studied the dish as if judging a contest. Frank Marino, however, wasted no time. While the others waited for Bonsal to complete his calculated response to Savenko, Marino decided it was now acceptable to dig in, which he did with gusto, breathing loudly through his nose as he carved into the thick beef medallions.

"Now that's what I call food," he said. "Hits the spot." He scooped up a large forkful of potatoes au gratin, washed it down with a gulp of wine, and requested a refill by tapping his goblet with his cat's-eye pinky ring.

"Since we're speaking frankly," Bonsal said, "I must say that we take a keen interest in activities close to our borders. We find it curious that the Soviet Union, which has never shown any interest in the nations of the Caribbean, has recently begun to establish a relationship with Dr. Castro and the people of Cuba."

Tatarenko had taken her first bite of food while pretending disinterest in the exchange, but now she laid her fork on the plate and joined in. "Why would our country be any less interested than yours in the future of Cuba? This is, unless you consider proximity a factor in diplomatic relations, as if our nations radiated a halo of influence on surrounding states."

Bonsal began to slip to the defensive. "The US administration takes a particular interest in protecting our allies against oppression and suffering."

"This we have in common," Tatarenko said.

To Lucy, the maneuvering was pointless to the point of boredom. "Oh, brother."

As soon as she blurted this out, she knew it was too late to squirm out of it. Even pulling a TV Lucy tactic like commenting on how great the food tasted wasn't going to cut it now. She went for the direct approach—after all, this wasn't her game. Might as well play the role of the naive Hollywood starlet.

"I mean, what's the point of pretending you see eye to eye?" She widened her own eyes. "I hear a lot of beating around the bush and not much straight talk."

"The lady's got a good point," Marino said. "What's the point of all this this and that?"

Lansky asked Marino to pass the salt and pepper.

"You do say what you think," Vilma said. "You would make an excellent revolutionary."

"My wife would only make a revolutionary if she were the general," Desi said. "I suggest you watch yourself, Prime Minister Castro. She might try to take over your country."

Everyone laughed except Lucy. Desi had been taking more potshots at her lately. Booze had made him cold, but sobriety was making him cruel. She knew he was struggling, but the last thing she needed was for him to become her personal heckler.

She tried her best to cut him some slack. "I'm no soldier, just a clown."

"You're too modest, Mrs. Arnaz," Vilma said. "You are a successful woman, quite wealthy—a household name, Dr. Castro tells us. Even those of us who haven't seen your television programs know of you."

"My wife has worked hard for her fame and fortune," Desi said.

Lucy shifted in her chair. Jumping to her defense very nearly blew away the stink he'd left with his last remark—or it would have had it not been more about him than her.

"Perhaps the role of revolutionary would be a noble application of your abilities," Tatarenko said.

Desi didn't bother to look up from his plate. "Now you done it."

"For people in your line of work, I suppose what I do is undignified," Lucy said to Tatarenko.

"I express no opinion on your profession," said Tatarenko. "I wish to say only that women have a new role in the social order, and you might be an excellent role model for young women."

The more Lucy tried to be direct, the more obtuse the Russian woman became. She took a different tack. "It's getting thick. She makes it sound like I'm a hooker."

This elicited a few tentative chuckles and a more boisterous laugh from Marino. Vilma translated for Celia, who nodded but didn't crack so much as a smile. Lucy had managed to break most of the tension, but it didn't last long.

Castro straightened his back and placed both palms on the table on either side of his plate. "We all know, each of us and the people we represent, what we want. There is no point in debating our motives. What must be determined is which affiliations will benefit Cuba."

"Everybody's got an angle," Lansky said. "It's a two-way deal, isn't it? I assume you understand that any deal you make has to be good for all parties."

"Then let's begin with you, Mr. Lansky," Castro said. "Tell us how your enterprises benefit Cubans."

Lansky leaned in, propped his elbows on the table, and clasped his hands together. "We run a legitimate business."

"On the up and up," added Marino.

This time, Lansky signaled Marino to cut his running commentary.

"You had a business relationship with Batista," Raúl said.

Lansky wasn't about to let either of the Castros paint him as a gangster, even if he was one. "He was the man in charge. Don't change the fact that tourists are good for your country. They come down here with pockets full of dough to spend in our establishments. It takes people to run hotels and casinos. Good jobs."

Relieved to be out of the hot seat, Lucy cut herself a final nibble of beef. Whatever kind of crap Lansky was dishing out, the man betrayed no lack of confidence.

"Many lives were given to relieve us of Batista's corrupt and oppressive regime," Castro said, slipping into oratory. "We will not forfeit the sacrifices the Cuban people have made for our revolution. However, Cuba cannot thrive in isolation. We must strengthen relationships with many nations, for trade, for security, and for the health and prosperity of our comrades."

"'Comrades,'" Desi echoed. "A word used by our Soviet friends."

"You prefer 'citizens?'"

Lucy folded her napkin and placed it on the table. "It's less scary for Americans—sorry, North Americans. I'm sure you know that paranoia about communism is running high in the States."

"I believe you've been accused yourself," Vilma said to Lucy.

It had been bound to come up.

"And found innocent," Desi added briskly.

"Accused," Savenko said. "So to Americans, communism is a crime."

Lucy couldn't resist. "Our citizens are free to believe anything they wish, as long as Uncle Sam doesn't think they're plotting to overthrow the government. For better or worse, communism has become synonymous with conspiracy."

Bonsal jumped in. "The US government does not wish to accuse any other nation of conspiracy. We favor peaceful coexistence."

"Coexistence is not possible," Tatarenko said. "We believe history will prove a society based on the dignity of the worker will prevail."

"I think we will not achieve much by debating the merits of capitalism versus communism," Castro said. "Cubans do not see any point in becoming the next Korea, a battlefield on which to play out your nations' contest. Let your political philosophies test themselves in practice rather than by military proxy."

In diplomatic fashion, Bonsal adopted a deferential tone that hardly disguised his confrontational question. "Prime Minister

Castro, would you not consider your agrarian reform law a step toward socialism?"

"Agrarian reform has been necessary to erase the echoes of colonialism. Such disproportionate ownership of property sustained a de facto oligarchy, a circumstance not conducive to political and economic equality."

Raúl jumped in on top of Fidel's dramatic pause. "Our own family has given up our land holdings in full compliance with this reform act."

After acknowledging his brother, Castro continued. "I stand firm that the Cuban people must determine their destiny, and this is why we will return to democratic process, hold elections, and choose leaders who represent the best interests of the people and not the interests of outside parties."

"The US is Cuba's most important trading partner," Bonsal said. "We wish to preserve this relationship."

"I'm certain you do," Castro said. "You will also understand that our national security requires that we diversify, to broaden our relationships so as not to be economically dependent on a single trading partner. As I said, your political and economic philosophies will play themselves out. As Mr. Lansky will understand, we will be wise to hedge our bets."

Lansky winked.

Bonsal, looking pale, attempted again to get the last word. "The US certainly supports Cuba's interests in expanding global trade. Healthy economic bonds are the foundation of trust."

"It should be the inverse," Tatarenko said. "An economic relationship not built on the foundation of political unity is nothing more than exploitation."

Bonsal lit up. "I could not agree more. The US and Cuba, as close neighbors, have enjoyed a fruitful and friendly relationship for many decades."

"Yes, for more than a century," Tatarenko said.

"It wasn't always under the best of circumstances," Bonsal conceded.

"Slave trade," Desi said to Lucy.

"You don't say," she sniped back. Somewhere along the line, he'd acquired the habit of making her look stupid by pretending to be helpful.

This topic was finally sufficiently touchy to silence the room, except for Marino, who was scraping his plate clean with his fork. Lucy took a final swallow of wine.

It was Castro himself who broke the tension. He rose as if to preside over the table. "It is time for some entertainment."

Everyone other than the Marxist brothers and the two soldier girls looked around as if they were expecting dancing girls to show up.

"We have cars waiting. Mr. and Mrs. Arnaz, please join me."

Lucy perked up. Havana's nightclubs had been legendary—right up until the revolution, that is. It was difficult to imagine where Castro might be dragging them off to next.

PAYOFFS & PAYBACK

*A*s they came to a stop at their apparent destination, Desi looked out the window of the sedan. "Why are there cameras outside? What's the big event?"

A doorman opened Lucy's door and offered assistance. Her heart sank.

"I hope this isn't for our benefit," she said. "I'm not prepared to appear on camera."

Castro stepped forward and took her arm while Desi circled around from the left side of the car.

"Who are these folks?" Desi asked.

"This is a Cubavisión news crew," Castro said.

Exactly what they'd been hoping to avoid.

"Mr. Lansky, welcome back to Club Montmartre," Castro said. "As you left it."

Clearly not fond of cameras, Lansky shielded his face with his hat and quickly turned his back on the lenses. This must have been his first visit to his own club since Castro and his revolutionary army had marched into Havana.

"Mr. Lansky," Lucy asked, "how long have you been away?"

"Year or so." Lansky inspected the facade of his club.

"Who's been minding the store?" Desi asked.

"We've taken good care of Mr. Lansky's property," Castro said.

A doorman greeted them, and Castro and Lucy led the way inside. The others followed, with Bonsal in the rear.

A band was playing inside, and about half the tables were occupied. It wasn't exactly the Hollywood and Wall Street crowd. The last time Lucy and Desi had visited the Montmartre, before little Lucie was born, it had been bursting at the seams with the rich and famous tourists. Although the guests were dressed neatly, they mostly wore the common outfits seen on Havana streets: guayabera shirts for the men and simple, calf-length dresses for the women. Lucy's slacks stood out among the curve-hugging dresses worn by the local women. The only women present who looked more out of place than she did were Vilma Espín and Celia Sánchez, in their olive drabs.

The host greeted Castro with no more or less deference than he would likely have shown any special guest, presenting himself with the Ellington-like sophistication of a man who took his job seriously, using the manners of a Latin gentleman. After quietly exchanging greetings with Castro, he approached Lansky. "Mr. Lansky, it is my greatest pleasure to see you again."

"Hector, thank you for managing things in my absence."

Hector showed them to a pair of adjacent tables with a view of the stage. Busboys wearing white gloves swiftly moved the tables together, reset the chairs, and lit extra candles. The Castro brothers remained standing until all the other guests had taken seats. Intentionally or not, they recreated their dinner seating order, leaving the broad side facing the stage open.

Lucy noticed Lansky taking a suitcase from Marino and placing it beside Fidel's chair. She glanced at Desi to see if he'd noticed. The picture was starting to take shape.

Instead, Desi teased her with a nod toward the dance floor, where three couples danced the mambo on the expansive floor in front of the band. He knew well that she wasn't comfortable with those sexy steps, and it had become a running joke he suggested at every opportunity. She would respond with a silent expression, "Are you kidding me?" After so many years on camera, they could carry on an entire conversation with nothing but facial expressions.

Now it was nothing but a taunt.

"How's business?" Lansky asked Hector.

Hector pressed his hands together. "It's quite complicated. Things are much different here in Havana now."

"It's fine, Hector," Castro said. "You may speak freely."

"The revolution, it has changed everything. Not so many tourists come now. The Montmartre has become a place that Cubans can enjoy."

"Does the revolution pay you well?"

Hector hesitated again, and Castro gave him the nod. "I have everything I need."

"And your family? You have what, six kids?"

"It is now seven."

"Plenty of food on the table."

"Sí, señor, yes, yes. And speaking of which, what may I bring for you and your guests?" He looked back and forth between Lansky and Castro.

Lucy couldn't blame him. How was he supposed to know who was hosting this party? She was glad not to be in his shoes.

"We will have the Spanish wine," Castro said.

Lansky raised his glass. "I would like to thank you, Prime Minister Castro, for taking good care of our property. It's been a good year for you and your country, and we look forward to a prosperous future under your leadership."

"President Urrutia closed down all gambling establishments over one year ago."

"I assumed it was temporary, until things quieted down and life could get back to normal."

Castro shrugged congenially. "I wasn't personally in favor of these measures at the time, which left hundreds without jobs. Over time, however, I have been relieved that the loss of these establishments has had more of a positive than a negative impact on Cubans."

Like any experienced negotiator, Lansky remained poker-faced.

"My associates and I have invested heavily in hotels, nightclubs, and casinos which bring thousands of visitors to Havana. Visitors who like to have a good time and spend large sums of money. Tourism is a big part of your economy. I have the numbers." He tapped the table with one finger, as if pointing to an imaginary ledger.

"I do not doubt you," Castro mused. "Do you also have the numbers to show where all that money goes once it's spent by the rich tourists?"

Lucy turned her ear toward Lansky. There weren't a whole helluva lot of people willing to take on the Mob.

"Do you know how many children have been raped?" Castro continued with quiet intensity. "Do you know how many Cubans have been prevented from enjoying these establishments? Do you know how many maids, waiters, dancers, and prostitutes are starving while you and your associates fill your Swiss bank accounts? You call yourself a legitimate businessman, yet you deliver suitcases full of money to the very highest leaders of this country to strengthen your grip."

Apparently, Marino wasn't just carrying his luggage everywhere they went.

Marino looked to his boss for direction. Lansky ignored him, maintaining his outward composure. It didn't take long for the other shoe to drop.

"Batista took advantage of his situation," Lansky said. "He treated his people badly. And that's why you and your compañeros have won their hearts and loyalty. Let's work together to bring legitimate business back to the country, good jobs, prosperity. Win-win."

When Hector and a server arrived with several bottles of Castro's favorite wine and a tray of glasses, Castro beckoned him and whispered into his ear. Hector disappeared back into the kitchen.

A few seconds later, half a dozen men wielding chainsaws emerged through the double service doors. In unison, they pulled the starter cords, and their saws roared to life.

Castro saluted them with his glass.

Gasoline fumes filled the air, overpowering the scent of tobacco. Lucy pulled Desi close. She covered one ear with her free hand.

"I guess you are about to get your answer," Joffrey called to Lansky.

The men fanned out around the large club. Two of them began sawing the substantial bar into segments, as if they were breaking down timber. Sawdust fishtailed into the air and dusted the dance floor like snow. The other men hacked away at the fine wooden chairs and tables, reducing them to splinters and shredded red upholstery.

The other patrons hastened out the front door, although it was clear that the men were not there to harm anyone, clearing the way and waiting courteously for everyone to exit. Finally, Castro rose and invited them all to follow. Lucy trotted right on his heels. Hector and the waiter gathered their glasses and fell in behind them.

The remaining staff began carting out the dismembered fixtures and furniture, down to mahogany paneling stripped from the walls and various carved ornaments that had decorated the railing posts, booths, and other fixtures. They piled the debris in the street as the Cubavisión crew filmed the proceedings.

When they were outside and far enough removed from the mayhem of the chainsaws to be heard without shouting, Desi spoke to Castro. "There's not enough light for those cameras."

"Sí, bueno." Castro took the bottle of Chivas Regal that Lansky had given him and poured its entire contents over the pile of broken wood, shaking loose the final drops. He handed the empty bottle to Bonsal and struck a single match. As the pyre roared to life, Lucy detected the fleeting aroma of burning whisky, which must have taunted Desi.

She marveled at Castro's bravado. No doubt Lansky and friends would come after this arrogant young politician, but he appeared to be goading them on. He had just unseated a dictator backed by these same gangsters—and as much as she hated to admit it, by the US government as well. If the revolutionaries could take down a government with such an enormous advantage in military might, the Mafioso boys might not have the balls to make Castro angry. God only knew how far Castro had already extended his reach beyond his island dominion.

The fire cast a pleasant warmth in the cool, damp evening air.

Castro had ordered the men to spare a couple of tables and enough chairs for the entire party. The band set themselves up on the sidewalk and struck up a cha-cha.

Bonsal would have nothing of it. He made his perfunctory apologies, as any diplomat would have, and invited Joffrey to join him in a black taxi, one of many that had gathered to watch the festivities. A few dozen men and women in green fatigues had taken positions along the street and at either end of the block.

Raúl handed Castro the suitcase. He popped the latches and pulled out a bundle of bills. Marino lunged, but one of the guards knocked him back and pointed his rifle point blank at his belly.

Castrol fanned the stack of bills a couple of times.

"You see," he said to Lansky, "I saved you much trouble. You already have my answer."

He stood and proceeded to toss the cash onto the pyre, one or two bundles at a time. As the horrified onlookers gaped, he closed the case and politely returned it to its owner, lingering next to Lansky, towering over him by more than a foot.

Marino stood close to his boss, looking as tough as possible. But even a Cosa Nostra hitman knew when he was outgunned and outnumbered.

Three of Castro's men showed Lansky and Marino to their waiting car.

Marino turned just before he got in. "Thanks for dinner."

MIDNIGHT MESSAGE

*L*ucy and Desi finally returned to their hotel room just before 2 a.m. Desi crushed out his final cigarette of the evening and took his turn in the bathroom before Lucy started her evening beauty regimen. She opened one of her suitcases and found her negligée.

"At least no one was shot tonight," she said.

"Not yet," Desi said from behind the closed bathroom door.

"Did you get a load of Boris and Natasha?"

"Boris and Natachacha? Who?"

"Na-ta-sha. The Russians." She paused to see if he would catch on. "From that cartoon show Lucie loves, Rocky and Bullwinkle."

"Boris and Bullwinkle. I got no idea what you're talking about." He emerged from the bathroom, stripped down to his boxers and undershirt, slipped into bed, and rolled over on his side.

It took so little for Desi to transform into an overgrown child. Eydie and Carol called it "middle man syndrome." As long as their husbands were neither too happy nor too angry, in a middle mood, they acted like adult men. Otherwise, they were either buying themselves toys or throwing little-boy tantrums. Desi was more complicated than that. When he was happy, the toys he chose were more often boobs and ass than chrome and horsepower. And when he was angry, he usually picked a hot fight before giving her the silent treatment. Or maybe she picked the fight, but only when he'd been an ass—usually, unless she was feeling particularly bitchy. Not all their fights were about important things, but from the beginning, arguing had been part of their relationship. Maybe passion always had two faces, ecstasy and rage. Probably bullshit.

Tonight, Desi's anger was a mystery. Other than being deprived of booze, she couldn't think of anything she'd done. "That was some show he put on."

"No kidding."

Although she preferred her own collection of skin cleansers and creams, she sniffed the lotions and soaps the hotel had left for them. Castro might have transformed the grand Hotel Habana Libre into his headquarters, but they'd continued some of the luxury touches, at least for Lucy and Desi's benefit. "He gave Lansky the boot. Maybe he's legitimate."

"Or maybe he wants a better deal. Don't be so gullible." He punctuated the insult with an over-the-shoulder glance, then returned to his "do not disturb" position.

"I'm the one who's gullible. Look who signed us up for the CIA."

He spoke at the facing wall. "I'm not the one who signed up to be a Red."

Enough already. "You should know a bluff when you see one."

"What if it wasn't a bluff? You want to throw away everything?"

He was right. The risk was too great. Congressman Velde and the House Un-American Activities Committee had gone easy on her. Someone in Washington had protected them, and it had only been a matter of time before that someone had called in the favor. Still, that wasn't a good enough reason to let Desi off the hook. She couldn't help herself.

"What are we doing here?" she asked. "If we've got spies here already, then we're just wasting our time."

"Every decision I make is for our business."

"So you're saying you make all the decisions. I've got nothing to say about it."

"You don't have to make no decisions because I take care of all the business so you can do your part."

She hurled a towel at him.

"My part?" she said, fuming. "You mean, the part of the clown."

"All of a sudden—tonight—you want to argue about who makes the business decisions."

"There *is* no argument. We make the decisions together."

"You mean, I tell you what we should do, and you agree."

"You think I'm stupid." She wadded up her nightgown and threw it down on the bed, but the soft satin landed with all the wallop of a feather. "You could've let me know twenty years ago."

"Here we go again with the reruns. I didn't say you were stupid. You're the star. You're America's Sweetheart. But I run the business. You could have told me twenty years ago you'd be so nuts."

"You know what America really thinks?" She wanted to stop herself, but the demon had already gripped her. "I'm the sweetheart. You're the drunken playboy."

When Desi was done with a fight, he ended it with a coup de grace. "I don't care what America thinks so long as they keep watching TV and buying Jell-O and cigarettes. The studio will go on long after you've lost your looks."

She didn't need to see his face to know he was pleased with himself. She'd seen the look of satisfaction plenty of times. But he had a point. Their sinking marriage wasn't the only thing threatening her career. Mother Nature was catching up with her.

At this point in any argument, one of them would usually leave the room and slam the door. Tonight, Desi wasn't budging, and there was no place to go. She wasn't about to walk off steam in the middle of the night on the streets of Havana. The only sanctuary was the bathroom. She could have a bath and not give him the satisfaction of climbing into bed beside him until she was good and ready. Hopefully, he'd be asleep by then. At least if he'd been drunk, he would've had the courtesy to pass out by now, so she could fume in privacy.

She drew a bath and was about to step in when someone knocked on the main room door. She wrapped herself in the white terry robe, embroidered with the Hilton crest, and peeked out into the room.

"Are you going to get that? Who the hell would be knocking in the middle of the night?" She grabbed her clothes and scurried back to the bathroom in case she needed to get dressed again in a hurry. Desi didn't stir. "Desi! The door."

"I don't hear no door."

The knock came again.

"You get it," he said.

"I'm not answering the door in the middle of the night."

Without getting out of bed, he rolled over onto his back.

"Who's there?" he shouted.

"Room service," came a muffled voice.

"We didn't order no room service." He rolled toward Lucy. "Did you order room service?"

Standing inside the bathroom doorway, she shook her head silently. He rolled back over and planted his head in the pillow.

A folded piece of paper slid under the door.

Desi didn't see it. She did.

I have important information for you, but you must speak to me aloud only as a steward. Everything else we discuss must be in writing.

SHE OPENED THE DOOR, and the steward rolled in a trolley, which was set elegantly with china coffee cups, a pitcher of coffee, and a miniature vase of fresh flowers. A three-tiered serving dish displayed a variety of petit fours, cookies, and cucumber sandwiches, like an English tea service. Also on the cart were a small pad of paper and a pen.

"You can leave it over there," she said, pointing to the space by the window.

While the steward uncovered and arranged the items on the tray, she quickly wrote a reply to the first note.

Dulles said no cloak-and-dagger on this trip. Why are you here?

"Would you like any milk or sugar in your coffee?" the young man asked. He read her note and then tore the sheet off and replied.

The director wanted to assure you that you were not on your own after your crew was detained. No need to worry. Everything is going according to plan.

Lucy looked him in the eye as if silently asking, "Are you serious?" She wrote on the page below his words:

What plan? I thought we were here to make a picture.

He replied:

Do not be alarmed by what you see here. You're in good hands.

It was too late to not be alarmed. They'd never discussed any kind of plan. Nightclub demolition and gangsters weren't the sort of thing she had expected to include in a frivolous little travelogue. This was not what they'd signed up for.

She wrote:

What kind of plan? We're here to make a picture, not for this cloak-and-dagger crap.

He wrote:

Yes, that's what I meant. You can be sure we'll be keeping an eye out for any trouble.

Words of little comfort.

The steward tore off several sheets, stuffed them into his pocket, and studied the pad at an angle to make sure the remaining pages were free of bleeding ink and telltale engraving. Then he spoke.

"Please accept this complementary refreshment."

"That's very kind," she said, playing along for safety's sake. "Do you have any orange juice?" She displayed her dissatisfaction with sternness bordering on a sneer.

The steward acknowledged her concern with a nod but offered no further reassurance or explanation. "I'll have some sent up immediately."

"Thank you, but don't bother. I'll be ready for sleep soon." She played along by offering a tip from her handbag, which he refused before he left.

She closed the door quietly so as not to disturb Desi.

"What was that all about?" he asked, without moving so much as a hair.

That's what she wanted to know. "Coffee."

"Who needs coffee at two in the morning?"

It was almost 3 a.m. now, but she didn't respond. She didn't like that word, "plan." Since when was there a plan? The only plan she knew about was to make Castro's glory picture, and they hadn't shot frame one yet. She knew Desi was holding some cards close to the vest, but it was useless to ask him about it. Not that he could pull off a lie. He was good at many things, but keeping secrets wasn't one of them. He just wouldn't bother to tell her the truth.

She took just a couple of sips of coffee and did the only thing she could do. She returned to her bath.

LET'S MAKE A PICTURE

At midmorning, Lucy slipped into the back of a black 1957 Lincoln next to Desi to be driven the mile or so to the Havana waterfront, known as El Malecón. Their driver deposited them into the midst of a bustling on-location film set presided over by Castro himself.

Overnight, Castro had transformed from soldier and statesman to an excited child. He was issuing orders to a dozen men and women, specifying where to place cameras and deploy parasol reflectors. Given the location and the morning light, he'd made some surprisingly good decisions, however inappropriate it was for him to second-guess the director. Lucy could feel Desi tensing up in anticipation of a confrontation.

Castro welcomed them eagerly. "You see? I've made all the arrangements. Like a Hollywood producer, no?"

The CIA team assigned to support them was nowhere to be seen.

"Where is our crew?" Desi asked.

"They have returned to your country," Castro said, "along with all your equipment. When you return, you'll find it all properly handled and accounted for. We have cameras and other equipment you need. We also have fine filmmakers in Cuba."

Like that Nazi propagandist, Leni Riefenstahl. Lucy slipped her hand into the loop of Desi's arm, hoping to lend a bit of restraint.

Desi gave the set a quick once-over. A couple dozen men and women were setting up sun reflectors, mounting cameras on tripods, and roping off the area.

"It's your show," he said.

Lucy carefully retracted her arm from Desi's. He'd folded too easily. This man had never put up with anyone stepping on his toes, not sponsors, not network executives, not vain actors who questioned his direction. Even more reason to suspect he hadn't let her in on the entire scheme. She'd get to the bottom of it later. Right now, creative control was the least of their worries.

James Martell, their undercover CIA sound man, had promised they'd be under the constant protection of his dozen trained men. Castro had obviously seen right through that flimsy charade. Or maybe he hadn't but didn't want to take any chances. Either way, they were up a creek. Although CIA Director Dulles had assured them that other agents were operating in Havana besides Joffrey, whom they'd met at dinner the previous evening, how would they know where to turn if things went sour? Now they were depending on unseen, unrecognizable guardians to come riding to their rescue.

Castro finally made eye contact with Lucy. He must have been reading her mind. "I give you my word, you will be well cared for." He turned to Desi. "You will have a capable crew at your disposal for the making of this film."

She snuck a look at Desi. Nothing but his best poker face. Castro had shipped off their ersatz crew, who also happened to be their only protection, and he hadn't blinked an eye. Was he ready to fold, or was he bluffing? Either way, she wouldn't get a decent night's sleep until they got back to LA. The sooner, the better.

Castro turned to face the sea, placing his hands on his hips. Cloud shadows played over undulating blue water. "I am told you had a visitor last night."

Exactly the kind of thing she'd worried about when they accepted this deal.

Desi took the cue before it soured into a guilty silence. "Yeah, some joker came to our room. Very late. Said he had a complimentary meal for us."

"I was told of a man wandering the corridors," Castro said. "An autograph hunter, perhaps. You have many fans."

"Well," Lucy said, "it was rather rude of him to be disturbing us so late. I do have to admit, though, that it's flattering to know we have fans even in your country."

"Nevertheless, he won't bother you any further. He was apprehended. We made it very clear to him that it's not acceptable to disturb guests."

She didn't need a mirror to know she'd gone pale. Thank God he was more comfortable looking at the sea than making eye contact.

Castro raised his voice to be heard by everyone over the sound of surf. "We open with the seaside."

"The beauty of Cuba," she said, "a tropical gem in the Caribbean."

"Sí sí, yes yes. I also think North Americans like beaches."

This was no beach. The Malecón was a sweeping avenue that ran along Havana's waterfront, rimmed by the shoulder of a massive concrete seawall. A procession of waves rushed the sliver of sand and leaped up through jumbled rocks below the seawall, here and there spraying up and over the barrier, raining down on people and vehicles. Despite the unpredictable sea, a steady stream of locals, including some determined winter sunbathers and a few who looked like tourists, passed by the set, detouring around the barricaded area.

With his coarse beard and head-to-toe green fatigues, Castro looked hopelessly out of place next to the toned, tanned young women and men here. For that matter, he looked odd compared even to the less shapely folks with round bellies and butterball butts. Not unlike the beaches back home, Havana's stone and concrete waterfront was inhabited by a cross section of humanity, plump and lanky, short and tall, young and old. But here, there were no zones favored by white or black folk. Skin tones ranged from milky to chocolate and every shade in between. This country was either further along in race relations than the US or maybe had been forced to abandon segregation because its freely mixing population had already blurred the racial lines. In any case, it was unlike anything Lucy had experienced at home or in Europe.

As grips bustled about setting up reflectors, Castro introduced Desi to his very young local filmmaker. "I've asked Señor Jorge Herrera to assist you with this production."

Herrera, who couldn't have been more than twenty, if that, made no effort to hide his annoyance. Even in Cuba, the kids had high opinions of themselves. Lucy expected Herrera would learn a thing or two from Desi, in spite of himself.

"We must begin," Castro said.

She took a back seat, following Desi's lead.

"What are we shooting?" Desi asked Castro. "You got something in mind?"

Castro handed him a stack of pages a couple of inches thick, bound with metal tabs.

"What's this?"

"The script."

Lucy raised her eyebrows in disbelief, until she realized she was being observed by Castro's entourage. The script had to be at least eight hundred pages, more than a little long considering that an average two-hour feature film ran about one hundred and twenty pages. Desi needed both hands to hold it. He looked at Lucy, hefting the manuscript to demonstrate its weight. She was just as dumbfounded as he was.

"You, of course, are the artist," Castro said. "It's merely a starting point."

Lucy looked over Desi's shoulder as he thumbed through the script. It contained page after page of speeches at various locations—a school, a hospital, a factory, a stadium, a plantation, and so on. Castro looked on expectantly, like one of those hopefuls who'd occasionally managed to corner them outside the studio. Desi usually tried to appease them by thumbing through their scripts and asking them to send them to him at his office. He never had time to read any of them, but he didn't want to be rude by brushing off fans. For a man with so much power, he remembered where he came me from, and he believed it never hurt to give a little encouragement. For every script sent to him, he had his secretary send a signed thank-you letter explaining that it wasn't right for Desilu, but he wished them well in their careers—both cold and compassionate at the same time.

There would be no polite rejection letter for Prime Minister Castro. It was going to be a long day—make that a long week.

"This is what you want to shoot?" Desi asked.

"It's sufficient." Castro tapped the pages in Desi's hands.

"It's certainly substantial," Lucy said.

Castro handed Lucy her own copy, lifted from a crate dragged over by one of his assistants. She took a seat on the concrete seawall so she could rest the script in her lap, then switched from her sunglasses to reading glasses. Under her big floppy sun hat, she began reading from page one.

She didn't get far before calling Desi over. "He's expecting me to read this on camera." She started mouthing the lines silently to herself, then aloud: "'… the people of Cuba have broken the bonds of oppressive northern aggression.'" She held it up for Desi to see and lowered her voice enough for the sound of crashing surf to cover her words. "They'll string me—us—up for this."

He paged through his own copy, reading lines to himself, and shrugged. "What's the difference? It'll never see the light of day."

She hoisted the script to hide her face from view. "How do you know? Because a bunch of government stooges said so? I'm not buying it. Unless you spoil the footage yourself, you can't possibly know where it'll end up. He's got his own crew, for God's sake."

"I'll think of something. Let's do it his way for now. We'll fix it in post. It would take weeks to rework this script."

She set down the script again on her lap and glanced back at Castro, who was waiting politely for them to finish their conversation, occupying himself by instructing the crew and soldiers to finish unloading equipment from the nearby panel truck. For his benefit, she kept a smile on her face and placed her hand on Desi's forearm. A nice touch, she thought—a happy husband-and-wife team talking through a few details. "If we don't do something about it, it'll take months to shoot," she added.

One man started a generator on a trailer apparently unhitched from the truck. The machine belched black exhaust and made a racket that rattled Lucy's bones. A cannon-bang of backfire made her heart skip a couple of beats. Castro waved his arms at the man until he shut down the machine. He then had a couple of soldiers heave a power cable down from the truck and uncoil it across the street. They dragged the business end into the nearest shop. Passing cars and trucks thudded and rattled over the thick line, a less nerve-racking noise, yet still too much for a film set.

Satisfied that he'd solved the problem, Castro signaled them with a sweep of his hands.

Back in the day when they worked their toughest deals together, Desi used to stir the pot while she played peacemaker, all the while slipping in everything they wanted in the first place—almost everything, anyway.

"Set him up," Lucy said.

Desi tucked the script under his arm and headed toward Castro.

She continued turning pages as if she were still reading, openly eavesdropping. If the two of them together couldn't handle this joker, they might as well pack it in, sell the studio, and move to Peoria.

"It's very long," Desi said.

Not the point, but maybe he could talk Castro into cutting the politics.

"The folks at home will like pictures," he continued. "Not so much the talking."

"And this is why I chose this location as the background for our message." Castro held his hands up in the director's gesture he'd learned from watching too many movies, framing the scene in a rectangle formed with his thumbs and forefingers. "Show the children playing along the water, the mothers taking sun." He placed his hand on Desi's shoulder, as if confiding in him. "Before the revolution, only the tourists and wealthy Cubans could enjoy the seaside. Most Cubans cleaned their hotel rooms, waxed their fine automobiles, cooked their meals, and blended their daiquiris. Now these pleasures are available to all Cubans."

Desi ran his fingertip across the open script. "Yes, that's what it says in here."

That was it? He was putting on a half-baked show, and she couldn't tell whether it was for Castro or for her.

A woman approached and led Lucy back to a folding director's chair next to a short wooden table where she had laid out cosmetics, brushes, and a hairbrush. She introduced herself with gestures as Ximena and began stretching a net over Lucy's hair. Lucy cringed and forced a smile. No one but Irma had touched her hair in years. How she looked in Cuba didn't worry her so much, but she'd better come back looking no worse for wear.

Ximena must have been a beautician, because she obviously had no knowledge of stage makeup. Lucy borrowed the hand mirror and inspected the girl's handiwork. The eyes were lovely but understated. She took an eye pencil and demonstrated how to darken the lines, to which Ximena responded with wide-eyed and lip-biting dismay. One of the grips, an attractive young man, noticed the communication breakdown and helped Lucy explain how to exaggerate her features so they'd come out looking natural on film.

As Ximena prepared Lucy for her first scene, Lucy listened to Desi's ongoing consultation with Castro, who either didn't trust Desi to manage the project on his own or couldn't control his enthusiasm. It wouldn't surprise her in the least if the cocky military leader of a bloody political takeover proved unwilling to relinquish control over his propaganda masterpiece.

"I've asked for the lines to be written to cards," Castro said, "as the speeches may be difficult to commit to memory without advanced preparation."

"My wife does not work from cue cards," Desi said.

Flattering—but maybe it was time for an exception. She hoisted the script from her lap and held it out in front of her, demonstrating the challenge by pinching the twenty-six pages containing the first speech. There was no chance in hell she was about to memorize this bullshit.

This time, Desi got her message. "In this case, maybe it's a good idea."

He tried to fold the script over so he could hold it in one hand, but it was too thick and he had to prop it against his chest. He took out his pen and began making notes. Lucy suspected he was trying to work out some shots, but there wasn't much to do if they were actually going to shoot to the script. She already knew how he'd set it up. He'd put one camera on her, framed in a medium shot with the surf and sky in the background. He'd send another camera further away to catch some wider angles, including beauty shots of the boulevard and Havana's skyline. He'd send the third crew roaming the promenade for B-roll, strolling pedestrians taking the sun. Then he would cut it all together later, with her reading Castro's meandering speech as a voice-over. Castro's ode to himself—and Lucille Ball's Hollywood swan song.

"Okay," Desi called out, "everyone take your places."

Castro offered Lucy his hand to help her to her feet. She'd seen many men in uniform during her USO days, not to mention Desi when he served, but Castro was a different kind of fellow. She didn't doubt the sincerity of his courtesy, but in comparison to his behavior toward the other women in his cohort, it felt condescending, as if she was too delicate to manage on her own—or worse, just plain fragile.

She handed her script to the young woman acting as production assistant and took her place on the X mark Desi had chalked on the pavement in front of the camera. The Malecón waterfront stretched behind her into the distance with the city skyline to her right, where it would appear through the camera viewfinder at screen left. She'd chosen to wear a calf-length sundress, white with a pink and orange floral print. Along with her bright red hair, gently breeze-blown, she would contrast nicely with the blue Caribbean and earthy city tones in the background. White parasol reflectors filled the shadows with diffuse sunlight, making her fair skin appear to glow from within, especially in contrast to her darkly outlined eyes and candy-apple red lips.

Castro sent one of the soldiers into the street to stop traffic. A driver several cars back leaned on his horn until another soldier ran back and gave him the what for, which started an argument, until Castro waved to catch his attention. The man abruptly dropped his protest.

Desi spoke to the more distant cameramen through a walkie-talkie, telling them what footage to capture of the surroundings before they began shooting her monologue. Finally, he turned off the radio to silence its crackling static and peeked through the viewfinder of the primary camera to check the framing for himself.

Just above the reach of the camera's lens, a man lowered a boom over Lucy, dangling a microphone wrapped in a puffy gray wind-muffler. Desi adjusted the focus. He'd soften it for her to give her, as he said, a more youthful appearance. At home, it was no secret that Lucy preferred a little age-reversing camera trickery. Desi gave Herrera some brief instructions, no doubt explaining his intentionally imperfect settings, before yielding the viewfinder back to him.

In the script, Lucy had noticed a few awkward phrases—likely translation errors—and considered whether it mattered if she recited the speech verbatim, especially given how unlikely it was that the final film would be shown anywhere outside of Cuba. She suspected Castro would scrutinize every word, however, so she'd need to take care. Otherwise, she'd just end up doing multiple takes.

SAY WHAT?

"Roll film," called Desi.

Herrera raised a hand to signal that his film was rolling.

Desi looked over at him. "In Hollywood, we say 'speed' when the cameras are ready."

"Sí, speed," Herrera said.

"Slate."

The snap of the clapper board signaled the synchronization of the camera and sound recording. The production assistant called out, "Scene one, take one," which he'd also scrawled on the clapper board in chalk.

"Action," Desi called.

Lucy began. "'Today we are visiting beautiful Havana, Cuba, the gem of the Caribbean…'"

Castro nodded at Desi his satisfaction at finally being underway.

"'…Free from the tyranny of corrupt dictators and exploitation by ruthless imperialists and criminals, the people of Cuba have finally realized the vision of José Martí and taken charge of their own destiny.'"

Speaking it aloud was even more unnerving than reading it to herself. Castro mouthed the words as she spoke them, which she found distracting. Had they been in a studio, the lights would have prevented her from seeing anyone behind the cameras, but outside in open daylight, she had to concentrate to prevent her eyes from tracking their movements, one of the challenges of location shooting.

Desi rubbed his forehead and wiped his hand down over his face, his habit whenever he disliked the way a scene was playing.

She continued reading the endless lines, working hard to anticipate breath breaks in Castro's long sentences. It would have been easier to get through this ridiculous crap if she'd had time to rehearse. She was flying blind and had to anticipate lines by reading ahead of what was actually coming out of her mouth, a skill usually practiced by sight-reading musicians that also came in handy for guest appearances on live television.

"'The imperialists have finally been dispossessed of their illicit land holdings, freeing the Cuban people from the bondage of—' Whaaat?" She coughed and tried to cover her outrage. "'...from the bondage of corporate slavery.' I'm sorry. It's my age. I'm afraid my eyes aren't so good anymore, and I'm too vain to wear glasses."

Fidel nodded to the cue card girl, the same young lady who'd taken Lucy's hat, urging her to move in toward Lucy. Herrera, peering through the eyepiece, guided her with hand signals to the closest spot out of camera frame.

"Keep it rolling," Desi said. "Pick it up from the next line."

After twenty minutes, Desi had to call cut so they could change the film magazine.

Castro waited patiently, scratching a few changes in his own copy of the script. When the camera was loaded and ready again, he held up a hand as if calling time-out. "I wish to start again."

Desi sighed audibly. "We just ran through four thousand feet of film. Are you sure you want to waste it?"

"You make many tries when you make movies?" He looked to Lucy for help with the terminology.

"Takes," she offered, plastering on a smile. She was exhausted. She had never in her life concentrated so hard to maintain continuity on camera. She could hardly bear the thought of repeating that entire speech. If this footage ever made it out to the public, they would string her up as a traitor. And she'd have her own government to thank for it.

"Yes, yes. Let's have another take." Castro was jubilant at the prospect of starting over, the mark of a true perfectionist, a characteristic he shared with Desi. Except, apparently, on that particular day.

"You are very good," he said to her. "It's the words. I want to make some changes." He took a seat in the folding chair that had been set up for him and disappeared into thought, scratching out and rewriting lines.

She sat in the chair beside him and looked over his shoulder. "I wonder…"

Desi sighed.

She got it. He wanted her to dummy up and get on with it, but he sure as hell hadn't convinced Castro to tone down the political diatribe. She dismissed Desi's unspoken plea with a twitch at the corner of her mouth.

Desi lit up a cigarette and turned his attention to a curvaceous women strolling by. While Lucy spoke with Castro, she kept one eye on Desi. She wasn't so much bothered by his attraction to the scantily clad women. She never held it against him when his eyes wandered. When he made love to her, she felt like a member of that club, sexy by association, and these Cuban gals were quite lovely, with their cute figures and a tendency to walk as if music were playing in their heads. It was Desi's hands, lips, and cock she wanted him to control. Fortunately, the Cuban beauties were out of reach, at least right now. At the moment, she was more concerned about how he wore his stress like a suit—more like a straitjacket—especially when he didn't have booze to take the edge off. He was chain-smoking, but at least he was coherent. Sobriety might not have been as traumatic for her as it was for him, but she'd become so accustomed to drunken Desi. She had to readjust to sober Desi.

Castro angled toward her. "You are unhappy with the words?"

"I have a few ideas. Do you have a pen?"

He transferred the hefty script to her lap and watched her strike through several passages, silently mouthing the alterations to himself. He hummed from time to time, which made her pause to check whether he was agreeing or disagreeing with her alterations.

She licked her fingertip and used it to flick through several more pages. "I was just thinking, if you want to win support from the American people—"

"People of the United States," he corrected.

"Yes, from the US Americans…"

He nodded acceptance of her more succinct terminology.

"You may want to take a less accusatory tone."

He stepped forward to better hear her over the roar of the surf. "It's not meant to be taken personally."

"I'm sure," she said. "Some might take offense at some of these statements. I mean, is it true that people in the States have profited from the sweat and blood of Cuban workers?"

"Yes, absolutely true."

"But not all."

"Many."

"Some."

Clearly exasperated, he crossed his arms. "How would you say it?"

She pointed at the offending passage and read through the next page. "You could skip that part altogether. Maybe just focus on the positive?"

"Ignore one hundred and eighty years of slavery?"

She had to appeal to his ego or his pride—or both. "You've already won. You'll get more from the US by making friends."

"Like Lincoln at Gettysburg," he said thoughtfully.

Desi joined them. "What's this about Lincoln?"

"The Civil War," she said. "You know, 'Four score and seven years ago…'"

"Now we're having a history lesson?" He opened his arms wide. "Let's shoot before we lose the light."

It was only about ten o'clock in the morning, but by noon, the overhead sun would drown out all the shadows. They needed the angled light to add depth to the filmed images. They couldn't continue in the afternoon because the sudden change in the sun's position would cause an obvious continuity break. Desi might have been impatient with her, but he was just as meticulous about the cinematography as she was about the script. Neither of them could stand to make a piece of garbage. If they lost the morning sun, they'd have to continue tomorrow.

"You wish for me to be conciliatory," Castro was saying. He removed his cap and scratched his head. "How would you say it?"

"This is just a suggestion," she said, waiting for him to acknowledge his understanding. "First, I'd remove all the inflammatory statements. Focus on the positive. The future. What the revolution has done for Cuba."

"How can I explain what has come without comparing to what was before?"

"It's implied. You want US Americans to appreciate the culture and opportunity."

He pounded his fist into his other palm. "And the social justice."

He would keep circling back to the same argument. The only way to get through to him was with a direct approach. "Yes, sure. But you can't throw political philosophy at our people. Their eyes will glaze over and they'll label you—and me—as crackpots."

"That's very insulting to both us and to your people."

"It's just the way people are. Folks at home are riding high. Ever since the war, we in the States have had it pretty cushy. It's not so easy for US Americans to empathize with the pain and suffering your people have overcome, and rubbing their noses in it won't make them feel guilty. It'll just make them disinterested. People are simple. The first thing that comes to their minds is 'what's in it for me?'"

He refitted his cap. "This is the essence of our struggle."

He was a different kind of animal. He wasn't just playing a role. He was inseparable from his politics.

"Let's say we make a travelogue," she said.

His expression indicated he didn't understand.

"We'll capture the sights and sounds. Show them the adventure awaiting them in an exotic paradise."

"Insufficient. We will proudly proclaim the social advances we are making. We're not a playground for wealthy North Americans. We are a country of seven million people recently freed from bondage and prepared to participate in global trade and political advancement, not as lap dogs, but as first-class members of the global league of—"

"It's too damned long," Desi declared in Spanish.

This brought silent shock from the crew and those assembled to watch the filming and get a close look at their hero. Castro himself seemed stunned. Apparently, it was not customary to interrupt the prime minister when he was speaking.

Castro took another copy of the script from the stack and thumbed through it. He paused to read, mumbling the lines to himself. Disgusted, he dropped his script on his chair and marched off, stroking his beard.

Lucy followed. Maybe she could keep him from putting them in front of a firing squad. "He's right, you know."

"So you agree?"

"It plays a little long. A lot long."

"It's a good story, no?"

"I'm sure there's a good story somewhere in there, but it's a little buried."

"I talk too much."

"I wouldn't know."

"I have much to say."

"It seems so. Maybe let the camera do the talking."

Castro looked sullen. "You are certain those words will not achieve our goal."

She placed her hand on his chest over his heart, which took him by surprise. "You have to appeal to their hearts, not their minds. Sell them the dream."

She was winning him over, but now she would need to come up with something to say. If she could talk him down from the hot air speeches, she might just save her own neck. "Paint the picture. Let la revolución speak for itself." A little pandering couldn't hurt.

Castro nodded at the script. "What are your recommendations?"

"Give me a minute." She asked the girl for her glasses and sun hat.

He took three puffs on his cigar. "You may continue with your changes, but I must approve."

"Of course."

Desi tapped on his wristwatch and then followed her down the sidewalk to the privacy afforded by the roaring surf. "Eight hundred fucking pages," he snarled while maintaining a movie extra's neutral expression.

"He's a wordy fella."

"Thirteen, fourteen hours of film." Desi placed his hand on the small of her back and guided her out of the path of the sea spray. "That could take months to shoot. I can tell you one thing right now, I'm not sticking around to make Castro's commie epic."

She flipped open the script to a random page, cradled it in one arm, and traced a line with her finger as if explaining an idea. "Don't look so defiant. He's watching."

"Why bother fixing it?" He loosened his posture and lit them each a cigarette. "You're wasting your time."

"What do you suggest?"

"We play along. Two weeks. We shoot for two weeks. That's it. We'll keep the cameras rolling as much as possible, and you deliver the speeches. Burn through the whole damned thing in single takes. Then we drop it in the can and give it to him as is, over and done. We got our own show to shoot."

"Do you have a hole in your head?" She crossed her arms, hugging the script against her chest. "Are you expecting me to recite twelve hours of his Red bullshit and hand it over to him to spread all over the world?"

"Dulles said they had a way to keep it out of his hands. We'll give everybody what they want, and Castro won't have a clue."

"And what if Castro outsmarts them? We'll lose everything—the studio, the house. They'll run us out of the country."

"Better keep your eyes peeled for a nice place to live, in case we have to take up permanent residence."

"You're making jokes." Lucy said.

He nodded in the direction of Castro and crew. "Let's get it over with."

He was right about one thing: they might be wasting their time. It made no difference whether the script was eight hundred minutes of film or eighty. If it got out, they were ruined. Somebody would make a movie about this someday, like a Greek tragedy. She'd fallen into the cracks of her own life. The heroine who'd sown the seeds of her own destruction long ago—not so far-fetched. Melodrama sold soap.

Castro was pacing around the cordoned set, reciting his crazy speeches to himself while puffing on a fat cigar. Desi quick-stepped back over to his station beside Herrera and his camera.

Lucy handed the script back to the girl and sat in her chair so Ximena could put her windblown hair back in order. Desi pointed at the sun. She gave him the "one minute" finger.

Castro flipped through several pages. "It's the same."

"We'll shoot it as is," Desi said.

Castro's face crinkled with satisfaction.

Most of the other hands on the set stood around smoking while they waited. As Ximena brushed at Lucy's eyeliner, an older man, maybe in his sixties or seventies, wandered across Lucy's field of view, shaking the stands that held the reflectors and lights and checking them for steadiness. He happened to approach one and catch it just as it was about to tip over in the wind. He grabbed a couple of chunks of broken pavement from the edge of the street and weighed down the feet, then went back to prowling around.

Castro looked up momentarily and exchanged greetings with him. As Castro turned toward Desi, the man pivoted to follow. He pulled his hand from his pocket, and Lucy caught the glint of metal—a switchblade.

ACCIDENTAL HERO

Desi flinched as he realized what was happening just behind Castro. The crew member was gripping a switchblade knife blade down, ready to plunge it into his target.

Desi leaped forward, barreling Castro off his feet. Castro used his considerable strength to throw Desi off, and his elbow smacked against the pavement. He ignored the pain.

"Somebody stop that man!" he shouted.

The man with the knife was already fleeing. The crowd of onlookers parted to let him pass, but one of Castro's bodyguards tackled him easily, and they went down hard on the pavement.

Castro sprang up and pulled his pistol on Desi.

Another bodyguard called out to his boss and pointed at the assailant, face down on the ground with a heavy boot on his back. Castro took a few seconds to assess the situation. He lowered his gun, walked over to the assailant, and told the guard to bring him to his feet.

Blood streamed from a cut above the man's left eye and from his nostrils.

Castro looked back at Desi and then again at the assailant. "One of you is a hero."

The man stared at the pavement, refusing to make eye contact with Castro. He appeared to be silently reciting something to himself —a prayer, maybe. The knife lay open on the ground a few feet from where Desi had tackled Castro, but Desi knew better than to move a muscle right now. Lucy stood frozen at the edge of the silent crowd.

Castro picked up the knife and brought it back to face the assailant. "Did you plan to kill me with this blade?"

The man continued to recite prayers to himself.

Castro placed the point of the knife at the assailant's chest. "Who sent you? How much did they pay you to betray these people?" With his free arm, he made a grand, sweeping gesture at the surrounding crowd.

Rubbing his elbow, Desi tried to get Lucy's attention, directing her with his chin to look away. She didn't need to see what might happen next.

"I don't know," the man said in a tiny voice. Blood trickled over his lips and fell in droplets on his shoe.

"You don't know? *I* know. The one who sent you was a thief and a coward."

"Sí, sí."

"Are you a thief and a coward, too?"

"Sí, sí, sí."

"I don't think you are. You were willing to sacrifice your life. This is not the act of a coward. No, I think you are the victim." Castro was nothing if not Shakespearean. If they tried to make a show about him, no one would believe it. He was too over the top even for the TV audience.

The man had no answer for this. He had stopped his blubbering prayers. The gash on his forehead, torn open by the pavement, threatened to expose bone.

Castro looked around, making eye contact with many in the crowd, then returned his attention to the man. He lifted the man's chin and looked into his eyes. "You have been told that I have stolen the country."

"Sí."

"You have been told that the revolutionaries—some call them the Fidelistas—serve communist masters bent on world domination."

"Sí, your honor."

"You have been told that the revolution has been constructed only to turn Cuba into a tool of the Soviets to expand their power into our hemisphere, to land on the doorstep of the United States."

"I don't know."

Castro was beginning to exceed the man's political knowledge and affiliations.

"You don't know—this I believe. Someone has paid you to perform an act of historic significance, treating you as an ignorant peasant, easily intimidated. They have used their power and money to influence you. Do you think what you were about to do was right?"

"I don't know."

"You do not. This is not your fault. Power is maintained by those who perpetuate ignorance and desperation, by those who withhold sustenance of mind and body, making the masses dependent. This is not freedom."

And then Castro was silent. Everyone was silent. The man was silent.

Castro began to press the knife into the man's chest. The crowd, including Lucy, gasped, and many looked away.

The blade folded, clicking back into the handle.

"Take this knife," Castro said. "Give it to the man who put you to this task. Tell him if he wishes me dead, he must come and see me himself. You are free to go."

Desi shifted uncomfortably and rubbed his sore elbow. Capra himself should have been directing this scene. Castro must have seen a lot of movies.

The bodyguard hesitated to release the man's arms, which he held twisted high behind his back. Castro nodded reassurance.

As soon as he was released, the man fell to his knees and begged for forgiveness.

Castro took his hand and tugged him to his feet. "You must have that wound treated. You"—he gestured to the bodyguard—"take him to the clinic."

He spun and pulled Desi to his feet, crushing him in a bear hug and then holding him by the shoulders at arm's length. "You are a hero of the Cuban people."

Desi nodded, wincing at the pain jolting into his hand from his elbow. Just what he needed. If he was learning anything about Castro, it was that the man had a gift for exaggeration. This was the kind of thing that the reporters would eat up. The government boys had better do their job and keep it from getting out.

He broke away from Castro and went to Lucy, who was looking at him in complete disbelief.

She drew back one hand and punched him in the chest. "What if the knife had gone into you instead of him?"

He reached for her. "The knife didn't go into nobody."

"You're an idiot!" She was blazing.

"What was I supposed to do, stand around and watch a crazy man stab someone? I apologize. Next time I see a murder about to happen, I'll mind my own business."

"Your husband saved my life," Castro said with a new kind of open warmth. "I know of no greater act of friendship."

Lucy's face matched her hair, and Desi knew she was about to blow.

"You son of a bitch," she shouted at Castro. "You promised us safety—guaranteed it! It's not my husband's job to protect you from all the crazies you pissed off by taking over the country."

"My sincerest apologies," Castro said. "I hope you will forgive me."

She shoved her script into Castro's chest and turned her back against the breeze to light up a smoke.

"We did not take over the country," Castro corrected her. "We reclaimed it."

"To-may-to, to-mah-to," she tossed back over one shoulder.

Fidel looked to Desi for translation.

Desi obliged. "It's a song. Gershwin. You know, 'You say...'"

"Sí, sí. Ella Fitzgerald, Louis Armstrong." He sang the "I say to-may-to, you say to-mah-to" lyric with gusto, and Desi struggled to maintain his composure. Castro placed one large hand on his shoulder. "Today, you have forged a bond between our nations."

Whatever. It wouldn't last. Desi cupped his sore elbow in the other hand. "Can we shoot the scene now?"

Castro backed up a few steps, took his seat, and extended both arms, palms up in deference to Desi. "Proceed."

A FRIEND OF LA REVOLUCIÓN

They joined Castro after dinner in his office, a converted hotel room on one of the upper floors of the Hotel Habana. The beds had been removed, replaced by a nondescript table that served as a desk, along with a round dark walnut table presumably for meetings and several carved wooden chairs with seats upholstered in tropical floral patterns. Lucy chose one to settle into. Not exactly a comfortable place to relax after an exhausting day.

"It's time for celebration." Castro selected a bottle of wine from a small collection arranged in a row on a side table at the back wall. He studied the label. "It's a good one." He held the bottle out for Desi's approval.

"My husband doesn't drink," Lucy said.

Desi accepted the bottle and read the label. "I can speak for myself."

She wanted to trust him, but he'd never given her reason to do so.

"It's old," Desi said.

Uncharacteristically, Fidel chuckled—not so much at Desi's observation, it seemed, but more out of delight. "1945 Herederos del Marqués de Riscal. It's a very special Spanish wine." He uncorked the bottle and poured its contents into a cut crystal decanter, twisting the bottle with a final flourish to stem the flow of sediment. "We'll let it rest." He sniffed the cork and then offered it to Lucy.

She shook her head and crossed her arms. The assassination attempt replayed over in her head. "Who do you think was responsible?"

Rather than sitting behind his makeshift desk, Castro turned one of the chairs from the conference table to face them. He placed the decanter and two wine glasses on the table, close at hand. "Was it the work of your government? I can't be certain." He'd apparently gotten her drift. "In such matters, and in the midst of social transformation, no one is beyond suspicion. Señor Arnaz, you are as knowledgeable as any other Cuban. What is your theory?"

Desi had been fidgeting with his cigarette lighter. It was that time of the day when his cravings badgered him, and the musky, fruited aroma of the wine wasn't helping. He was a ticking time bomb. "How the hell would I know?"

"Your government may wish to sow the seeds of insurrection, or they may land their armies on our shores. However, no matter how prominent your celebrity, these are not things they would share with entertainers." He must have noticed Desi's nostrils flare at the dig, because he quickly added, "That is for your safety. It is best you should remain ignorant."

She certainly appreciated her own ignorance, but she could only wonder whether Desi was in the same position.

"In any case," Castro was saying, "it makes no difference. Many people want me dead. They think by removing me, they will kill the revolution."

She might have written off his confident defiance as an act, if not for the eye contact. A blowhard would've gazed off toward an imagined crowd of admirers or up to the heavens while spouting off. This fellow was different. In ordinary conversation, at least with new acquaintances, he was tentative, uncomfortable. But his passion compelled you to look him in the eye and size him up for yourself. Still, it was one thing to defy the opposition and something else to stay out of their crosshairs.

"Must be hard fearing for your life all the time," Desi said.

"How do you protect yourself from so many enemies?" she asked.

"I do not. If I devoted my attention to self-preservation, then my work would suffer. This would serve the assassin's purpose. Whether my heart were to continue beating in my chest or not, I would be dead. The revolution doesn't need me, but I need the revolution. Living in fear is the same as slowly dying. The body remains, but the spirit is lost."

"What if the revolution fails?" she asked. "What would become of you?"

His expression flattened. "I could ask you what would become of you if something happened to your children. What would your life be then?"

The question stabbed like a threat, though it was too brazen to have been intentional. No words were necessary. Her bewildered expression must have served the purpose. Desi, however, wore an expression of relentless skepticism.

"You see, Mrs. Arnaz, the pain for me would be no less. If the Cuban Revolution were to die, I would perish with it."

"The captain goes down with his ship," Desi said, with a hint of mockery.

Castro offered cigars, which Lucy refused this time. The first one had knocked her for a loop.

"Who else knew where we'd be filming today?" she asked.

"You have an investigative mind," Castro said.

"It's an actor's business to get inside other people's heads."

He nodded. "Someone who was present must have disclosed our location in advance."

"Either that, or the crazies are everywhere and that one just got lucky—well, not luck. I mean he thought he got lucky, not that it was a good thing."

"I understand your meaning. And I understand that you may have concerns about your own safety. Many people are protecting you while you are in Cuba—so much that they missed the attempt on my own life."

"You mean your people are watching over us," Desi said.

He nodded. "We have a secret security guard, just as the president does in your country. I have instructed my guards to put your safety ahead of my own. But they are not alone. Are you aware your government is conspiring to overthrow the revolution?"

Apparently, she wasn't the one in the know about that particular question. "If you mean do we know about some such plan, then we're not well connected enough to be trusted with that kind of information—are we, dear?" she added to Desi.

Desi feigned disinterest by seeking the optimal puff on his cigar. "But I wouldn't be surprised."

"No," Castro said, "it's what we expected."

"How will you find them?" she asked. "The one who informed the assassins."

"The traitor will reveal himself."

"Or herself?"

"You need not worry. You cannot be a traitor because you are no Cuban. You come here openly and honestly with skepticism on behalf of your comrades—"

"Fellow Americans," Desi said.

"North Americans."

Desi crossed his arms and spoke around the cigar held in his teeth. "To you, we are North Americans. To us, we are Americans."

"North Americans," Lucy said, playing the diplomat, "are not so careful with words. We like things short and sweet."

"That has nothing to do with it." Desi had become far more sensitive to her tendency to amend and correct him than he'd been in the past. "To us, we are Americans, all two hundred million of us. You are Latin Americans. It's a matter of prospectus."

"Perspective."

Another button pushed. She couldn't help herself.

He took a deep pull on his cigar and blew out the smoke slowly.

"I will continue to say North Americans," Castro said. "You may freely observe and study revolutionary Cuba. However, any attempt to overthrow our government would be considered, under all international law, an act of war. It could be said that a deliberate distortion of the truth in order to insight or justify an attempted overthrow would also constitute aggression. I trust this is not your mission."

"It's your script," Desi said.

"This is insufficient," Castro said.

"Insufficient?" Lucy said. "If you don't mind me saying so, your script is already a little on the long side."

Castro softened to a smile of self-deprecation, and he held his palms up to indicate the thickness of the manuscript. "Sí, it's very long. I have a reputation for talking too much."

Desi and Lucy shared his chuckle, both careful not to suggest that they were laughing at him rather than with him. It was a welcome break in tension.

"You must make your own opinion," Castro said.

Desi said nothing.

They'd known before they arrived that this would be a fool's errand. Whether they improvised their own script or shot Castro's, he was the one holding all the cards and would show precisely what he wanted viewers to see. Time to take off the kid gloves.

"Are we making a travelogue to attract North American tourists back to the Cuban tropical paradise, or are we making a picture celebrating the revolution?" she asked.

"One and the same," he said. "Cuba is a paradise because of the revolution."

"For many, Cuba was an appealing playground before the revolution."

"Because they couldn't look behind the scenes, as you say, and rarely outside of Havana or the coastal resorts. They saw only what was constructed for their enjoyment. They remained blissfully ignorant of the price paid for their pleasures. If North Americans are truly the compassionate people we all believe them to be, then they will be shocked to learn the truth of the past and delighted for the liberation of Cubans from oppressive exploitation."

"It ain't fun and games for everyone in the States, either," Desi said.

"Most people in the States work hard every day. Why do you think it should be different?"

"It is different. One who works hard every day should always have food to eat, and shelter, and enough left over to enrich their minds and spirits. Cubans have enjoyed few privileges."

She accepted his challenge and raised the stakes. "If you want North Americans' approval, then I suppose you'll have to show us—them—the bad as well as the good."

"This is an interesting word, approval. Revolution is a struggle, and ours has just begun. We need no approval."

"Then what in hell are we doing here?" Desi's agitation was intensifying as Castro downed one glass of wine after another, with no mercy or concern for his discomfort.

"Why did you protect me today?" Castro asked him.

"Gut instinct."

"Some part of you must not see me as a devil. If you recognized no redeeming value in my life, you would have reacted differently."

Desi tucked in his chin indignantly.

"Not consciously. I don't suspect you are a man who would condone murder. However, in the deeper recesses of your subconscious, you might have recoiled in the normal way that we are compelled by instinct to protect our own lives, or you might have instinctively shielded your wife."

"She was yards away," Desi said, dismissively.

"Instead, you put your own life in jeopardy, and you did so without forethought. This expresses both your personal nobility—Cuban courage, possibly—and your willingness to postpone judgment."

"I'm not here to judge you. I'm here to make your picture."

"Judgment may not be your purpose, only your nature. Though God warns us against judgment, he requires us to govern ourselves."

The innuendo was wearing thin. The adrenaline of the day had given way to exhaustion, and Lucy wanted to turn in, but fatigue let curiosity get the better of impatience. "How do you judge us?"

"I choose not to indulge my judgmental instinct."

"Bullshit," Desi said.

Her sentiments, exactly. Castro's holier-than-thou declaration stretched credibility, although open belligerence might not have been the wisest reaction in the present circumstances. Yet if Desi was succeeding at pushing Castro's buttons, Castro wasn't showing it. If Castro had any violent instincts—and he had waged a bloody civil war—he had the ability to put a lid on them. For one thing, he sure could have dealt with Lansky more harshly. Who knew? Maybe he still would. And maybe she and Desi both needed to exercise more tact, at least until they better knew their host's boiling point.

"The instinct you showed today when you placed yourself in danger to protect me, that is a part of your being," Castro said. "This compassion exists in most people. The North American people who possess such compassion will be moved by the achievements of our revolution. It cannot be otherwise. Like the two million colonists who declared your country's independence from tyranny two centuries ago, Cuba's seven million people wish to be left to our own history, without interference. But you are correct. There are certain things, as you've already seen, that are not so good. A partial truth is worse than a lie. You shall see everything."

He was playing right into Dulles's hands, although she wasn't so sure she wanted to see everything. Legions of disfigured revolutionaries and loyalists could put a damper on their tropical getaway.

For a control freak like her, this situation was unnerving. She and Desi shared that trait, a source of friction that required no shrink to figure out. Castro made it a threesome. He was determined to be the one pulling all the strings. They were at his mercy, and his concession to pull back the curtains—the curtains he chose—was nothing more than a demonstration of superiority. Maybe it wouldn't have been half bad if Desi had been working some kind of scheme to put him in his place.

She conspicuously checked her wristwatch and permitted herself an exaggerated yawn. "Pardon me, I'm very tired."

Castro apologized for keeping them so late and offered to walk them up to their room, which they politely declined. He promised "very interesting things" for the next day, clasped Desi's hand and thanked him again, and bid them good evening.

Good morning would have been more like it, Lucy thought as she staggered along the long hallway. It was hours past midnight. With so many more "very interesting things" just beyond the next sunrise.

STEPS

The next morning, after a Cuban breakfast of fruit, bread and butter, and strong café con leche, they were escorted to join Castro in his waiting car. Lucy noticed he was comparing articles side by side from multiple newspapers spread across the back seat. She gathered from the pictures and multiple languages he was keeping a keen eye on what was being written about Cuba—and him—in papers from around the world.

In the fashion of diplomatic protocol, the car displayed both the American and the Cuban red-white-and-blue flags, one mounted at each front fender, Stars and Stripes on the right, the host country's flag on the left. Perhaps it was out of respect for Desi's heroics the day before, but they'd suddenly become more conspicuous. The guards, who served double duty as hotel doormen, showed them each to the doors on either side of the car, leaving Castro in the middle. Castro stacked and tidied the papers to make room for her and Desi.

Escorted by rifle-bearing men in jeeps ahead and behind, they threaded through the narrow streets of Old Havana.

Castro narrated the ride. "You can see that only one year after the start of the revolution, life in the capital has returned to normal."

Sure, if soldiers with guns on every corner was normal. It might have been a speech lifted from the script. Lucy couldn't detect much difference between Fidel's everyday patter and his written words. He was a habitual orator, which noticeably grated on Desi's nerves. Desi flipped through the pages of the script as if browsing a magazine, and every time Castro spoke, Desi exhaled audibly—and apparently unconsciously. If Castro noticed—and he wasn't the kind to miss things—he pretended not to. Probably used to it.

While Castro narrated his guided tour, Lucy read the passing faces of the people walking along the streets, looking for signs of joy or despair. They were flat, what you'd expect from folks in any big town going about their business. If this was a staged event, she could detect no attempt to make any particular impression. Occasionally someone would catch a glimpse of Castro and wave. Only once did she notice a negative reaction: a couple, maybe in their forties, who looked in the direction of their motorcade and then quickly turned their attention forward and quickened their steps. In one case, Castro asked Desi to roll down his window so he could return a greeting from a young mother who had encouraged her little son and daughter to stop curbside and wave to the premier. If he had seized power as a despot, it certainly wasn't apparent, at least not in this part of town. Of course, the working folks had little reason to oppose Castro and plenty of reasons to welcome him.

They cruised several streets, clearly not on a direct route to their mystery destination. Castro pointed out a few historic buildings, both from earlier colonial times and those relevant to revolutionary activities, especially apartments where his movement had taken shape when he was a student, and a few notable for their notorious pre-revolutionary residents. She tried not to be rude by looking at her watch, but Desi, not in the mood for niceties, self-consciously checked the time every couple of minutes.

After nearly an hour tooling around town, they pulled up and stopped in front of the University of Havana. The broad marble steps reminded Lucy of the Capitol building in DC, or maybe more appropriately, the Low Memorial Library at Columbia University in Manhattan, complete with an Alma Mater statue.

"The birthplace of the revolution," Castro announced. He leaned across and pointed toward the flight of stone steps.

His sudden proximity made Lucy uncomfortable. If Desi had leaned across her in the car, she would have placed a hand on his back or shoulder. To make way for Castro, she shrank into her seat, clutching her handbag. He was an imposing enough figure at arm's length—tall, fit, with a coarse beard. Close up, despite his soft voice and pleasant manners, he was just plain overwhelming—kind of like Betty White's shaggy Saint Bernard, Stormy, she cracked to herself.

After a pause in which he was apparently lost in his own memories, Castro unlatched Lucy's door and invited her to exit. One of the men from their armed escort tried to assist Desi, but he was out before the soldier reached him.

"You never had the privilege of attending our university," Castro said to Desi, matter-of-factly. "Perhaps this is why you lack knowledge of our history."

Another of Desi's buttons that didn't need pushing. Desi hadn't attended any university. He'd arrived in the States with his father, penniless after the Bolsheviks had chased them out of Santiago de Cuba, where his father had been the mayor—and wealthy to boot, with multiple homes and a private island. In Miami, they'd carved out a niche in the decorative ceramic tile business. The only schooling Desi had had after that was to improve his English.

For Desi, pride was two-faced. Despite his delight in pointing out to his Hollywood peers that he'd managed to beat them at their own game without a college degree, he was still sensitive about his lack of education. She could jump to his defense, but that would only be throwing gasoline on the fire. Instead, she angled up the first three steps and surveyed the grand staircase as if she were a keen architectural scholar.

The film crew had already arrived, and Lucy greeted them in broken Spanish.

Desi flipped back and forth through the phone-book-sized script. They were shooting out of sequence. When he found the right scene, he folded in the corner and flipped through the pages, shaking his head. Today's speeches had been longer than yesterday's until Lucy had gone to town on them. She showed her marked-up script to Desi, and he asked the production assistant to pencil Lucy's changes into his copy and update the huge stack of cue cards.

One of the cameras stood on its tripod at the top of the steps, looking down. Another pointed up from the bottom. The third was off to the side, no doubt prepared to pan with them as they ascended the steps to the heights of Cuban scholarship.

As soon as he'd lit up his cigarette, Desi joined the middle cameraman. Castro bounded up the fifty-some stairs with the effortless grace of a gazelle and took a position at the top on the broad terrace. He looked out over the plaza below as if he were about to deliver one of his famously long speeches. By now, he was so accustomed to making political sermons that he should have been tired of the whole business, but he clearly relished the idea.

A smattering of young people trotted up the stairs and on through the imposing Roman-style portico, most likely students rushing to classes. A few began to notice Castro. Others lingered along the margins, including a little girl watched by her mother, playing under a magnolia tree, standing on its roots and reaching with all her might for its branches as if determined to climb. She consulted with her mother, her little voice reverberating off the stone steps and surrounding buildings. Her mother wisely offered no apparent encouragement.

Lucille caught up to Castro, coughing and trying to catch her breath.

"Cigarettes," Castro said. "They choke your lungs."

"What about those fat stogies you smoke?"

"No inhalation. The pleasure of tobacco without the unpleasant effects on the breathing."

A woman at the edge of the steps stood watching them closely, not making any effort to hide her interest. She wore a fashionable calf-length dress of kelly green topped with a gauzy white sweater, and on her feet, open-toed white heels. She carried an extra wrap, possibly fur, draped over her arm, and clutched a small handbag. She was too far away for Lucy to make out her jewelry, but a glint here and there hinted at diamonds.

Perhaps this was one of their CIA handlers, what Castro would doubtlessly call an accomplice. Or maybe another Russian. Or maybe just someone who happened to be there. With all the spy games going on, Lucy's imagination cast every person as potential friend or foe, like little Lucie and Desi Jr. spotting dragons and pirate ships in cloud formations. Lucy glanced at Castro. Despite the woman's conspicuous beauty and overt attention, he avoided acknowledging her presence. In fact, he appeared to be making a special effort to turn his attention in every direction but hers. This cloak-and-dagger stuff was entertaining, at least up until the actual dagger appeared.

Desi finished giving his instructions to the three cameramen and joined them.

"Many impassioned speeches have been given here," Castro said. "Riots have occurred. Blood spilled."

The nearest cameraman repositioned his tripod to capture Castro head on. The other two had once again set themselves up to capture wider angles.

The mystery woman finally ascended the steps and closed in. It was obvious from Castro's glances and his pointed refusal to greet her that they were no strangers.

The woman spoke first. "I knew you would bring them here. You are very predictable."

"This is Señora Natalia Revuelta Clews," Castro said, without looking in her direction. In an impatient, dismissive monotone, he added faint praise. "She is a great friend of the revolution."

"Call me Naty," the woman said.

If she had been in Lucy's neighborhood, they'd have already put her in pictures. She had bright green eyes and a delicate, Hepburnesque figure—enough to put Desi in a trance. Who was she? She was too well dressed to be a member of Castro's proletariat.

She sidled up to Castro, which made him visibly uncomfortable. His stance stiffened again, and he pinned his hands at his side as if resisting contact.

Lucy decided to break the ice and turned her face squarely on Desi. "You can start breathing now."

Desi sneered at her, and not in the playful way he used to have when she'd caught him eyeing a pretty young extra.

Naty smiled at him, silently thanking him for the flattery.

Lucy motioned between Naty and Castro. "You're close?"

"Let's say I put him in this uniform," Naty said.

"Señora Revuelta sewed many uniforms for our comrades in arms," Castro said. "Although the señora comes from a background of wealth and privilege, she has demonstrated great sympathy for her fellow Cubans, in words and deeds. She has supported the revolution in every way possible."

"Yes," Naty said, "in every way."

Lucy wasn't born yesterday. These two had obviously been more than comrades. In Hollywood social life, she'd witnessed the aftermath of many failed romances. She dreaded the role of bitter divorcée, which she hoped to avoid.

The little girl who'd been playing under the tree came bounding up the steps. "Tío Fidel! Tío Fidel!"

"*Pequeña* Alina." Castro lifted the girl, and she threw her arms around his neck.

"This is your daughter?" Lucy asked Naty.

The woman who'd been watching the little girl, who Lucy had mistaken for her mother and now recognized as her nanny, kept her distance.

"Sí. Alina," Naty said to the girl, "these are very famous people from the United States, Señor y Señora Arnaz."

Castro's affection toward Alina was as apparent as his disapproval of Naty's uninvited appearance. If his face had been any redder, his beard might have burst into flames. Alina laid her head on his shoulder, smiling silently, a look she'd seen countless times from little Lucie with her daddy. There wasn't much for a little child to say to a couple of strangers. Naty's introduction had obviously been more for their benefit than for Alina's.

Castro raised his voice. "Señora, you are familiar with our guests?"

Naty paid no attention to his forced pleasantries and kept her attention on Lucy and Desi. "Have you only just arrived?"

"Two days ago," Desi said.

"Then you've already had plenty of time for indoctrination."

Neither Lucy nor Desi found words.

"I'm only teasing." She placed a hand on Desi's arm, then broke away and looked around with affected wistfulness. If she had actually been discovered by Hollywood, she would have needed some acting lessons.

"The Arnazes have come to tell the story of the revolution to the North Americans," Castro said. "They will dispel their fears about the future of our nation."

"I wonder who has the greatest fears," she said. "Do the *Yanquis* fear us more than we fear them?"

Castro spoke calmly to Alina. "We have no reason to fear the North Americans, do we?" He then turned to Naty. "As our guests will show, we are a progressive country, as prepared for economic and social growth as any state in their nation."

"You might begin by not calling it a revolution," Naty said. "Revolutions are unnerving to those not among the victorious."

"You mean the losers," Desi said.

"The losers and the outsiders," she said. "Why not call it the Newly Liberated Nation of Cuba? Perhaps when they see how far we've come, they'll make us a territory."

Castro disengaged, refusing her taunt.

Naty offered Lucy her hand. "I want to show you something."

Desi checked with Castro before summoning the camera crews to follow.

Naty walked Lucy through the tunnel-like portico. Her clicking heels reverberated against the marble walls and floor. They emerged on the other side of the terrace, overlooking a large square plaza. Scattered young people crisscrossed the patterned stone plaza. The campus buildings were elegant, as was much of the architecture in Havana, one of the positive contributions of the Spanish colonists. Fidel and Desi followed behind the ladies but gave them space.

An onlooker who'd noticed Castro from below in the plaza shouted, "Viva la revolución." Castro raised his fist in acknowledgment. The exchange caught the attention of others, some of whom halted in place and appeared to be waiting for the next shoe to drop.

Naty puffed up her chest and pantomimed stroking a beard. "This is the heart of intellectual life in Cuba," she said in a put-on masculine voice, stealing some of Castro's thunder with more than a touch of mockery, which Castro appeared to take in stride. "This was it. I stood here. Fidel stood where you are. We met on this spot."

Castro tipped his head in acknowledgment.

"As students?" asked Lucy.

"Sí. We, many hundreds, came to remember the Spanish student massacre from the first revolution. Slogans were shouted. There was much chanting. And then Fidel began speaking about justice and how many had died on these steps, and yet how we were still oppressed by a new form of colonialism. I knew at that moment that this man was different. He stood for something. He was very impressive."

Lucy knew where this conversation was heading, and it put her off balance. The aphrodisiac of charisma had worked on her, too.

"We were both married to others, but we connected on a different level. Through the mind."

Desi signaled "cut" to the cameramen with a finger slash to his throat.

"No," Castro said, "we must document even those truths that make us uncomfortable."

Desi revoked his previous direction with a cranking motion, and the cameramen returned to their viewfinders. If Castro really wanted this scene in the final cut, Desi would work it in without the melodrama. No matter what you were selling, Americans couldn't resist a pretty face, especially when it came with a nice figure.

"Weren't there many passionate men at the university?" Lucy asked. "You said this was the place that students came to debate each other and to hold political rallies."

"Then, as now, when Fidel spoke, everyone else stopped to listen." Naty nodded in the direction of the crowd. "By this time, he had educated himself to such a degree and his mind was so strong and clear that he could take apart any argument and piece it back together with the precision of a Swiss watchmaker. When he was done, the person with whom he had taken issue would believe that he had shared Fidel's position all along. This was the skill that would have made him a brilliant attorney, and also what made him the leader of the revolution."

Castro appeared to be giving his full attention to Alina but no doubt had absorbed every word of Naty's gushing flattery. If Lucy shared Naty's attraction to self-made men, she also shared Castro's unapologetic need for attention.

"He does go on about the revolution," Lucy said.

"Even in moments of intimacy." Naty blushed.

Lucy gave one of her patented wide-eyed looks, hoping to lighten the mood while communicating that this subject was making her uncomfortable.

Naty pointed at her, waving her finger. "That's it!"

"That's what?"

"That's Lucy. I was beginning to wonder why you were so much less funny in person."

She smiled wryly. If only she had more to laugh about.

Alina was thankfully too young to register the full meaning of their exchange, although she responded to the melodramatic tone of the conversation by squirming in Castro's arms. He put her down and urged her to continue her explorations. She ran off toward a promising-looking tree beyond the plaza below, followed by the nanny, calling after her with warnings in Spanish too rapid for Lucy to interpret. If it had been her and little Lucie, she'd have been urging her not to get dirty and to take care with her clothes.

Onlookers had continued to gather. No longer passing through, lost in their own thoughts or conversations, they had begun to linger, their eyes turned toward the visitors and film crew on the terrace.

"Fidel educated me," Naty was saying. "Filled me with such passion. We've had a very productive relationship."

"As mentor and protégé," Castro said. "Señora Revuelta has a keen mind."

Sensing that her face had gone flat, Lucy put on her most polite smile. This woman showed no remorse whatsoever for their illicit affair. Just the opposite. She worked Castro with those emerald eyes and the graceful gestures that brought out her many physical qualities. Lucy would have liked to hear Mrs. Castro's side of the story. They might have seen eye to eye on this subject.

"It was inappropriate," Castro said.

Had he sensed Lucy's disapproval? Strange that he'd felt the need to own up to his own sins to a couple of actors from the States.

"She is married," he added.

"And so were you," Naty said.

"Only in the beginning, and then I divorced her."

"You left me because I was still married."

"It was a factor."

"I was not good for your image. Not like Celia."

Castro grunted, at an unusual loss for words.

"He couldn't be seen with a woman of society," Naty said. "Not good for the revolutionary image. I'm sure it was Che's doing. He always despised me."

"Yes and no," Castro said. "He despises what you represent. It's not personal."

"He refused to be in the same room with me," she confided to Lucy.

If this had been an argument between a couple they knew personally, Lucy would have excused herself and dragged Desi along for a cigarette. But both Fidel and Naty were clearly playing to their audience. Cheater or not, Naty was a spurned lover, and she apparently needed this scenario to get some things off her chest. Besides, it made Desi squirm, and that wasn't all bad.

Naty turned to Lucy. "I supported his revolution from the start, you know. I gave money. I worked my fingers to the bone on a sewing machine. Me, a society woman, too good for the soldier."

Difficult to choose sides. They were both cheaters. Still, if Castro had truly cared for her, he might have found ways to rationalize their relationship instead of reasons to ends it. Just as she had? Reasons for leaving. Reasons for staying. All the same. As soon as you needed reasons, all reasons were meaningless.

Lucy touched the back of her neck. "So the women supported the revolution too. I mean, making uniforms and cooking meals, I suppose."

"Many women compañeros fought bravely alongside the men," Castro said.

Lucy didn't dare ask Naty whether she had carried a weapon. No matter how it came out, it would have sounded condescending.

"Did you shoot the enemy?" Desi asked.

Like that.

"No," Naty said. "Not me. I am no killer. Not like one of Fidel's soldier girls. How can a woman who has given life take the life of another woman's son? I did what I could. I myself sewed this uniform." She placed her palm on Castro's chest, who promptly removed it.

"He may be watching, as you were watching us." Castro scanned the courtyard and the street below.

"I know you don't fear Orlando. He trembles when he sees you."

She was laying it on pretty thick.

"He trembles with anger," Castro said. "A man with money can accomplish many things, and a cuckolded man with money is dangerous, especially in the company of a woman scorned."

"Is that what you've done to me, scorned me?"

"I think you see it this way," Castro said. "I have my role in the revolution. I must not be seen as a puppet of the elite."

Naty spoke directly to Lucy, as if they were close confidants. "At least he labels me elite. This is better than calling me a whore."

Lucy's jaw dropped. Desi patted his chin to remind her not to leave her mouth open. He found it unflattering. That was why he'd come up with her wide-eyed shock take. But that comic reaction would have chafed in this situation. Better neutral than drooling.

"The women of the revolution are to be revered," Castro said. He was becoming visibly agitated, refusing to make further eye contact with Naty. "You shall soon see."

"Some men appreciate our feminine charms," Naty said to Lucy as if no one else were present. "He prefers them in green fatigues, which I provided. I don't know which excites him more, the boots or the rifles. Speaking of which, have you met Celia?"

"Naty!" shouted Castro. "Many women fought for our freedom. Many died. Do not let your personal feelings cloud your judgment."

She was visibly shaken by his reprimand. She'd overstepped, and she knew it. Whether it was a performance designed for Lucy and Desi, Lucy couldn't guess, but she suspected their presence had weakened Naty's inhibitions. Naty was looking to Lucy for allegiance from someone she perhaps considered a worthy feminine accomplice. Although she couldn't help but empathize with Naty, she declined the implied invitation to take sides.

"Desi has always said Cuban women were strong," she said.

"And beautiful," Desi added, drawing Naty's gaze. He might have been using his own misguided charm tactics to defuse the tension. Not the direction she was heading.

"I think the story of the role of Cuban women in the revolution would make a great angle for our film," Lucy said.

"You mean it's not already there?" Desi asked.

"It's touched upon," Castro said. "As you've noted, the script was already quite lengthy."

"It would be my pleasure to share my story," Naty said.

"Sí, sí," Castro said. "Should we interview you in your home?"

"You know that isn't possible," Naty said.

"Of course. I shouldn't be insensitive." Now that the cat was out of the bag, he was just punishing her for her intrusion with embarrassment. "We'll contact you to schedule a filming."

"I'm certain you'd be not only be interesting but stunning on camera," Lucy said, stealing the opportunity for Desi to drop another compliment and soften the sting of Castro's needling.

Castro folded his arms, dismissing Naty. Lucy and Desi took the cue and smiled their farewells. Once Naty registered Castro's meaning, she pivoted on her heels and strode off to collect Alina and the nanny.

A considerable crowd had filled the plaza—hundreds, and not just students. If this had been a stunt planned for Desi's and Lucy's benefit, it had been well organized. There were no obvious crowd wranglers.

"Speaking of cameras," Desi said, "the light is good. Let's get what we need."

Castro nodded to the onlookers and turned to leave through the portico. "No speeches here."

Lucy adopted her professional posture, approaching Castro as if to consult with him. "You said this was the birthplace of the revolution. Isn't this the most appropriate location to reflect on those events?"

"Peace and quiet will speak for our victory."

An admittedly artful choice. Castro was full of surprises.

"Tomorrow, Mrs. Arnaz," he continued, "you shall have your story of our female compañeros."

"That's not in the script," Desi said.

LADIES' LUNCHEON

*L*ucy chain-smoked three cigarettes and tried to focus on the local architecture as the driver drove deep into a Spanish colonial-style neighborhood somewhere in Havana. She'd never felt so out of place. She had openly protested being separated from Desi that morning, but the driver assured her that while Desi was tending to production details with Prime Minister Castro, she was to be the guest of some of the revolution's heroic women, all anxious to meet her.

Most of these houses were two stories tall, some three, with decorative details and clay tile roofs just like their own home in Beverly Hills. Everywhere she'd visited in the Caribbean, the architecture was similar, with molded, carved, and wrought iron ornamentation reflecting whether it was built by Spanish or French settlers, although they'd often borrowed from each other to create a charming look unique to the islands. If Castro had arranged for her to meet with women revolutionary soldiers, this hardly seemed like the appropriate setting. Maybe Naty had taken him up on his offer to make her own appearance on camera.

The driver stopped in front of a lovely home painted white, well kept, with neatly trimmed palm trees and maintained flower beds in the front. Intricate iron railings, painted aquamarine, edged two upper terraces. A veranda extended from three sides of the first floor, sheltered by a colonnade. A low garden fence matched the house's detail work. A gate off to the side opened to a clay tiled walkway that curved toward the entrance portico. The driver helped Lucy out of the car and left her at the gate, not bothering to wait until she was safely inside.

Vilma Espín, whom she recognized from their welcome dinner, emerged from the front door, quick-stepped down to greet her, and ushered her through the gate. When they'd first met, the petite Vilma had appeared comically overwhelmed by heavy green gabardine, as if playing dress-up in her daddy's uniform. Today, she looked downright cute in a simple embroidered dress and flat shoes.

Vilma escorted her up the path and into the house, which was elegant but sparsely furnished. The other three guests awaited: Celia Sánchez, Melba Hernández, and Haydée Santamaría. Vilma was clearly the youngest, possibly Castro's age. The others looked to be in their late thirties or early forties. Like Vilma, all three wore simple outfits, Melba and Haydée in dresses and Celia in an embroidered peasant blouse and a navy skirt. Over their clothes, they each wore a grease-stained apron as if they'd been preparing a feast together, although Lucy smelled nothing cooking.

Once among the women, Lucy's anxiety began to subside. She welcomed a respite from the testosterone-fueled revolutionary bravado. She'd always preferred the company of confident women. When she was modeling in New York and then later learning the show business ropes as a young contract player in Hollywood, she'd shunned the girls who behaved like sheep, doing whatever they were asked, even when it meant certain inappropriate compromises. She'd been just as impatient as any of them for success, but it had to be at least partly on her own terms.

Her encounter with Natalia Revuelta the day before had reminded her how easily instinct could overpower principles. Naty had been charmed by Castro's masculine charisma and intellect. Lucy had herself fallen for a bad boy, and she understood how Castro, a real rebel with a real cause, filled the bill for Naty—just as Desi had done for her, with similar consequences. It remained to be seen whether these gals had a better grip on their senses. At last she might finally get the real story. She was far more interested in what less privileged Cuban women were up to while the men were shooting at each other.

This house, though, suggested that her hostess was no Cuban peasant, at least not since the revolution. The front parlor was brightly lit by sunlight streaming in through tall, arched windows. The terra cotta floor tiles were sun-bleached here and there, contrasting with darker areas once covered by rugs or large furniture. The women took their seats in carved wooden dining chairs arranged around a four-legged coffee table of relatively poor quality. Probably not an original furnishing of the house. The gathering might have been a regular tea party if not for the rifles propped against each chair. Time for another smoke.

It was immediately clear that the one most comfortable speaking English was Vilma. She offered Lucy a seat between herself and Haydée Santamaría. As soon as Celia poured Lucy a cup of coffee, the women picked up the rifles and laid them across their laps. Without comment, and as if it were as natural as knitting, they began disassembling them, arranging the parts neatly on tea towels laid out on the table between them.

Lucy was familiar enough with polishing the silver for a party, although it was usually done before the arrival of the guests, but this was a first. The women meticulously cleaned each part of the weapons, stuffing a small wad of steel wool through the barrels with a long rod and lubricating the moving parts with oil dripped onto cloths from a small can they passed around. While polishing the guns, they nibbled on cakes and sipped strong coffee from bone china.

As a celebrity, she'd become accustomed to breaking the ice. "Typical. I guess men are the same everywhere."

The women looked at her and then at Vilma, hoping for additional translation, but Vilma only shared their confusion.

She tried to clarify. "So typical of men that they'd expect the women to clean up after them."

More confusion.

She began to feel embarrassed that her attempt at relating to these young ladies was landing with a thud. She pointed at one of the weapons. "The soldiers—I see they have you cleaning their guns."

Vilma interpreted, and the smiles returned to their faces.

"These are our own weapons," Celia said.

Lucy had known several women in the States who were skilled marksmen. Hunting and skeet shooting were popular pastimes back home in Celoron, but she'd never been comfortable around guns, especially after the tragic target shooting accident that had crippled a neighbor boy and bankrupted her family. And she was pretty sure these women weren't sportsman. "I suppose you needed your own weapons during the war, to defend your homes."

"We didn't hide in our houses," Celia said. "We are soldiers of the revolution."

"You fought in the war?"

"La revolución," Melba corrected her. "Sí, yes." She mimed firing a rifle at an unseen enemy.

Lucy twitched with each imaginary shot. Melba must have noticed she was making her uncomfortable, because she rubbed her palms together as if washing her hands of the unseen weapon and went back to pampering the real rifle in her lap, as if that was somehow less disturbing.

During her USO tours, Lucy had met plenty of women who'd served in the Women's Army Corps. WACs, they called them. They worked in all kinds of job, from secretaries to mechanics. But those women didn't carry guns. Lucy found it difficult to imagine these women shooting other human beings, much less killing them. She preferred not to ask whether any of them had ever taken a life.

"Melba and Haydée fought at Moncada," Celia was saying.

"Was that a famous battle?" She felt slightly embarrassed at having to ask, but she'd never had much reason to follow what was happening down here. After two wars, she'd had enough bad news for one lifetime. And Desi didn't pay much attention either, except for what little showed up in the paper. If he'd shown more interest, it might have piqued her curiosity.

"It was the first," Melba said. "We attacked a military barracks near Santiago de Cuba in the town of Moncada, a very famous day in Cuba, twenty-sixth of July. It became the name of our revolutionary movement, *Movimiento 26 de Julio*."

"And you succeeded?" asked Lucy.

"No," Melba said. "We went to prison."

She could hardly imagine. In show business, women had two ways to succeed. They could play snake charmer to the simple creatures Hollywood moguls carried around in their boxers, or they could talk tough, which was far more effective at masking vulnerability. She had chosen the latter strategy, making acting a useful skill on camera and off. Maybe these women were also acting, playing the reverse roles, gentle and feminine, covering for the killers they'd become.

"We were imprisoned for only seven months," Melba was saying, "because they didn't believe we carried weapons."

"Was Prime Minister Castro in prison, too?"

"Much longer," Vilma said. "Fidel was sentenced to fifteen years. Others, including Raúl, thirteen years, ten, or less."

"How did they escape?"

"Batista freed them after only one year—the ones who were still alive, exiled to Mexico," Vilma said. "Batista believed by showing compassion, he could win back the trust of the people. Fidel is certain he was released to be hunted by assassins."

"It looks like Batista made a big mistake."

"Sí. When Fidel returned to Cuba, we all fought alongside him in the Sierra Maestra."

Some of this, Lucy knew in a vague way from an interview of Castro done secretly by a Herbert Matthews for the *New York Times* a few years before, more famous for the daring work of the reporter than for anything Castro said at the time. When Castro and his followers came back to Cuba, they had hidden in the mountains from Batista's army.

All the parts from the dismantled rifles laid out on the table left no room to put down her coffee cup. At least in dozens of pieces, the weapons were harmless. "This is not how a group of gals would typically spend an afternoon together back in the States."

Vilma chuckled along with her and finally translated so the others would join in. "It wasn't so much an activity for ladies before the revolution. It became necessary."

"But the war is over. You've won."

"*Yanquis*," Haydée said. "They will come."

Haydée scrutinized Lucy for a reaction, possibly hoping she'd spill the beans, as if she'd have been trusted with some secret invasion plan. She could have protested her suspicions, but it would have made no difference. The truth was that she couldn't be sure the US government wasn't planning some kind of military operation. With Castro's communist tendencies, it wasn't so far-fetched. Since she could offer neither reassurance nor denial, she returned to the relative safety of guns. "Do you carry those things everywhere?"

"Not to the bath." Haydée, of all people, had made a joke. She was less stiff than she looked.

"We still must act more serious than the men," Melba said. "The revolution might have changed our status, but men are still men, especially Cuban men. Their ideas are not so easy to change. Now that the shooting is done, they expect us to stir our bean pots."

"Those of us who have bean pots," Celia said. From Celia's bare ring finger, Lucy surmised that she was unmarried.

"It's very important to keep our weapons in fine condition," Vilma explained.

The women who spoke no English smiled at her. Finally Haydée politely asked, via Vilma as interpreter, how Lucy was enjoying her stay in Cuba.

"It's always been a lovely country," she said.

"This is not your first visit, then." Celia flipped over her reassembled rifle, startling Lucy. "It's not so normal, this."

"This is certainly new to me," Lucy said. After the usual delay for translation, the women shared a warm laugh with her. "What was

Cuba like before the revolution? I only knew it from Havana, which was a wonderful city."

Even after Vilma translated, none of the women seemed anxious to respond to her question, as if she had just made a great faux pas. It didn't matter much. As long as she had to be here, she might as well dig for the truth. Castro said they had no secrets. She had never been one to beat around the bush, and she wasn't about to start. What were they going to do, shoot her?

"The rich remained rich," Celia finally said. "The poor remained poor. Isn't this true in your own country?"

Celia seemed determined to drag her into an argument in which she wasn't interested. The others looked up from their polishing tasks like preoccupied baseball fans alerted by the crack of a bat. The relentless political talk was wearing thin.

"So unfortunate that it came to war," Lucy said. "Sometimes I think men just have naturally bad tempers. They can't resist a fight."

"In your country, labor organizes and demands rights for themselves."

She was well aware. Long before she'd joined the Screen Actors Guild, Lucy had grown up with her eccentric grandfather Fred's passion for workers' rights. He'd never stopped complaining that "fat cats live on the blood and sweat of the working man." He'd insisted every member of the family take up the cause—and that's how she'd ended up in this situation. If she'd known then how much aggravation would come from registering to vote as a socialist, she'd have joined the Republicans and lied to her card-carrying grandfather.

"My grandfather was a great supporter of the labor movement."

"Then your grandfather would have been welcome here," Melba said.

"Labor unions never succeeded in our country," Celia said. "Those who dared challenge the wealthy, who controlled all the land, they were all sent to prison."

"Or murdered," Haydée said.

Celia polished her rifle with renewed vigor. "Many were tortured. Many died."

Without looking up from her task, Haydée spoke. "In prison, they brought me the eyeball of my brother Abel, gouged from his skull. This was their threat. I did not cooperate. Then they brought to me the bloody testicle of my fiancé, Boris. I told them, 'If you did that to them and they didn't talk, much less will I.' They murdered them both."

Lucy forgot to breathe. She must have looked as light-headed as she felt, because Vilma jumped to steady her in her chair.

"I'm sorry," Lucy said. "I didn't know."

"Of course not," Melba said. "How could you?"

Lucy wasn't sure whether these women considered her friend or foe. Despite her grandfather's teachings, she'd become one of the people these women appeared to despise. Why had Castro sent her here? To weigh her sympathies? To bend them in their favor? Either way, they were bound to be disappointed.

She shifted in her chair and opened her handbag for a cigarette. "I imagine Prime Minister Castro would be particularly disappointed with my husband. He must think of him as a traitor."

"Fidel holds disloyal Cubans in greatest contempt," Melba said. "However, Señor Arnaz cannot be a traitor because he was forced from the country against his will and can't be held responsible for the indoctrination he received in your country."

Indoctrination? That was a funny way to look at what happened to a man who'd been kicked out of the country with nothing but the shirt on his back who then made himself into one of the most powerful men in Hollywood. If American life had made an impression on Desi, he'd returned the favor.

"I can tell you, Señor Arnaz was no fan of Batista's." It was true, although his disdain for the deposed dictator didn't make him any more supportive of Castro and what Desi called his "gang of commie thugs." Unease wormed through her body. Castro must have believed she'd be more open to the justification for a bloody civil war if she heard it from these women, as if they had some kind of sisterhood. "I'm beginning to get the picture."

Their response was muted. Common English expressions only

elicited bewilderment. "I mean, I think I understand why Prime Minister Castro arranged this tea party," she added.

"You can be sure that almost anything Fidel does has a political motive," Celia said.

"He's obsessed with his revolution," Lucy said.

"Our revolution," Haydée said. "Obsession to one person is dedication to another. Dedication to the principles that made la revolución necessary."

"He doesn't mean to be disrespectful," Vilma said. "He wants to test his dedication in debate. He has no patience for those with no opinions."

"Sometimes, he apparently shares his thoughts with the help of bullets," Lucy said.

"What makes Fidel a great revolutionary is that he uses violence only against those who impose injustice through violence of their own." Celia patted her rifle.

That remained to be seen. Of course, the missing and the dead would be invisible. An outsider would never know they'd ever been there, much less what had become of them. Lucy twisted her lips into a sardonic smile and crossed her arms. The four Cuban women froze. Apparently Lucy's unwelcome skepticism required no translation.

MATERNAL INSTINCTS

Oddly, Haydée, the sternest among them, was the one who broke the tension, smiling broadly as she spoke in Spanish.

Vilma translated: "Besides, we find you and your husband very funny."

Lucy breathed a sigh of relief and took a long drag on her cigarette. Celia joined her in a smoke, the same Soviet brand that Castro had offered.

"I wish I could agree," Vilma said. "I think you show in your television program that women are weak and silly. This is unfortunate."

"We only mean to make folks laugh," Lucy said. "A break from the daily grind. Our shows don't contain any hidden messages."

"But they do," Vilma said. "It's inescapable."

"We don't blame you," Celia said, jumping in as if her cork had popped, "but you'll understand we must speak our minds. You see, what you show us in your program, your silly Lucy person, and Ricky Ricardo, they reflect the culture of your country."

Silly? Yes, no argument there. Silly and harmless.

"And perpetuate it," added Vilma. "It's as if you're saying to the men and women who watch your program, 'These roles for you are good, wholesome, the way it should be.'"

Diplomacy was exhausting, especially for someone accustomed to speaking her mind. She was going to have to take charge of this conversation. "I see it this way. Ratings tells me that Americans relate to our show. It's a two-way street. If they didn't like what they were seeing, they'd turn the dial. We have three networks in the US, plenty of choices."

"Yet they don't turn the dial," Melba said.

"Thankfully."

"Because they believe what you show them."

"I'm not so sure anyone thinks that Lucy Ricardo represents the ideal wife. As you said, she's more than a little silly."

"But everything shown to an audience is propaganda," Vilma said. "Lucy and Ricky represent a certain ideal of life in your country."

"One that many people call the American dream," Lucy said.

Celia leaned forward. "What is this American dream?"

It wasn't a challenge. Celia's expression had shifted from furrowed intensity to forthright curiosity.

"It's simple," Lucy said. "Most would say that it's about having a roof over their head, children, maybe a reliable automobile, and of course, a good job that pays the light bill and puts three square meals on the table. Oh, and a family vacation once in a while."

Speaking these things aloud reminded her how fortunate she'd been—and also what she'd been missing. On television, Lucy Ricardo had it made. She had an adoring husband. She had dreams of stardom. She had her best friend close by. She was a wife, a mother. Too bad playing the part didn't bring her to life. Lucy inhabited Lucy Ricardo like one of those split personalities, except hers only got to come out when summoned. If only their roles had been reversed, with Lucille Arnaz the character played by Lucy Ricardo, to be stashed away in a suitcase when she wasn't needed, like Edgar Bergen's Charlie McCarthy. Maybe Lucy Ricardo was so appealing to fans because Lucille had invested her with so many of her own desires. That was the real American dream, the dream itself —chasing the carrot on the stick. She'd created Lucy, and now she envied her. Of course, that's what imagination was for. Maybe it was time to count blessings and spend less time dwelling on fairy tales.

"It's still funny," Haydée was saying, again avoiding eye contact with any of the other ladies.

"What's funny, Haydée?" asked Vilma.

"The *I Love Lucy* show," Haydée said. "It's a funny program. And Mr. Arnaz is very handsome."

Vilma hesitated to translate.

Lucy knew enough Spanish. "Yes, he is."

Melba had begun reassembling her rifle. "In the future, perhaps you'll portray a woman's strength." She finished fitting the gun's components into place and tested the mechanisms. The vacant snap of the trigger set Lucy's teeth on edge. "In the United States, most women's fortunes are due to the accomplishments of their husbands. In your case, however, you are partners in business and therefore share equal credit for your wealth and fame."

It was a backhanded compliment, coming from someone who expressed disdain for material gain, but difficult to refute. No point to false humility. Lucy's dipsy alter ego had launched their careers, but Desi was the hard-nosed negotiator who'd brought their dreams to life. Things might have been much different for her—for both of them—if they'd never married.

"It's frightening sometimes," Lucy said.

Celia was quick to tug on the loose thread she'd just exposed. "What makes it frightening?"

"If something were to happen to him—or to me, for that matter. We're practically one person."

"For us," Vilma said, "it's difficult to think of such things. We've lost many. We must continue."

Celia gave her reassembled rifle a final polish and laid it on the table. She poured herself another cup of coffee and milk, and then sitting upright like a model with perfect posture, she straightened her colorfully embroidered blouse. "No one, not one man, not one woman, should be absolutely dependent on another individual. It is harmful to both."

Surely even these soldier girls could understand partnership. "Don't soldiers depend on each other for their lives?"

"We do," Melba said. "It's a practical matter. We all depend on each other for our material needs. I don't think that's what Celia meant."

After Vilma caught her up, Celia shook her head. "No, not physical strength." She locked her hands together, shaking them as if one were struggling against the other. "The mind. The heart." She emphasized her words by touching her own chest and temples.

"The spirit," Vilma added.

"Sí, espirítu," Celia said. "We must have strength in our spirit. This is something we cannot gain from others, even from God."

"Is marriage a kind of partnership?" asked Lucy. "Don't a husband and wife depend on each other for strength?"

"It must be," Celia said, "although I haven't had the privilege to experience this. The wife must never be the servant of the husband. Every day, they must choose each other."

Choice was a luxury Lucy sometimes thought she lacked. Truth be known, there was always a choice, provided you were willing to accept the consequences. The lesser of two evils.

Haydée placed her hand on Celia's. "Celia makes herself too busy to be bothered with getting married." Celia accepted Haydée's gentle tease with a warm smile. "She has many important things to do."

"Raúl and I married one year ago," Vilma said cheerfully. She was clearly the youngest among them. She, Haydée, and Lucy wore rings.

"That's what we call keeping it in the family," Lucy said.

"I think you were asking something more," Celia said. "You and your husband are partners in both marriage and profession."

"It does make things more complicated," Lucy said. She tried to redirect. "Don't you think, Vilma?"

It didn't work. Celia moved to the edge of her seat, clasped her hands, and waited with anticipatory silence for Lucy to elaborate. While Haydée kept a good poker face, Celia showed keen interest in everything said, whether by Lucy or one of the other women. And now Lucy had opened a fresh can of worms. She'd come here to poke around in Cuban business, not to air her own dirty laundry.

"Well, you know..." Lucy stalled, collecting her thoughts. "Desi and I met on a movie set, and we've worked in show business together ever since. Sometimes it's difficult to separate work from marriage."

"So you are together at all times," Vilma said. "Very romantic."

"Yes, well..." She cast her eyes downward. She'd been trying not to expose herself too much to these unfamiliar women, but her defenses had begun to slacken. "Sometimes we're so busy we hardly see each other, unless we're filming the show."

"You miss him," Vilma said.

Not the easiest question to answer, especially if she had to explain herself. "I miss who he was."

All movement ceased. It's possible they were all holding their breath. Had this been live theater, she'd have been thrilled by their riveted attention. But this wasn't theater. She'd carelessly exposed herself, and their anticipation chafed.

She tugged a handkerchief from her handbag. Celia came to her side, placing a hand on her shoulder. Lucy realized that while she enjoyed the admiration of millions of strangers, she'd never had the comfort of even one. Despite her youth, Celia reminded her of her own mother.

Until recently, her mother had rarely spoken to her about her relationship with Desi. It wasn't that DeDe was timid about sticking her nose in other people's business, but she might have shared Lucy's fear that their marriage was the mortar that held all their lives together, that it needed patching at any cost. Her mother might have changed her tune, but they both knew that if the marriage crumbled, it was sure to take everything else with it.

For a moment, Haydée spread the fingers of her right hand over her own tummy, not with the distress of indigestion but with tenderness. Lucy smiled through her tears. Haydée wasn't showing at all. Lucy knew the feeling. Once she'd known she was carrying, she couldn't stop thinking about that child growing inside her. No matter how small, she could've sworn she felt it. As soon as she'd learned she was pregnant with Lucie, she'd become more than Lucille, the daughter, the actress, the wife. She'd become a mother.

She smiled at Haydée. "I wonder whether your baby will change how you feel about carrying that rifle."

"Haydée has no children," Celia said.

"Not yet," Lucy said.

The others quickly looked at Haydée, who still had her hand on her tummy. Haydée pursed her lips and said nothing.

"Haydée Santamaría Cuadrado," Melba said, shifting to a motherly tone, "why didn't you tell us?"

"I wasn't certain until this morning."

"This is wonderful news," Vilma said, as they huddled around Haydée in her chair, each leaning down and hugging her in turn. The flurry of Spanish elation required no translation.

Nothing in Lucy's life had been more fulfilling than the births of her two children. Her marriage with Desi might have been rocky, but children had given them something, someone to focus on other than themselves and their careers. At least that was what she'd hoped for.

"Motherhood may take time away from your revolutionary activities," Lucy said.

Haydée reverted to sternness. The others stood behind her as in a tableau. They shared not just a warm affection for each other but a sisters-in-arms camaraderie that would never be available to an outsider like Lucy.

"I don't think so," Haydée said. "Like you, my work will continue. The revolution is for the children, to make a world without suffering."

"Even with that?" Lucy asked, pointing sharply at Haydée's rifle. "Will you still be willing to use that once you are a mother?"

"More," Haydée said. "I will protect my children and their freedom with my life, as I have protected all children in my country." She gripped the weapon with both hands, holding it defensively at an angle across her torso, as if shielding herself and her unborn child. "Does not the lioness protect her cubs from hyena?"

The women finished reassembling their rifles and wiping off the last drips of oil. It was pointless to ask whether they all shared that sentiment. They were peas in a pod.

"You must meet some of our children," Vilma said.

"You have children?"

"The children of Cuba." Vilma began clearing the cups and saucers while Melba removed the oil-stained towels from the coffee table. "We will take you to meet your husband and Fidel. They should be ready for you by now."

Lucy gave at last dab at her eyes and bent down for her purse. She would have preferred to return to the hotel. She needed more of Desi's sniping and Castro's philosophizing like a hole in the head.

"Will you be carrying those?" She gestured at their gleaming weapons.

Celia had stationed herself at the door, where she waited for the others to collect themselves, a soldier in lamb's clothing. "That won't be necessary today. We wouldn't want to frighten the children."

FIDEL AND DESI'S NICE CHAT

*D*esi's driver recognized him and engaged in the usual banter about how funny the show was, that Lucy is crazy, and so on, along with questions about why he was in Havana. He answered only that he'd been away for too long and wanted to see what was happening down here, visit with a few old friends.

They pulled up in front of a plain building, uncharacteristic for Havana, two stories of windowless block walls painted white. It reminded him of the austere sound stages at their Cahuenga studio. The driver remained in his seat and pointed Desi toward a door near one end.

Inside he was greeted by Castro, Castro's brother Raúl, and four other fully uniformed men, a couple bearded and a couple bare-faced, all standing. One of the others looked familiar, but Desi couldn't place him. The room was actually a studio, although apparently not currently in use, with coils of black cable stacked along one wall and dozens of unlit stage lamps hung on overhead battens. Dramatically, three fresnel lamps projected a pool of harsh white light straight down onto a square table and single chair set on the wood-planked floor roughly in the center of the room. The contrast obscured the outer recesses in shadow. More showmanship. Not surprising. Politics and show business weren't so different. Why should this schmuck be any different?

"Buenos días, Desi," Castro said. He invited Desi to sit, which he did. Desi plopped his copy of the script on the table.

Desi skipped the formalities. "Where's Lucy? I thought we were meeting her."

In spite of his less than deferential tone, Castro offered him a cigar, which Desi accepted and then lit with his own lighter.

"Mrs. Arnaz is still visiting with our compañeros," Castro said.

With all the olive green gabardine, they looked ready to pose for a class picture, or maybe some crazy re-enactment of one of their heroic battles, which wasn't going to come off too good in a big, empty studio. He hoped like hell they hadn't planned some kind of black-box theatrical crap.

"Your wife, she is a strong woman," Castro was saying.

What was that supposed to mean?

"Before we go," Castro said, "I have some questions."

"You should discuss your script with my wife." He patted the block of bound paper. "She's better with those things." Better her than him.

"It's not the script I wish to discuss." Castro passed out cigars to the five other men. "I am compelled to ask you why you treat Mrs. Arnaz with such animosity?"

This is why Castro dragged him here, to stick his nose where it didn't belong? This bastard had stepped over the line, and Desi didn't mind saying so. "Maybe you should mind your own goddamned business." If not for the heady effects of the potent cigar, he'd have already punched the son of a bitch.

Castro took his anger in stride, as if prepared for that reaction. "You are known as America's Sweethearts, no?"

He wouldn't give this man the satisfaction. He said nothing.

"So it is a pretense."

He tried again to close the subject. "I don't mix private matters with business."

Castro persisted. "You mean, except in your marriage."

"That's different," he snapped. "We built our careers, our business together. I don't know you from Adam. Don't worry how my wife and I talk to each other. She's a tough lady. Tough as any of your soldier girls."

"Maybe so. One who is passionate is also vulnerable, including Celia, or Haydée. Or Lucille."

The others nodded agreement.

"Now you're a shrink, too? What about Naty? Do you treat her with respect?"

"I never mistreated her," Castro said.

"I don't think she sees it that way."

"Sí, she is heartbroken, but I never said anything to her that wasn't the truth. We knew what we were doing, and I told her our association would not be possible after…"

"After what? After you became the supreme leader?" Desi was accustomed to working on his feet. Without movement, he was becoming restless. "You talk about your affair as if it were a business relationship."

"So do you," Castro said.

It was a right hook. Desi couldn't deny that their marriage had been tangled up with their work so much that the two had become inseparable. If not for the kids, they'd have had little reminder of their personal lives—not that they'd given little Lucie and Desi anywhere near half enough attention.

Castro could see as plainly as anyone that he and Lucy were no longer the sweethearts they portrayed. Maybe they never had been. She'd never understood him. He'd never understood her. They were opposites. Funny thing—the sparks that flew between them in their personal lives had probably come from the same electricity that powered their professional partnership. With the show winding down, that energy had only one outlet, and it was about to blow.

Desi sighed. "This is why you brought me here? To give me marital advice?"

"It's your unique relationship as both business partners and spouses, along with your endearing image, that we hope North Americans will respond to, that will inspire acceptance and cooperation with free Cuba. If your relationship is changing, it could jeopardize the effectiveness of our message."

So now their divorce was about to get another project canceled? One they'd never wanted in the first place? Good riddance. "We've been married twenty years come November. We don't always talk sweet no more. Don't worry about us."

"Forgive the intrusion. The subject is closed." Castro paced the circumference of his theatrically lit stage. "Let's instead discuss your reasons for being here."

Oh, now he got it. He'd had a little interrogation defense training in the army. Castro had been warming up his temper, loosening his tongue. "I thought I was here to make a picture about your coup."

The compañeros stiffened as if called to attention.

Castro chewed his cigar and crossed his arms. "There was no coup."

"Your Fidelistas marched into Havana and kicked out Batista. That sounds like a coup to me."

"Batista's army could have removed the bastard at any time. That would have been a coup d'etat. The revolution is a popular movement. The country's military was an instrument of murder. We put an end to them. The people sent their message to Batista, and he fled like a spineless jackal."

To-may-to, to-mah-to. "And you want us to show the world the glorious achievements of your great revolution. I got it."

"That is precisely the purpose. Yes, your words are well chosen, a film to share the glorious achievements of the revolution—omitting the sarcasm."

"If you ask me, the folks up north will respond better to palm trees and beaches. What you want is a propaganda film. That's it."

"All film is propaganda," said one of the other men. Desi finally recognized him as Che Guevara.

"Okay, like I said, it's your show," Desi said. "Besides, you already wrote the damned thing. My wife and I are professionals. You'll get the product you asked for." Judging by their location and the cast of characters assembled, they were about to stage a scene glorifying the leaders of the revolution. He didn't recall anything like that in the script, but he'd hardly read half of it. "Where's the crew?"

"They will meet us at our next location," Castro said.

"So what are we doing here?" No food. No coffee. Not even chairs. Just the boys and their cigar smoke hanging in the shaft of light.

"When you arrived, I explained that we have nothing to hide," Castro said. "We want you to see for yourselves what the revolution has done for your people."

"My people?" asked Desi.

"The Cuban people," said a third bearded man he didn't recognize.

"Now I have a request of you, to share what you know about your government's intentions toward Cuba."

"You're asking me?" He studied the cigar's leafy wrapping as if he was appraising a glass of wine. "I'm a bongo player. Wha'do I know about the government?"

"They sent you here."

"You invited us."

Castro waited for him to give up the pretense. Even with his mouth shut, Castro talked too much.

"I see what you're doing. My name is Desiderio Alberto Arnaz y de Acha III. I was born in Santiago de Cuba on the second of March, 1917. I live at 1000 North Roxbury, Beverly Hills, California, United States of America."

"Are you going to say the same thing over and over again?"

"That's what you're supposed to do when you've been captured by the enemy."

"So you think I am your enemy."

"Sorry." He leaned back and crossed his legs. "That's right—you're just one of the fellas. Good friends kidnap their buddies and take them to a secret location."

"You don't know where you are?"

"Of course I know. But who the hell else does?"

"Who should know?"

"My wife, for one. Maybe someone from the embassy."

"I apologize if it seems inappropriate, but we must speak in private."

He looked around at the five men surrounding them and raised an eyebrow.

"Private between you and us. They are trusted compañeros."

"Anything you can tell us could help prevent unnecessary conflict," Raúl said.

"How should I know? Like a say…" With one hand he tapped a few Rhumba beats on the table. "…I'm an entertainer."

"Sometimes you don't know what you know," Castro said.

"Say again?"

"We notice things. People. Activities. We don't always think about them. Then later, if we think back, we can put it all together. It tells a story."

"What's this show all about?"

Another man spoke from the shadows. "This is no show. Things like this we take very seriously."

Guevara stepped into the light. Nice entrance. Very dramatic. What a putz.

"You look like your picture," Desi said. "You boys got quite a propaganda machine going."

"The difference between us," Guevara said, "is you sell tobacco and soap, and we sell freedom and dignity."

"No more," Castro said. "I promised not to insult our guests."

"There are many who wish to put an end to la revolución," Guevara said.

Desi looked at Guevara as if he was wasting Desi's time.

"You may think you know," Guevara said. "You know nothing."

"This is exactly what I've been saying. I think you are not as nice as Uncle Fidel," Desi said. "Is this your good cop, bad cop routine? I don't know what you plan to get from me. You invited us down here. I got plenty of better places I could be."

"This is very upsetting to us," said Guevera. "The bastard who stole this country for his own profit was starving his own people to death. Your government claims to oppose dictators. Yet when we removed one of the worst of them, they refused to acknowledge our legitimacy."

"Maybe you should look at it from their side," Desi said.

"I'm not interested—" shouted Guevara.

"Wait, wait, wait," Castro said. "Let's understand what Señor Arnaz is saying."

"Thank you." Desi adopted his negotiation posture, dropping his shoulders and crossing his legs. "You boys are talking big about socialism. You sound like the Russians. If there's anything the Americans worry about, it's the commies. We're all afraid of the bomb. Americans love their freedom—even their freedom to be bastards and fuck everyone else if necessary to get what we want."

"American filth," Guevara said.

"Plenty. But not everyone. Like I say, we are terrified of the communists. That's why we went to Korea."

"This is the propaganda of the capitalist pigs who need to exploit the people."

"Maybe yes, maybe no. Forget about good and evil for a second. Your people believe what you tell them. Our people believe what the government tells us. The Russians build a bomb. We build a bigger bomb. Back and forth."

"We are not the Russians."

Desi wagged a finger "Not yet," he said. "You talk like Russians with the wrong accent. You scare the hell out of our government. I'll tell you right now, Lucy and I didn't want to come here. Uncle Sam said we needed to do it. Lucy had a communist grandfather. We couldn't afford to lose our business. You think they make it tough for you. We're citizens. We're America's Sweethearts. And that only makes it easier for them to screw us over. Too much to lose. So we're here making you a movie. That's the story."

"Like Korea." Guevara turned to Castro. "I told you. Cuba is next."

"You expect an invasion?"

"Don't you?" asked Castro. "We've made the big American companies angry. They are not so happy with us. The Mafia is puny. They may have a few guns and not so much brains. They show up again, I shoot them on sight. The only way to take this country away from the people is with military force."

"We got plenty of that. Enough to take down Hitler." Desi lit up another cigarette. He blew a plume of smoke into the beam of the floodlight. "If the US government wanted to take Cuba, don't you think they would just come and do it? Do you really think they need me and my wife to tell them whether it will work? Of course it will work. The only question is why they didn't do nothing already."

"The Russians."

"So you do have a deal with the Russians."

"What do you think?"

"I think you got a sweetheart deal here. Ike don't want the communists taking up residence in our part of the world, but he won't risk another world war over a little island. Plus we already got Guantánamo."

"For now," Guevara said.

"You planning to stage a takeover?"

Guevara leaned over the table to face off with Desi. "I say yes, you tell Eisenhower yes. I say no, you tell Eisenhower no. Either way, he won't know." He pounded the table once with his fist, paused, and stepped back five or six paces.

"All I can say is we've got big guns. Bigger than yours. So if you decide to pick a fight, make sure you got some friends in your corner, like your pals Oleg and Tatiana. You're gonna need all the help you can get."

"That sounds like a threat," Guevara said.

Desi folded his hands on the table, a tactic he'd used in countless negotiations to pre-emptively declare himself the presumptive victor. "Who am I to threaten? Do I look like a general? I'm only putting myself in your shoes."

"What did the CIA want you to find out?"

"You already know the answer to that question. Let's say I tell them what I've seen down here, like a bunch of Russians and gangsters offering deals. You said it yourself, you've got no secrets. I don't know anything they haven't already figured out."

"This is our point exactly," Castro said. "What could you do that no one else could do from US soil?"

"Maybe they just wanted us to keep you busy."

"Or maybe something else," Raúl said.

"You think they're using us." Desi paused to ponder. It was more fact than theory. "Sure, why else would we be here?" He dropped his cigarette to the worn plank floor and crushed the butt. "I got another question."

Castro glanced at Guevara for his approval. Guevara gave him the "sure, why not?" look.

"Aren't spies supposed to be in disguise? I don't mean to brag, but me and the wife, we're pretty famous. Why would anyone expect us to be spies? Never mind. I get it. No one would ever expect us to be spies. Ridiculous."

"No one would expect you to be more than spies," Guevara said.

"What are you talking about?"

"No one would be in a better position to make an attempt on Fidel's life than you or your wife." Guevara banged his hand on the table again. He was a dramatic bastard.

Desi looked at Castro and Guevara and back at Castro. "Listen, I think a lot of people want you dead. The both of you. You haven't exactly been making friends."

"Assassination is a serious matter," Guevara said.

"I think you forgot who saved his life."

"These are techniques used commonly by operatives to misdirect their targets."

"Anything I did could be a trick."

"Exactly."

"Exactly."

"Then how do you know what's a trick and what isn't?"

"Maybe you don't even know."

Desi stood. "Are you screwing with me?" Castro's men closed in. "Tell these fuckers to back off. They make me nervous. Listen, you pompous ass. I've had to put up with hour after hour of your philosophical bullshit. Three days. You've talked my ears off. Lucy's ears off. I think we got your point. You are Jesus H. Christ, sent to save humanity from the capitalist pigs."

Castro straightened into his most solemn stance, towering over Desi and Guevara alike, and delivered a declaration. "I don't need instruction from God to know what is right. If such God exists, he may speak through me, but no more so than through any other man who stands for justice."

Desi closed in on him. They would have been nose to nose, had he another four inches of stature. "So now you're everyman."

"I am one man."

"Fuck you and all your Fidelistas. If I had come here to kill you, it would be done by now. I don't piss around with nothing. I didn't get to be a big shot by farting around."

"You have a high opinion of yourself," Guevara said. "This pig thinks everything is about him."

"Are you calling me a pig, you two-bit gangster?" Desi leaped at Guevara and tried to land a punch, but the experienced guerrilla quickly subdued him, twisting his arms behind him.

"Che, let him go," Castro said. "Try to act like grown-ups."

Guevara let him go, and Desi rolled his shoulders until he was sure they were still in joint.

"I'm no killer," Desi said, "but I know how to do a job once I sign the contract."

"I didn't think so, but I had to ask. My friend Che worries."

"You are a shit," Desi said.

"I am a shit," Castro said. "This brings me back to my previous question."

Desi put his hand on his forehead. Enough already.

"Why do you treat her so badly?"

Desi arched his eyebrows in disbelief. "What did she do, recruit you as a marriage counselor? Or is this part of your God complex?"

"It's part of my God complex, if that's what you need to believe. It changes nothing. You are married to an extraordinary woman. She is at least your equal. She is beautiful. She has intelligence. She has affection."

"Affection," Desi said. "You don't know nothing about my marriage. Don't you have more important things to worry about than my personal life?"

"You see?" Castro turned to Guevara. "Did you see what he did?"

Guevara nodded.

"What? What?!" Desi said.

"Repeat what you just said."

"What part? The part of you being a shit?"

"No, the last part."

"I said stay out of my personal life."

"Not your exact words, but same idea. 'My personal life,' you said. What about her?"

"Our personal life, same thing."

"No, not the same thing." Castro spoke again to Guevara as if Desi were no longer present. "Would you say that it's the same thing?" Guevara shook his head. Castro glanced at each of the other men present. They all weighed in, muttering, "no, no."

Desi took his seat again. He waved Castro on, shaking his own head in exasperation.

"Whatever you do next, Señor Desiderio Alberto Arnaz y de Acha III of Beverly Hills, California, you must ask yourself what is the most important thing in your life."

"I need a drink."

"You continue to make my point for me."

"Where is my wife?"

"We had to check out your stories, like in the movies. We will go to your wife now."

SCHOOLED

Lucy and the more petite ladies fit easily into Melba's black Cadillac. Lucy wasn't exactly large, but at five foot seven, she was the tallest among them, rivaled only by Celia, who must have been a good five-six.

"This is a very nice car for a soldier," Lucy said, "although some people at home do think of it as a kind of tank."

At first the women were puzzled by the word "tank," until Vilma explained. It certainly dampened her punch line. Timing was Lucy's comedic strength, and she wasn't accustomed to a delayed response. Once clarified, the small quip managed to get a smile from Vilma and Celia. Not so much from Haydée and Melba. Serious bunch.

The outside temperature must have been in the seventies, and the crowded car with the black paint job and big windows added several degrees. Lucy felt as if her face were melting. LA was warm but less humid. The other women wore no makeup and seemed unaffected by the heat. They must have thinner blood. If she hadn't been seated in the middle of the back seat, the apparent position of honor, she would have opened the window a crack.

They traveled a couple of miles. The streets narrowed.

"The people here are very poor," Haydée said.

In one street, the car barely squeezed past a fruit cart. Vendors sold cabbages and potatoes, dry beans and rice, and a little fruit, mostly bananas.

Celia, who was sitting behind Lucy, leaned forward to speak to her. "These streets used to be filled with children during the day."

Lucy's blood turned cold at the implication. "Are you saying something happened to the children?"

"Yes, we will show you."

She stiffened. "Can't you just tell me?"

"I don't think it would be meaningful."

She closed her eyes to prepare for some kind of horror. She'd seen plenty of war photos. One time on the USO tour, she'd comforted a badly injured GI who must have been about eighteen years old. He'd died squeezing her hand. That had been difficult enough. If there was anything she couldn't bear, it was the deaths of children. At seven and eight, her kids' faces reminded her always of their vulnerability.

They pulled up to a building where Desi and Castro were waiting outside, smoking—a cigarette for Desi, Castro puffing his usual cigar. One of the cameras captured her arrival.

It would be inaccurate to say the building was nondescript because all the buildings in Havana were ornate, not like the barren Bauhaus monstrosities rising in New York and Chicago. There was no glass and steel here. Not that the facades were covered in marble or granite, at least not all of them. They were shaped from concrete and brick, with details of ornamental wrought iron and shuttered windows, even a few flower boxes. With its streets paved of cobblestone, instead of the asphalt Lucy was used to back home, the city had postcard charm, but the building they approached gave no hint on the outside of its purpose or contents. She prayed it wouldn't turn out to house a mortuary.

Inside she heard the sounds of children's voices, some speaking in unison, a few laughing, and breathed more easily. Another cameraman filmed a young woman leading a tearful little boy down the corridor in front of them. The boy looked back at them over his shoulder and stumbled; he would have fallen if not for the woman's firm grip. Curiosity briefly interrupted his sobbing, until he felt the gentle tug of his escort and resumed his upset. The third cameraman, prompted by Desi, shouldered his camera to capture Lucy's every reaction. A school. They had brought her to a school. She amused herself by imagining a bunch of little tykes running around in fatigues, with BB guns slung over their shoulders. Good little revolutionaries.

"Only sixty percent of Cubans can read," Haydée said. "The people of Cuba cannot take responsibility for their own future until they can all read and write. Education is the foundation of political freedom."

"What were the children doing before the revolution?"

"You may ask them yourself," Celia said.

They ascended two flights of stairs to the third floor of the building. Lucy's pumps reverberated down the corridor. The other women wore practical, soft shoes like rubber-soled Hush Puppies, except for Celia, who wore flat leather sandals.

Melba opened a door and led Lucy into an ordinary classroom. Sixteen girls sat in four rows of smallish student desks facing a young teacher with a noticeable smear of chalk dust on her dark blue blouse, poised to write on the blackboard, chalk in one hand, an eraser in the other. Judging by figures and faces beginning to mature from childhood, the girls looked to be around age thirteen.

"Buenos días, señoritas," Celia said.

"Buenos días, Señorita Sánchez. Buenos días, Señorita Hernández. Buenos días, Señora Espín. Buenos días, Señora Santamaría…" the girls chanted in unison before subsiding into whispered chatter. The wide-eyed students were starstruck, and not with Lucy. It was the revolutionary heroines they recognized.

Castro remained outside the classroom.

"We are sorry to interrupt," Celia said to the teacher, who waved off the unnecessary apology, trailing a cloud of dust from her chalkboard eraser.

"We are honored to see you," the teacher said.

Celia offered introductions, first in Spanish, and then in English for Lucille. "Señoritas, this is Señora Lucille Arnaz, a famous American television star, who has come to learn more about Cuba and the revolution."

The girls chanted again, "Buenos días, Señora Arnaz."

"Sí," the teacher said. "And I am Señorita Ramallo." The teacher put down the chalk and eraser, shuffled the dust off her hands, and offered them both to Lucy.

"What a lovely group of young ladies," Lucy said, looking at each of the girls in turn, wanting to make them comfortable with her presence, although they clearly had no idea who she was, much less what she was doing there.

"Perhaps some of the girls could introduce themselves to Señora Arnaz?" Celia asked the teacher.

After an exchange in Spanish, which Lucy took to be about translation, the young teacher asked the girls for volunteers. Several raised their hands. The girl she selected began to speak in Spanish, and Vilma was about to begin interpreting when the teacher interrupted and asked her to step up to the front of the classroom and speak directly to Lucy.

The other girls stopped chattering, leaving no sound but the whirring of the two cameras' electric motors. Desi had moved the cameramen to opposite sides, one on Lucy, the other on the child, far enough away not to frighten the girl.

"Me llamo Lucinda," the girl said in a tiny voice with no expression. "Lucinda Alvarez Muñoz." She was too timid to make eye contact.

"That's very similar to my name," Lucy said. Lucinda was one of the smaller girls, and youngest in appearance. "I have a little girl at home named Lucie, so that makes three of us."

"My middle name is Lucila," Vilma added before translating.

Lucy crouched down. "That makes four Lucys. We should have our own ladies' club."

Even after translation, the girl showed no more comfort. The teacher offered Lucy her chair so she could comfortably sit face to face with the petite girl.

"How old are you, Lucinda?"

"Twelve years." Even with Lucy directly in front of her, the girl looked away to the side.

"My Lucie is almost ten, so you are older than her."

"Sí, señora," the girl said.

"Do you like school?" Lucy asked her.

"Sí, señora."

Lucy looked to Vilma for some kind of direction. Although she adored her own kids, other than them and Keith Thibodeaux, who played Little Ricky on the show, she had little experience with other people's children. She didn't easily relate to children, especially when they didn't speak English.

Vilma spoke to the girl, who reluctantly looked up to Lucy, still expressionless. "Tell Señora Arnaz where you live."

"*En La Habana, distrito Centro.*"

"And what did you do before you became a student at this school?" Vilma asked her.

Lucy found this an odd statement. Didn't most children play before they started school?

"I worked in a club," Lucinda said.

"In a club?" Lucy asked, taken aback by Vilma's continuing translation.

They nodded to her to continue her conversation with Lucinda.

Lucy almost choked on her next question. "What did you do in the club?"

"I was an entertainer."

"Did you dance on the stage?"

"Sometimes," the little girl said, almost too quietly to hear her—not that Lucy would have understood all her words. "Mostly I would be with the men."

Lucy tried and failed to hold back a tear. Words stuck in her tightening throat. "What does she mean, she would be with the men?"

Celia encouraged Lucinda to speak. Barely audible, the little girl said, "I pleasured them."

"But she's a child." With a handkerchief she'd slipped from her handbag, she dabbed the tears welling in her eyes. "This is what you wanted me to see? This little girl?"

Celia nodded. "All of these girls."

Nausea slithered in Lucy's gut, and the heat seemed to press down even more oppressively. She resisted the urge to run from the building. If she fled, they'd have thought she was disgusted by them. She would have preferred to embrace them all, but that too would be strange, since they knew nothing about her; it would make her feel better, but the girls wouldn't understand. She could hold this little child, though. How could she not?

Lucinda let Lucy wrap her arms around her. Behind the girl's shoulder, she wiped more tears from her eyes. "Thank you for telling me about yourself," she whispered in English. Lucinda wouldn't understand the words, but her body softened a little, and Lucy felt she had reached her, at least touched some part of her to let her know she was loved. And then she thought how selfish it was to believe that making herself feel better could diminish in any way the suffering this child had endured.

Señorita Ramallo had the girls line up and one by one to curtsy to Lucy. When they'd all taken their seats again, Lucy blew them a kiss and thanked Señorita Ramallo before marching out into the corridor, down the stairs, and straight out to the street to compose herself, fixing her makeup while the others said their goodbyes and trailed after her.

What a miserable country. No wonder Desi never missed it. In this moment, just being a woman felt like a burden. Rotting from the inside. Desi appeared on the sidewalk and tried to comfort her, but his touch made her skin crawl.

Despite Hollywood's rampant lechery, only a couple of hotshots had ever made moves on her, and none had ever forced himself on her or blackmailed her. Sure, there were a few unwanted pats on the ass and a whole lot of innuendo. Men were men, and she'd signed up for Hollywood, where sex was part of the currency. But she'd never had to prostitute herself for her career. Yet it was so much a part of the business she often wondered whether she just didn't have what the bastards were hungry for. Or maybe they were waiting for her to offer, and that's why she never landed the big parts while she'd still been a "stable filly" at RKO.

Thankfully, she'd gotten the last laugh when she and Desi bought out those bastards. It might have been Desi's wheeling and dealing that turned that sinking ship around and put them on top, but that never diminished her joy at beating them at their own game. How many abused workers fantasized about topping their bosses and giving them the shaft? She wasn't going to earn any points with the big man upstairs for such thoughts, but as long as she didn't rub anyone's nose in it, there was no harm in a little private gloating. When she was a kid, she'd once asked her minister whether thoughts of sin were just the same as sinful acts in the eyes of the Lord. He said they were, but she figured if the standards were really that high, heaven must have had a pretty high vacancy rate. Nothing a few prayers couldn't cure.

Plenty of desperate young women had succumbed to the Hollywood succubus. Hollywood hopefuls—a few with talent, some stunningly gorgeous, most pathetically inept—groveled at the feet of starmakers, pursuing their dreams at the mercy of seedy sexual politics. Often, powerful men forced themselves on the aspirants, the more conniving bastards duping them into believing they were the apples of their eyes with the added bonus of a shot a stardom. A steady stream of girls desperate for fame and fortune chased the "carrot"—and if the career didn't pan out, well, there was always that promise of marriage someday, and a hefty revolving charge account to boot. Whether driven by naïveté or blind ambition, many had made their choices.

This was different. These children had no choice. Lucy tried to resist imagining the abuse little Lucinda had endured. She conjured a flood of fond childhood memories to drown the horror, but they drained away in the rush of this waking nightmare. She hadn't been the victim, yet she couldn't shake it off.

There was no point in asking what monsters had done this to innocent children. She knew. She might have even known some of them—the sick, wretched scum, more than a few of them emissaries of the LA bacchanal, who'd found themselves a lawless playground just a hop, skip, and a jump from home, where they could live out their depraved fantasies scandal-free.

Neither was there any point in asking Castro why he'd felt compelled to show her Batista's legacy of crushing misery. As a trained lawyer, he was compelled to make his case, at once passing judgment on the Yankees he apparently despised for supporting a loathsome dictator while seeking their acceptance, as if asking for pardon in exchange for penance.

Lucy made a beeline for the equipment truck, climbed into the passenger side of the cab, and slammed the door shut.

RED RISING

*L*ucy finally remembered to breathe, sitting motionless, facing forward, her gaze locked on a glint of sunlight reflecting off the chrome-trimmed tail light of a Bonneville parked farther up the street. It was if she'd taken a bad fall and had the wind knocked out of her.

Desi stepped up beside the rolled-down window of the equipment truck and handed her a cigarette. That was when she realized her hand was shaking.

"Careful," he said. "You drop that, this old jalopy may blow."

She was in no mood. He must have thought he could cheer her up, but she was too numb for humor.

The script called for them to shoot a speech at a school. It didn't say anything about the traumatized children she'd meet there. The setup hadn't exactly put her in the mood to smile pretty for the camera. For all its bulk, Castro's eight hundred pages of endless political drivel omitted the essential details of a shooting script—settings, setups, a cast of characters. Apparently, he was planning to fill in the rest on location. If it had been anyone else, she'd have said the omission reflected ignorance about filmmaking, but she suspected that wasn't the case with Castro. He knew exactly what he was doing. He hadn't hidden his expectation that she and Desi would stand in for an entire nation, so she wasn't surprised that he seemed determined to shock them into concession and acceptance. But if there was anything she despised, it was manipulation. Dirty tricks were an insult to her profession.

Desi went back to speak with Castro. She knew by his delivery that he was covering for her again. There had been a time, whenever she'd had a bad moment—call it a temper tantrum—that Desi would have smoothed things over, making excuses for her, holding things together. Not anymore. More often than not, he was her target. This time, he was handling Castro while expecting her to get a grip so they could finish the day's work.

Not so fast.

She fought with the stubborn door latch and stepped down from the truck, bearing down on Castro and halting toe to toe with him. She stabbed at the air in the direction of the building, as if she could muscle her point home. "Why wasn't someone protecting those children?"

"Batista failed. Worse, he permitted it—this, and more. If it were possible, I'd execute Batista personally." He patted his sidearm. "I pray I may yet have the opportunity."

"That would make the both of us feel better, but it won't do shit for those children."

Castro was a kid, at least twenty years younger than she was, yet he absorbed her rage like a devoted father. He was playing the hero, working from a second script, one inside his head. She resented manipulation, and yet she'd fallen for it. Was it a setup? That little girl was no actress. Lucy could see right through Castro's tricks, and yet she knew she wouldn't have been moved as deeply had she only read the words and not looked into that child's eyes. Did the ends justify the means?

"Perhaps we should postpone the filming until you are feeling less distressed," Castro said.

She was a professional. She'd been rattled more than once, and it had never prevented her from doing her job. Regardless of Castro's designs on power, this was a story worth telling, and telling stories was her job—their job.

"Set it up," she said.

Desi complied, directing the camera crews with broad gestures like a traffic cop and rattling off instructions in Spanish. Meanwhile, she bent over in front of the truck's side mirror, wiping away her running mascara until Ximena led her to a chair and took over.

Thankfully, Desi was a filmmaking genius who'd managed to make her look twentysomething—or at least early thirtysomething—through nine seasons. Natural sunlight was not the friend of an aging screen actress. Like an artist painting with light, Desi strategically placed parasol reflectors to cast a soft glow over her face from in front and a little below, while she consciously released the tension from her mouth, eyes, and forehead to smooth away shadow-deepening wrinkles. It worked to her advantage at times like this that Desi admired feminine beauty and had the skill to accentuate its best qualities.

Lucy lost herself in the long speeches she was about to deliver. It wasn't practical to transcribe them all to cue cards, which went against all her professional instincts anyway. There was no way to act natural on camera while reading. If nothing else, your eyes would always give you away. It was a common problem on TV variety shows, which audiences didn't mind so much because the bits were mostly broad comedy and didn't need to appeal to anything but their sense of humor, but they'd never tolerate wandering eyes in a movie or in a TV drama or sitcom. Whether or not this picture they were making would ever see the light of day, Lucy wasn't about to compromise her craft, which meant she'd spent most of the night memorizing some of driest material she'd ever seen. A TV test pattern would have been more entertaining.

When the lights, reflectors, cameras, and mic boom were all in position, Desi gave them the signal and off she went. He never signaled to her once she'd begun, for the same reason that she didn't use cue cards: the camera was quick to pick up an actor's distractions.

She'd deliver her lines, oblivious to anything happening behind the cameras, until Desi called "cut."

Odd how nervous the lens made her. She'd practiced for so long not to notice the cameras, even when they were bearing down on her for a tight close-up. Now she had to force herself to peer deeply and directly into the dark cyclops staring back at her. It was also no small task to stand still, given her aptitude for physical comedy. She'd never learned what to do with her unoccupied arms while delivering speeches and now found herself holding her hands together at her chest. Before Desi gave her the signal to start, he silently modeled with his own body for her to drop her arms loosely to her sides.

"'The popular Cuban Revolution had ended centuries of oppression, sponsored by nations determined to take advantage of Cuba's rich resources and defenseless citizens,'" she began. "'The foundation of our modern democracy will be the education of our people. Deprived of access to schools and books, Cuba's illiterate children were enslaved. Under new universal public education programs, Cuba's children are now free to grow and flourish. As Thomas Jefferson said, "An educated citizenry is a vital requisite for our survival as a free people." Education is the first step toward a democratic republic.'"

As usual, Castro mouthed the words silently as she spoke them.

"'The children attending this school in the heart of Havana come from a multitude—'"

"*Cortad*, cut, cut," shouted Castro.

"What are you doing?" Desi asked.

Ignoring his objections, Castro addressed her directly, thumping his open script with his fingertips. "This is incorrect. You skipped some words: 'Yet Cubans have been denied this privilege by the actions of the nations who have demanded it for their own people.'" He waved in Desi's direction. "Please, please, again."

Of course she'd skipped some words. There were plenty that needed cutting. "I made some changes."

Desi said nothing.

"We agreed to discuss any changes," Castro said.

She marched over. "What is this crap? You will not heap all the guilt for every horrible thing that has ever happened here on American shoulders."

Castro pointed at her chest. "Ask yourself why you feel so strongly about this."

"What are you, a shrink? Don't play mind games with me. If you're implying that I feel guilty for the shit that's happened here, you're wrong. Outrage is not the same as guilt."

"I don't accuse you. I accuse your government."

"You must be crazy." Her voice increased in volume. "The US government does not sell children into sex slavery."

"They've done nothing to stop it."

"What do you think you're doing?" She was now in full prima donna form, and she knew it. Desi knew it. She could see from Castro's darting eyes that he knew it too. "Do you know anything about your audience? Are you looking for their acceptance? Or maybe you think you'll inspire a revolution in our country."

"The revolution requires no inspiration from me," he said, his composure finally breaking. "It is coming. The people of the world demand it."

What a line. "They do, do they?"

Sometimes Lucy Ricardo popped out like a mental homunculus. Had this been a regular contract, she would have just read her lines and walked away with her check. But she wasn't going to allow herself to be filmed accusing her own country of abusing children for profit. "Americans have no reason to revolt. We don't fear our government. In case you hadn't noticed, we've beaten a whole bunch of fascist bastards to protect our freedom—and by the way, you're welcome."

"Freedom is not the property of Americans alone."

"Stop talking in circles." She rearranged the chair the crew had set up for her, turning it away from the sun, plopped herself into it, and waited for Desi to sort things out.

Desi approached. "Let's try something different."

He knew as well as she did that the words Castro was putting in her mouth were career suicide, and that wasn't part of their agreement, either with Castro or with CIA Director Dulles.

"Let me speak with my wife."

He tapped her on the shoulder, and they walked a few dozen yards down the block, not out of sight but far enough that the rumbling of passing vehicles would afford them some privacy.

He lit her a cigarette, and after giving her a few seconds to settle, he became cool and detached, speaking in a flat tone, as if he was directing any old production at home. "Let's do it the way he wants. We'll cut it later."

"And what if he keeps it? He can ship the whole damned thing off to Winchell and make fools of us."

"Now you see what I'm saying." He raised his eyebrows in a full and satisfied performance of "I told you so." "I got a better idea. You don't look so great on camera today."

She arched her eyebrows. "Thanks."

"You're trying too hard to put this shit out of your mind. We'll tell him we're going to record it as a voice-over. We'll get more footage in the school—you know, smiling kids, happy, happy. We can record the speeches later."

She crossed her arms. "I'm still not saying all that bullshit." She knew he was mostly humoring her but that he could, if he was serious, fix it in postproduction.

"Let's get it over with," Desi said. "I sure could use a drink."

She didn't dare ask whether he was serious.

She blew smoke up into the air and maintained her best version of cold detachment, complete with upturned nose, while Desi went to do the talking. He convinced Castro that they were putting her on camera too much, and he needed to let the images do more of the work. "Picture's worth a thousand words," and such. Castro relented, and they finished picking up shots here and there, much to the frustration of the teachers trying to run their classrooms. Desi made sure they had enough raw footage to cut into something less accusatory.

Once they climbed back into the car taking them back to the hotel, Castro spoke to them through Desi's rolled-down window.

"Tomorrow you shall meet one who is responsible for what you have seen today."

Lucy nodded her acknowledgment so he would back off and let them leave. This rabbit hole was leading straight to hell. Castro signaled the driver with a double tap on the car's roof.

BIG FISH

*T*he next morning, after two hours in the car, they arrived at a marina. Lucy immediately recognized the captain of the rugged, black-hulled *Pilar*, dominated by a large open cockpit and a partially shaded aft fishing deck.

"Welcome aboard," Ernest Hemingway said.

"Mr. Hemingway," she replied. "You stuck around for the fireworks."

"It's Ernest, Mrs. Arnaz."

"I'll call you Ernest if you call me Lucy."

"Agreed. And not exactly, Lucy. When things got dicey, I spent a little time away. Just came back—couldn't stay away from paradise. Don't you agree, Desi?" It was a taunt.

Desi waved him off. "To me it was just home, and then it wasn't. Too much blood here. To me, LA is paradise."

"I'm afraid we'll never see eye to eye on that account," Hemingway said.

The *Pilar* was stocked with deep sea fishing rods and reels. Despite their minor squabble, Desi lit up for the first time in a month, at least in her presence.

"Is this how you give the spies and assassins the slip?" she asked Castro.

"Best to let things quiet down," Castro said. "At the start of a revolution, there is anxiety. As the leader, I must set an example. Life must continue. How do you stop a child's tantrums, by appeasing him? No. After much bloodshed, peace must become the normal state. Peace makes peace; bloodshed makes bloodshed. We continue to cultivate the new cycle: sow seeds of peace, harvest its fruits, and repeat the cycle. Besides, I still have many things to show you."

Rather than roll her eyes, she twitched a smile.

"The revolutionary poet." Hemingway patted Castro on the shoulder.

"I think you mean Che," Castro said. "Che speaks poetry. As our guests will tell you, I make speeches."

"You can say that again," Desi said.

"But don't." She blurted it out before she could catch herself.

Castro and Hemingway glanced at each other and shared a laugh.

Castro wagged a finger at her. "The humor swims just beneath the surface. It strikes at the perfect moment. This is your genius."

If only it worked that way more often. The she might have an easier time living up to expectations.

Hemingway and Castro untied the mooring lines and jumped back aboard. Castro shoved the boat away from the pier, and Hemingway pulled around to point out to sea. He throttled up the noisy engine, and gasoline fumes gave way to the fresh aroma of ocean air.

As they bounded over low swells, droplets of salty spray landed on her lips.

"Ernest, are you appearing in our production?" she asked.

"No, no," said Castro, answering for him. "He wants to make sure he maintains good relations with the US so he can return whenever he wishes."

Hemingway wanted to maintain relations? What about her and Desi?

"I might have beaten around the bush a little more than that," Hemingway said, "but that's about the size of it."

"Mr. Hemingway is a friend of Cuba."

"Let's just keep that between us."

"Your government suspects I am a dictator. I have no need to dictate to people who will defend themselves against imperialistic oppression."

"A noble servant of the people," Hemingway said. It was clear he had a friendly relationship with Castro, who accepted the sarcasm with no hint of offense.

"So you are antidemocracy," Desi said.

"This is not my meaning," Castro said. "I said imperialism. A democracy need not be imperialistic. Must not. The people must choose, but they must believe that all humanity shares 'these inalienable rights,' as your Declaration of Independence says. You cannot be a true democracy if you exploit the people of other nations to advance your own prosperity."

"Exploitation or opportunity? You can choose words to change meaning. American companies create jobs around the world."

"You imply that those jobs benefit workers," Castro said.

Seemed simple enough. She licked away the salt from her lips. "By making them financially secure."

"If that were so, we wouldn't be here today."

"People who work for pay are free," Desi said. "People who work for no pay are slaves."

Although Castro was just a young man, he reminded her of her grandfather. Like Grandpa Fred, Castro had a talent for sucking people into debate whether they were interested or not.

"I think you're being a little unfair to us North Americans, Dr. Castro," she said. "We're so often called upon to make great sacrifices in order to protect the freedom of others."

"Like Korea?" Hemingway asked. "Some good friends were killed in that mess. The problem is how can you be sure that you are on the right side of justice?"

"We went to Korea to stop the Reds," Desi said.

Castro scanned the horizon with his binoculars. "Troubles

continue in all parts of the world. Do we choose sides based on the will of the local people or for the benefit of our own?"

Hemingway tapped Castro's shoulder and had him take the wheel.

"You didn't fight in this one," Lucy said to Hemingway.

"No." He trapped a sardine in the bait bucket with his bare hand and then yanked a large hook through its jaw. It wriggled on the hook as he raised his rod, preparing to cast his line. "No more mercenary fighting for me. I'm an old man now."

"A tough old man," Castro added from behind the wheel.

"And how do you feel about imperialism?" she asked Hemingway.

While Desi baited his own hook, Hemingway unreeled more fishing line and then set his pole in the deck-mounted rod holder. "Put that way, you give me no option. Of course I oppose imperialism, which strictly defined is the exploitation of foreign people and resources for the benefit of the occupiers. I think we can all agree that that's bad behavior for any civilized nation."

Gulls followed a few feet off the gunwales, waiting for their chance to swoop in and steal the bait. Hemingway shooed them away. "Once these buzzards get a taste, they'll call in the whole damned feathered air force." He grabbed for the wing of the closet gull, but the bird dodged him effortlessly. "Go do your own fishing," he shouted.

She declined Hemingway's offer to bait a line for her. She preferred to enjoy the sun and breeze. "You disapprove of American activities abroad."

"Not all. Time will tell."

"What about Cuba?"

"I have my opinions, but I think Fidel's purpose is to let you form your own. I think it's best not to influence."

"It's a little late for that," Desi said.

"Maybe so."

She moved beside Castro at the helm, aligning her gaze with his binoculars. "How can you look for fish with those? I'm no expert, but don't they usually stay underwater?"

"Usually, but the big ones will jump into the air, especially when they are hunting," Hemingway said. "When they're hungry, they take the bait."

Castro handed her the binoculars for a look. He pointed her in a promising direction, where the water looked a little more restless.

Desi and Hemingway cast their lines. Castro hadn't spoken for a couple of minutes, a sure sign of something unusual. While the other men played out their lines, she fiddled with the focus of the binoculars and scanned the horizon.

Castro held them on a steady course. "Better hold on to something."

Maybe a hundred yards off their starboard side, the water ripped into a wake as if trailing an invisible boat, threatening to capsize them. Lucy steadied herself by gripping one of the wall brackets used to stow the fishing poles. Desi and Hemingway moved to the side and held on.

A tower rose into the air. The surface of the water mounded and then split open as if plied by an upside-down boat hull. Water cascaded off the deck of a surfacing submarine.

The sub dwarfed the *Pilar*. It had to be at least three hundred feet long and must have stood a good three stories to the top of the conning tower, which bore a familiar red star. The Russians must have felt left out. She more than half expected Savenko and Tatarenko to appear atop the tower. "That's some fish."

Hemingway twirled a scoop net in his hand like a tennis racket. "Not sure I can land this one."

She passed the binoculars back to Castro. "Your Russian friends have decided to join us."

"The Soviets, more accurately," Hemingway said. "*Zdravstvuyte!*" he shouted to the windowless black submarine.

Castro continued to pilot the boat as the submarine matched their trawling speed. The wake had shoved them off to port a few yards.

Desi put his hands on his hips. "So you've got the Russians to protect you."

"I think they are curious," Castro said, "just like the North Americans."

"Maybe we should chase them out of here," Hemingway said. "We could ram them with our little ship."

"Yeah, that'll show 'em," Lucy said.

"A humble tropical isle remains the quarry of imperialist conquest?" Hemingway racked his fishing rod, popped open a bottle of beer, and sat, swinging his ankles up onto the gunwale as if the appearance of an enormous submarine were an ordinary occurrence.

"Humble?" Desi said. "A year ago, Havana was more like a tropical playground."

"For the depraved and overprivileged, which were often the same thing. And all that to line Lansky and Batista's pockets."

Apparently satisfied that they were no threat, the submarine to pulled away.

Castro had remained uncharacteristically quiet.

"Nothing to add, Prime Minister?" Lucy chided him.

Castro cut the engine. "Even I know when to let others do the talking."

Lucy followed him to join Hemingway and Desi on the fishing deck for a final look at the hulking vessel.

"That makes one of you," Desi said.

She shot Desi a look and retreated again as far as possible from the sun and his ridicule to the shade of the open cockpit, as the boat rocked in the sizable waves of the passing wake. Desi sat in the fisherman's chair fixed to the deck. She landed in the lightly padded captain's chair behind the wheel. Unnerved by the presence of the massive vessel, she unconsciously swiveled back and forth until she realized she was amplifying her own seasickness.

Outside on the aft casting deck, Hemingway and Castro steadied themselves on foot, absorbing the wild bucking with bended knees, each perfectly balanced and gripping nothing but a beer bottle in one hand and a cigar in the other. Castro stared down the submarine, which powered on, leaving them bobbing behind.

"Our revolution continues to attract interest," Castro said.

"My only regret," Hemingway lamented, "is that I'm blank to all but the most obvious writer-prone wisecracks."

"What the hell is he talking about?" Desi asked Lucy.

"Moby Dick." She considered rubbing his nose in his ignorance, but better instincts prevailed. Besides, there was no need. Castro and Hemingway had generously contributed the setup. Desi's own ego would deliver the coup de grace.

"Thanks for not making me say it," Hemingway said.

She smiled. "It was just hanging there. Like drool."

He pointed at her, acknowledging her wit. Three of them chuckled; Desi did not. Nothing rubbed him the wrong way quite as much as finding himself the odd man out. It was the perfect taunt to a man who reveled in being the center of attention.

"So, captain," Hemingway asked Castro, "what's the next move?"

"Is it possible I've been watching the wrong adversary?" Castro asked.

"The Russians won't invade," Hemingway said.

"How are you so certain?"

"Too close for comfort." Hemingway pointed with his thumb at Lucy and Desi as stand-ins for the entire US. "The Soviets will try something more insidious. Offer some kind of deal. Get inside."

Castro swept his arms like an umpire calling an out. "We just ejected the colonists."

"I would exercise extreme caution," Hemingway said. "They may show up soon with an attractive offer. I wouldn't trust them. They may see an opportunity here to expand their influence, especially in light of your socialistic tendencies. The Bolsheviks have a reputation for brutality. Some people say you're following their example."

"I'm known for brutality?"

"Suspicions abound," Hemingway said.

She hadn't seen pictures, but it was no secret that hundreds if not thousands had been executed, even after Batista had fled the country. Dulles had shared a few specific names and asked them to pay particular attention to such stories.

"You haven't exactly conducted a bloodless takeover," Lucy said.

Desi held his head in his hand.

"War is never bloodless," Hemingway said. "The manner in which blood is shed is what separates hero from villain."

"The revolution ended in brutality." The clean-shaven parts of Castro's face flushed. "I stand before God naked and prepared for his judgment."

"That will serve you well in the afterlife," Hemingway said.

So that's what it took to ruffle Castro's feathers. She spoke directly to him. "Ernest and I are saying there is an impression. Whether it's true is another matter."

"It's the entire matter." Castro crossed the deck like a trapped bear. He covered the distance in a couple of steps. "I am ready to show you something. Reel in the lines."

After they stowed the fishing gear, Castro spoke briefly with Hemingway, and Hemingway throttled the engine to full power.

"This should be interesting," Hemingway said.

They were headed away from shore. "Aren't we going the wrong way?" she shouted over the noise of the wind and spray.

"He's taking us to Isla de Pinos," Desi explained. "Machado built a prison there."

She took a seat in the deck chair beside Desi. She was still disgusted with him, but she needed answers. "Who's Machado?"

Desi got up and sheltered just inside the pilot house to light himself a cigarette. "Gerardo Machado. Dictator before Batista helped kick him out. Machado built the prison to lock up pretty much anyone who disagreed with him."

"I myself spent two years there," Castro said, "a political prisoner of the Batista dictatorship."

Hemingway had to shout to make himself heard over the engine and spray. "Thousands have spent their last days there. It's been a dumping ground for the most reviled criminals."

Castro pointed at himself with the butt of his cigar. "And most feared adversaries."

She gazed at the receding shore. "Sounds like a lovely place. I hope we don't have reservations."

ISLE OF THE DAMNED

*A*fter an hour crossing open water, they docked at Nueva Gerona on the northern coast of the Isla de Pinos. On the dock, the cameraman named Felipe was already filming their arrival. So much for spontaneity.

"This wasn't in the script," said Lucy.

"It's a work in progress," Castro said.

Quite the showman. Lucy flashed him a brilliant smile. "I don't suppose that Russian sub was part of your story."

"You overestimate me. I don't have such relations with the Soviets to ask for their participation."

"Crying shame," Hemingway said. "I would've given you credit."

A small caravan had assembled, led by a flat-bed truck packed with lights, stands, and the riveted black travel crates that held the other cameras. One of the grips rode in the cab with the driver, while two others crouched in the back among the gear to keep any of it from bouncing out. The remaining members of the film crew had squeezed themselves into a green Ford woody station wagon.

Lucy piled into the middle back seat of a waiting Lincoln Continental with the others. The car smelled a little of sweat and bait, mixed with the spiced orange scent of her Florida Water cologne.

Hemingway crossed his arms, trying to be polite by minimizing contact, while Castro chatted with the driver in Spanish and Desi stared out the window.

"Are we still in Cuba?" she asked.

"We are indeed." Hemingway rolled down his window and hung his arm outside. He leaned forward to ask Desi, "You know it?"

"Never been," Desi said.

"Nor have I," Hemingway replied.

Castro bit the butt end off a fresh cigar and offered them their own, though he refrained from lighting up. Just a few minutes from the marina, they turned on to a straight road leading across a broad expanse of fields toward a cluster of round buildings.

"What is this place?" Lucy asked.

"It ain't no Hotel del Coronado," Desi said. "And that ain't no golf course."

The grassy field was filled with row upon row of brown dirt rectangles that looked like recently filled graves. Perhaps it was a cemetery for fallen soldiers, Cuba's version of Arlington.

"Machado's model prison," Hemingway announced. "Presidio Modelo."

Not the graves of heroes, then. Hoping for the best, Lucy tried to guess the ages of the graves. Many looked recently filled. For every unmarked grave that remained exposed, she wondered how many more had grown over. In so much space, it could've been thousands.

Castro traced a loop in the air with his finger, and the driver took them all the way around the central round building, which looked like an oafish facsimile of the Central Park Carousel house, its first floor rimmed with squarish arches. Four more stark, round buildings stood outside the circular drive, identical to each other and taller than the one in the middle.

The film crews, whispering to each other in Spanish, unloaded the flatbed.

Castro unceremoniously barreled toward the entrance of the nearest building, lighting his cigar and trailing fat puffs of smoke like a heaving steam locomotive. A steady murmur issued from inside, which increased in volume.

Hemingway jogged to catch up with Lucy and Desi at the doorway. "Looks less ominous than I'd expected."

"A real country club," Desi said. "We're shooting here?"

"Sí. Please," Castro said.

The cameramen and crew drew up behind, awaiting Desi's instructions.

Desi flipped through pages. "It's not in the script."

If Castro was usually overprepared with his saga-length script, this time he was unprepared. Desi didn't respond well to poor preparation.

"What are we supposed to shoot in here?" he said. "You got a funny way of bringing back the tourists."

"I promised I would show you everything," Castro said. "Does a prison not tell you the character of a government?"

Desi looked at Lucy, raised his arms in a silent "what the hell am I supposed to do?" gesture, and began pacing around.

Lucy's eyes adjusted slowly to the gloomy interior. The cylindrical building's interior was wide open, an atrium rising from a circular expanse of bare concrete. The sheer scale of the place, along with its unbroken curvature, made it difficult to take in all at once. At center stood a stout masonry tower rising half way to the roof, resembling an indoor lighthouse. Barred cells lined the perimeter of five floors, beginning on the second level. Wherever the angle of view reached the main floor, prisoners looked down between the bars at them. Two or three had whistled when Lucy entered, but most just stared. She supposed it had been a while since they'd seen a woman. Whenever she inadvertently caught the eye of one man or another, he waved, some with a slightly psychotic glaze.

"Are these men political prisoners?" she asked.

Castro stiffened. "We hold no political prisoners." He tilted his chin up, punctuating his claim with pride.

He spoke to one of the guards in Spanish. Desi didn't bother to translate.

"Is it not illegal in your country to conspire to overthrow the government?" Castro added. "Your government, like ours, must imprison those who do so."

She tucked her chin in surprise. She'd pushed a button. Other things had set him off into a diatribe, but this time, he'd slapped back.

"Hell, if we did that, we'd have to lock up all kinds of crazies," Hemingway said. "We have a lot of big talkers in the States. We can't lock up every Tom, Dick, and Harry who sits on a barstool fantasizing about rounding up his own army. It's all 'sound and fury, signifying nothing.'"

"The problem is, how do you know who's just a talker?" Lucy asked.

"It's not so easy," Castro said. "For some of us, we know only what we are told. We believe in this god or that. We prefer this food or that. We pledge loyalty to these laws or those. A difference of opinion does not become treason unless the dissenter chooses to betray his country out of self-interest, and with harm to his fellow citizens."

"Fidel, my friend," Hemingway said, "you are a true soldier-philosopher."

"You mock me," Castro replied, with no hint of malice.

"Not at all. But I don't quite know what to make of you."

"We punish deeds, not thoughts. To kill ideas is to kill culture. Don't you agree, Señor Desiderio Arnaz?"

"I agree absolutely. Traitors must be punished," Desi said.

Lucy assumed Desi's implied indictment wasn't lost on Castro, but he offered no response. Hemingway buttoned up his lips, although he appeared to delight in the sparring.

The guard returned with a man in ragged prison clothes. He looked to be about forty or so, with the fair complexion of a Spaniard.

"Señor Fidel," he said quietly, eyes down.

Castro placed a hand on the man's shoulder, an odd gesture for a captor. This was the second time he'd put on this show, demonstrating empathy for his detractors. "These people are guests in our country. They are famous North Americans."

"Sí," said the man. "Lucy and Ricky."

Lucy couldn't help but be touched at being recognized by someone who seemed so unlikely to be in their audience. The vanity was a perk she felt she'd earned by bringing people like this prisoner a little respite from their difficulties.

"This is Señor Xavier Medina Cordero," Castro said. "We are old friends. We attended school together at Colegio de Dolores."

"That was my school," Desi said.

Lucy looked at Desi in surprise. "You two went to the same school?" Although he looked much older, Medina must have been close to Castro's age.

"Sí," Desi said.

"Not at the same time," Castro said.

"Maybe ten, twelve years ahead of you," Desi said.

"We all have much in common," Medina said cheerfully.

"Señor Medina was a soldier." Castro gestured for Medina to proceed. "He will tell you."

Medina looked to Castro for a nod, which was given, and came to life like a puppet. "I was a fighter." He raised an imaginary rifle to his eye, pointing politely not at any of them but at an imagined foe in the distance.

"You fought for Batista?" Desi asked.

"Sí. I fought to protect my village."

"The people were told we were murderers and rapists," Castro said. Seeing that Medina was missing some of the conversation, he translated his own words.

"Sí, sí, asaltantes. Very dangerous men."

Lucy had no desire to pass judgment, but Castro wasn't going to let them off the hook. He had an axe to grind.

"What do you think now?" she asked Medina, reading his eyes for any signs of fear or intimidation.

"While I was away in the mountains, Batista's men came to our village. They took the boys. Gave them guns. Told them they must fight. If they refused, they would go to prison. When the Fidelistas came to Bueycito, the boys waited for them. The Fidelistas surrounded them."

She covered her face as if Medina's story were unfolding before her. She dreaded tales of carnage, even if they were tempered with acts of heroism. Stories like this came to life all too easily for someone who made her living from her imagination.

Desi clenched his fists. "They were only boys."

With previously undisplayed impatience, Castro raised an open hand, commanding Desi to withhold his outrage. Desi was startled into silence.

Medina continued. "The boys were taken by surprise. The Fidelistas fired their weapons over their heads. The boys ran in all directions, straight into the arms of the waiting enemy. Captured. One boy was shot, but not by a Fidelista. His friend, very scared, fired wildly. He shot him in the back. The Fidelistas rounded up the boys. One of the Fidelistas carried the wounded boy to the nearest house. He was himself a doctor. He tried to save the boy, but he could not."

Lucy recalled that little neighbor boy shot accidentally in their own back yard. A blood-soaked shirt. A child dying. "You knew that boy?"

"Sí, he was the son of my friend. A good boy. Fifteen years only."

She needed a chair. Desi must have seen her wobbling, because he came to her side and put his arm around her waist. He hadn't completely abandoned her yet.

She braced herself with a hand on his shoulder. "This changed your mind about the Fidelistas?"

"They came and took the guns away from the boys and made them go back to their mothers. They told them they would not have to worry about Batista's soldiers."

"After the Fidelistas went to Havana and took over the country, I went home, Bueycito. My wife told me this story. This was when I knew I had fought on the wrong side."

"And yet here he is, in prison," Lucy said to Castro.

"The punishment is symbolic," Castro said. "We can't allow our enemies to go completely unpunished."

Desi sneered.

"Not so symbolic to him," she said. If Medina's story was true, he was just someone who'd got caught in the middle of a fight he didn't ask for. "Who's supposed to get the message? While you're making an example of this man for your enemies, you just may be scaring off your friends."

"You find this unpleasant. And you are correct. It is not desirable, only necessary." Castro instructed the guards to return Medina to his cell.

This man had acted out of fear, not malice. She stepped to Medina's side and placed her hand on his shoulder, stopping Medina and his escorts. "Cruelty breeds cruelty."

"We must be strong," Castro said.

"If you want the support of the North American people," she said to Castro, "you're going to need to start showing compassion."

He displayed one palm. "Strength." He displayed the other palm. "Compassion." He clasped his hands together and paced away, making a circuit of the floor.

The building fell quiet. Hundreds of prisoners whose cells were within sight stood gripping the bars, as if Castro were about to decide not just Medina's fate but theirs as well.

With Desi's help, Lucy asked Medina about his wife and children. Until the revolution, he said, he'd led a farmer's life. Not easy. Yet he expressed no bitterness, only contrition. When she asked the name of the boy who had died, he choked up. He wept.

From somewhere above, a prisoner called out, "Medina libre!"

Castro looked up and scanned the cells. Lucy followed suit. In the circular chamber, it was impossible to pinpoint the source of any sound. The shout was repeated, but Lucy couldn't tell whether the voice was the same. Then a few more called out. Castro spotted one and pointed in the prisoner's direction. The man raised his arm through the bars of the cell, as if challenging Castro. Soon others joined, and the calls grew into a chant. The reverberations multiplied the deafening chorus.

Lucy covered her ears.

Castro returned to face Medina and raised his open hand over his head, silencing the chants. The reverberations persisted for several seconds. With dramatic flair, he waited for complete stillness.

Then he orated for the benefit of his captive audience. "Today, Señor Xavier Medina Cordero shall return to his family."

The prisoners erupted in deafening cheers and whistles, again intensified by the curved walls. Lucy covered her ears.

Medina sank to his knees, but Castro lifted him back to his feet and embraced him. Medina held Lucy's offered hand for a moment, saying nothing, before one of the guards led him away.

"Bullshit," Desi said.

"You disagree with Fidel's decision?" Hemingway said.

"How much did you have to brainwash that man to make him think you were doing him a favor? Did you torture him?"

The middle of a prison didn't seem like the best place to tell off an unpredictable guerrilla leader, but Desi was right. Castro's staged display of mercy more than likely was just a ploy, not only for her and Desi's benefit but to inspire loyalty and good behavior among the hundreds of other men impatient for their own freedom.

Despite Desi's antagonism, Castro remained calm. "You may examine him if you wish. He has no wounds or bruises."

Hemingway observed quietly, taking no side, appearing only to await Desi's next volley.

"You don't need to beat a man or make him bleed to fuck with his head."

"He didn't seem like a man who'd been tortured to me," Lucy said.

"I didn't ask you, woman," Desi snapped.

Lucy recoiled. It was that time of day when Desi's demon crawled out from under its rock.

Desi stabbed the air after Medina. "You mean to tell me that man, who fought against your revolution, suddenly had a change of heart? Just because of a dead boy? Without your war, that boy wouldn't have died."

Castro maintained his composure. "I promised to show you everything. You will have your own conclusions."

Lucy stood back alongside Hemingway. Castro might have been

up to something. Or maybe not. Unlike Desi, she hadn't jumped to the horrific possibility of torture; she'd confined her doubts to simpler deceptions. It was too horrific to imagine darker alternatives.

But now Castro dragged Hemingway into the argument. "Ernest, you lived in the shadow of Batista's tyranny. Which is more likely, that Señor Medina was forced to fight the revolution by intimidation or threat, or that the revolution has broken his mind and body?"

"I'd prefer not to speculate," Hemingway said, "but I've seen my share of broken soldiers, and I have to say, Desi, in Señor Medina I see a man in his right mind."

"Men like this," Castro said, "awakened from Batista's deceptions, they would not survive outside."

Desi's face flushed. He spat his words. "You're saying you throw them in prison for protection? What kind of bullshit is this? *Mierda!*"

Castro showed no hint of provocation. "We cannot protect every man and his family. Batista's gangsters must believe these men remain loyal. That is why they wait here, disguised as the resistance, until the true criminals are eradicated."

"Eradicated?" Lucy asked. "Do you mean jailed?"

"Some, yes."

"I told you," Desi snapped at her, as if no one else were present. "It was what we saw in the news. They've rounded up everyone who was against them and blew their brains out—in the streets for everyone to see."

She didn't remember arguing this point. Regardless, since he wasn't getting any satisfaction from trying to antagonize Castro, he was directing his anger at her, as usual.

"We must excise the murderers and torturers," Castro was saying, "as was done at Nuremberg."

After spending several hours with Vilma and Castro's other female followers, she had to believe that Castro's government couldn't be completely brutal. "So you'll try them first."

"Of course we will. We are not barbarians. When I completed my studies and became a doctor of jurisprudence, I swore to uphold the law. Justice is the basis of my entire existence." Whenever Castro declared his principles, he appeared to puff his chest and erect his already substantial frame at least an inch taller.

Desi chafed. "So you're completely committed to upholding the law that you yourself make."

"The universal laws of human dignity," Castro said. "I will not deny that we arrested, tried, and executed hundreds of war criminals."

"Thousands."

"Hundreds." Desi had pushed too many buttons. Castro's expression hardened, and he gestured with clenched fists. "We hunted and captured the vermin who ruthlessly murdered men, women, and children suspected of sympathy to the revolution. These men were not armed soldiers. They were citizens of what was once a democratic republic, until Batista enslaved the population to line his pockets. When he feared the flow of money would stop, he became desperate. He ordered squadrons of his men to drag citizens from their beds and execute them or lock them in his filthy prisons until they starved to death or perished from untreated wounds and diseases." He wiped sweat from his forehead with a handkerchief, hung his head as if praying for the lost, and then looked Desi directly in the eye. "I freely admit to dispensing justice."

And then he walked away.

NO HOLDS BARRED

"This is democracy?" Desi asked Hemingway.

"This is not the United States of America," Hemingway said.

"You can say that again." Desi marched from the building. Framed by the doorway, he flailed his arms in a rage-filled tirade to himself.

Lucy didn't follow. No point. He'd have a smoke and pace around. He reacted badly whenever she infringed on his anger.

"There's that Cuban passion," Hemingway said.

"Yeah, passion. He's nervous—I think we're both a little nervous about looking sympathetic on camera."

"Pardon me for saying so, but it looks like you two are having a little trouble being sympathetic toward each other."

She raised her eyebrows.

"Didn't mean to offend," he said.

She shook her head in amazement. What rock had he been living under? Not that it was any of his goddam business. They were here to make Castro's picture, not for anybody's marital advice. No matter that she'd actually hoped this trip might help them patch things up again. "I hate to tell you this, but you may be the last person on earth to get that news flash."

"I'm not much of a gossip hound."

Apparently. Still, whether or not it was any of his business, no need to pick a fight with the man for expressing concern. She let him off the hook with a pursed smile.

She didn't blame anyone for their curiosity. Here they were at the peak of their success and popularity, and their personal lives were an all-too-visible mess. She'd asked for fame, and that meant living in a fishbowl. Somehow, Desi's drinking had remained off limits, and she preferred it that way. Too easy to backfire. She couldn't be sure anymore which had come first, the booze or the battles, but she sure as hell didn't want to become known as the prima donna Hollywood bitch who'd driven her loving husband to the bottle.

Above them, some of the men had begun chanting, "Fidel, Fidel, Fidel." Up on the third floor, Castro was circling in front of the cells, shaking the hands of hopeful prisoners reaching through the bars.

Castro began shouting commands to the film crew in Spanish. One turned his camera upward and followed Castro from cell to cell, and a second checked his film cartridge, then rushed up the stairs to follow Castro as he greeted and spoke with the prisoners. Two assistants gradually unspooled power cables behind them from coils slung over their shoulders, while flooding the scene with light from handheld reflector lamps.

Lucy's squinted to shield her eyes from the harsh movie lights. She could hear Castro speaking but couldn't make out the words.

"Why don't we join the festivities?" Hemingway suggested.

"Is it safe? It doesn't look safe."

"I think we'll be fine."

She didn't feel particularly reassured, but Desi was still walking off his version of the delirium tremens outside, and Castro wasn't coming back down.

Hemingway let her lead the way up the clanging steel stairs. Good thing she was wearing her boating shoes. Heels would have poked right through the grating. They found Castro inside one of the cells seated on a cot facing another prisoner with a chess board on an overturned wooden crate between them.

They paused outside the cell, hidden from Castro's view behind the glare of the movie lights.

Hemingway spoke first. "You've chosen an odd time for games, unless your objective is on-the-nose symbolism."

"Or only, I play a game of chess," Castro said.

Hemingway shielded his eyes against the intense flood lamps and peered over the railing. "I see Desi hasn't returned."

"He's sulking somewhere," Lucy said.

"He needs a drink," Hemingway said.

"That is exactly what he doesn't need."

A guard dumped a bucket of soapy water into the hole in the floor that served as a toilet and left.

"Come." Castro urged them forward into the cell.

Lucy had never set foot inside a real prison cell. She pushed through a barrier of anxiety, crossing the threshold between the rusted iron bars. The tiny cell wasn't large enough for the four of them, and the toilet hole, despite the rinsing, emitted a putrid odor. Without concern for offending her hosts, she applied more cologne to her neck.

"Señora Arnaz, Señor Hemingway," said Castro, "I present to you Señor Eduardo Castañeda."

Castañeda moved his bishop a few squares, taking out Castro's knight before tipping his head in Lucy's direction. He winked and then spoke a few words to Castro.

"He says you are a beautiful woman, an unusual sight in the castle," Castro said. "You must forgive his forwardness. He speaks truthfully that these men have not been visited by a woman in many months or years."

She partially covered her face with her hand. The cologne clinging to her fingers helped mask the stench of excrement and sweat. "Castle? Wouldn't it be more like a dungeon?"

"Only if it were underground," Hemingway said. "The translation is off. Should be more like the citadel or the stronghold. Not so fairy tale-ish."

At Castro's invitation, she took a seat beside him on the cot.

Hemingway leaned against the bars.

"Eduardo and I played basketball together in school," Castro said.

In his circles, nepotism had a flip side. "I'm certainly glad I was never one of your childhood friends," she said.

"For what reason?"

They waited until the answer dawned on him, and he chuckled. He wagged his cigar in her direction. "This is more of the funny."

He offered Castañeda a cigar, which Castañeda took without hesitation. Smoke soon filled the cell. The strong aroma of cigars had never offended her, but the cocktail of stenches in the air made her feel more than a little green around the gills. Shadows of the bars thrown by the flood lamps striped their faces and hung in the haze. She felt like the femme fatale in a scene from a George Hill prison picture.

"From teammates to rivals," Castro was saying.

"You opposed the revolution?" Lucy asked.

Castañeda raised his chin. "I did. I do."

"You weren't bothered by Batista?"

"I was a successful businessman," Castañeda said. "When the Bolsheviks came to steal our homes and our land, the government of Fulgencio Batista y Zaldívar stopped them."

"Then it's true that Batista stopped the Bolsheviks," Lucy said. "He sent my husband and my father-in-law away to protect them."

"The Bolsheviks called themselves communists," Castro said. "They aimed to murder those who had wealth or power."

"I thought the revolution also took property from landowners," Lucy said.

"Sí, comunista," Castañeda said, aiming his finger pistol squarely at Castro.

Castro shook his head at Castañeda's accusation. "Unlike the Bolsheviks, the revolution does not assassinate the innocent. Wealth itself is not a crime. But the desire to acquire wealth corrupts the soul, harming the wealthy and the poor alike. My own family bestowed our land to the reform. This protects all Cubans, even those whose souls have been corrupted by excess. The Bolsheviks were only criminals."

"Like Stalin," Lucy said.

"Castañeda speaks truthfully," said Castro. "Batista stopped the Bolsheviks. But why? He coveted power. Once they showed him how to rule by fear, he exterminated them and adopted their methods."

"People also died during the revolution."

"Many. Soldiers died honorably in combat. Innocent civilians died at the hands of murderers, whom we have captured. Many have been executed—hundreds."

Death hung in the air. Maybe it was the ghosts of everyone who had died in this hellhole. She felt trapped, unable to escape the cell without making a scene, yet also curious.

"Thousands fled to escape justice," Castro said.

"What will you do when they return?" Castañeda asked.

Castro's demeanor hardened. He leaned over the chess board and interrogated Castañeda with his eyes.

"There is only talk," Castañeda said. "You know how prisoners speak. One man expresses his hope. In the next cell, words are heard. Hope becomes possibility." He traced an orbit in the air with his finger. "Rumors circle the tower, grow into prophecies."

"I hope you do not choose to withhold information," Castro said quietly. "There are consequences."

He stated his threat without concern for his guests' presence. He touched his holster—whether as a threat or to reassure himself, Lucy couldn't tell. He shielded his eyes from the film lights, squinting across the vast chamber at the inmates in their locked cells.

"Rumors," Castañeda said.

"You mentioned you were imprisoned here," Lucy said to Castro.

"This was my own cell for nearly two years."

She crossed her arms. It was as if she'd found herself inside his bedroom. The concrete walls pressed in. She'd trained herself not to react to flinch or squint at the glare of stage lighting, yet now tilted her head down, shielding her eyes. What was his story? Prison might have transformed him from cruelty to compassion, or from compassion to cruelty—or perhaps it had left him unchanged, stoically committed to principles he'd held since childhood, a political prodigy.

Castro switched his rook and king.

Castañeda grunted with satisfaction. "You see, I have you on the run."

"You are a man of many talents. I had better keep an eye on you. Someday you may break free of Presidio Modelo and come looking for me."

"I swear it." Castañeda moved his knight. "*Comprobar.*"

"Check," Hemingway repeated.

Castro returned his attention to Lucy. "That was the birth of the revolution, the twenty-sixth of July, 1953, an attack on Batista's men at Moncada."

She'd set him off again. He explained in painful detail how the small band of one hundred forty rebels had attacked the Moncada military barracks, demonstrating the events with the chess pieces—the white king representing himself, of course. Their operation had failed when they were surprised by an unexpected patrol.

"How did you expect to defeat Batista with only one hundred and forty men?" she asked.

"Men and women," he emphasized. "Melba Hernández and Haydée Santamaría fought at our side that day. We needed to ignite the passions of our people, and the only way to do that was to show them they were not helpless in the face of oppression. We took up arms and attacked head on. It was costly. Many died. I was spared by the actions of a single man, an enemy soldier who felt the first light of justice dawning over Cuba."

"Ernest is right. You have a gift with words." As long as he didn't feel patronized, a little flattery couldn't hurt.

"Thank you." He composed himself, even wiped a tear slowly forming in his left eye. Lucy couldn't tell whether it was a reaction to her compliment or the resurgence of painful memories.

From memory, he restored the chess pieces to their game positions.

Castañeda nodded agreement with the board before considering his next move. "How is Fidelito?" he asked.

"I struggle to break him free of his mother's influence. He does well in school. Your children—have you received news of them?"

"They are fine. I assume no harm will come to them."

"I gave you my word."

Castañeda took Castro's bishop with his queen, which gave him broad control of the board. What determination. And the nerve, taking on a professional army. What kind of man inspired admiration in his own captives?

"What happened to the man who saved you?" Lucy asked Castro.

"He joined our cause."

Castañeda addressed Lucy. "He was a traitor to Batista. It seems that there were traitors on both sides."

"A traitor in the cause of justice is a hero."

Something didn't add up. "And Batista didn't execute you? You say he was a bloodthirsty dictator. Why did he let you live? And how did you escape this prison?"

"I can tell you, escape would have been possible," Castro said. "Many would have helped us." He touched the heads of several pawns on the board, as if making a roll call of his allies. "But that's not how we left this place. Batista allowed his advisors to convince him that killing me and Raúl would accelerate a rebellion."

"You would've been a martyr."

"Sí, martyr. It is said the same in Spanish."

"But he would have stopped the revolution."

"With or without Fidel Castro, la revolución was inevitable. It was only a question of when, and who would speak for the people." If his humility was disingenuous, it was a marvelous put-on—not surprising for a politician. "Batista underestimated our will. We remained imprisoned for only two years, which was our time of political education. He knew he couldn't hold us indefinitely. Many would have come to our aid. And as we've spoken of already, execution would have accelerated our cause. Instead, we were exiled to Mexico. He planned to set us free and have his secret guard hunt us like animals."

"Wasn't that unwise?"

"Very much. But only if you believe he had any good option. We went to Mexico and built an army."

"An army of eighty." Castañeda took Castro's second knight. "Check."

"Eighty-two," Castro said. "We returned to Cuba trained and armed for battle."

"And that was when you took over the government? Eighty-two of you?"

"We were cut to pieces again. Only thirteen of us survived. We took refuge in the mountains and prepared ourselves once again to fight for the freedom of the Cuban people."

"From one hundred and forty to thirteen. How on earth did you plan to fight Batista's army with only thirteen men?"

Castro took one of Castañeda's pawns—not a particularly aggressive response to Castañeda's last capture.

"One by one, we built an army of men and women fueled by passion for freedom. We fought Batista's army all across the island. We would come out of nowhere, inflict great suffering upon them, then disappear again into the forests and mountains. They never knew when or where we would materialize. Inevitably, their will was broken."

"Why inevitably?"

"Those who fight on behalf of tyranny are doomed to failure. Only a just cause can sustain a crusade. With no ideology, they have no place to stand."

"So you do lock up anyone who doesn't support your beliefs. Didn't you say you were building a democracy?"

"This man is a prisoner of war."

"Isn't the war over?"

Castro unholstered his pistol and carefully laid it on the chess board between the remaining pieces, careful not to disturb their positions.

Her stomach lurched, and she kicked back on the cot, bumping the board with her leg and toppling a few chess pieces. She pressed herself as far from Castro as the tiny cell would afford.

Castro fiddled with his cigar as if he hadn't a care in the world.

When Castañeda reached for the gun, Castro made no attempt to stop him. He waved off the guard who leaped into action.

Castañeda raised the gun squarely to within a foot of Castro's face.

Lucy shielded her face with her script, as if a stack of paper would stop a bullet or a shower of blood. In the brief moment when she clenched every muscle in her body and squeezed her eyes shut, she heard the hammer snap.

No shot was fired.

She should have known it was another of Castro's stunts.

Castro held out his hand, into which Castañeda laid the gun. "Many have sworn allegiance to the criminals and imperialists. The revolution continues until no threat persists."

"Are you completely out of your mind?" Lucy said, hyperventilating now that it was over. "He could have killed you."

He held up a fistful of bullets. "He could have, had I allowed him."

Castañeda smirked and wagged a finger at Castro. "One of these days, you will forget to empty the chamber."

Castro took Lucille's hand, which was still shaking. "I meant no harm. As I explained to your husband, we punish deeds, not thoughts."

"You're a son of a bitch." She gripped his hand tightly, regardless, trying to steady herself.

"Yes, I am told so." He studied the board, his subtle eye and chin movements betraying the angles he was working out in his head. Finally, he announced, "You almost had me." He slid his remaining bishop into position. "Checkmate in three more moves."

"I will beat you someday." Castañeda laid down his king, conceding the game. "I will prepare more."

They laughed.

Very funny. The sheer stupidity of these antics, this machismo one-upmanship made her want to slap the smiles off the both of them.

Castro rose and invited Castañeda to embrace, like a brother visiting from abroad. He slipped two more cigars into the pocket of Castañeda's threadbare shirt. "Adiós, amigo mío. When you change your mind, I promise to give you back your freedom. For now, you cannot be trusted."

"Nor can you," Castañeda said.

Castro directed Hemingway and Lucy out of the cell. The guard slammed shut the door with a steely clang that reverberated around the circular walls.

Lucille walked beside Castro, with Hemingway several paces behind. "Are these people prisoners of war or political prisoners?"

"You are not afraid to speak your mind," he said. "As long as the revolution continues, we must imprison the enemy."

"And the revolution will continue until when?"

"Until those who would drag us back into the slavery of imperialism have capitulated."

"Or died."

"That is a possibility. Some will choose to die for their beliefs. As I said, we've spilled much blood for our freedom. I would expect nothing less from our enemies, who hold their beliefs as firmly as we do. We will let providence choose who lands on the side of justice."

"What if providence chooses against you?"

"So be it. I can only follow my own conscience."

"And ask millions of others to go along for the ride."

"This is another of your expressions," Castro said.

He often made observations in lieu of asking questions, seeming to step outside of the scene to digest a thought. She imagined some tiny clerk in his noggin, stepping away from the controls to file each bit of information.

"If you mean the Cuban people have embraced my beliefs," he continued, "then yes."

Except the ones who hadn't—and wouldn't. She pointed firmly with an outstretched arm in Castañeda's direction, and Castañeda nodded back as a host would acknowledge a departing guest. "What will happen to him?"

"He will either change his heart, or he will live here until it no longer beats."

Her shallow breathing and dry mouth continued until they were outside again. The prison's yellow exterior glowed in the slanted tropical sunlight. If not for the iron-barred windows, it could have passed for a decrepit hotel.

Hemingway caught her eye and modeled a deep breath. She flushed her lungs and filled them with fresh air. She was ready to get back on the boat and return to Havana. This had already been the oddest day of her life.

The roar of a crowd spilled from the unglazed window openings of the next building.

"Sounds like a disturbance," Hemingway observed, which did nothing to calm her nerves.

Castro raised his hand to silence them and then cupped his ear. The noise had turned into a rhythmic chant. He directed Lucy, Hemingway, and the film crew to follow.

"I think we've located Señor Arnaz."

HAIR TRIGGER

For a moment, Lucy couldn't move. She wasn't so sure she wanted to see what Desi was doing inside, or what was being done to him.

Castro drew his pistol and jogged ahead. She rushed to follow, while Hemingway urged her to stay back from the entrance.

They found Desi in the middle of the rotunda, quarantined from the gloom by a shaft of sunlight, all the prisoners shouting at him. He was craning his neck, scanning the circular cell blocks, as if looking for familiar faces. Lucy recognized enough of the words the prisoners were shouting to know they weren't expressing their admiration.

"They're hollering obscenities," Hemingway confirmed. "I wouldn't feel comfortable translating for you."

"I hate to say, but I've heard them all before. I might have uttered a few myself. It helps to communicate with a Cuban in his native tongue." She wasn't proud, but she also wasn't apologetic. She and Desi were both foul-mouthed.

When the men on the lowest levels spotted Lucy, the noise died down, although a few of them shouted another type of obscenity directly at her, accompanied by piercing whistles. The men above the second cell block, however, had no view of the ground floor. A man on one of the upper tiers was shouting questions, which were being answered by another man below, apparently the designated reporter.

The men glared, not with lust but with seething rage. She'd never been the target of such corrosive hatred. Even the actors and crew she tormented on the set when she became possessed by perfectionism showed only nervous fear, never loathing, and she'd given a few of them good reason to dislike her.

"May I ask them a question?" she asked.

Castro waved his arm deferentially. "You are entitled to pose whatever questions you may wish of the accused."

Castro, Hemingway, one of the cameramen, and a guard followed her up to the second level, where she searched dozens of faces for eyes that appeared the least possessed by rage. She glanced back over the railing. Desi had stepped out of the glaring shaft of dusty sunlight piercing the shadowy interior and pivoted to watch from below.

Hemingway interpreted for her when she finally stopped before a prisoner.

"Why do you dislike us?" she asked the man. "We never did anything to you. We never did anything to anyone in Cuba."

Another man nearby shouted, "*Sucios estadounidenses.*"

"He says we're filthy," Hemingway said.

The man continued, Hemingway interpreting as rapidly as possible. "Your words—you did nothing. *Yanqui* garbage left us naked, surrounded by these monsters who claim they fight for freedom. They steal only for themselves."

In the dead air, thick with the putrid stench of sweat and excrement, she couldn't help being repulsed by the prisoner's wretched condition. He wore a heavily stained, sleeveless undershirt full of holes. His coarse beard was matted and tangled. His oily, thinning hair clung to his scalp, barely hiding festering sores. She kept her distance, backside touching the railing, avoiding the odor by breathing through her mouth. Disgusting. Her tongue had become dry and pasty. She tried and failed to fan herself with the massive script.

She turned to Castro. "Why is there so much brutality in your country?"

"This is what we fight against," he said.

"By perpetuating it?"

He faced the man within the cell. "It is fascinating you choose this cell. Ask this man what he did, why he is imprisoned here."

She found it difficult to look at the man. Castro waited patiently. She looked to him again, half expecting him to retract his invitation, but he nodded again in the man's direction and ordered him to speak to her.

"I was a proprietor," the man said, "a man of business. When these communist swine came to tear down Cuban society, seizing what they wanted by force, I protected my property by serving my president, Fulgencio Batista y Zaldívar."

She heard him say "Capitán something-or-other Rodríguez," which she assumed to be his name, but Castro didn't repeat it during translation.

"By the communists, you mean this man?" She gestured toward Castro. Apparently, Castro and Rodríguez were reluctant to utter each other's names, as if each intended to nullify his adversary's identity.

"Sí, yes." The man spat on the floor, barely missing her shoe.

"And you were captured."

He nodded. "The rebel criminals came to my home after President Batista left the country. They tied my hands and ankles, and they brought me here."

She looked to Castro, who nodded his affirmation of the story.

"Even after the rebels, as you call them, succeeded in overthrowing Batista, you were taken prisoner. Do you know why?"

"My business was too attractive to these thieves."

"What business were you in?"

"Entertainment."

His evasive answers suggested something she probably would prefer not to know, but Castro was relentless. He ordered the guards to enter the cell. They twisted Rodríguez's arms behind his back, and Castro pressed him for a more specific answer.

"I ran a brothel."

Castro could no longer contain himself. "He is the merchant of children. This is the man who tortured the little girl Lucinda. You met her at the school. I'm certain he violated her himself."

Fainting wasn't a habit she struggled with, but she had to steady herself against the railing. Hemingway offered his arm as well, which she rejected. She couldn't stomach the touch of any man.

"The worst of these vermin have abused—tortured—their brothers and sisters." Castro again unholstered his pistol and shoved in a magazine.

This time, Lucy ducked behind Hemingway, who willingly shielded her. She hadn't read every word in Castro's script, but she was pretty sure there were no execution scenes.

"What the fuck is going on up there?" shouted Desi. He rushed up the steel stairs.

Someone shouted in English, "Hey! Here comes fucking Ricky Ricardo!"

Someone else repeated, "Sí, aquí viene Ricky Ricardo."

Laughter filled the echoing chamber like the studio audience in some twisted nightmare.

Castro held out the weapon. "Mrs. Arnaz?"

What was he suggesting? That she shoot this man? She stepped out from behind Hemingway, a few steps closer to Castro to get a better read of him.

"There will be no consequences," Castro said.

One cameraman trained his lens on Lucy's face, the other on Castro's. They were harshly lit by the brilliant flood lamps. Castro cast a looming shadow across the wall curving away behind him.

This was no way to convince her, or any of the folks at home, that Cuba should be their next vacation destination. "So says you. Some of us don't believe in cold-blooded murder."

"Murder is a crime," he said. "Execution is justice."

"What about this man's trial?"

"He has confessed to selling the flesh of children."

"I didn't hear a confession." She stepped out from behind Hemingway, approached the man behind the bars, and peered into his eyes. He said nothing. Denied nothing.

She stepped back and accepted the pistol from Castro.

"What the fuck are you doing?" Desi shouted.

It was time to see some terror in this arrogant bastard's eyes. The guards yanked his arms behind his back and slammed him forward into the iron bars. If he weren't still conscious, she'd have assumed his skull had cracked.

She raised the weapon at the putrid wretch's wedged face, aiming as best she could remember Grandpa Fred had taught her. She'd seen Castro load the gun. Or was the cartridge empty?

The guards stood well out of the way, cranking Rodríguez's arms in their sockets. His eyes narrowed, and his jaw locked, but he remained silent.

"If this man lives, what will you do with him?" she said.

"Eventually, he will waste away and we will bury him in the fields, to rot among the other vermin."

She turned the barrel on Castro.

The other inmates within sight gasped and murmured. Those in cells behind Castro dropped to the floor.

"*Muerte a Fidel!*" shouted someone.

Those who couldn't see what was happening shouted questions at those who could.

"Lucy, what in fucking hell are you doing?" Desi bellowed. "Put down that gun."

Castro didn't react. "Mrs. Arnaz will make her own judgment."

She wasn't born yesterday. What a setup. This son of a bitch was trying to brainwash her. Next thing, she'd be waking up in green khakis. "Enough games."

"This is no game," Castro said. "To you I may be a devil, no different than these murderers. I have killed many men—too many."

"Then I should shoot both of you."

"You're not shooting no one," Desi said. He stepped toward her, apparently thinking he'd take the gun, but she only pointed it at him next.

"Maybe you too," she said. "I've had enough of this bullshit from all of you."

Castro stood his ground and silently ordered his guards to keep their distance. "It may be disturbing, but it is no bullshit."

"Shoot us both," said Rodríguez. The guards twisted his arms until he grunted, but despite the pain, he spit his defiant words. "A cheap price for his life."

"This man has the courage of a lion," Castro said. "Fortunately for us, he is securely caged."

"I don't see it," said Hemingway.

"What in hell are you talking about?" Desi said.

Hemingway crossed his arms. "It's not her style. Doesn't fit the image."

She wasn't so sure. She had a temper, not her most attractive quality. And more than once she'd thrown a thing or two at Desi. Could she pull the trigger? Maybe not. But she'd give her left arm to see Castro break a sweat. "You don't think I can kill one of these bastards."

"Just a personal observation," Hemingway said. "It'd make a great story, though. Either way, you'd be a hero to somebody."

"I'm not sure I'd have much to lose. Might be worth it." With Hemingway's ribbing to take off the edge, she found herself able to lower the gun. She dangled it in the air by its grip until Castro retrieved it. "Is it loaded?"

He swept an arc with the gun. The inmates on their level and the level above ducked instinctively—and uselessly. Castro aimed at the base of the central guard tower and squeezed off a shot.

Lucy jumped out of her skin. Shards of brick and plaster flew from the telltale dust cloud. The noise reverberated off the hard, circular walls for several seconds, until the only sound that remained was the whirring gears and chattering gates of the cameras.

Castro signaled the guards, who shoved Rodríguez onto his cot. His spine struck the steel frame, and he finally let loose a groan. Lucy allowed herself some satisfaction that he'd suffered greater discomfort as a result of their visit. Too bad he'd get over it.

When they emerged from the grim prison block, the sun was low in the sky, only a couple of hours before sunset. Castro remained inside for several minutes, no doubt planning some other sadistic games or signing death warrants.

Still shaking, Lucy needed Desi to steady her arm while he lit her first cigarette, and the next.

"I thought we were making a fluff piece." Desi shook his head. "He didn't need us to make his picture. He needed fucking Ed Wood."

He told the camera crews to pack up. When Castro finally emerged, Desi shook his head to warn him off. Castro wisely kept a little distance, exchanging some words quietly with Hemingway.

Lucy finished her cigarette, threw the butt on the ground, and stamped it out. "I've seen enough of your new Cuba," she called to Castro. "I'd like to go home now."

TURNING BACK

Back aboard the *Pilar*, Lucy found the sea breeze even more refreshing than on the way out to the island, despite the evening chill. It was the next best thing to a bath or shower, which she desperately needed to rinse away the day's horrors. Castro had taken the helm. She sat with Desi in the aft deck chairs while Hemingway and Castro chattered in the cabin. The roar of the engine drowned out their words. She held on to the gunwale with one hand as the speeding boat skipped over lazy swells, misting them with salt spray splashed from the bow. She rubbed her arms for warmth. There was a time when Desi would have noticed her goose pimples and wrapped his arms around her.

"I think we have enough," Desi was saying. "This was a real show-stopper. This will really sell the revolución to the folks at home."

Oddly enough, Desi's sarcasm was one of the things she found endearing about him, especially when he made a mess of his English. It took the edge off. When the footage leaked out of her leveling Castro's own gun at him, she'd either become a national hero or a mental patient.

Despite Desi's harsh feelings toward Castro and his revolución, she'd come to Cuba thinking their film would show life had returned to normal. If Castro really did want Cubans to prosper, it made sense to encourage tourists to come take advantage of the Caribbean beaches and spend their American dollars in the hotels, shops, and nightclubs. That, they could have sold to Americans. Too bad Castro was barking up another tree entirely.

Desi might not have noticed or cared that she was chilled, but Hemingway apparently did. He went below deck and fetched her a green mackinaw jacket, which she threw over herself like a blanket. They could make the return voyage in about three hours at sixteen knots, he said, give or take.

But somewhere in the middle of the Gulf of Batabanó, well out of sight of land, Castro throttled down, cut the motor, and set them adrift.

Apparently neither surprised nor concerned, Hemingway remained with Desi and Lucy at the aft to enjoy one of Castro's cigars while Castro climbed the ladder from the port gunwale to the roof of the pilot house. Hemingway's binoculars dangled from his neck. What he expected to see in the fading light, Lucy couldn't begin to guess. Another submarine?

"What's the problem?" Desi asked. "Don't tell me we ran out of gas in the middle of nowhere."

Castro silenced him with an open palm. He planted himself in a wide, steadying stance, absorbing the boat's rhythmic rolling. With the binoculars he scanned the horizon, pausing a couple of times to listen for something.

Lucy scooted her chair around parallel with his gaze. A single, lengthening jet contrail glowed in the sky, a streak of neon in the rays of sunlight still reaching the heights.

"More subs?" said Desi.

Castro silenced him again.

Lucy exchanged bewildered glances with Desi.

"It's very quiet," she said.

"Too quiet," Castro said.

"What do you mean, too quiet?"

Desi bounced his knee nervously. "We're going to be stuck out here in the dark."

Castro continued to scan with the binoculars. "Our enemies have made a great show of their reconnaissance. Boats, planes skimming the waves, they circle us like sharks. Tonight they are silent and invisible."

"It could be," Desi said, "they just aren't there."

Lucy moved inside the pilot house. Although it was open at the back, it would provide enough shelter from the wind and spray to keep her from freezing to death. Desi remained aft.

"What's this guy's game?" she asked Hemingway.

"He's not playing any games, you can be sure of that. This has been a bloody mess, and I mean that literally. Fidel is an idealist, along with his compadres, including his own brother and especially my namesake, Che."

"Che?"

"Ernesto Guevara. Goes by the nickname Che. These men have conditioned themselves to violence. But they aren't bloodthirsty, just young idealists. Once they'd watched a few dozen of their fellow revolutionaries die, many of them bound, gagged, and executed on the spot, they lost every last shred of compassion for Batista's sympathizers. And rest assured, Batista was not the type who deserved compassion."

She pulled the coat more closely around her like a cloak. "But they picked the fight. What about the men they killed in the name of their cause?"

Hemingway found a rag in one of the storage lockers and used it to polish the inside of the windshield. "Soldiers who fought for Batista were fair game, in their estimation. Before the revolution, I spent many years on this island, and it was peaceful. That's the funny thing about tyranny—peace masquerades as tranquility."

Castro's heavy boot steps thudded across the cabin roof and down the short ladder.

"You should ask Fidel," Hemingway added. "He'll happily share his thoughts on that matter."

"I have no doubt," she said. Another joke shared at Castro's expense.

"What thoughts shall I share?" Castro asked.

"What thoughts will you not share?" Hemingway replied. "Our friend Fidel here is a natural storyteller, even if he does tend to talk too much."

"Yes, I talk too much. We are both men of words. It's a good thing we are also men of action." Castro patted Hemingway on the back. "*Adelante.*"

Hemingway nodded, started the engines, righted their course, and throttled up to full speed.

Castro took a seat on the bench opposite Lucille. While Hemingway occupied himself with navigation, they settled in for what she hoped would be the uneventful remainder of their voyage back to mainland Cuba.

"Are you anticipating trouble?" she said.

"Before a storm, there is stillness."

"The calm before the storm."

"Sí, we have the same expression in español. When the rhetoric ceases, the diplomats stop talking, the ships disappear, the skies are clear. This is a warning sign."

No question this fellow had more than one screw loose, so it came as no surprise he was tilting at windmills. "You're saying that the less activity you see, the more likely an invasion?"

"When you put it in words, it sounds crazy, no?"

Better that he knew rather than someone needing to break the news to him, with God knows what consequences. "I wouldn't worry too much about sounding crazy. All politicians sound crazy now and then."

Castro unholstered his pistol and inspected it. "I'm political, but I am no politician. I'm a revolutionary."

She'd had enough of that damned gun already. She took a breath of the fresh sea air, but she could swear it was tainted with gunpowder tang leftover from Castro's demonstration at the prison. "There's a difference?"

Apparently convinced his weapon was ready for action he stowed it again. "Politicians shape opinions but go no further. Revolutionaries are like Che, a doctor—once we recognize the disease, we cut it from the body."

Desi ducked inside the pilot house but remained on his feet, leaning against the port dash panel. "I've got no patience for bullshitters."

"Yes," Castro said, "you've already said I am full of shit."

"I changed my mind," said Desi. "There's a difference. Full of shit means you don't know nothing. I think you know plenty. A bullshitter is special. Look it up in Webster's. 'Bullshitter: someone who never does nothing he says he's gonna do.'"

"Who'd have thought bullshit could be so nuanced?" Hemingway said.

"What should I do?" Castro said.

"To start with, how about elections?" Desi said.

"As I have said, elections will follow when militias disband and make room for political parties." Rather than stiffening at Desi's accusations, Castro softened his posture, crossing his legs. "I have another definition: someone who presents lies as truth."

"That's a funny one, considering what you brought us here for."

Touché. Desi hadn't lost all his zing.

Castro kept his eyes on the horizon. "If you believe I show you lies, and yet you film them, then that makes you a bullshitter. If you believe what I show you, and yet you protest that I deceive, then that also makes you a bullshitter. You think I'm a bullshitter. I think you're a bullshitter."

"Finally," Lucy said. "It's good you two finally see eye to eye. I'd hate to think you'd never find anything in common."

One hand on the wheel, Hemingway was keeping an eye on Desi and Castro in case their verbal argument came to blows. Desi took a few long pulls on his cigarette, stepped to the rear, and flicked it overboard. Castro remained at ease—but then, he was carrying a pistol, and Desi knew better than to pick a fight with an armed man, at least when he was mostly sober. He'd come home more than once with a black eye, but never any bullet holes.

Castro offered Desi a cigar in truce, and Hemingway took a swallow from his mug.

"What about you?" Lucy asked Hemingway. "How did the two of you become pals?"

"I do admire this young man," Hemingway said. "I would say we're friendly, but I'm no Fidelista. Not enough of a beard. Too old for shooting." He held out a tremoring hand. That wasn't age. Desi had shown similar signs. Hemingway might have had a couple of decades on Desi, and the booze had done more damage, but Desi was catching up.

"You are an honored guest of the Cuban people," Castro said.

"That right there is the bullshit. I appreciate the sentiment, but I'm nothing but a Yankee tourist who's overstayed his welcome."

Castro stood and peered forward through the windshield. "Your presence has significance."

"I think he means you've endorsed the revolution," Lucy said.

"Ernest is a born revolutionary," he replied mechanically, without turning in their direction.

Hemingway looked over his shoulder and winked at Lucy. "I'm a meddler, for sure."

"It looks to me like you've chosen sides," Desi said.

"I sure don't miss that bastard Batista. I'd have sent him off to hell myself." Hemingway offered the wheel to Castro, who obliged, and ducked into the cabin. He came back with a couple of cigars from his own stash, along with a bottle of whisky and four ceramic cups. "It's too bad he managed to postpone his one-way trip to the afterlife."

"They used to watch us all the time," Castro said, as if speaking to himself.

"Maybe they lost interest," said Hemingway, who apparently understood who Castro was referring to.

"Who lost interest?" Lucy asked.

"The US Navy. They've been circling ever since Batista warned them the Fidelistas were gaining ground."

"Not ground," Castro said. "The revolution was not about territory. The people gained the courage to demand their freedom."

"Does he ever stop?" Lucy asked Hemingway, as if Castro weren't present.

"He's the genuine article, revolutionary through and through."

Castro acknowledged Hemingway's apparent compliment by patting himself over his heart. "Everyone is political."

Thanks to Grandpa Fred, Lucy'd had her fill of politics as an adolescent. Her empty stomach churned. In his enthusiasm for their delightful tour of the prison, Castro had forgotten about such frivolities as food and drink. Maybe it was for the better. She'd never been susceptible to seasickness, but she needed a break from the rank cigar, fish, and man-sweat odor of the pilot house. She stood and moved aft to steal a few breaths of fresh sea air, leaning over the gunwale just in case.

The first few stars dotted the darkening sky. Hemingway flicked on the red and green running lights. "Just because I was raised with politics doesn't mean I'm political."

Hemingway left the wheel to Castro again and offered Lucy a box of soda crackers.

"A fish knows nothing of the water in which he swims," Castro said.

"Fish? What the hell is that supposed to mean?" Desi said.

Lucy wiped away a crumb that had stuck to her lipstick. "He means we believe certain things we don't even know we believe. That's our politics."

"I didn't ask you." Even when he needed an answer, Desi had come to dislike when it came from her. "That don't mean we go around making everyone else believe the same as us."

"You don't have to," Hemingway said. "That's what we hire Uncle Sam for."

"You cannot deny your influence on the thinking of others," Castro said.

Desi began pacing the deck like a lion at the zoo. "I'm still trying to figure out what we're doing here."

"You don't trust me."

"Should I?"

"Trust can only be earned. I had intended to earn yours."

"You talk a big game, but I don't see you putting your money where your mouth is."

"Unlike you."

Desi's face flushed. He took a deep draw on his cigar and held the smoke in his puffed cheeks before letting it drift out through his parted lips.

"What's that supposed to mean?" Lucy said.

"Your husband contributes to the resistance."

Desi remained silent.

She took a seat again in the open air, where despite the chill, she felt less motion sickness. The occasional spray on her face took her mind off her stomach. "Doesn't surprise me." It did. Was the prison tour a warning? Or a threat? "How much?"

"One fight at a time," Desi said. He crossed his arms and squared off with Castro. "So I got no secrets. How about you tell us the truth?"

"Let me know when it's my turn," she added.

"I promised to show you whatever you asked to see," Castro said. "Today I showed you the unfortunate yet necessary side of revolution. As you say, no secrets."

"Some revolution—more like a coup," Desi said. "I'll tell you what I want to know. Where's the democracy? When do your liberated compañeros get to choose their own president?"

Castro took a Patton-like stance, cigar hanging out of his mouth, hands folded behind him. "The time will come."

"You'll decide for them." Desi spit out a flake from the cigar he'd bitten off while gritting his teeth. "You don't know nothing about democracy."

"It's possible you are correct. We Cubans have never experienced democracy. Those who have been elected have always collaborated with outsiders to usurp our constitution. We have much to learn."

Whenever Desi tried to back him into a corner, he found a way to turn it around. Playing along might better move the conversation along.

"How will you know when the time comes?" she asked.

He pointed out to sea. "There are still those out there who wish to control us for their own purposes. Democracy cannot succeed until we are a secure as a sovereign nation."

"Maybe if you had a democracy, you'd make more friends."

"You mean the North Americans. We do not, will not, seek Yanqui approval. We will choose what is best for ourselves and not what the empire imposes upon us."

"Empire?"

Castro turned his attention forward again, scanning the horizon like John Wayne in *The Sea Chase*. "They will soon return."

The posture might have been Wayne, but the delivery was pure Laughton. Castro might have been correct that *Lucy* fans learned to imitate what they saw on television, picking up habits from Lucy and Ricky or Ozzie and Harriet, but they weren't alone. She couldn't decide whether Castro was vigilant or just plain delusional. If he started building up defenses to match his paranoia he was liable to raise suspicions in DC he was up to something undesirable, which could easily blow up into a self-fulfilling prophecy.

How exhausting to see—or imagine—only threats and enemies in all directions. "How do you know the ships aren't still out there?" Lucy said. "You couldn't see them from here."

"They'd make their presence known," he said. "Their planes fly back and forth to Guantánamo. They test their artillery. At night they sweep the skies with searchlights. Our own pilots haven't reported any sightings since three days."

"Do you really think our military would start an invasion while we're here?" The words had barely left her lips when she knew the answer could go either way. What better way to keep Castro guessing?

"I wouldn't underestimate certain elements of the US government," Hemingway said, "especially while Nixon has Eisenhower's ear. Be a hell of a kickoff to his presidential campaign."

She pulled Hemingway's coat high up under her chin. "You mean the part about America's Sweethearts dying in the fight against the commies? Maybe coming here wasn't such a great idea."

"Maybe?" Desi said.

"It wasn't my idea."

"It wasn't your idea to join up with the Reds?"

She kicked off her shoes and tucked her feet up on to the chair, under the coat. "Here we go again."

Desi pounded the back of the other fishing chair, then rubbed his hand. "Not again. Still."

"I thought it was my idea," Castro said to Hemingway.

Hemingway shrugged. He clearly wasn't about to get himself into the middle of their quarrel.

"I hope the whole damned US military shows up," Desi said. "Better than if the Russians come first. Then we got ourselves a bigger mess."

"I frankly don't know what the big deal is," Lucy said. "What do you think, communism will spread from Cuba to America?"

"Socialism." Castro raised his cup of whisky as if offering a toast.

Desi let loose as if Castro and Hemingway weren't present, as they had both done so often when they'd pushed each other's buttons in front of friends or crew—or the children. "Stupid woman, you don't know nothing. Why don't you call up your friend Dulles and tell him you're hosting a welcoming party for the Reds? We can end up like the Rosenbergs." He flailed his hands so fast that the burning ash end flew off his cigar and landed on his head.

Lucy jumped up to brush it off before his hair caught on fire. Desi flinched. He must have thought she was about to smack him, because he blocked her with his forearm, knocking her flat to the deck.

Castro stepped between them. Hemingway throttled back to an idle and, drink in one hand, helped Lucy up with the other.

Castro held his ground in front of Desi. Desi's nostrils flared.

Lucy held on to Hemingway's arm. Despite more battles than she could count, Desi had never struck her. She knew this hadn't been a direct attack, but he should have known better. Hemingway waited for her to nod before stepping back, and Castro followed suit.

Desi took a seat in a chair facing out to sea and lit a cigarette. Hemingway and Castro returned to the pilot house. None of them spoke for the final hour of the voyage.

They tied off at the dock around eight thirty.

"You will all be my guests for dinner tonight," Castro said.

"I appreciate the invitation," Hemingway said, "but I'll need to take a rain check. I'm beat."

A long, drawn-out meal with Castro was out of the question. The only thing that appealed to Lucy at that moment was a couple of Alka-Seltzers and a warm bath. Then maybe she'd be able to stomach a quiet meal in their room.

"It's been an exhausting day," she said. "I think we'd better get some rest."

No need to ask Desi whether he agreed.

They made their farewells to Hemingway at the dock and left him to finish securing the *Pilar*. She welcomed the peace, warmth, and cushy seat of the car during the ride back to the hotel. This was more her style. She'd been expecting beaches, palm trees, nightclubs, and dancing in the streets. Instead, they'd gotten guns, gangsters, spies, soldiers, prisons, and tortured children.

"Prime Minister Castro," she said, "not that I don't appreciate your hospitality, but you need an experienced journalist to properly tell your story."

Castro shifted his enormous frame in the passenger seat to face her. "It is a complicated tale. You bring a unique perspective, and the trust of your fellow citizens. However, if you wish, I will arrange for you to depart tomorrow."

Desi crossed his arms. "A deal is a deal. We finish the job."

Now he was standing on principle. Or maybe he actually believed that Congressman Walter had dredged up more dirt on her. "I'm ready to go home."

"As soon as we're done."

She flipped through the pages of the enormous script and raised her eyebrows at him. For crying out loud. He couldn't be serious. Unless Castro agreed to major cuts, they'd be shooting for months.

For all she cared, Desi could stay down here as long as he wanted. Whether the committee went after her or this film got out—which seemed certain—their careers and the studio were already doomed.

She was going back to the children.

Desi dozed off, preferring to lean against his car door rather than her shoulder. In the front passenger seat, Castro had turned on the dome light and was reading a well-worn paperback he'd retrieved from the glove box.

Lucy closed her eyes and occupied herself by counting her worries.

CHANGE OF PLANS

As they approached the Hotel Habana, Castro ordered the driver to stop half a block short. All day, whenever he'd detected—or imagined—something out of the ordinary, he had tuned in like a hound. It made Lucy jumpy, seeing him constantly listening and looking for the next sign of potential danger. Then again, while political disagreements at home could be heated, they rarely involved guns.

She peered out the window just as several men in front of the hotel spotted them and headed down the next street. Castro stepped out of the car for a better look, partially shielding himself behind the open door. Two guards stood in front of the hotel, the tips of their cigarettes arcing up and down with each puff. Other than the group of young men who had disappeared around the corner, Lucy could detect nothing unusual.

Castro set one of his two bodyguards from the car to following them on foot. He leaned down to look into the car. "We are taking extra precautions on your behalf." He was clearly trying to hide his concern, and she was nervous enough to play along.

Desi stirred, opened his eyes, and asked what was happening.

"Something fishy," she said.

He closed his eyes again.

She leaned forward for a better view through the windshield. The bodyguard stopped to confer with one of the hotel guards, patted him on the shoulder, and entered the lobby.

A bright flash erupted from an upper-story window, followed by a thunderous boom. Castro dove back inside the car. The shock wave shattered the car windows and blew out the storefronts across the street. Desi threw himself across Lucy as pebbled glass showered the car interior, and debris clattered onto the roof.

Smoke and dust rolled down the hotel's facade and billowed into the street. Orange and yellow flames raged within the cavity that had been a guest room. Lucy counted the floors up from the ground. Their room?

Castro left them in the care of the driver and the other bodyguard and ran into the hotel, pushing between the guests and uniformed officials spilling into the street. One man had apparently broken his ankle and was being carried away. Bystanders on the street were helping each other.

"That's our room," Lucy said to the bodyguard, who only pointed and nodded with typical Fidelista stoicism. "Was our room, I mean."

A fire brigade arrived and while they unfurled their hoses, a couple of the firemen helped a guest who'd attempted to climb down from his second-floor terrace. The black smoke billowing from the gaping hole in the hotel faded to gray. The firemen raised their ladder and began dousing the flames.

Lucy could've sworn she saw Castro at the open ledge, waving to her from inside, as if she should be comforted now that all was well. It wasn't.

Another car skidded to a stop behind theirs. The doors were thrown open, and three more of Fidel's soldiers sprang into action. Two took defensive positions at the front and rear of the car, while their own driver helped Lucy get out. The third soldier assisted Desi, who'd wrenched his knee when he twisted to shield her.

Lucy pivoted on her heel but saw only pandemonium in all directions. She choked back her horror by latching onto one fleeting thought: had any of their things survived the explosion?

"Up in smoke," she said.

She hadn't brought anything of great value other than her coat, which she was now wearing, but she'd need fresh clothes for the trip home. She'd go shopping, then. So disappointing. She had adored some of those outfits. Who could say? She might find something new, even prettier. What better excuse for a new wardrobe than having the old one blown to kingdom come?

Her heart was still racing, and all she could think about was shopping. Such absurd thoughts, yet all she could manage.

Desi limped around, pausing a couple of times to massage his sprained knee.

She needed no further justification. "I want to go home. Tonight."

Desi nodded, returned to the car, and spoke with the Fidelistas standing at the ready with their rifles in hand. He offered them smokes. Lucy couldn't make out what he was saying, but it better have been about travel arrangements.

The men nodded but didn't budge. One of them nodded in the direction of the hotel and said something about Fidel.

Desi hobbled over to her. "They won't do nothing unless they get it from Castro."

"It didn't look like you put up much of an argument," she said.

Another four soldiers came running from the direction of the hotel and surrounded them. One of the soldiers, a woman, spoke to Desi in Spanish. He told Lucy that Castro had sent them to provide protection. This should have been comforting, but it had the opposite effect. Protection from what? Or whom?

Desi moved in close and put his arm around her. Even if he was only reacting to the drama, she welcomed his embrace. One minute he could scorch her with his words and the next minute, melt her with his touch. Nothing like snuggling up after a bomb blast in front of a raging inferno to fan the flames of passion.

The woman soldier directed them into the back of a second sedan; she took the front passenger seat, standing her rifle between her knees. One of the other soldiers banged on the trunk of the car, signaling them to drive away.

Before they rushed off to God knew where, Lucy asked them to stop and retrieve her handbag from the other car. "Are we going to the airport?"

Desi spit something in Spanish at the woman soldier.

"No," she answered.

"Why the hell not?" Lucy said.

Apparently catching her meaning from her tone, the woman continued speaking.

"Too dangerous," Desi said, interpreting. "Castro thinks we're under attack."

Lucy was shaking so hard, Desi had to light her a cigarette and hand it to her. "Whatever gave him that idea?"

The woman was still speaking.

"She says Castro wants us to go to a safe house for now, until he's sure there's no more danger."

"Tell Prime Minister Castro," Lucy said to the solder, "my husband and I don't feel safe. We'd like to go home as soon as possible."

The soldier spoke again with Desi.

"She says we got to tell him ourselves."

They took a circuitous route, possibly to throw off anyone who might have been tailing them, although in Havana even the most direct routes wound every which way. Lucy and Desi were tossed back and forth as the car sped around turns. They held on to each other for stability, sliding as one across the black vinyl seat. Desi tried to anchor them by gripping the door handle, but accidentally unlatched it and had to yank it shut again before they took another fast corner and flew out.

They were let out at a private home, where they were received by a woman about their own age and a young man, who showed them to a bedroom.

"Where are the cameras when you need 'em?" Lucy said.

"It'd make a good pilot," Desi said.

"Except for the actual blowing us up part."

"That's the thrill."

The room was cramped, with nothing but a double bed, a couple of nightstands, and a small dresser for which they had no use, since they had nothing with them but the clothes they were wearing. The room was lit harshly from overhead by one small frosted glass ceiling fixture.

They sat together at the foot of the bed. Before all hell had broken loose, Lucy had been craving a bath. The boy had shown them a tiny bathroom outside their room, and the idea still appealed to her, but she was too nervous to leave Desi's side. No, not nervous—downright terrified. Although Desi, fidgeting with his cigarette lighter, wasn't exactly the picture of strength and calm. He didn't have to say it: he needed a drink, and if she'd had one, she might have offered it and had one herself.

"Why us?" she said.

"Why do you think? Because whoever's watching us thinks we're on his side."

"I'll tell you, I'd rather side with him than with Lansky and Batista."

"They're all crooks. Either way, somebody gets killed."

She was reluctant to remove so much as a shoe in case the opportunity to get out of there presented itself. Desi tried to pace the tiny room, tripping over her feet. After the way he'd reacted earlier, she'd half expected the crisis, as terrifying as it was, to bring them closer again. Instead, he was withdrawing. It was bad enough that he resented her for stealing center stage in their careers. But now that her circumstantial political past threatened to tear down his own accomplishments, his resentment had flared into hatred, threatening to char every last bit of the affection that might have still mended their splintered marriage.

"What now?" she asked. "You think he's really expecting us to stay here all night?"

"I got no idea what he knows." He went to the small window and pulled aside the curtain.

"What he knows?" Not what she was talking about.

"You heard him. He's expecting the marines to land at any minute."

Something didn't add up. This wasn't just Desi's poor English scrambling his meaning. "What are you looking for? We're supposed to be in hiding out in a safe house, and you're standing in the window like a sitting duck."

"The spooks must be looking for us."

"I don't know if he's protecting or hiding us, but his soldiers are all over the place. He doesn't want us to fly the coop."

"There's no place to go. He shut down the airport."

The maid prepared them a simple supper of shredded beef, fried plantains, and Cuban bread. Despite not having eaten for more than twelve hours, Lucy had little appetite. When the maid offered them cold beer, Lucy held her tongue. Desi drank. There went nearly two months of sobriety. With uncharacteristic moderation, he limited himself to two bottles before asking for coffee.

By 2 a.m., it was clear they wouldn't be leaving until morning. Lucy couldn't bear the thought of sleeping on clean sheets without first bathing. After picking at dinner and three or four cigarettes, she finally calmed down enough to try going alone to the bathroom. She rinsed out her underwear in the sink and draped it over the rim of the bathtub to dry. Wrapped in her towel, she returned to the bedroom and slipped under the bed covers, nude. She hadn't slept without a nightgown since little Lucie was born, except on those long-forgotten special occasions.

Desi needed to bathe as much as she had, but he lay on top of the bed covers, fully clothed except for his shoes, as if expecting to leave at a moment's notice.

"This was a huge fucking mistake," he said, speaking at the ceiling.

She was too exhausted and anxious for another argument. She rolled onto her side, away from him. He didn't so much as place his hand on her hip. He showed no interest in offering her either affection or comfort.

Neither of them slept much. Her eyes popped wide open at the slightest sound—a passing truck, a barking dog, the creaking bedsprings whenever Desi turned. Each time she awoke, she lay still until she convinced herself she'd only imagined an intruder, and then she listened to Desi's breathing. More often than not she found him awake, too. They both should have downed a couple more beers.

In the morning, the maid told Desi they were free to help themselves to clothing from the owners' wardrobes. In the small closet of the master bedroom, Lucy found no slacks but did find a knee-length dress. Her underwear had dried enough to wear; she preferred their slight dampness to garments belonging to a stranger.

Desi bathed and dressed without underwear. The master of the house must have been slightly shorter and possibly a little wider than Desi, because his slacks fit only with the help of a belt. They were about an inch short, so Desi tried to wear them a little low on his waist, which only increased the bagginess. He finally settled for flood length rather than a sagging crotch. He was not a man accustomed to ill-fitting clothes. Fortunately, a handsomely embroidered guayabera shirt, mostly black with a broad brown vertical breast stripe, helped to hide the cinched waistline.

Rather than blending in, despite Desi's Cuban origins, they both looked more than ever like a couple of tourists. Desi must have felt guilty for taking the finest clothing he could find, because he tucked a folded wad of cash into the pocket of another shirt hanging in the closet.

Lucy had some blush, eyeliner, and lipstick in her purse, which was sufficient to put on her face, although her eyebrows were a little lighter than she liked. Her hair was completely flat, but she had her scarf. She'd lost her sun hat in the confusion, and she couldn't find one in the house with a brim wide enough to shade her face. She'd pick one up as soon as they could do a little shopping.

Another typical Cuban breakfast of bread and butter, fruit, and coffee awaited them, along with the daily newspaper, *Revolución*, for Desi's benefit. Lucy had little appetite. Her stomach churned from a combination of nerves and the shredded meat stew they'd eaten late the previous evening.

Although she couldn't see the street from the dining room, she heard multiple vehicles pull up outside, engines idling. The maid answered the door.

Ambassador Bonsal entered, along with Castro.

"Good," Lucy said, draining her coffee cup. "Now we can get out of here."

"I came to make sure you were uninjured," Bonsal said.

"Why hurry? It's only been a dozen hours since some crazies tried to blow us to kingdom come."

"We had no way of locating you."

"This is my fault," Castro said. "For obvious reasons, we moved you to a protected location, and I was preoccupied. You'll be pleased to learn that we know which group is responsible for this act of sedition."

"Oh well, now I feel much better." She was on her feet, headed for the door. "We're ready."

"Prime Minister Castro will escort you himself to Guantánamo," Bonsal said, "where you can safely depart the island under protection of the US Navy."

Guantánamo? That was at the other end of the island. They were maybe seventy miles from Miami at most, and now they were heading in the other direction—with Castro. "You must be joking. I thought that's why you were here."

The maid offered Bonsal and Castro coffee in blue, gold-rimmed cups and saucers. The scrolled handles were so small that Castro had to hold his cup by encircling the brim with his beefy fingers.

"The embassy doesn't have the personnel or equipment to assure your safety," Bonsal said.

"If we can't fly to Miami, how in hell are we supposed to fly to Guantánamo?" She glanced at Desi, expecting him to chime in any second. He sure as hell knew how to put his foot down.

"We will travel over land," Castro said.

"I assume you mean by car and not by mule. How far is that?"

"A thousand miles, maybe," Desi said.

"Six hundred," Castro said.

"What's the difference?" she said. "Six hundred, a thousand. Someone wants to kill us, and you're taking us on a road trip."

Expressionless, Desi repeated her concern. "My wife is not so comfortable with your plan."

His wife was not so comfortable? What the hell was he talking about? Castro was planning to drag them from one end of the island to the other with crazy bombers on their heels, and both Desi and Bonsal seemed to think that was a great idea.

"If they had wanted to kill you," Castro said, "they would have succeeded. They only wanted to frighten you."

"Whoever they are, they're very good at their jobs," she said.

"What if we don't go to Guantánamo?" Desi asked.

Bonsal placed his cup on the saucer and checked his watch. "As US citizens, you have the right to seek refuge in the embassy. However, we have no way of knowing when you will have the opportunity to leave. Could be days, could be weeks. Once you are inside the embassy, we will have to insist that you remain in the building at all times until safe passage can be arranged. The insurgents are well armed."

"Very well armed," Castro added, with a look toward Desi, "thanks to certain benefactors."

Talk about looking a gift horse in the mouth.

Lucy cut them off before Bonsal and Castro could launch into another verbal scrape over who was doing what to whom. "We have to get back to LA."

"We will deliver you safely," Castro said. "You may trust me."

Trust him. Now look who was the comedian.

The maid had already folded and packed their dirty clothes into a large cloth bag with wooden handles, which she presented to Lucy.

"If we're going all the way to Guantánamo," Desi said, "let's get moving."

"You're buying into this?" she asked incredulously.

He shrugged. "We got no choice. The sooner, the better."

He'd been avoiding eastern Cuba for twenty-seven years. "Too many bad memories," he said. Now, of all times, he was ready for a homecoming.

SO LONG, HAVANA

*L*ucy had expected to be whisked away discreetly. Instead, Castro had assembled a small convoy of drab green trucks and jeeps emblazoned with Cuba's flag. The shiny black Lincoln in which she and Desi were riding stood out like a sore thumb—or a sitting duck. Celia was riding in the passenger seat. She explained that since she was from Desi's hometown of Santiago de Cuba and overdue for a visit, she'd offered to serve guard duty on what Castro was calling their "mission," an oddly grand and intimidating name for a road trip.

They left Havana on the main highway, the Carretera Central, a two-way, single-lane road running the length of the island through the interior. Their drive would take them through several of Cuba's smaller cities. Two vehicles rode ahead of them, the jeep in which Castro himself rode and an open truck carrying eight soldiers with arms at the ready. Another jeep and three trucks trailed behind. Lucy tried to get a look at the rear of their caravan in the driver's side mirror, but the forward-most truck blocked her view of the last two vehicles.

All the windows except Lucy's were rolled down, ventilating the car with a steady breeze, tainted a bit by the exhaust from the troop carrier. She held her hair in place with the one scarf she'd had with her the day before.

The Carretera Central was not so much a freeway as a tree-lined country road. They drove past lush, green crop fields dotted with tall palm trees, grazing livestock, churches, and ornate colonial-style buildings painted in bright pastels—coral pink, aquamarine, yellow, sea blue—along with many shacks and small houses. More than once, they had to slow to pass a horse cart carrying melons or caged chickens. Other than one piece of battered and twisted artillery lying a few yards past the shoulder, and a few mostly hand-painted political posters, there was little evidence of a recent civil war.

Castro was instantly recognized everywhere along the way, returning greetings with a robust wave of his hand or a salute. When he wasn't playing parade marshal, he looked around incessantly like an owl on the hunt. Lucy appreciated his vigilance, although she assumed he was primarily concerned with the impending invasion.

She polished a smudge off her wristwatch. They'd only been traveling for half an hour. The road conditions and slow-moving truck and horse traffic didn't permit high-speed travel. They must have been averaging no more than forty-five miles per hour. At this rate, the trip would take at least fifteen hours. After a few hours, both she and Desi managed to doze off, catching up on lost sleep.

A bump jolted her out of a shallow nap. Could have been a flat tire, but they hadn't stopped moving. The convoy had pulled off the highway and was jouncing up a potholed road.

"We're not there already?" she asked Desi.

"No," said Celia. "We are making a stop."

The vehicles in front of them were kicking up a brown cloud. Celia fiddled with her wing window to deflect the dust, but it hardly made any difference. Lucy and Desi rolled up their windows. The driver did not do so until Celia, who had apparently noticed Lucy coughing and grimacing, instructed him. It was early afternoon, and the tropical sun rapidly heated the air inside the still car. They all fanned themselves. Finally, Desi opened his window an inch or so, and the others relented as well, including Lucy. The driver, a little more so.

Hoping to escape the worst of the dust, Lucy scooted toward the middle of the wide bench seat beside Desi. He placed his hand on her thigh, although he hadn't so much as looked in her direction for most of the drive. It seemed more like reflex than an actual display of affection. She stared dully out the windshield ahead as the convoy rumbled onward.

* * *

Their convoy pulled up in front of a small church, a plain structure with smooth adobe walls painted bone white and a single bell tower topped by an octagonal cupola. In lieu of carvings or other ornamentation, the tower was painted from top to bottom with wide horizontal stripes in a contrasting putty color at the corners, resembling dovetail joints, entirely decorative and a little carnivalesque.

Castro had said nothing about stops, although they could hardly drive from one end of the island to the other without a break. Still, a church didn't seem like the ideal rest stop.

Another jeep arrived, delivering three more soldiers in olive drab uniforms. They all wore untrimmed black beards, which amplified their intimidating appearance. If uniforms were meant to make soldiers all appear alike, a thick beard certainly completed the revolutionary costume, in tribute to their chief, Fidel.

The men appeared agitated, quietly speaking into each other's ears and holding their rifles at the ready. One approached Castro's jeep and spoke to him, pointing upward. Celia left the car and joined them. Castro removed his visored cap for an unobstructed view of the sky as the man traced out a line overhead.

Desi rolled down his window for some fresh air. "These boys smell something cooking."

"You think it really is an invasion?" she said. "They're not gonna show up while we're here, are they?"

"Who knows? Maybe it's the Reds. Or maybe that's why the geniuses in DC really sent us, to keep Castro busy."

"If that's true, that is the most idiotic plan I ever heard, and I play the queen of idiotic plans."

"Play?"

Wounded, she scoffed dismissively at his tease, which masked genuine ridicule.

"In an election year, who'd expect it?" he said. "Could be smart."

"Listen, if you and I can think of it, then he's already figured that out."

Although she was trying to find some humor in the situation, on the inside, her stomach turned. The last place she wanted to be was in a war zone. If Eisenhower really did plan to make a move, she hoped the CIA had enough sense to get them out of there before any bullets started flying. Odd how this new worry helped her cope a little more easily with fleeing from assassins. Just imagine, war as a welcome distraction—like cutting off a leg to distract yourself from the sting of a paper cut. She cringed at the absurdity of her own thought.

Celia returned to the passenger seat and twisted around to face them. "Señor Arnaz, perhaps you will tell your government they should not invade Cuba. You are a successful businessman, a Cuban, and very famous. They would listen to you."

She must have assumed Desi wanted to prevent a US invasion. Or maybe she was sizing him up to see where he really stood. They'd been sent to gather information. Castro knew it. Celia knew it. It wasn't so far-fetched that whatever they might report could prevent another idiotic war.

This was such a small country. If Castro hadn't grabbed the property of a few big American companies, the US government might have never taken the slightest interest. Money trumped politics—money and fear. Red paranoia had Americans on edge, even with McCarthy dead and gone. Sooner or later, Americans believed, someone would drop the bomb and set off World War III. And that was reason enough to make sure the Russians didn't set up shop next door.

"What a crazy country," she said.

"You don't know the half of it," Desi said. "Revolutions are the national pastime in Cuba."

"I mean the States. Why can't we leave these people be?"

"Sí, please," Celia said, as if they had direct line to the White House.

Four of the soldiers in the other trucks had disembarked and were taking up positions at either end of the street. The others, after receiving instructions from Castro, drove off.

"What in hell are we doing at a church?" Desi said. "We don't need to pray. We need to get the hell out of here."

"Maybe that's what we should pray for." She tapped him on the shoulder to get his attention on the activity behind them. The camera crews had been trailing their caravan and were now busily unloading and setting up their equipment.

"There are reports of some trouble ahead," Celia said, "west of Camagüey. We'll remain here until Fidel is certain that there is no danger."

Comforting to know that they might be fleeing the frying pan only to drive into the fire. "Can't we drive around it?"

Celia tapped her wristwatch without even looking at it. "It would add many more hours to the trip than we will spend in a delay here."

Castro had a way of getting what he wanted. Lucy clasped her hands together. "And just to pass the time, we'll shoot more of our picture." He'd try to get every bit of work out of them he could, and if the footage ever made it stateside, Dulles's boys would grateful for the coverage—a win for everyone except for her and Desi.

Desi stamped out the cigarette he'd been smoking and went inside the church.

The sun was beating down on the motionless sedan. Lucy followed him in, if only to find shade. No point in trying to calm him down. She wasn't any happier with the situation than he was. Fine with her if he stewed in his own juices.

The interior of the church was almost as plain as the exterior, with two rows of slat-backed pews and a few icons. A painting of Jesus hung in a bulky gilded frame behind the altar, flanked by two more life-size and lovely images of Jesus painted directly on the wall. The altar itself was a simple, cloth-covered table.

Desi stood facing the altar with his hands folded behind his back.

"I thought you said this was no time to pray," Lucy said. "Not that you ever do."

"Maybe it's time to start."

"What were they pointing at?" She took a seat in the second pew. "In the sky, I mean."

"A spy plane must have flown over."

As far as she'd noticed, not one plane had flown over since Castro had shut down the airports the night before. "I didn't hear anything."

"They fly too high."

"What can they see from way up there?"

"Special cameras," Desi said.

He hadn't even turned around. He could have been thinking through their situation, or maybe he was just as frightened as she was and didn't want to show it. God forbid he should ever look weak. If only he'd known how pathetic he looked when he was soused.

"Top secret," he was saying. "They could probably take a nice snapshot of Castro looking up at them." He took a seat in the pew on the opposite side of the aisle. "Castro's paranoid. Nuts. Do you see any ships or warplanes? I don't."

"Nothing but a huge Russian sub." If she hadn't seen it with her own eyes, she would've agreed that Castro was hunting shadows.

"Sure, everyone wants a piece. That don't mean they're about to land on the beaches."

She considered using a Bible to fan herself but decided that was not an appropriate use of the good book. Instead, she used her hand, with little effect. "Maybe there's a good reason to take over. If Castro gets in bed with the Russians, they'll be close enough to skip stones at Miami. Big ones."

"It makes no sense," Desi said. "The navy already has Guantánamo. The Russians aren't that stupid. If they want to make trouble under our noses, they'll go into South America somewhere. Argentina. Chile, maybe. Not Cuba."

"What makes you so sure? Khrushchev is as much a nut job as any dictator."

"Including this one." He looked at her for the first time since they'd entered the church. "Nothing is going to happen while we're here. They're just doing a little spying. It makes perfect sense. They want to see what the Russians are up to."

Wishful thinking. He didn't know any more than she did. "I hope you're right."

He stuck a cigarette to his lip but knew better than to light up inside the church. "Our boys will come looking for us soon."

"And what are we supposed to do in the meantime?"

"What we're already doing."

And let Castro stretch a two-day drive into two weeks or worse? "Keep shooting his picture? How come you're so calm about all this?"

"I got faith in our government. They want pictures—I'll give 'em pictures."

No question, Desi was a patriot like most refugees, especially those who'd struck it rich. But that didn't explain why he was playing along while Castro dragged them all over hell and gone. If he didn't buy Castro's freedom and glory shtick, then he had to have some other ace up his sleeve.

"We're almost halfway to Guantánamo," he said. "When we get there, we'll hitch a ride back to the States. No more of this bullshit."

She knew he was trying to keep her from panicking, but he had a little shake of his own going. Part of it was from too many hours without booze, but it always got worse when he was nervous.

They both noticed the sound of a car pulling up outside. He was back.

"He'll get what he deserves," he said.

No point in asking how. Somehow, this kind of secrecy ached more than any of the cheating. This time, he wasn't motivated by impulse, and it wasn't her trust he was violating. Now, he no longer trusted her.

Sunlight spilled in through the door as Castro entered alone, his cap in one hand and his script in the other.

"Whatsoever a man soweth, that shall he also reap," he recited. "Galatians chapter six, verse seven. I will accept the judgment of providence."

KINDRED SPIRITS

As usual, when caught with his pants down, Desi played it cool, flicking his lighter on and off as if he had the upper hand.

Castro removed his gun belt and placed it on a table just inside the church's entrance—not the kind of reverence Lucy would have expected from a so-called godless communist.

"I notice you're keeping that as far from me as you can," she said, nodding in the direction of the pistol.

"Do you think you might choose differently next time?" He joined her on her pew, leaving a respectful space between them. "We will remain here only a short time, a few hours at most. You are Catholic?"

"Me? No, Protestant. My husband is the Catholic in the family. Yourself?"

"It is very difficult to be born in Cuba into any other faith."

"So you're religious."

"I am not. I prefer the wisdom of the church to its metaphysics."

Cigarette still hanging from his lips, Desi headed for the exit, shouldering the door open and lighting up on the way out.

"He does not like me," Castro said.

"Now you and I have something in common."

Castro raised his eyebrows. "He is your husband."

That was open to interpretation. She touched her ring and then displayed it for Castro, twiddling her fingers. "I do remember marrying him."

He removed his green cap. "Do you find prayer helpful?"

Intentionally or not, he had reminded her to remove her scarf from her hair. She folded and refolded it in triangles on her lap with unnecessary care. "What've I got to lose?"

"Do you pray for favor or for strength?"

"Why one or the other?"

"If there is a God, I think he expects us to use his gifts. Favors make us weak, the enemies of strength."

"I could certainly use some strength about now."

"You have nothing more to fear. You will soon return home."

He didn't know the half of it. "I'm not so sure home is any better than here."

He tucked his chin and raised his eyebrows. "I might agree with you that your home country is disagreeable, but I suspect your reasons for thinking so are different than mine."

She'd tipped him off, and he'd hit her with his spotlight. "Prime Minister Castro, you are wise beyond your years."

"Politics and bloodshed age a man rapidly."

She hadn't intended to confide in him. Their lives were as different as beans and caviar. Yet she'd opened her own can of worms, and judging from his undivided attention and uncharacteristic silence, he wasn't likely to let her put the lid back on.

"I have no right to complain," she said quietly.

"You have more than you need," he said.

Very comforting. True or not, he could have chosen a better moment to finally lay into her, unless he'd been waiting all along for an opportunity to make it sting as much as possible.

He pointed at her. "But no matter your material circumstances, you do have the right to act on your own behalf."

So she wasn't just a whining, spoiled brat. "Have you ever been a situation where whichever way you turned, the odds don't look so good?"

"It's unavoidable in my profession. You ask a telling question."

She suppressed tears by gazing at the flickering votive candles on a table at the side of the church. "I think I'd like to light a candle."

He rose and waited for her to lead the way. On the table, in a wooden rack, stood several dozen candles in glass containers painted with various images of Jesus, Mary, or one of several saints.

"Which is Cuba's patron saint?" she asked.

"They call her Cachita," he said, selecting a candle bearing her image. "Our Lady of Charity. It is said she, the mother of Christ, came to Cuba with the child and visited people of all races and means—Spaniards, slaves, natives."

She took a five-dollar bill from her pocketbook, but before she could slip it into the slot of the offering box, he stopped her and replaced it with Cuban pesos. "Difficult for the priest to exchange." She offered the bill to him, but he declined it. With a match from a box on the table, she lit the candle and set it in the rack among those lit by other worshippers. She lingered, mesmerized by the flickering flames and the colorful translucent paintings they illuminated from within.

Two of the cameramen entered with a clatter, the oak and steel legs of their tripods clattering against the door. Herrera brought Lucy her copy of the script, which Castro had so thoughtfully brought along for the ride. Why let a little thing like attempted assassination get in the way of making a picture?

"What do Cubans expect from Cachita?" she asked.

"What do worshippers expect from any of their saints? Hope. Relief."

"Is the revolution the answer to their prayers?"

"Whether there has been divine intervention, I cannot say. What I have seen with my own eyes is the spirit of the people."

"The people we're running from right now?"

He narrowed his eyes. "We don't run from our enemies. If every Cuban had supported the revolution, it would have been unnecessary." He strolled around the perimeter of the church, pausing at each religious icon hanging on the left and right walls. Opposing mirrors hung on either side of the sanctuary, and at each one, he appeared to gaze into his own eyes as if contemplating his soul. "The people have chosen to live as equals."

Under what conditions? If the news coming out of the Soviet Union and China could be believed, the communists wanted to con everyone into believing that bare subsistence was noble. Not to her. If she had to be poor again, she'd still want to know she had a fighting chance to make a better life for herself. "In what way will they live as equals?"

"Now you ask the question for which your government has asked you to find the answer, a question rooted in fear. They want to know is Fidel a communist? They reduce social order to black and white, democracy or communism. Good and evil."

He drew a cigar from his pocket and rolled it between his thumb and fingers before thinking better of it and putting it away again. While he'd implied he doubted the existence of God, he showed respect for the institution of the church, or at least what it meant to his people. That already made him different from the Soviet and Chinese Reds—the 'godless communists,' as McCarthy had called them relentlessly.

"What your people truly fear is dictatorship," he said. "This is not communism or socialism. Dictatorship is the enemy of democracy."

She caught up with him before a simple painting of the Virgin and Child. "Is Cuba a democracy?"

"It was before Batista."

"You'll bring it back?"

"We have already removed many of the thieves who stole our democracy."

He might have assumed she'd take his dodge as a hint and let it go. She had no such intention, and not just to satisfy the fellas at Foggy

Bottom. He'd promised no secrets. Time to put his money where his mouth was. "That's not what I asked."

"As I explained yesterday, we must put our democracy back together piece by piece." He laid his hands upon one another, alternating left and right as if laying brick.

"Wouldn't it be better to let them decide for themselves? You talk about freedom…"

"I would if I could. They are like vulnerable children, inexperienced in the world. If I do not protect them—as you, a mother, should understand—they will become victims again. Predators will descend on them like vultures and take away everything they've won, and possibly worse, punish them for daring defiance. The backlash would be vicious and relentless. Given the opportunity to regain the upper hand, those who've lost power once will spare no punishment to prevent it from happening again."

"So you cage them to protect them."

"You see a cage." He banged the side of his fist against the adobe wall. "I see a stronghold. We are united."

"And you are king."

"If the king is one to whom all look for strength and to set the standard of justice, then I accept your characterization."

It was difficult to challenge a man who could turn any criticism into praise. That made him even more frightening, in a way. His confidence left no room for compromise. To Fidel Castro, compromise was a weakness, as if it were one of the seven deadly sins.

"You're their protector?"

"I defended the revolution," he said defiantly. "A soldier shoots the enemy."

"Or the enemy shoots the soldier. Either way, someone is getting shot."

He seemed to vacate his eyes. Lucy awaited his return.

"I was not always so vengeful," he said, turning back to her. "As a child, I went to school. I played baseball and basketball like other boys. I didn't think about injustice, except when I thought I was being mistreated by my guardians."

"Guardians? What happened to your parents?"

"They sent us away to school. It was in difficult circumstances. A strict household. I disliked it. I made trouble."

How about that. But he wouldn't make up a story just to win her confidence—too obvious. She sat down again at the end of the nearest pew. "I lived with guardians, too."

"You lived with your mother's family," Castro said, "after the death of your father."

"Yes, but my mother lived with us. We were all together for a couple of years. Then when my mother remarried, she and Ed, our stepfather, ran off to Detroit to find work. She didn't want to burden our grandparents with both of us. Freddy was only three and enough of a handful, so they separated us. I lived with my stepfather's parents. Very old, very strict, very sour Swedes." She pursed her lips and narrowed her eyes. "We couldn't even have mirrors in the house. It would make me vain, Grandma Peterson said." She rubbed her crossed index fingers together in the gesture of shame. Grandma Peterson might not have been so wrong about that one.

She'd become a rebel, too. Maybe not the life-and-death sort, but as a teen she'd given her mother a run for her money. She'd never have expected to have one thing in common with this man, not in a million years. He might have planned his revelation. He might have known her entire history all along. It didn't really change anything. Growing up fast had made her more serious than other children, and it might have done the same to Fidel.

Fidel towered over her. She scooted over and invited him to sit.

"You have been told much about me, about Cuba," he said.

"I don't believe everything I hear. Hatred will rot your heart from the inside."

"Fear is as potent a poison."

"Must it be one or the other, fear or hatred?"

"I could ask you something similar." He shifted and turned himself to face her fully, his bent knee resting on the seat.

"It shows, then." She planted her feet on the floor, straightened her back, and smoothed the creases from her skirt.

"You fear what will become of you when you are no longer married." He spoke it as a foregone conclusion.

"He's the wheeler-dealer in this family. He makes a lot of things happen in the four hours of the day before he passes out on his couch."

"Wheeler-dealer?"

"Another expression. He's a good negotiator. Gets what he wants—what we want."

"You're not a wheely-dealy."

"I get what I want a different way. More of a meany-bitchy." She covered a smile; he wasn't getting it. "I push our people—actors, crew—to do their best work. Some call it 'demanding.' It doesn't work so well when you're trying to talk a network into buying your product—can't just bully them into it. Desi's the smooth talker."

"What do you want?"

"That's an odd question." She picked up one of the Bibles from the pew and leafed through it. It was in Spanish. Her mind hopped from one recognizable word to another as Fidel left her to puzzle out his question. "Is that a roundabout way of asking whether we're happy?"

"Only you. Are you happy?"

"I love what I do."

"And then you go home."

"Yes, to my children. I have a good life." When it wasn't a battleground.

"You have everything you need."

There had been a time when she couldn't imagine being on her own, especially before little Lucie was born. She felt herself becoming defensive. "Not everything. Who says we're entitled to everything?"

"This is true. We all must bear a burden from time to time. That for which we sweat makes the rewards sweeter."

It was a little corny, but not bad for a man whose native language wasn't English. "For a warrior, you really are quite the poet."

"Warriors are the greatest poets. I think you understand that. Yet I think some things in our lives do not need to call us to battle."

For a warrior, he had an awfully romantic take on relationships.

Or maybe because he was a warrior, he idealized romance. "Aren't all relationships complicated?"

"Complicated, yes; painful, no. Why do you allow it to continue?"

"That's the million-dollar question."

"Ah, for the money." He turned to face forward again and leaned on the pew in front of him.

She scrunched up her face as if she'd just had a whiff of a pigsty. "Please. I'm not that simple. It's another expression. I may be bourgeois, but I'm not completely shallow. I love the fame too."

The quip fell flat. He either took it at face value, an even greater character flaw, or dismissed it as deflection. She couldn't tell which. He nodded and briefly lifted his hand in invitation for her to continue.

"He's a bastard, but he's always been my bastard." Remembering where she was, she looked guiltily around for other worshippers. Although they were still alone, she lowered her voice to a near whisper, as if compensating for the transgression of swearing in church. "That man breaks my heart almost every day. But it's true, we're not just husband and wife. We're partners. It's show business. Some unhappy people stay together because they think it's better for their children. For us, it's because of what we've built together. Our little empire. Neither of us could stand to see it crumble over our personal problems. Too many people count on us."

"And now you speak of a cage," he said.

It was becoming stuffy in the old church. The air wasn't moving at all. She smelled burned paraffin and smoke. One of the votive candles must have burned out. "Responsibility can be either a trap or a privilege."

"You mean responsibility to the workers."

"Yes, the workers. They're artists, craftsmen, technicians. We employ hundreds. Good jobs. Good pay. It's like a big family, really." It was fulfilling to have so many counting on her. Some might say she enjoyed the power. The truth was, it made her feel useful.

"This is fear speaking again. You tolerate betrayal as a necessary sacrifice. You deceive yourself. A worthy sacrifice nourishes the soul.

You say hatred rots you from the inside. Betrayal, too. You must end it."

He was new to the game. He'd learn soon enough that you didn't always get what you wanted. Try to eliminate every last bit of betrayal, and you'd be liable to end up alone. "Easy for you. You lock up the traitors and throw away the key. Without Desi, I'd have nothing."

"You underestimate yourself. One cannot know oneself until one is tested."

"And you don't know me." A little sincere flattery never hurt, but with Fidel, it was difficult to detect his motives.

"What I have witnessed of you has been unexpected."

"You aren't still holding that little gun incident against me, are you?"

She'd made this trip hoping the adventure would rekindle the sparks that had brought her and Desi together, a working honeymoon doing as a pair what they loved most: making pictures. She hadn't completely given up yet on their marriage, and she sure as hell wasn't ready to accept marital advice from a young militant who'd had no evident romantic success of his own.

"I mean that you are not the person I took you for," Fidel was saying. "This is a lesson for me."

"You aren't married, but you have a daughter."

"You are observant."

"Anyone could see right through Naty," she observed, "and when it comes to Alina, you too."

He nodded and stared in the direction of the alter. "I was married once. Not to Naty. I have a son also, Fidel Ángel, called Fidelito. My former wife, Mirta, and her family opposed the revolution."

Or maybe Mirta had become impatient—lonely, even. Whether it was Fidel's obsession with his revolución or Desi's booze and women, no woman chose to play second fiddle. "Could've been nothing to do with politics. I hate to tell you this, but Mirta might have felt neglected."

He crossed his arms defiantly. "She knew of my devotion, as you say, before we were married. Her family, Batista sympathizers, they turned her against me."

"I'm just saying, betrayal may be in the eyes of the beholder." It felt oddly satisfying to put him on the defensive. He wasn't impervious after all. "First your wife, and then Naty, neither one of them fit into your plans."

"Sí," he said stoically, and as far as she could see in his eyes, without remorse. "I betrayed Mirta. With the revolución. With Naty. Have you betrayed your husband?"

"I certainly never cheated on him. I wish he could say the same." The words stuck in her throat. What a time for confession. She was no Catholic, and Fidel was no priest, but at least she was in a church. "Like you, I have a passion for my work to the point of exhaustion. I might have neglected him."

"When affections fail, there is no blame—and also no excuse. I might have chosen to save my own marriage. I did not. Two people enter into relationship, two people leave relationship."

Of course she knew she had something to do with the failure of her marriage, up to a point. She'd thought long and hard about what she might have done wrong—until she'd made herself sick. No matter what she'd done or not done, said or not said, it was hard to see past the cheating. Fact was, it no longer mattered how much of his or her ego and insecurities had beaten the life out of their marriage. It looked like they'd finally reached the end of the line.

She sighed. "You must be disappointed. You were expecting America's Sweethearts to speak on behalf of Cuba, and here we are, a bickering couple on the verge of divorce."

"So much the better. You are in the midst of your own personal revolution. This makes you a worthy role model."

How fabulous that her own misery could prove beneficial to others. Maybe she wasn't just playing the clown. Looking for another distraction, she strolled along the walls of the church, feigning interest in the statues and painted icons. He shadowed her, his hands clasped behind his back. How patient of him to let her ruminate on the wisdom he'd so generously imparted.

The door creaked open, and Desi returned with the third cameramen. "How much more time are we going to waste here?"

"Celia will return soon," Castro said.

Desi took a seat in the back pew near the exit, arms and legs crossed like little Desi when he didn't get what he wanted.

Lucy took advantage of his reappearance to change the subject. She put on her reading glasses and placed her palm on the script, as if preparing to play along. "You want to show us Yankees that Cuba should be trusted…"

He pounded his fist into his other hand. "I want the people of your country and your government to accept our right to self-determination. I have no interest in earning their trust."

"Doesn't one require the other?"

He dismissed the idea with a sweep of his arm. "It shouldn't."

"Believe me, it does," she said. "To the folks at home, this looks like a communist takeover. Cuba was a nice little tropical paradise in the Caribbean. Now a bunch of bearded men in green fatigues show up and overthrow the government, and suddenly all the fun comes to an end. That makes you the bad guy."

"I did not start the revolution. The people of Cuba did. I accepted the call to action. I am their servant. The revolution began before I was born."

Desi grunted. Apparently, his presence had snapped Castro back into character.

"You disagree," Castro said.

"No, I agree," Desi said. "Absolutely. That's all this country is about, is revolution."

"How about that? Something else you two can see eye to eye on," she said. "So when will the revolution end?"

"There will be revolution until we end tyranny everywhere in the world," Castro said.

"Sounds like job security for you." Desi might have been a master negotiator, but when it came to an argument, he swapped contempt for rhyme or reason, a weakness she knew all too well.

Herrera left and returned with two of the other crewmen carrying parasol reflectors. He pointed at the high clerestory windows, through which sunlight streamed in. "Señor Desi, we should begin soon."

The men arranged the reflectors to diffuse the sunbeams, spreading their light into the shadows and recesses, softening their contrast throughout the interior of the church. On film, the effect would be subtle, but to the naked eye, the church's subdued charms had been washed out.

Fidel set his script aside on the pew beside him and looked at Lucy. "You are a paradox."

"Prime Minister Castro, you flatter me. That sounds like the beginning of a come-on."

He wrinkled his brow in confusion.

He spoke English, yes, but once again it was evident he hadn't mastered its quirky expressions. "A romantic advance, a flirtation."

His frown deepened. "That was not my intention. I meant politically."

Sarcasm was utterly lost on the man. It was either the language barrier or his literal, philosophically flooded mind. "Are you saying I'm a hypocrite?"

"I mean only that you obviously do not accept the subservient role of the wife."

Here we go again. "If you mean cooking, cleaning, and taking care of babies, no. I'm too busy for that. I have a career. I've had a career since I was very young."

"You are a successful artist and woman of business, yet you depict a woman on your TV program who aspires to exceed her circumstances and yet fails all attempts, reminding her and your audience each week that her role in society is chosen for her."

"That's a paradox?" Desi raised his eyebrows. "She's an actress."

Lucy rankled whenever she was attacked for making women look silly and helpless. Lucy Ricardo was not a stand-in for all women. She laughed to shake it off and threw it back at him. "You asked us here to take advantage of our public image, to support your own cause. Isn't that hypocritical?"

"It might have been," Castro said. "Thankfully, however, it is Lucille Ball who speaks for Cuba, not Lucy Ricardo." He gestured to Herrera to continue setting up. "We will shoot you in the church."

Lucy wrinkled her nose at him. "And maybe without saying 'shoot.'"

PEACEMAKER

When Lucy had finished dutifully reciting her speeches, she followed Fidel through the small crowd of onlookers now filling the back of the church. He shook each and every hand and kissed quite a few cheeks. When they finally reached the exit, his gun was gone from the table. He glanced around quickly and then stepped outside.

Sunlight reflected off the white walls of the church's tower like the parasol reflectors inside, softening the shadows in the street. Castro stood in the pale shade, lighting his cigar. Lucy retied her scarf over her hair. A hat would've been better protection from the sun, but she hadn't had a chance to buy one. Someone around there had Fidel's pistol. She didn't know whether to play along or run for cover. He was cool as a cucumber.

Desi came out with some of the folks who'd lingered to meet him. "I need some more smokes." A couple of his new admirers offered to escort him down the street. He was none the wiser.

Fidel appeared at Lucy's side. "Is your spirit refreshed?"

She nodded and indulged his determination to carry on their conversation as if nothing were out of the ordinary. "Faith brings us all together, like music. Everyone's the same in the eyes of God. It's comforting."

"I am certain of some divine providence, for otherwise I could not stand here." He took three big puffs on the cigar, gently releasing them toward the sky as if setting them free. "I have spent many hours in harm's way and have passed unscathed. Since I possess no divine powers of my own, I must assume that I am protected by something greater than myself. This is how I know I am on the path of righteousness."

Apparently his revolutionary tendencies extended to his religious beliefs. He did things his own way.

"Righteousness. Now there's a preacher's word—good old-fashioned fire and brimstone. That's what I grew up on. Scary as hell."

"There again. You said you weren't funny."

"It wasn't on purpose. I mean, scary but more entertaining. The Catholic Church is so solemn." She accepted a light; he carried a few wooden matches in his shirt pocket, no showy lighter. "Those people in there came to see you. God was not the first one on their minds."

"It was good that I removed myself. If one is to believe in God, in anything, then one must not be distracted by false idols."

Parishioners trickled out of the church, returning to their shops and homes. As they passed, saying their final farewells, Fidel kept an eye on a trio of young men at the end of the street who were watching the proceedings. One turned his back as if trying to prevent anyone from reading his lips. Lucy could see they didn't share the churchgoers' enthusiasm for Castro's presence.

Everywhere they ventured, it was clear that nothing had been settled yet in this country. A constant state of tension hung over them. Despite the placid tropical climate and fanning palm fronds, the politics were so thick they hung in the air like the humidity, at least around Castro, who never appeared to step outside his ideological bubble.

She resisted the temptation to hide behind him. Why disappoint him after all his flattery by abandoning her dignity? "Is it time to go now?"

He fully disengaged from the dwindling admirers, fixing his gaze on the three men. "I do not think so."

"We're alone here." It wasn't strictly true. Two of his soldiers were standing across the street in the shade, but their intimidating presence only increased the likelihood of violence. Some of the parishioners scurried away, but others, including some later arrivals, stopped to watch, like a showdown at high noon.

Castro stepped out into the middle of the street. One of the men said something to their third companion, nodding toward Castro. The third man turned around. He held Castro's gun and crossed his arms in defiance.

"As I said, providence shines upon me," Castro said. "Those 'fellas,' as your husband would say, they distrust me. They look for signs of weakness. Let me speak with them." He motioned to his soldiers to stay put and then left Lucy behind, lost in disbelief.

A few more men who'd been scattered in small groups along the street joined the first three.

"Buen dia, amigos," Castro said as he reached the gathering mob. "I sense that you may have concerns you wish to share."

The cameramen had come back outside. Herrera set up his tripod and continued filming.

The three men looked at each other, speechless. Whether he was motivated by courage or arrogance, or both, Castro approached his opposition with neither bravado nor caution. His arms dangled loosely at his sides. His bodyguards were at least one hundred feet away as he faced the man who had his gun. One of the other men kept patting his right hip as if checking for his own weapon, a potentially deadly tell. Fidel must have been truly possessed by the essence of Cuban machismo—or maybe 'Fidelismo,' given the trend, most likely of Fidel's own making, to name things after him.

The parishioners behind Lucy had formed their own small contingent in the middle of the street. What a bunch of unarmed locals hoped to accomplish was beyond her. Fidel managed to inspire loyalty that bordered on fanaticism. That must have been what he meant when he claimed his revolution was a popular movement. As more folks joined each of the opposing groups, the street filled in what was shaping up as some kind of standoff, with Castro in the middle.

Herrera carried his camera tripod up onto the truck for a better view. Now that kid had balls. He was a sitting duck up there. He'd have made one hell of a war correspondent. He panned back and forth to catch the faces of both Fidel and the disgruntled men.

"Sí," the man in front was saying, "we are still suffering. A year after the revolución, we still have nothing."

The other two men showed considerably less confidence at close quarters. She couldn't blame them. Castro had at least six inches on them, and his soldiers had rifles. By the time any of them could pull out a weapon, they would have been finished. In their shoes, Lucy would have pissed her pants by now. Cockiness was an unfortunate consequence of male youth.

Castro gestured with cigar in hand for the man to proceed with his list of grievances and listened calmly, nodding.

Desi returned and worked his way through the crowd to Lucy. "The hell's going on?"

She nodded in Castro's direction. "You tell me."

The man was speaking loudly, making his points for the entire gathering. The crowds shouted at each other. Both used Fidel's name, but the tone was distinctly different. There was no mistaking the chant 'Viva Fidel! Viva la revolución!' What the other side was chanting, however, sounded nothing like praise.

Fidel raised his hand, silencing them all, and began speaking directly to the young man.

"What are they saying?" Lucy asked.

Desi hushed her but began interpreting.

"My brother died for nothing," the young man said.

"I am very sorry for the loss of your brother." Castro bowed his head for a few seconds. "We lost many brothers."

"But what for? We had good jobs. They are gone now."

"Who did you work for?"

"The United Fruit Company," one of the other two said.

Castro repeated the words so everyone could hear.

Folks at both ends of the street booed and shouted. "*Demonios Americanos*," she heard, American devils. More than ever, she was a fish out of water.

"How much did they pay you?"

"Enough," the first man replied.

"Today you have no jobs?"

All three men shook their heads.

"You say you bring us freedom," said the man with the gun. "The only freedom we have is freedom to starve."

"Do you not have your own land now?"

"What good is land with no machinery? How can we grow anything? And if we did, who would buy it?"

"These are complicated questions." Castro shrugged and launched into one of his speeches. In his own palm, he traced imaginary pictures—diagrams or numbers, she couldn't tell which. He appeared to be laying out a plan for them in great detail. Some of the onlookers closed in for a better listen. The three original detractors huddled closely around him, following his scribblings as if they could actually see markings. He was surrounded.

High overhead, the sun cast but the shortest shadows. Lucy found a spot in the shade, leaning back against the front of an apartment building. The men's voices reverberated in the narrow street.

"What's he saying?" she asked Desi.

"Sacrifice for the common good. Social justice. The usual Red bullshit. Have you checked whether this is all in the script?" He walked away to join one of the cameramen. Not Herrera. Desi was no coward, but he was also no fool.

Lucy continued to eavesdrop. Despite her limited Spanish, she could follow the direction of the conversation. She was a visual artist. Most of her humor depended on sight gags and facial clowning. If Fidel was being insincere, he was giving an Oscar-worthy performance.

Anger shifted to curiosity as Fidel's detractors fell under his intellectual spell. One of the three original men began to nod slowly. The man still holding Fidel's gun wore his skepticism with set jaw and furrowed brow.

Fidel capped his sermon by lacing his fingers together in what she took as a symbol of unity.

The skeptic holding the gun asked a question. Finally, after listening to Fidel's response, his face softened. Fidel held out his hand, and the man handed over the pistol and holster. Fidel then firmly shook the hand of each young man and watched them amble off, talking energetically among themselves. Whether Fidel restored democracy then or later was irrelevant to those young men or any of these other people struggling to make ends meet. Some would blindly follow him, if only because he was all they had left to believe in.

Fidel returned to join Lucy and Desi on the shaded sidewalk.

"Your gun really gets around," she said. "What did you tell them?"

"I encouraged them to form a community with their neighbors and assured them their hard work would bring them success."

"And they bought that?" Desi said.

Lucy stood and dusted herself off, then presented her backside to Desi. "Darling, do I have dirt on my ass?"

Fidel looked politely away. "I make a convincing argument—with a little help from Jesus: Every kingdom divided against itself is brought to desolation; and every city or house divided against itself shall not stand."

A man who claimed no relationship to God and then quoted him chapter and verse. Go figure. She took a couple more swipes at her backside and then shrugged it off.

Celia returned in a jeep and briefed Castro in serious tones, pointing as if blocking actions on a movie set.

Desi refrained from translating for Lucy. "You get the point. It's a shitshow out there."

Half a dozen military vehicles roared up in a line, and Lucy took a step back. A few soldiers piled out, and it quickly became clear they were Fidelistas. Castro consulted with the driver a canvas-covered truck, outlining some kind of very specific instructions. She asked

Desi what they were saying, but he only shrugged. The engine noises drowned out their speech.

Castro came back around the front of the truck. "For your safety, I will ask you to ride in this vehicle. We'll make it as comfortable for you as possible."

"What's wrong with the Lincoln?" Desi asked.

"For the next few miles, I would like for you to be not so visible."

"Incognito," she said.

"Sí."

She lifted the rear flap and peeked inside. It was filthy and musty, not to mention hotter than hell. She scrunched her face, an expression she borrowed from her alter ego. "You want us to ride in the back of that truck?"

"For a few hours, until we reach Camagüey."

"If it's so dangerous out there, maybe we should stay put."

"This is just for extra safety," Celia said.

Desi stomped out the butt of his cigarette. "And that canvas is supposed to stop any bullets."

"Bullets are expensive and scarce. The traitors will not waste them shooting at unseen targets."

"You see?" said Lucy. "Perfectly safe."

Fidel directed them toward the rear of the truck. "You will find Camagüey a more hospitable place to stop for the evening. We have many friends there."

Celia unloaded a steel box from the truck and positioned it to use as a step, and Fidel helped Lucy into the truck. Celia reloaded the box and pulled the flaps most of the way closed, leaving a narrow opening for fresh air and light.

Inside the truck, the only seats were hard benches along each side. They'd ride sideways, facing each other. There wasn't much to hold on to, so they wedged themselves into the forward corners for support. Several metal crates, identical to the one they'd used as a step, were lashed to brackets in the floor. Most had handles on either end, which they could grab if they truck tossed them around too much. With any luck, the road to Camagüey would be paved and gentle.

"As far as I'm aware," Lucy said, "that's the first time anyone has referred to me as a target."

"As far as you're aware," Desi said.

"That's more than I can say for you. I'm sure more than a few angry husbands have imagined a bull's-eye on one part of you or another."

"We're surrounded by crazies with guns, and you want to pick a fight now."

A fight was just about the only thing she could think of that would take her mind off the situation. After Fidel had single-handedly prevented a riot and possibly, once again, his own assassination, she'd thought they were free and clear. With a few hundred miles to go, that was obviously wishful thinking.

"I hope this joker knows what he's doing," Desi said.

"He certainly handled that situation back there," she said.

He prepared to light up until she pointed out a No Fumar plaque on the back wall of the truck. She toed one of the steel boxes, all of which were likely packed with ammunition.

He stuffed the cigarette back into its pack and took a swig from a bottle he'd untucked from his waistband—no doubt another purchase he'd made that morning. He stretched out on the bench. "You two had a nice talk. It looks like you're falling for his bullshit."

"It may be bullshit, but it's gotta be better than before the revolution."

"Revolution? He's already brainwashed you. What do you care? This ain't your goddamned country. And since when are you a political genius? Maybe you should leave the politics to the politicians."

He knew exactly how to press her buttons. She braced herself against the wall and shoved a crate in his direction. To her disappointment, it barely touched his shin. "Are you saying I don't understand the shit these people have put up with?"

"Don't get involved. Do you want to ruin everything we worked for? This guy is nuts. You see what he's doing. Before you know it, we'll have communists crawling all over the place. They'll jump like cockroaches from this shithole straight to the States. Next thing you know, we're standing in bread lines."

"Okay, Mr. Yames Bond," she said, twisting it tightly for every last whiff of sarcasm. "I'll tell you one thing, I can't tell which of you is crazier."

One cheap shot deserved another.

He clenched his jaw. Too bad. A good fight would've passed the time, taken her mind off things. Truth be known, neither of them had the strength nor the will anymore.

"Just keep your head down," he said with an air of finality. "We don't know what kind of crazies are out there."

THE BEARDED ONES

*L*ucy's hips and tailbone chafed against the hard bench seat, and exhaustion began to catch up with her. Maybe the stuffiness of the canvas enclosure was depriving them of oxygen, or the truck's exhaust was asphyxiating them. She curled up on the bench with her backside pressed snugly against the wall, propped her head on Castro's fat script, and dozed off.

She awoke when a sharp turn nearly rolled her onto the floor. Desi, too, had barely caught himself. They both sat up and hung on to cargo straps as the truck rumbled across a rough surface and lurched to a stop. She exchanged silent glances with Desi. He had no more idea than she did what was happening or where they were. He pulled out a cigarette in anticipation. Out of habit, she checked her appearance in her compact mirror and fussed with her hair until she conceded to herself it was not only futile but ridiculous.

Someone released and pulled back the rear flaps. Desi hopped down off the truck and immediately lit up, leaving her high and dry. Celia again dropped a crate on the ground to help Lucy exit more gracefully. She disliked the pampering, but she feared injury—or worse, embarrassment—if she tried to play tough.

The convoy pulled in side by side in a gravel lot behind rickety wooden bleachers that were loaded with people, judging from the volume of chatter and laughter and the forest of legs visible between the benches.

"Now we're stopping for baseball?" Desi said to Celia.

"This is Camagüey," she said.

"I know where we goddam are."

Lucy smiled at Celia apologetically. "He wakes up cranky." She moistened her fingertip on her tongue and paged through the script. "I saw it. It's in here." She held up the script for Desi to see, but he barely glanced at it.

"Where is he?" Desi shouted. He shook his head and paced a few yards up the line of vehicles.

Celia didn't bother to respond to Desi's receding backside. She might have dressed as a soldier, but she was no country bumpkin. She had grace and manners and clearly felt no obligation to tolerate Desi's rudeness.

The crew wasted no time. They were already shuttling cameras and other equipment to the field. Herrera approached Desi and asked him a question.

"We ain't shooting no more." Desi walked away from a stunned Herrera.

Herrera consulted with Celia and then instructed the other five men to continue setting up.

Lucy and Celia followed Desi through the gap between the two sets of bleachers, which ran alongside the third and first base lines. Desi chose the shadier left side, and they climbed about two dozen rows to the top.

The seats were surprisingly full. They had started back down when a middle-aged man on the end of one row called to them.

"Señor, señoras, por favor!" He stood and asked the other folks to scoot over to make room for them on the end of the bench.

Celia took a seat one row down. Her seatmates greeted her enthusiastically by name as Señorita Sánchez.

"Muchos gracias," Lucy said to the man. At least she could exchange niceties in Spanish, if not carry on a conversation.

"Americano?" asked the man.

"Sí."

"It's okay. I know the English. I am Manuel Constantanios." He extended his hand, and she accepted.

"Thank you for making room."

"Baseball. Everyone welcome."

He leaned in and offered Desi a cigarette, then Lucy. They still had plenty of their own, but it would have been rude to refuse. They could pick up the next round. A smoky haze hung over the heads of the spectators.

The outfield ended at a high chain-link fence with a green scoreboard at center field. Same as home; baseball was baseball, and Cubans had learned to love it as much as Americans had. A man stood on a raised platform directly in front of the scoreboard, hanging a board painted with the number one for the first inning and zeros for everything else. A few players on both teams snapped balls back and forth. Judging from their faces, it looked as though they were warming up for a father-son match, with one team full of bare-faced boys in blue jerseys and the opposing team, visitors in white shirts, made up of bearded men. The local team's pitcher threw sidearm fastballs that thwacked into the catcher's mitt. With each pitch, he high-kicked the leg opposite his throwing arm.

"Why do they throw so funny?"

"That's the way we learned. Cuban style." Desi picked up Lucy's copy of the script and thumbed its pages absentmindedly. "What's he plan to shoot? I got no idea how to cover a ball game, but I know it takes more than three cameras. This ain't no movie set."

"You just need a couple of shots," Lucy said. "It's okay to cut corners."

Despite his bad habits, Desi was a perfectionist when it came to his work. The entire staff marveled at his ability to maintain high standards. She'd once overheard some of the crew on their set joking that Desi walked around with so much alcohol on his breath, if the fire marshal ever dropped in, he'd shut them down—"one spark and the whole place would go up."

This whole production was beneath Desi's standards. She had to keep reminding him that it would never see the light of day, but he always responded the same way. And what if it did? If he was going to be accused of supporting the Reds, at least he'd have done quality work. Funny that he cared so much about his work and not so much about his marriage.

"Maybe it's just about Cubans having a happy day at the ballpark," she observed.

He closed his eyes and breathed loudly through his nose. "Now you're going to explain to me how to direct?"

He could find fault with everything she said. It used to be only once in a while when he was particularly irate, although not necessarily with her. She was just the target of his sour mood. Now she took the brunt all the time, and not just since he'd given up drinking.

Everyone jumped to their feet, including Celia.

Once Lucy put on her glasses, she was able to make out the team name on the uniforms of the bearded men. "Barbudos," she read aloud off one of the white uniforms.

The crowd chanted, "Bar-buuuu-dos. Bar-buuuu-dos."

"What's that mean?"

"Bearded ones," Desi said. "Now I seen everything."

"I seriously doubt that."

Taking the pitcher's mound was their host, Fidel Castro, wearing baseball whites. This fella was full of surprises.

Castro waved his cap, and the crowd took their seats.

"Jesus Christ, the ball-playing dictator," Desi said. "Who would believe it?"

"This is definitely something Americans can relate to. It's too bad we can't get a series out of this. Or maybe we should."

"That's a great idea," he said sarcastically. "Our next big hit. Better yet, maybe you should leave the ideas to me." He lapsed into silence, whether for emphasis or out of remorse for snapping at her for no good reason. It made little difference.

"Is he going to make another three-hour speech?" she asked. "Maybe he's just throwing out the first ball."

"It's an exhibition game," Celia said. "The Barbudos raise money for the schools."

Desi shook his head in continued disbelief and scanned the bleachers, apparently looking for a refreshments vendor. A couple of boys were selling paper-wrapped sandwiches.

"Nobody drinks beer?" Desi asked.

"This is baseball," Señor Constantanios said. "We must respect the game. We have the great *pasión*. Drink makes the fight." He demonstrated an air punch.

Lucy sprang to her feet. "Some of us don't need alcohol to enjoy everything we do." She squeezed past Desi.

"Where the hell are you going?"

"Might as well make myself useful."

"Now you're the director?"

"You're not gonna do it."

"This I gotta see."

She trotted down the stairs to the field and joined the camera operator at first base. Herrera and his camera would focus on the batter and catcher, while the third would cover the rest of the field. As long as they were there, Lucy hoped to enjoy a ball game without the constant stares and whispered conversations that accompanied celebrity. Desi thrived on his ability to command an audience at the drop of a hat, and if either of them was a celebrity here, it was him. That was evident from the people spotting and pointing him out to each other in the stands. Even with her dyed hair and pale complexion, in Cuba she was rarely recognized as anything other than a foreigner. Here she could stand on the field and feel invisible.

Up in the stands, Desi wiped some sweat from his brow with his handkerchief. A man bounded up the stairs and handed him a baseball hat. Desi thanked the man with genuine warmth. Nothing phony about Señor Desi Arnaz, neither the good nor the bad.

Herrera asked her whether to focus on Fidel or the batter.

"Wherever the action is." She wasn't much interested in filming the game. She'd only wanted to needle Desi.

From a distance, he looked like a kid in that cap. Things might have been different if they'd been high school sweethearts. She'd had glimpses of Desi the boy whenever he was fronting the band, working an audience, playing the hell out of those conga drums. Those were the hands she'd imagined exploring her body. But maybe back then, he wouldn't have been the Latin bad boy who'd given her goose bumps.

The other Barbudos took their positions. Castro remained on the mound, adjusting his cap and pounding the ball into his glove. It reminded her of that day at Gilmore Field when Bill Frawley and Desi had dressed up in uniforms, acting like they were going to join the Hollywood Stars PCL team on the field. When the team manager started arguing with Frawley, he and Desi had put on a good show, clowning it up for the fans, complete with dirt kicking and hat throwing.

When everyone was set, Castro faced the batter. He nodded at the catcher and hurled a breaking fastball. Castro wasn't clowning. He was there to play, along with half the cast of his revolutionary soap opera. Lucy expected the opposing team to go easy on them. Who'd want to show up the dictator and his cronies? Plus, wouldn't it just be polite to let them win? No such thing. By the end of the second inning, the local team was up three runs to zero. Their pitcher was a monster. He threw a mean knuckleball and used crazy arm motions to goad the Barbudos into swinging at some wild pitches.

Finally, in the third inning, Castro knocked a grounder into left field, right past the third baseman, and made it to first base. The fans weren't any easier on the regime than their team was. They hooted at Castro and cheered when the pitcher struck out the next batter.

Then a fella Herrera identified as Laudelio Reyes came to bat. He was slightly smaller than Castro, but he put some real wood into his swing and clobbered the ball. Castro reached third, and Reyes landed on second.

Lucy spotted Desi trying to get her attention. He was trying to give her instructions, pointing at each cameraman and then where he should point his lens. Either his instincts had kicked in and he couldn't resist a challenge, or he wanted to remind her she didn't know what she was doing—which was true. How was she supposed to know how to shoot a baseball game? She crossed her arms and cocked her head in the best show of defiance she could manage at that distance.

Another one of the Barbudos was taking his warm-up swings, with Castro shouting encouragement from third base, when a thunderous boom rolled through the stadium. Lucy ducked instinctively, but everyone else looked up. A white contrail was penciling itself across the cloudless, deep blue sky, the telltale sign of a jet high overhead.

A sonic boom. A military jet.

Celia snapped to her feet.

"*Yanquis*," Lucy's bench neighbor said. "Very curious."

The Barbudos and home team players spilled out of their dugouts. On the field, play had halted, with all eyes on the sky. The thousands of spectators stood, shielding their eyes from the glare of the sun as if joined in a salute. Castro locked his sight on the path of the distant plane, which gleamed momentarily in the sunlight, as if in acknowledgment.

From the stands, Desi was frantically cranking his arm, signaling the cameramen to keep rolling. This was the kind of thing that they were here to see. He must have sensed or hoped that something interesting was about to happen. She hoped it would not. She wanted him to stop gesturing, as if he might magically cue a bomber squadron.

Castro, too, was exchanging hand signals with his teammates. He called them all into a huddle at the mound and began issuing orders. Celia hurried down to the field to join them. It was obvious something serious was happening. In California, sonic booms weren't unusual. Occasional flyovers by jets out of Edwards Air Force Base had ruined more than one take. Even the acoustic padding in the studio walls and roof couldn't block out that kind of racket.

Desi would have wanted Herrera to move in for closer coverage of the Fidelistas at the mound, but she wasn't about to push her way into the middle of that business. And it was a good thing, too. Out of nowhere, a pair of fighter jets skimmed low over the field, their shadows sweeping them silently at first until the disembodied roar of their engines came up behind as if in tow.

Castro yelled after them, pulled his pistol from his waistband, and fired uselessly. One of his shots tore into a corner of the scoreboard. The crowd in the stands ducked in a wave as the crack of gunfire reached them, and Castro's teammates scattered to take shelter under the stands, leaving him defiantly shaking his fist at the long-vanished jets.

Lucy braced the top of her head, as if that could somehow protect her from whatever came next. The CIA had promised they were not planning to antagonize the Cuban government while Lucy and Desi were in the country. This seemed like bad timing.

"I think the game will not continue," Herrera said.

Fans began filing out of the stands, and the local team finally threw in the towel and funneled off the field. It was as if a storm had rolled in and rained them out.

"Do you think there will be bombs?" Lucy asked Herrera.

"Maybe yes. Maybe no."

She hadn't really expected a useful answer. She was just worrying aloud. She left Herrera and joined the crowd leaving the stadium, watching for Desi. There were still times when, for no good reason, she felt safer at his side.

She wondered what kind of plan the Barbudos could have been formulating. It didn't seem like they could have much of a response. Cuba had no air force of its own. One thing was certain: if she and Desi had been sent in to give Castro a false sense of security against an American invasion, she'd have some words for Dulles, and maybe Eisenhower himself. Nixon and Eisenhower had probably cooked up this scheme together. She'd sue the whole goddam government.

Then again, thanks to Castro's little shell game, the US government had no way of knowing where in the country they were at that moment. It's possible the planes had been sent to track them down. Desi must have been thinking the same thing, because when the planes made a second pass, he'd waved. It seemed unlikely that anyone in the air could pick either of them out from that crowd. Regardless, their appearance had given Castro a new mission. Even in the face of overwhelming force, he'd never back down. He was not that kind of man.

The camera crews were heading for the truck.

Desi came running. "They must be looking for us."

The air felt charged, as if she were standing on a fairway in the middle of a thunderstorm. She leaned on him long enough to shake a pebble from her shoe. "Either that or they really are about to invade."

"Unless the marines are already landing, they wouldn't tip him off with planes. You don't win a war by warning your enemy you're coming."

War? A wave of panic swept over her. "We can't stay here."

He glanced over her shoulder. "Here comes more trouble."

She turned around. Castro and Celia were jogging toward them along the third base fence, and Castro was waving them in.

"Now where's he going to drag us?" Desi wondered.

"This is of the utmost importance," Castro called. "We are checking with all our coastal observation stations to determine whether an invasion is imminent."

Not wanting to further antagonize the man, she held her tongue. Cuba had to be defenseless against American forces. "What will you do if they do come?"

He stiffened. "You know something you have not disclosed?" He had already transformed from host to soldier and now hardened as if he were a stern captor.

"Just guessing," she said with a shrug. "Although I'd prefer they waited until we were out of the way, it seems like only a matter of time. How will you respond?"

"Shoot them." He was serious. "This situation is very dangerous for you."

Desi poked a finger toward Castro. "Is that a threat?"

Castro became contrite. "No, Señor Arnaz. Your government may not know your location. If that is true, you could be caught in the middle of a combat situation. I promised your safety. I take my pledge seriously."

"Then you'll get us out of here right now?" Lucy asked.

"Not possible," Celia said.

Castro nodded. "We have already closed down all travel in and out of the country. Now it is shown why this is necessary."

"Why can't you drop us off at Guantánamo?" Lucy asked.

"We cannot approach the enemy base during a conflict," Celia said.

"Where do you plan to take us?"

"There are many places within Cuba that provide refuge," Castro said.

"It would be unwise for us to share strategic information with enemy operatives," Celia added.

Desi put his hands on his hips. "So now we're the enemy."

"If the shoe fits…" Lucy said.

"You're holding us hostage."

Castro halted his accusations with a raised palm, took a notepad from his shirt pocket, and began writing. "We will take you first to a safe place within the city of Camagüey, where you will wait for further arrangements." He tore the note from the pad, folded it in half, and handed it to Celia. "We have more friends than enemies. We will soon be on our way again."

"On our way where?" Desi asked.

"Arrangements will be made." He marched away.

Outside the stadium, Castro ordered the camera crews to set up their tripods again and point their lenses at the sky. He would catch the invaders in the act. This man wasn't just a soldier; he was a lawyer. If Eisenhower had ordered a secret operation, Castro would have his own evidence.

Only eerie silence remained now that the chattering fans had dispersed and most of the military convoy had roared away. The planes had vanished as quickly as they'd come. It should have been just another sunny day in Cuba. The anxiety was all in their heads.

At least, that was what Lucy hoped.

RESISTANCE

*L*ucy was relieved to travel by sedan and not again in that cargo truck. Camagüey's closely packed houses all had similar colonial styles with columns or arches and various ornaments. They were painted in bright pastel colors—yellow, blue, coral, seafoam green. After many turns and a few alleys barely wide enough to pass through, they arrived at a traditional stucco house with a red tile roof, a Mediterranean style similar to Betty and Harry's home down the street from them in Beverly Hills.

Lucy and Desi hadn't spoken during the ride. Although Castro hadn't accompanied them, they were sure the driver would be listening for any hint that either of them knew what their fellow *Yanquis* were up to.

"Is the home of Dr. Alfonso Lopez, a physician, a good man," said their driver. "He tak-ed great care of soldiers during the war."

Before they had a chance to knock, Dr. Lopez greeted them at the door. He walked with a cane and, unlike most Cuban men, wore a neatly pressed, vested suit over a starched white shirt and paisley tie.

Like many of the older men Lucy had met in Havana during previous visits, the doctor was distinguished and mannered, a Latin gentleman. His home was small, orderly, and clean. He invited them to sit in his small parlor, which was furnished modestly with a sofa and a pair of carved wooden chairs with upholstered seats. Gold brocade draperies were drawn closed, and although the late afternoon sun still shone outside, the room was lit by a crystal-shaded floor lamp and a Tiffany lamp on a corner table. Also on the table stood a few family photos, including a hand-tinted portrait of a young woman. A single book and a pair of glasses lay on the coffee table. Instead of Cuba's ubiquitous aroma of tobacco smoke, Lucy detected a faintly floral scent in the room.

She sat in one of the carved chairs near the curtained window. Desi sank into a corner of the small sofa. The doctor took the other end of the sofa and studied her for a long time.

Finally, a little embarrassed, she broke his gaze by looking around the room. "You have a lovely home."

"Thank you," he said. "It's very small."

She smiled warmly. "In America, we would say it's cozy. We're sorry to barge in on you. Prime Minister Castro sent us here while he tended to some government business. We don't mean to share our troubles with you."

He picked up his wire-framed glasses and polished the lenses with a handkerchief before putting them on. "This is no trouble. The troubles were much greater before."

"You're a medical doctor?" She adopted a friendlier posture, sitting forward on her chair, feet on the floor, and hands pancaked together. She noticed Desi looking her over, which he did whenever she acted a little girlish, a remnant of the impatient attraction he'd once shown for her. Now, the expression was tainted with disdain.

Dr. Lopez nodded. "I studied medicine at the University of Pittsburgh."

"That explains your excellent English."

"My wife is obsessed with how well we speak," Desi said.

"'We'?"

"Latin men."

The doctor smiled in way that appeared genuine and not simply polite. "As an actress, words are important to you."

"Why, yes," she said, teasing Desi with a sidelong glance, "that's so true. What my husband fails to mention is that he's made a good living making fun of his own broken English."

Dr. Lopez stiffened. "I'm sorry, I forgot to offer you refreshment."

"We're fine," she said. "We don't want you to go out of your way for us. We're uninvited guests."

"This is not true," he said. "Fidel told me some time ago he would bring you here."

Some time ago? So Castro really was jerking them around. She smiled grimly. "He's surprisingly well organized."

Desi forced a deep breath through his nose.

"Celia told me you have been traveling uncomfortably for many hours," Dr. Lopez said. "When my sons return, we will have a meal."

She would have raised another polite objection except it was pointless, and she was starving. Desi would be more than ready for a hearty meal.

"Would you like a beverage? Cerveza? Café?"

"Coffee, please," Desi said. "I'm dying for some coffee."

"If it's not too much trouble," she added, "I wouldn't mind a cup myself."

They followed him into the kitchen.

"Fidel tells me you came to Cuba at his invitation," Dr. Lopez said.

"He asked us to make a picture about the new Cuba," Lucy said. "We thought it was meant to bring back the tourists."

"And what do you think of this 'new Cuba?'"

"It's a little sad."

The doctor looked up from measuring the water into his coffee pot, inviting her to continue her thought.

"It's just that we were here a couple of years ago, and Havana was a lively city, an exciting place to visit."

"And very decadent."

She'd been aware of the bawdiness, the bare-breasted chorus girls prancing across the stages of the Tropicana, the burlesque entertainment. To a man like Dr. Lopez, that would have been enough to qualify as decadence. She wondered whether he knew about the nauseating depravities that few tourists, and likely fewer Cubans, had been aware of. "I had no idea what was really going on. Such horrible things."

He put the pot on the stove. "And yet you find Havana more sad than before?"

"I don't quite know how to say it," she said. "The worst of its sadness was invisible before. Now it's sad in a different way."

"It's like one big ghetto," Desi scoffed.

During their orientation in Washington, Officer Bradley had warned them to assume they were under constant surveillance. It was not only possible but likely that Castro had sent them here so that Dr. Lopez could wheedle hints or clues out of them. If so, it was a futile plan. They weren't exactly privy to any secrets.

"The sadness before was invisible only to those who chose not to see it," Dr. Lopez was saying. "Except for those forced to flee, the same families live there today. It's not easier for them, not yet."

He scooped coffee generously into a tin pot, ran water directly in over the grounds, and placed the pot on the stove. The thought of strong coffee reminded her that she was dying for a smoke, and she knew Desi must have been too, but her nose told her that Dr. Lopez was not a smoker.

Right on cue, Desi patted his pocket, checking for his lighter. "Castro's already a dictator."

"What about other parts of the country?" he asked. "Have you ever visited our city before?"

"Desi's never brought me all the way out here—so far from Havana, I mean."

He nodded at Desi. "Understandable. You lost many people and your home when the Bolsheviks savagely raided the country."

He directed Lucy to one of the upper cupboards. She took down three powder-blue cups and saucers rimmed with gold and arranged them on the countertop.

"Unless he holds elections," she said.

"He will do what he thinks is best for Cuba," Dr. Lopez said. "He is a young man. He is vulnerable. He is arrogant. He is courageous. He is fearful. Complicated, yes."

The coffee came to a boil, and Dr. Lopez turned off the gas. He transferred the three fine cups and saucers to a tray and decanted the coffee slowly, careful not to agitate the grounds and holding a tea towel under the spout to catch drips. Lucy smiled unconsciously, imagining such strong coffee eating right through the delicate china.

Dr. Lopez nodded toward Desi, who was still fidgeting with his lighter. "I think you are wishing to smoke. Let us go to the patio."

He carried the serving tray out through the living room and dining room, where a glazed door opened into a small courtyard at the back of the house. They sat on chairs with seats and backs woven from leather strips, at a circular table inlaid with a colorful mosaic depicting a bullfight. They were surrounded by clusters of white jasmine flowers, the source of the scent Lucy had noticed inside the house.

Before their first sips of coffee, Desi lit a cigarette for Lucy and himself. He politely offered the doctor one as well, and the doctor just as politely declined. The coffee was as strong as Lucy had expected. She was becoming accustomed to this potent Cuban brew, flavorful and fresh.

"I am told your visit has not been uneventful," Dr. Lopez said.

She clasped her hands under her bosom, elbows extended as if preparing to recite *The Rime of the Ancient Mariner* in Mrs. Stevens's class. "It's been a tourist's delight. We've watched an elegant nightclub demolished and all its furnishings burned in a grand bonfire..."

"...been to a prison..." Desi added.

"...ridden in a boat nearly capsized by a Russian submarine..."

"...and took in a ball game..."

"...where we were buzzed by warplanes." She knew they were performing. Must have been the caffeine. "Other than nearly being blown to smithereens in our own hotel room, I'd say it's been a regular holiday in paradise."

Dr. Lopez shook his head in amazement. "And how do you find your host?"

The bombing must have already been old news, because the doctor had skipped right past it. If they'd displayed any visible injuries, perhaps he might have taken more interest. As it was, he wasn't so susceptible to their dramatic flair.

"Fidel?" she said. "A bright young man with a very big chip on his shoulder."

Dr. Lopez placed his hand on his own shoulder and asked Desi a question in Spanish, obviously asking Desi to explain the expression. About the only word she understood was "machismo."

The doctor nodded. "He has seen very much blood. Suffered in prison. Watched his companions die. All manner of torture and horrific crimes have been perpetrated against him, against the men and women of his army, and against the people who supported him." He tapped his leg with his cane—an artificial limb.

"You lost it in combat?"

"I lost it in torture. They wrapped a rope around my leg and twisted it until the blood no longer flowed and the leg died. Then they removed it without anesthesia using a bayonet and a carpenter's saw heated with a gas torch to stop the bleeding."

It was good she was already sitting, or she might have ended up flat on the floor. She glared at Desi. He'd supported those monsters—with their money.

"Castro came to your rescue," she said.

"No. He was far from here at the time. I was saved by the courage of Huber Matos, a great hero. Unfortunately, now labeled a traitor and a prisoner of the revolution."

Lucy cradled her cup in her hands to soothe them. "You were willing to give your life for the revolution."

"It's not something you think of when you first take a position. I only wanted Batista gone. Courage was a side effect of placing myself in harm's way. I did not take a weapon, but I did administer aid to enemies of the state."

"Batista's men, when they captured you, this is what they did?"

"Rebellion is like an epidemic. It spreads. To stop it, those in power must quarantine the infected ones. Eradicate the virus. I've come to understand how far power will go to protect itself."

Dr. Lopez retrieved the coffee pot from the kitchen and poured them each another cup. Desi lit fresh cigarettes for Lucy and himself.

"What have you observed?" Dr. Lopez asked.

Lucy and Desi both hesitated. Could they trust this man? To her relief, Desi turned the question around with a master negotiator's technique.

"Is there something we should've seen?" Desi asked.

"You've seen a country in disarray, no?"

"What else is new?" Desi rounded off the tip of his cigarette into an ashtray the doctor apparently kept for guests.

"The threat is constant," Dr. Lopez said.

"We've noticed," she said.

"One cannot sleep safely in such a place," Dr. Lopez said.

It was late in the afternoon, and the courtyard was now fully in shadow. Goose bumps covered Lucy's bare arms, and she wrapped them tightly around herself. The doctor retrieved blankets. Lucy asked if they could move inside, but the doctor said it was safer to speak as far from the street as possible, which didn't make her any more comfortable.

Desi was fidgeting, shaking his leg, paying less attention to the conversation than his cigarettes, which he was chain-smoking. Part of this agitation was his craving, which increased late in the afternoon. Part might have been the chill, but he had to be as uneasy as she was with the direction of this conversation.

"This is the country of broken promises," Dr. Lopez said.

"But you supported this revolution," she said.

"I truly believed in the 26th of July Movement." His expression flattened as if he were replaying a difficult memory.

Lucy sat back. She and Desi would need to continue to measure their words. Maybe that prison visit really was a veiled threat.

"I'm sure things will improve over time," Desi said.

If Castro really had assigned Dr. Lopez to needle them for hints of their loyalties, Desi wasn't taking the bait. Another day or two and they'd be on their way home, where he could bad-mouth Castro to his heart's content.

Dr. Lopez leaned forward and folded his hands on the table, his walking stick propped in the crook of his elbow. "We are at a critical moment in our history." More drama. Cubans loved to make speeches. "I will tell you something. Fidel is a utopian. He is noble of purpose. However, he might have underestimated the magnitude of this undertaking. One does not transform an entire country with speeches, no matter how thorough the scholarship or prophetic the wisdom."

"Everyone seems to love the man," she said. "Wherever we go, folks come out in droves for a glimpse of their hero—usually, at least. They may be a little impatient for things to get better, but they mostly trust Fidel."

"Fidel?" said Desi. "Now you're on a first-name basis?"

Fidel was how he was known to Cubans, but it was true, she did feel that the distance between them had closed in these few days. He had crafted his image just as she had her own. There was nothing new about the fraternal bond that grew between flesh-and-blood humans inhabiting celebrity personas.

"He is widely admired, but not universally," Dr. Lopez was saying. "His impatience is creating victims, and victims become enemies."

"Have you advised him?"

"I have spoken with him. You have been in his company for several days. Does he appear open-minded?"

"My wife seems to have won Castro's confidence. They enjoy many long talks." Desi feigned jealousy, which the doctor read with the intended humor.

"He does enjoy the companionship of beautiful ladies."

She felt herself blush. "I will take that as a compliment." Flattery at home usually lacked sincerity, and at any rate, was becoming less common these days. She'd surprised herself with her vulnerability, and she thought she noticed a glint of genuine delight in Desi's eyes, too.

"As it was intended, although your attractiveness, physically and in spirit, are widely known."

"It never hurts to hear it from a charming gentleman such as yourself."

"Okay, okay," Desi interrupted. "This a wonderful love story you two are cooking. Let's not get carried away." He took another puff, blew a smoke ring, and winked at Dr. Lopez.

Desi had broken the tension. He was a sharp cookie.

"I've done a lot of listening," she said, "and I can't say the man is open to outside thinking."

Desi tapped his fingers on the table as he always did when he became impatient.

"Fidel has absorbed the teachings of many great philosophers. He finds it difficult to heed the arguments of we who are less well read than himself. He can recite Marx and Hegel's words to you from memory, and he has come to believe, not as the faithful but with conviction of the educated and practiced, in justice according to the socialist doctrine."

"He's a communist," Desi said. "Not exactly news."

"Your government must be concerned about the encroachment of Marxism near your shores."

"Cuba is still a tiny island," Desi said. "It's not so much a threat."

"That may depend on alliances."

Desi counted it out on his fingers. "So a communist dictator"—one —"who talks to the Russians"—two—"and seizes the property of American companies"—three. "Just like any other banana republic."

The doctor planted his walking stick like a king's staff. "Socialism is attractive to the Cuban people. I proudly call myself a socialist. Cubans have suffered too long under the thumb of colonial oppression."

"But you sound just like Fidel," Lucy said.

"I fought in the revolution. I believe in the cause. Now I fear for our freedom, which we won with our sacrifices." He tapped his artificial leg again with his cane. "Speeches fail to quell the people's impatience. So he resorts to force. The more threatened he feels, the harsher his actions. This I cannot condone. He will never restore peace and prosperity for the Cuban people through intimidation."

"Why tell us?" Lucy asked. "We are actors, comedians, not politicians."

"Were you not sent here by your government?"

She reminded herself they were still bound by secrecy, as much for their own protection as out of responsibility. Castro might have seen right through them, but there was no sense in broadcasting their affiliation with the CIA. "We accepted Castro's invitation."

"Because you were anxious to take a vacation in the aftermath of a civil war?" The doctor sat in his chair with his feet firmly planted on the tile floor and his hands resting on the top of his cane. Nothing Desi said would have convinced him they were in Cuba voluntarily.

"It's really no secret," she said.

Desi rolled his eyes.

She brushed him off by turning in her chair more in Dr. Lopez's direction. "Well, it isn't. I don't know why everyone pretends with all this cloak-and-dagger bullshit—pardon my language."

The doctor nodded.

"He knew what we were doing before we even landed."

"He is a smart young man," Lopez said. "The most intelligent man I've ever known, with keen perception. Your situation does not lend itself to secrecy, and even if it did, he has a unique ability to see through any deception. It's why he still breathes today."

"You have a complex relationship."

Dr. Lopez cradled his coffee cup in both hands, as if presenting a newborn. "I love him like I love my own sons, but he is not ready to lead a country. He has the passion of a revolutionary, and much knowledge, but not yet the wisdom. I admire him. And I also fear what he may become."

"Sounds like the relationship many young men have with their fathers."

"He is Cuba's Captain Ahab."

"That makes us Moby Dick," she said. "I mean, the United States."

The doctor gaveled the stone floor with a double tap of his cane. "Precisely."

"I don't know what you're talking about," Desi said. "Lucy, what's he talking about?"

"The great white whale, Moby Dick," Lopez said. "Ahab was so obsessed with killing the whale who killed his friend that he was willing to sacrifice anything."

"Why would he fight so long," she asked, "just to throw everything away by spitting in the face of the United States?"

The muffled sound of a door opening and closing came from inside the house. She clutched the arms of her chair, half expecting soldiers to stomp in and drag them off.

The doctor must have noticed her white knuckles. "My sons have returned."

A young man leaned out the door into the courtyard and exchanged a few words with the doctor.

When his son had closed the door, Dr. Lopez continued. "Hatred for the US shapes Fidel's beliefs—beliefs he then mistakes for truth."

In the dusk, the garden walls closed in. Lucy wrapped herself tightly in the blanket. Why couldn't they have just passed through without getting tangled in the mess? The things they were learning from Dr. Lopez were like little time bombs, knowledge she'd prefer not to possess.

Whenever Desi was about to begin a difficult conversation, he repeated his posturing ritual. He moved his chair out a few more inches from the table, crossed his leg, and lit a fresh cigarette. It had become dark enough that the lighter's flame faintly projected their shifting silhouettes on the courtyard's shrubs and walls. This time, instead of holding the lighter for Lucy, he simply stacked his cigarette case and lighter on the table where she could reach them herself.

He shook his head. "I can't make no sense of this country no more."

"Then you understand," Dr. Lopez said. "Someone must stop Fidel."

Lucy didn't know who or what to believe. She had no doubt Castro was a socialist, maybe communist. That wasn't the point. Who was she to decide for Cubans who should run their country? And how?

She shook her head. "Dr. Lopez, even if we believed Fidel was the devil himself, what could we possibly do?"

He rose and stepped near the garden wall, cocked an ear, and listened.

This didn't bode well. No matter what Dulles had asked, she preferred to be entrusted with as few secrets as possible.

After a few silent moments, Dr. Lopez paced all the way around the table, as if lost in thought. Finally, he laid his hands flat on the table's mosaic tiled surface. "Remain in Cuba."

APPEAL

Lucy watched Desi take Dr. Lopez's former position beside the whitewashed garden wall. He exhaled smoke up toward the darkening sky and then crossed his arms as if waiting for the punch line.

"We've already gotten the message we're not welcome in Cuba," Lucy said.

"Loud and clear," Desi added.

"How on earth would it help for us to stay? And for just how long?"

The doctor also stood and leaned on his cane. "You are his bird in a cage."

"In the States, we say 'canary in a coal mine.'" She explained to Desi, "Coal miners used to take canaries underground. If there were poisonous gases, the bird would die, so the miners would notice and get out."

"You think I'm stupid?" he snapped.

"It's an expression. Moby Dick, no. Canaries, yes. How am I supposed to know what you understand and what you don't?"

Desi poked his own forehead. "Don't assume you know what I don't know."

Dr. Lopez politely waited for their bickering to subside. "Your own government will not allow you to be harmed in an invasion. When they remove you from Cuba, Fidel will expect the American invasion to begin. He'll station all his forces at our shores. He will not anticipate an assault from within."

"As my wife says, we're entertainers, not politicians. This is not our country."

"You are Cuban."

"I'm American," Desi insisted. "Everything I have is because of my country."

"This is the point precisely. Fidel will join the Soviet Union and bring communism to our hemisphere. The threat to Cuba is a threat to America."

"People far more powerful than us will stop that from happening," Lucy said.

"I'm sure you are correct. And the Cuban people will once again be caught in the cross fire. Who else will pay the price?"

Desi pounded the wall a couple of times with the heel of his fist. "I don't know, but I do know if you aren't careful, he'll throw you and your sons into one shithole of a prison and let you rot."

And they'd end up in the same place if Desi didn't put a muzzle on it. She raised her eyebrows at him, signaling him to simmer down before someone heard them and they found themselves looking up the barrel of a rifle.

He glowered but adopted his cool, businesslike tone. "You better hope Castro is right to suspect a coming invasion. He can't possibly resist the American military."

"If he's forged ties with the Kremlin, an American invasion could start the next great war, and this time it will be in America's back yard," Dr. Lopez said. "Is this what you truly wish for?"

She pressed her lips together tightly. Too many American boys had already died defending the world against fascists and communists.

Dr. Lopez shook his head and continued. "Better to take matters into our own hands before the next holocaust."

Desi had no response. She had rarely seen him speechless, but Dr.

Lopez was right. He knew it. Desi knew it. But that didn't change anything. Really, what could they do?

"It doesn't matter," Desi said. "It's crazy. If this place is about to blow up into war again, we want to get as far away as possible."

One of Dr. Lopez's two sons came out to announce dinner. As casually as if they'd been discussing no more than the weather, Dr. Lopez dropped the subject. "I think you must be hungry. Fidel asked me to keep you out of sight until he returns, so we will dine in."

The dining table had been set with china that matched the coffee cups, and several dishes were waiting for them. The house was filled with the aroma of roasted meat and earthy spices.

Doctor Lopez introduced Marco, the elder of his two boys, a very serious young man with a clenched jaw and furrowed brow. His anxiety was infectious.

"Unfortunately, we must serve ourselves," Dr. Lopez said. "For your safety, I had to send away our housekeeper."

She inhaled deeply and touched her tummy. "This is wonderful. This is just how we enjoy dinner in our own home with our children." She wouldn't know for certain that her appetite would overcome anxiety until she'd had the first bite.

They took their seats. As far as she knew, the food wasn't particularly Cuban, but it was well prepared. They had two roast ducks, a simple green salad, and rice pilaf flecked with herbs.

As the doctor carved the duck, his second son, Fernando, a boy of maybe seventeen, asked him a question in Spanish. Desi paused in the middle of serving himself the rice, apparently to hear how the doctor would answer, which he did in English.

"It's not possible," the doctor said. "Our guests have expressed their regrets but feel that it isn't their place to put themselves in the middle of our troubles."

Fernando left the table. The doctor called after him, but he didn't answer.

"He is disappointed," said Dr. Lopez.

Other than requests to pass the serving bowls and platter, they began their meal in silence. Marco was broadcasting signals Lucy wouldn't have been surprised to pick up with the fillings in her teeth. He breathed heavily through his nose, clanked his utensils against his plate, and practically inhaled his food.

Marco broke the silence. "We'll soon have enough men and weapons."

"It's suicide," Desi said.

"Some of those weapons have been paid for with your money," Dr. Lopez said.

She knew Desi had been helping Cuban refugees, but until Castro had spilled the beans, she hadn't known he'd been funding the Cuban resistance. They'd agreed to stay out of politics. If they went through with the divorce, she'd make sure he paid for that insanity out of his own share of their assets.

Marco pounded the table and nearly toppled the water glasses. "If you are not against Castro, why do you support the resistance?"

Dr. Lopez motioned at Marco to calm down.

"For protection, in case Castro and his thugs try to round up anyone who opposed the revolution," Desi said, "not for a massacre."

If the CIA had known about their money going to Cuba, then how could they have sent them into the country, into the hands of the man they were opposing? Lucy shook her head. Even if Castro never made the connection, she wanted no blood on her hands. "Absolutely not."

"We will finish the revolution," Marco said.

"Help will arrive soon," Dr. Lopez said. "The exiles."

She remembered Dr. Lopez's concern about being heard from the street. She lowered her voice. "You can't win. You'll either die fighting or in prison. And you'll take us with you."

Marco unleashed a tirade in rapid-fire Cuban Spanish. Lucy couldn't pick out a single word, but she caught the gist of it before Desi's interpretation caught up: "He will rule with chains and bullets to protect his revolution."

"Castro will get whatever he deserves soon enough," Desi added. "In the meantime, we're getting out of here—the sooner the better." He continued to enjoy his roast duck, as if they'd been at home casually debating politics over dinner with friends.

"I apologize for my sons' rudeness," Dr. Lopez said. "You are guests."

"We don't mind," Lucy said. "We're not the kind of people who shy away from tough talk."

"She's not kidding. My wife has a mouth on her."

She ignored his taunt. She'd save her energy for bigger things.

Marco twitched, apparently ready to fire off another volley of accusations, but his father silenced him with an expression that must have been burned into the boys when they were kids. Marco sank back in his chair like a defeated five-year-old.

"We had planned to ask you to help us leave Cuba," Lucy said. "But we understand that this would conflict with your wishes. It's probably best if we don't remain here."

Dr. Lopez shook his head and touched Lucy's hand. "If you wish to leave, I offer our assistance. Fidel entrusted me with your safety. He said nothing about holding you captive. My sons and I will guide you."

Marco grunted.

She set down her knife and fork. "We've been hoping to find our way to Guantánamo, but Castro has been running us all over the place."

She stood and began clearing the dishes. Dr. Lopez protested.

"I enjoy cleaning," she said. "It's how I relax. Calms my nerves."

"She's not kidding," Desi said. "She's the most famous woman in America and she still cleans the bathrooms at the studio. I wouldn't argue with her."

The doctor conceded, and Lucy continued collecting the dishes and then carried them into the kitchen. Dr. Lopez took the platter, and Desi pitched in by collecting the water glasses. They followed Lucy into the kitchen.

Dr. Lopez offered to take over washing the dishes and then resigned himself to drying. "When would you like to depart?"

From his tone, she knew he understood they wanted to get out of there that night.

"The sooner, the better," Desi said.

Lucy accepted the towel from Dr. Lopez and dried her hands. "Not that we don't appreciate your hospitality, Dr. Lopez. You've been so kind to us. In fact, the request you've made of us is flattering, and we want you and your family to understand that we have obligations to our children and to so many people who count on us. It would be selfish of us to take the risk."

"No need for explanations," he said. "I promised to ask. You graciously declined. All that is left is to fulfill your wish."

Dr. Lopez's sons walked out of the house into the courtyard. She could see the glowing tips of their cigarettes arcing back and forth and the gestures of frustration as they argued. They wouldn't let their father down, she was certain, but they wouldn't be happy about the situation either, and that was fine. To the boys, she and Desi would remain personae non grata.

Dr. Lopez gave instructions to the boys in Spanish before explaining his plan to Lucy and Desi. "I will drive you myself. We will take my car and drive directly to the American naval base."

"That's a ten-hour drive," Desi said. "We can't ask you to do that so late at night. And then you will drive home. No. It's too much."

"This is the only way. I gave my word. My car is parked outside. Marco will accompany us. We will share the driving." He went out to the courtyard and explained his plan to his sons while Desi helped Lucy in the kitchen.

There was little to do to prepare for departure. She located her handbag, which she'd left by the chair in the front room. Desi completed his usual pocket-checking ritual. They followed Dr. Lopez to the big, carved front door. He opened it to a silent sea of faces.

Lucy recoiled. Her throat closed. She'd faced plenty of crowds, but they were always full of enthusiastic, smiling faces, shouting to get her attention. When a crowd had gathered in Sancti Spíritus, Fidel had been there to work his silver-tongued magic. If this was another angry mob, either Desi or Dr. Lopez would need to talk them out of whatever they had in mind.

Dr. Lopez fired a rapid round of admonishment at Fernando. Although Lucy understood few of the words, the meaning was clear.

Desi whispered to her that Fernando had sworn to his father that he had not betrayed their trust.

Dr. Lopez moved into position in front of them, shielding them from the crowd. "It's possible you were observed."

Fernando, fuming with anger, pushed through the crowd toward a Chevy Bel Air. In the dim evening light, it looked black, but Lucy picked up hints of dark green in glints of light reflecting off the car's broad hood from windows lining the street.

The crowd pressed in and a man confronted Dr. Lopez.

Marco whispered the translation to Lucy. "He asks whether you will help them?"

"Help them with what?" she asked. "When did they have time to make a plan? I thought we were traveling in secret."

"There's no such a thing as a secret in Cuba," Desi said.

"Just like Celoron," said Lucy. "Word gets around in a small town."

Desi responded to the man directly. Although he spoke in Spanish, she recognized his apologetic tone. The crowd murmured like a bunch of movie extras. This whole experience had the feel of a cornball script, only with real guns and bullets everywhere.

The man who asked the question had his answer. His face furled in despair, and he turned and melted back into the crowd.

A woman shouted above the din. All Lucy caught was "Americanos..."

Another voice answered, and a few muttered in agreement.

Dr. Lopez and his sons closed in around Desi and Lucy. "It's better to go back inside."

A few people in the front began pushing. Marco shoved them back. He was surprisingly strong. Two men and a woman tripped on the feet of the people behind them and fell to the pavement.

Lucy knew when a brawl was about to break out, and this one was not going to go in their favor.

They backed in toward the door. Dr. Lopez practically shoved them back inside as Fernando joined Marco to hold off anyone who tried to squeeze in after them.

"They want to hold us here," Desi said.

"You mean kidnap us," she said.

"Two of the ladies said to lock us in the church. Maybe they think that's less sinful than holding us prisoner."

"I'm happy they figured out how to clear their guilty consciences ahead of time. It's always good to have a plan for your soul when you're about to commit a crime."

"They are desperate people." Dr. Lopez stood inside the door, wielding his cane at anyone who came too close. "I tell you, the revolution has not relieved their suffering, and they fear another Batista. I myself know Fidel would not commit such crimes against his people, but he will make mistakes, and the people will suffer nevertheless."

Fernando finally backed into the house, pulling Marco, bent at the waist, from behind.

It was Lucy who spotted the blood first.

PRECIPICE

It dripped on to Marco's shoe from his pants leg. Lucy recoiled in horror. "He's bleeding!"

Dr. Lopez opened Marco's coat. Blood soaked the young man's yellow shirt. "He is stabbed in the abdomen." He tore off his son's coat and ripped open his shirt. "We must put pressure on it."

Desi and Fernando reached in at the same time, and Fernando snarled at Desi like an angry dog. His father placed his hand on the wound. "Press here very firmly."

"Can you stop the bleeding?" Lucy asked.

"I can slow it, but the wound is deep. We must get him to a hospital before he bleeds to death." The composure in the doctor's genteel voice yielded to anxiety. He encouraged Marco to be strong while he stuffed cotton wadding into the wound. He listened with his stethoscope to his son's heartbeat. "He begins to enter shock. He must be warmed." He rushed upstairs.

Marco stared at Lucy with the terror of a child looking for motherly comfort. She moved to his side and placed her hand on his shoulder, and he clasped his bloody hand over hers. She flinched at the sight of it, then regained her composure and held on.

"I am frightened," he said.

Dr. Lopez returned with a blanket, which he tucked around Marco.

"You are strong," he said, doing what he could to dress the wound and adjusting Fernando's hand to apply effective pressure. His hands shook, and Fernando held his father's hand to steady it. The doctor nodded once to acknowledge his son's reassurance.

"How can we get him to a hospital?" Lucy asked.

Desi rushed to the back of the house to check the patio. "There is no other way out?"

The people on the other side of the door continued to shout. Occasionally they would chant, although it never lasted. They sounded more as though they were arguing with each other.

It was only a minute or two until one of the front windows was shattered by a large stone.

Lucy locked arms with Desi. "This is a nightmare. If we leave, maybe they will follow us instead of you."

"Are you losing your mind?" Desi let go of her and threw his arms in the air. "They'll rip us to shreds. You want to have a knife in you too?"

"What if we tell them what they want to hear?"

He began pacing in the cramped quarters from kitchen to front room, back and forth, muttering to himself in Spanish.

"It could work," Dr. Lopez said. "You must convince them that you will help us. They must believe you will take their request back to your president."

"You honestly think we can just tell hundreds of angry Cubans we will do what they want, and they'll just go home like nothing happened?" Desi demanded.

"I don't think we have so many choices, do you?" She held up a cigarette, requesting permission from Dr. Lopez, who nodded. Her hand was shaking.

Desi lit hers and one for himself.

"I'll go," she said.

"No," Desi said.

"What do you mean, no? Who else is going to do it? They'll be so surprised to see me alone that they wouldn't dare touch me."

Dr. Lopez gave a nod of agreement.

Desi rounded on him. "You too? You're telling me to let my wife walk out into an angry mob?"

Now all of a sudden he was concerned about her welfare.

"They are just people," Dr. Lopez said. "They are frightened."

"They stabbed your boy."

"One of them stabbed my boy, not all."

"And that crazy is still out there."

Lucy's stomach churned. She ran to the bathroom and puked up her dinner into the toilet. She rinsed out her mouth, cooled her face with the damp corner of a towel, and took a deep breath.

"Some protection." Desi was continuing his rant in the other room. "That bastard sent us here to be safe, and the whole town comes to hang us by our necks."

"Maybe that's what he planned," Marco said.

"If we don't get him help soon, he will die."

"I won't die," Marco told his father. "You will fix it."

Lucy strode out of the bathroom. "You're goddam right you're not gonna die." She headed straight for the door and grabbed the handle.

"Lucy, please don't go out there," Desi said.

There was a tenderness in his voice she thought had died years before. As soon as he moved toward her, she opened the door and stepped out.

The crowd went silent.

Too bad there were no cameras now. This would have been the best scene in the entire picture. The man with the knife stood in front of her. The crowd formed a pocket around him, separating themselves in a kind of collective denial of culpability. He dropped the knife and sank to his knees.

The knife remained within his reach, but she stepped toward the man anyway and placed her hand on his shoulder. "You must let Dr. Lopez take his son to the hospital."

From behind her, Desi interpreted in Spanish.

Desi and Fernando shouldered Marco's weight and walked him out of the house. A few shouts came from the back of the crowd, but those in front of them yielded. A tearful woman pleaded with Dr. Lopez for forgiveness. The doctor only nodded and took Lucy's hand. They pressed on, following Marco. The crowd continued to give way. Desi and Fernando laid Marco across the sedan's back seat.

Dr. Lopez climbed in beside him with his medical bag, tending to Marco's wound as best he could. "He must not go into shock."

Fernando took the driver's seat. Lucy and Desi squeezed in beside him, with Lucy in the middle. Fernando started moving even before Desi had closed his door. She looked back over her shoulder. The crowd hadn't begun to disperse. They stood motionless, silently watching them drive away.

Somewhere along the way to the hospital, they picked up a tail. It was a jeep, and the headlights camouflaged the faces of the driver and passenger. Good bet that one of them was Castro. The jeep was followed by a couple more vehicles. Lucy reminded herself to breathe.

Dr. Lopez opened a package of gauze and asked for help applying pressure to the wound. Desi turned completely around on his knees and reached down, practically falling over into the back seat. As he had done earlier with Fernando, the doctor instructed Desi where to place his hands.

When they arrived at the hospital, the doctor and Fernando helped Marco out of the car.

Fidel jumped out of the jeep behind them and immediately pressed Desi for a detailed accounting. Desi gave a lengthy explanation in Spanish, before they switched to English.

"You are uninjured?" Fidel asked Lucy.

"I'm fine," she said.

She pushed her hair back from her forehead. With Marco bleeding in the back seat, they hadn't had time or presence of mind to get their stories straight. No need to say anything about what they'd been discussing with the doctor. Another crowd of frustrated locals had come to ask for their help convincing the US government not to interfere with the revolution, and one man planning to take out his anger with the Yankees on Desi, calling him *"traidor,"* had mistakenly stabbed Marco Lopez. Simple—as long as she and Desi were both planning to tell the same thing.

They weren't.

"Some safe house you got," Desi said. "There must have been a thousand crazies after us."

"More like fifty," she said.

"You don't know nothing," Desi said. "It was already dark."

"What was their purpose?" Castro demanded.

"I'm telling you," Desi said. "Not everyone is so happy with your revolución."

Lucy pictured Fidel's security forces breaking down doors and rounding up dissenters. "They're impatient," she said, with feeble hope of preempting the imagined police raid.

"This is to be expected," Fidel said. "As you've seen, the revolución continues. We've arrested the man who committed this crime."

She didn't bother to ask what they'd do with him. More than likely, he'd end up in one of the prisons or worse, with or without a trial. Fidel had made it clear that armed resistance would be punished severely. She preferred to believe he would show the same leniency he'd offered the man who'd attacked him on the Malecón in Havana, though she knew that had been a performance and was unlikely to be repeated.

"We must proceed to Santiago de Cuba," Castro said.

"You mean to Guantánamo." Desi made no attempt to disguise his irritation with Castro's seemingly endless road trip. She couldn't blame him.

"We will go first to Santiago de Cuba and contact US authorities there to arrange the transfer," Castro said. "It will be a brief visit. You must have many friends there."

"I don't know no one there no more," Desi said.

"The reverse is not true," Castro said. "You are well known to the people of your hometown."

"Then it's a good idea not to tell anyone we're coming." Desi plucked a cigar right out of Castro's pocket, lit it for himself, and took several long pulls.

"As you can see, news travels very quickly in Cuba."

Lucy used her scarf to begin wiping the blood from the back seat of Dr. Lopez's car. "Maybe it's because you people talk so fast."

"Sí," Castro said, "we Cubans are in a great hurry to speak our thoughts, not like our Mexican brothers and sisters who recite Spanish like poetry."

Celia came out and said that Marco was now in surgery, and his condition was unknown. Doctor Lopez had insisted in watching the surgery in person. Fernando was waiting in the lobby.

Castro straightened. "The criminal has been apprehended, and Marco is in the hands of the fine doctors. There is nothing more we can do here."

FLIGHT PLAN

Under the cover of darkness, they traveled by car from Camagüey to Santiago. No flags fluttering from the front corners this time to mark them as VIPs, and no obvious escorts. Castro clearly wanted to attract less attention. The soldiers traveled at a distance ahead and behind them.

They entered a large plaza just after sunrise. Lucy was exhausted. She had dozed restlessly during the five-hour drive, waking at a fuel stop and at every pothole. Her compact mirror showed her eyes drooping with dark bags. Her hair was matted and flattened on the left side from resting her head against the coach panel. Her makeup had turned to paste. She looked ten years older, which worked out to about twenty years older than she would have wished.

She stepped out of the car into a familiar seaside aroma, pungent yet comforting, that reminded her of home. Santiago de Cuba, Desi's hometown, lay near the southern coast at the eastern end of the island. The city spread out along a narrow bay, not visible from the plaza. Although the air was cooler first thing in the morning under its gray marine cloud layer, in the heavy humidity her over-worn clothes stuck to her skin. As anxious as she was to get back to American soil, she ached for a bath. She primped her hair and sprayed herself with a little extra perfume before stepping out of the car. They had pulled up in front of a hotel at one end of a plaza, perpendicular to a grand, mission-style cathedral flanked by two high towers, much larger and more ornate than the church they'd visited in Sancti Spíritus. A huge statue of a spectacular winged angel watched over the plaza from high above the main portico.

Desi turned around a full three hundred and sixty degrees as if checking whether everything was as he'd left it twenty-six years earlier.

"This is the Hotel Casa Grande," Castro said. "You will have an opportunity to refresh yourselves. I will make arrangements to transfer you to the care of your government."

"You said this would be a brief visit. Why don't we go straight to Guantánamo?" Desi asked.

"Your government has given strict instructions to your military personnel not to venture outside the boundaries of their occupation."

Although Desi seemed content to play along with Castro's cat-and-mouse games, he continued to poke at his political sore spots. "You mean the naval base."

Castro poked back. "We will contact the occupation commander and arrange for a rendezvous point."

She wasn't looking for VIP treatment. "You can't just drop us off at the gate?"

"That would be dangerous. The gate is not located at the base perimeter. Given the relationship between the revolución and your government, it is not possible for me or my compañeros to travel inside the boundary."

By now the CIA should have caught up with them and smuggled them out of the country. It couldn't have taken more than telephone call to make arrangements at Guantánamo.

"Is it really that complicated?" she asked.

"Always with government bureaucracy, sí. This is true even in our own country."

For the past day and a half during their shell game, she'd felt safer, if not especially comfortable. Better than a pair of sitting ducks cooped up in a hotel room. If Desi wasn't going to press him, she would.

"Will we leave soon? Tonight?"

"Arrangements are being made," he said.

It wasn't as if they had a choice. They couldn't exactly call a taxi. Maybe once they were alone again, someone from the CIA would finally be able to contact them.

Castro tucked a cigar into Desi's shirt pocket and offered one to Lucy, which she declined. "You must not end your visit in a state of darkness. You will once again be guests of honor. Señor Arnaz saved my life. His own neighbors will host a celebration of his courage."

"Not necessary," Desi said.

Dr. Lopez and his resistance friends weren't the only ones using them as decoys or delaying tactics. Castro wasn't ready to let them go. He himself must have arranged for this hero's welcome. He hadn't been especially crafty about his tactics, and Lucy couldn't imagine he much cared whether they saw through him or not. He was holding all the cards.

She wondered how their new friends in the CIA were planning to keep all this craziness under wraps, or whether it concerned them in the slightest. If word got out at home that Desi had saved Castro's life, things would get ugly for them. They'd certainly never be able to set foot in Miami ever again—not that she particularly loved Florida's bugs and humidity. But if Castro turned out to be a dyed-in-the-wool communist, even a rumor of this trip would ruin them.

Lucy hung on Desi's shoulder with both hands. "Prime Minister Castro, I'm terribly sorry, but I'm afraid I haven't an ounce of strength left in me today. We'd prefer to skip the party and head for Guantánamo as soon as possible."

Desi remained silent. He'd picked a fine time to give up arguing.

"You will rest and refresh. The plans are made." Castro didn't wait for a further reply before excusing himself. His well-worn jeep left them in a cloud of exhaust.

* * *

SHE KICKED off her shoes and lay down on one of the two double beds. She felt stiff as a corpse, and sure she had the complexion to match.

Desi stretched out on the second bed with his shoes still on. "If we get separated, go to Guantánamo."

She propped herself up on an elbow. "What the hell does that mean? Separated? Where are you going?"

"Anything can happen with all the crazies running around."

"You're scaring the shit out of me."

He laced his hands together on his chest. "Good. You need to be scared. You been listening to his crazy babble for a week."

She lay down again and stared up into space, as if she could see clear through the ceiling. "Those blackmailing sons-of-bitches knew damned well they were sending us into a war zone."

He patted his pocket for his cigarette case but then apparently remembered the cigar Castro had given him. "Castro thinks we're protection. As long as he keeps them guessing where we are, he thinks Eisenhower won't take a chance." At least when he was sober, he had the sense to dangle his arm off the side of the bed where any loose ashes would land on the terra cotta tile instead of the bed covers.

"I hope he's right."

He studied the glowing end of the cigar and then moved the ashtray on the nightstand to the bed beside him. "Our boys probably know he's expecting something big. Maybe they got other plans."

She rolled onto her side. "What kind of other plans?"

He tucked his free hand under his head. "How the hell should I know?"

"So what do we do, sit tight and play along?"

He finally looked in her direction, but only as if to question her sanity. "Keep shooting his goddam revolution? What am I, Ed Murrow?"

His belittling stare burned a hole in her. She got up and went into the bathroom to wash off what remained of her makeup. She stood in front of the mirror and rubbed her temples. Her head-to-toe stiffness wasn't just from the eighteen hours in cars and trucks. She was wound up like a ten-day clock.

"It's not so bad," she called. "A bomb here, a bomb there. It's not like they're shooting at each other all day long."

He grunted. "I don't see no cavalry riding to our rescue. The best chance we have of getting out of here is to get ourselves to Guantánamo."

Finally he was talking sense. She dried her face, postponing a relaxing bath to slink back to the bed beside him and bury her face in the pillow, blocking out the morning sunlight leaking in around the ill-fitting shades and curtains. She didn't like being stranded with no one to rely on but a bunch of bearded boys with guns. At least they could take comfort that Fidel was smart—smart enough to know that getting America's Sweethearts killed or maimed would have serious consequences. With Red paranoia at fever pitch, Eisenhower would welcome an excuse to let loose on him.

Desi sat up and swiveled the phone so the dial faced him. "I will get us out of here."

"Are you planning to call in the marines?"

He dialed zero. "As a matter of fact, that's exactly what I'm gonna do."

He apparently expected the front desk to just connect him with the US Naval Base. She rotated her head on the pillow toward him. "You don't seriously expect that to work?"

It did.

"Hello," he said into the phone. "Yes, I need to speak with someone in charge." A voice she couldn't quite make out crackled from the receiver. He looked at her and shook his head. "You wouldn't believe me if I told you. Just say I'm an American citizen stranded in Cuba."

But when he finally got transferred to someone at Guantánamo with some authority, he didn't get much cooperation. Colonel Something-or-Other on the other end told him they were under strict orders: no US personnel were permitted on Cuban soil. The president wanted to prevent any suggestion that the US government and military were planning any action against Cuba, which was prohibited by the terms of their lease agreement for Guantánamo Station. However, if they could reach the base on their own, they could discuss their options with the base commander.

And that was that.

She sat up with her arms wrapped around her bent legs. "They're just going to leave us here?"

"If they won't come get us, we'll go there."

"How far?"

He pointed in the direction of the window. "Hundred, maybe hundred-fifty miles that way."

That didn't sound so bad, except for a couple of problems. "Over those mountains."

"We can go around."

She traced the bedspread's floral pattern with her finger: a cluster of yellow and lavender dahlias for the mountains standing between them and Guantánamo, green stems for meandering roads. "We have no car. What are we supposed to do, walk?"

"We'll take the bus."

She dismissed him with a look of disgust. She knew that her sneers particularly irritated Desi. He had once said it made her look ugly. If any of their fights had been worse than any other, that one had certainly been a winner.

"If we're going on a trip, I'm going to need to do a little shopping."

"I'm serious," he said. "We have to get out of here—and without anyone recognizing us."

Now all of a sudden, he was in a hurry. Nearly getting blown to bits hadn't done it, but the threat of a party—that was enough to send him packing. She got up and peeked out the window. "How hard can that be? Almost no one here has a TV set. Who's ever heard of us?"

"The ones who matter know us plenty good. And they got guns."

She found it both strange and annoying that after thirty years of living in the States, Desi's English could fall apart after a few days of speaking Spanish. Twenty years ago, it had been charming, even cute. Now it was like a bad habit. He might as well have been picking his nose or farting.

He yawned and stretched out again. Maybe not in so much of a hurry. He stared at the ceiling and practiced swinging the cigar toward the ashtray he'd positioned at his hip without looking. Sooner or later, he was bound to light the bed—or himself—on fire. He was working out a plan, his eyes darting around as if he were checking a rough cut.

"You gotta wash the rest of that red out of your hair," he said suddenly.

Lucy hadn't been out in public without her trademark hair since their first episode. Desi said she'd invented color TV, because the audience saw her as a redhead even in black and white.

He tamped out the unfinished cigar and laid it in the ashtray. "We'll sneak away from the party."

She had no idea how they were going to get away—Castro's boys were watching them around the clock—but she was too exhausted to argue. They'd need to wake up before the evening so they could pick up some fresh clothes, maybe a wrap for the evening. Not too many things, though—not when they might be running for their lives.

FAVORITE SON

They arrived on a short, hemmed-in block just as the moonless sky was fading from deep blue to black. Continuous apartment rows walled the street on either side. A small crowd had gathered. The clatter and laughter of men playing dominos reverberated from the brick and stucco facades. Chattering women chopped onions and colorful bell peppers with well-worn cleavers, tossing them into large pots teetering on tripod stands over gas burners. The aromas of garlic and musty cumin mingled with tobacco smoke. Lucy had never been a fan of cigars, even the ten-dollar Cubans enjoyed by many of their friends and business partners, but something about this concoction of spices, smoke, and salt air was tantalizing.

Desi was already making the rounds, chatting with the cooks and sampling their pots with nibbles from oversized wooden spoons. The older women fed him with the zeal of foreplay. Both she and Desi were better known than she'd expected. American television had been available in Havana for several years, but outside the capital city, very few Cubans could afford sets. TV was still a privilege of Havana's upper class. And yet here, Desi was still a star.

Tables were set out in the street, some black wrought iron with matching chairs of iron and wicker. Others were simple folding card tables draped with colorful tablecloths. Lucy had avoided wicker ever since Desi had teased her about the pattern a pool chaise lounge had embossed on her backside one lazy day in Palm Springs. The woven crosshatch had been so deep that when she flopped over, it had tanned itself into the backs of her thighs and stayed there for a week.

Castro had given the film crew the night off, mostly so Desi could feel like he was not working, but also because Lucy had more than once worried aloud about appearing on camera more often than she liked. The break was a relief. The more film they shot of themselves, the more likely they'd get set up or framed for collaboration. And besides that, she was less talented at putting on her best face than her regular hairdresser and makeup artist.

The cameramen and grips busied themselves by stretching strings of bare bulbs zigzag across the street, accepting bottles of cold beer in appreciation for their efforts. Moths homed in on the lights, and she expected to be swarmed by bugs at any moment, but the thickening haze of cigar smoke seemed to act as an effective repellent.

A band showed up one player at a time. They parked their instrument cases near one end of the street and went straight for the cervezas. A short, barrel-shaped man, sniffing and snorting as he chewed his stubby cigar, set up music stands, each shaped like a stumpy podium, three feet tall, with a rounded front painted red and decorated in elegant gold script with the name of the now-defunct Club Montmartre. The makeshift bandstand looked out of place.

It had taken a lot of energy to hold up under several days of perpetual stress, and under the pretty overhead lights and among the cheerful crowd, Lucy began to relax. Even if they were celebrities here, there was no one to impress. No deals at stake. No reputation to protect.

One of the trumpet players had already taken out his horn and walked around visiting while polishing the brass with a cloth until it gleamed. He had the same general build as Desi, around six feet tall and clean-shaven, an attractive fellow although at least twenty years

Lucy's junior. It didn't hurt to enjoy the view, and she had a soft spot for musicians, especially good-looking Latin ones.

Fidel must have noticed her wandering eye, because he gave her a wink. He was several paces away, playing his usual supervisory role with a group of six or seven teenagers. Lucy overheard him issuing instructions in rapid, staccato Cuban Spanish.

When she had first met Desi, she'd thought he was just a little nervous and spoke too fast. It wasn't long before she learned that Desi was not even the fastest of Cuban speakers. Some of the ladies would go off on a tear, usually when they were unhappy about something, which was more or less every ten minutes. Cubans had two speeds, languid and charming or staccato and impassioned.

Fidel sent the teens off in different directions and pulled up a chair beside hers. "Your husband is quite at home."

"It's not just because he's Cuban. Desi likes to work a room. Being the center of attention goes with the job."

"It's the same for politics." Uncharacteristically, he silently gestured for Lucy's permission to light up.

"Be my guest." It would hardly make a difference. The cloud of tobacco smoke hung in the still air. She took a cigarette from her purse, which he rushed to light for her.

"It's a beautiful evening," he said. "Many stars."

"Cooler now. Who's that gentleman Desi is speaking with?"

"That's Benny Moré, Cuba's most beloved band leader—El Bárbaro del Ritmo."

She had an impression of Moré from his record album covers but had never seen him in person. Desi had come to Cuba once to buy some of Moré's arrangements for his own band. Moré looked old for a man of around forty, and his suspenders and bow tie didn't make him look any younger. He held a drink in one hand and a cigarette in the other.

Watching other men drink was not easy for Desi. They carried on an animated conversation, each showing the other a little footwork. Even without hearing their words, Lucy knew Desi was repeating the story of how he had introduced the conga line to New York. A couple of the other musicians joined them to share a smoke and a couple of laughs.

"He certainly brings out the ham in Desi," she said.

Fidel smiled at her. Apparently he either knew that particular English expression or had got the gist. "You are the observer tonight."

"I'm a little bit of a hard-ass. Part of a woman's job is to keep her man in line."

"And part of a man's job is to keep a woman guessing."

She raised an eyebrow and shook her head. "That is one skill my husband lacks. I can see right through him and his escapades."

Men, women, and children of all ages gathered in the street and warmed themselves with tin mugs of black bean soup and plates heaped with pollo con arrozo. Children chased each other from one end of the street to the other. A little girl about little Lucie's age, seven or eight, hid behind Lucy's chair, and when her friends came looking for her, Fidel playfully shrugged them off her trail. The children smiled at him suspiciously and then continued their search, pretending to fire rifles at imaginary foes.

The little girl came out and touched Lucy's ring.

Fidel translated. "She says 'pretty.'"

The little girl gave them the *silencio* gesture and tiptoed off to surprise the others from behind. Her giggles gave her away.

The teens returned with colorful crepe paper decorations to brighten the brick-lined street. Although the buildings were painted in typical Caribbean fashion with bright pastels—green, pink, yellow—the street itself was gray and dusty. It needed a little dressing up. Two of the kids carted in a couple of potted palms, along with several large vases of flowers, possibly "borrowed" from the nearby hotel.

Lucy shivered and tucked her coat in around her legs. "Looks like we're settling in the for the evening."

"Uno momento."

Castro whistled to a couple of men unloading steel oil drums from the back of an old pickup truck. One of the men heel-rolled a barrel over to them. The other man dumped in a bundle of firewood, splashed it with some fuel—most likely kerosene, from the smell—and tossed in a match. Within a couple of minutes, the gas odor had subsided, and sparks rose through the cigar haze like rising stars, fading as if taking their places in the black sky.

A couple of bass drum hits signaled the band to take their places. Before they'd settled in, Benny had already counted them off. The piano player pounded out a bouncy montuno. Within moments, several couples began dancing wherever they happened to be standing. The cooks, too, set their hips to swaying.

"Music is important in Cuba," Fidel said over the blaring brass. "We are passionate people."

"I'm aware."

"Do you wish to eat something?"

She nodded. "I'm hungrier than I expected, but where do I start?"

"I'll have someone bring you something."

She stood and surveyed her choices. "No, let's walk. I'll follow my nose."

The impromptu kitchens were lined up along one side of the street so the ladies could chatter while they cooked and served. As soon as Lucy approached the first, the cook grabbed a ladle and scooped out a cup of dark soup.

"Is it spicy?" Lucy asked Castro.

"Not so much. This is the soup of Cuba. Black beans with onions and garlic."

She drew a deep whiff from the steaming cup. The cook grinned at her and handed her a spoon. She thanked her and took a taste. It was musty from the cumin, and thick. Good to get something warm into her stomach.

She kept checking in on Desi. "It's killing him."

Fidel furrowed his brow.

"I mean it's killing him to be watching the band and not fronting. I'll lay odds he's on the conga drums by the third number."

"Would that bother you?"

"I guess I'm a little jealous." She wrinkled her nose in embarrassment. "I've never admitted it before, but I do envy Desi's ability to perform at the drop of a hat."

"But you are well known for making people laugh."

She trickled a spoonful of soup back into the cup like Desi Jr. would do when he wasn't so sure he liked something. "Oh, I'm great with a script. Stage or screen, I can juice every line. The thing is, because I'm a comic, everyone expects me to be funny all the time. I'm just not that clever. I'm an actress, not a performer."

"And so Desi takes the attention." He mused on this, once again crafting some kind of counsel.

And then he delivered.

"Is attention so important?"

It wasn't particularly cold yet, but Lucy warmed her hands by wrapping them around the enameled tin mug. "It is when that's how you make your living. I know he's not working right now, but I've always loved watching him perform. He puts on a great show, he and his band."

"But it's something he does without you."

She looked away at the dancing couples scattered among the tables. "Once you get used to working as a duo, it feels a little like being cheated on. And God knows, Desi's a cheat. I don't know which is worse, the women or the applause."

He pursed his lips at her doubtfully.

"Okay, the women are worse," she relented. "But one kind of pain doesn't cover up for another. This is how it begins. Every episode follows the same plot: Pal around with the fellas. Make some music. Smile big for the girls."

"A television program?"

Just when he seemed to be catching on. "Not an actual show. I mean Desi's as predictable as a sitcom. Only the joke's usually on me."

He motioned in Desi's direction with an open palm. "I see a man enjoying himself. This is so bad?"

"I'm not so sure he's enjoying himself. Ever since Desi gave up drinking—it's not easy for him."

He clenched a fist, shaking it slightly. "This is a man of great strength. Not like Moré. Benny will most certainly drink himself to death."

She wanted to believe that Desi had finally come around, but it had only been a few weeks. Maybe coming to Cuba had been too much of a test. Booze was everywhere, day and night. The way Benny was waving that glass in front of Desi, she thought Desi would snatch it from him any second.

She'd hoped that when Desi was sober, he'd stop womanizing. When he was hammered, he could almost make the excuse that he didn't know what he was doing; sober, he might control himself and pay more attention to her feelings. But so far, that plan had been a flop. He more than made up for the booze with women and tobacco. He was a man who desperately needed nonstop stimulation, and she'd never had the fire to hold his attention. They both had enough to deal with every day just running the studio and shooting their own show. With two kids and a crazy schedule, she didn't have the time or inclination to play vixen.

Desi stood before the band as if he were about to take over from Benny. A few young women loitered near him, too shy to speak. He smiled and winked at them.

"I'll lay odds on it," Lucy told Fidel. "Five to one, he's on the congas by the third number."

"I would not bet against you, Mrs. Arnaz. Besides, I do not gamble."

He had a sympathetic ear, but the time for sniveling had passed. That and lack of sleep were making her impatient. She'd had only a fitful afternoon nap. If they were going to sneak out later in the evening, she'd need to be wide awake. "I wouldn't mind a cup of coffee."

When he rose to get it for her himself, she insisted that she needed to move around, get her blood circulating and warm up a little. They skirted the makeshift dance floor and walked down the sidewalk, where one of the cooks was percolating coffee over gas burners. He noticed her reaction to the now-familiar rich and bitter brew and offered her cream, but she liked it black and as hot as she could get it.

They positioned themselves closer to the band, where it became difficult to carry on a conversation. Desi was still a couple dozen feet in front of them and had no idea they were there. When Fidel stepped forward to join him, Lucy tugged his elbow, asking him to stay back while they tested her prediction.

After the second number, Benny called for the crowd's attention and then introduced Fidel.

Fidel excused himself and took Moré's place. "You will all be nervous now." He paused, and everyone in the crowd looked at each other as if not sure what dire announcement they were about to receive. "It is said that I make long speeches." A few chuckles here and there, a couple of whistles, and many smiles. "Tonight, I only wish to say a few words about our guests, Mr. and Mrs. Desi Arnaz." Applause and more whistles.

Desi turned back and reached out his arms to Lucy, and she joined him in front. He put his arm around her, resting his strong hand on her hip. He might have turned into a son of a bitch, but he still knew how to touch her—touch a woman, anyway.

He swayed his hips, nearly knocking her off her heels.

"Stop," she said coyly.

He did not.

It was a performance for the crowd, whose gentle laughter showed they'd been charmed.

He presented her on the dance floor. It couldn't have been more movie-like, and all the other dancers yielded the floor and began clapping to the rhythm. Desi knew how to put on a show, and at least he had the decency to include her once in a while. Wrapped in her coat, she wasn't exactly giving it her best, but he drew her attention from any impression she was or wasn't making.

He looked deeply into her eyes, and as usual, she fell for it. In some ways, she couldn't blame other women for trying to get their hooks in him. He had the looks, the charm—and let's face it, the money. And it wasn't as if she hadn't had her share of illicit suitors. She just knew how to play the game without breaking so many rules.

After a bit of whirling and dipping, they settled into a less flamboyant salsa, and others began to join in. Smiling couples orbited them and traded places for a chance to greet the famous Hollywood stars.

During the next dance, a slow bolero, Lucy realized this was the most relaxed she'd been in months. After the initial shock of being cut off from their contacts, she had come to appreciate the isolation. The lingering shock of the bombing in Havana faded in the midst of the music and laughter. For all its intensity, the entire trip had almost felt like solitude, free of agents and producers and all the Hollywood rigmarole. No one wanted anything from them here except Fidel, and he was calling all the shots anyway.

She could sense in Desi's body, too, that some of his tension had slackened. At moments like this, she ached for his touch. Evenings often began this way, though they had a way of going south.

In close embrace, with their voices safely cloaked by the music, she asked Desi whether he knew anyone at the party.

"Santiago is a city. Thousands live here."

"But your father was mayor. Haven't any family friends shown up?"

"Most of the people we knew are in Miami now. If not, they're in Costa Rica, Mexico—some other place without so many guns."

She couldn't see his eyes, but she could feel his facial movements as he smiled at others, most likely the prettiest women passing behind her.

"Do you miss anything about this place?" She looked up at the evening sky, as if it would reflect back an image of the Cuba from Desi's youth.

"I was a kid here. It brings back good memories. But look at this country. It's a mess."

"And you think he's going to make it worse."

"He's a commie. How can that be good?"

She glanced around to make sure Fidel was out of earshot. "He says he's going to hold elections. I can't tell whether he cares as much as he preaches. He may just be another power-hungry dictator in the making."

It was difficult not to trip on the cobblestone street. She wanted to kick off her high heels, but the pavement didn't look so foot-friendly, rough and probably cold. She'd have to tough it out as long as she had Desi in her spell.

The band began to play a conga and this, she knew, was the end of their dance. Moré prompted Desi by pointing him toward the conga drums, where the band's regular player was already making way for him.

"Go on," she said. She tried to spot Fidel to give him the 'I told you so,' but he was busy shaking hands and carousing with the crowd.

Although there were no spotlights in the street, Desi was glowing. Moré let Desi start the next number with a conga solo intro. Desi could make more sounds with those two simple drums than anyone she'd ever heard. When he let loose, he was all hands and elbows, knuckles and fingertips. He could play a drumroll that rose from a whisper to a *pop pop pop*, and she could swear every note was different, as if the drums were talking. He signaled Moré and the band with a final flurry of beats, alternating between the two drums, crossing hand over hand and finally counting off with a *thrum-thrum, thrum-thrum, thrum-thrum*. The band took his cue and practically blew the smoke out of the air.

Whether he believed it or not, Desi was in his element, and that scared her out of her wits. If she understood anything about Latinos, and especially Latin men, it was their penchant for passion, which would be directed at the nearest recipient. Unless she was vigilant, Desi's eyes, as well as his other vital sense organs, tended to wander. The more charisma he exuded, the more attention he attracted from both men and women. She was accustomed to attention herself, but it was different, mostly the usual celebrity nonsense or her beauty. Her beauty had been her ticket to Hollywood, and she enjoyed being beautiful and glamorous. But with Desi, although it twisted her up inside with jealousy bordering on rage, his talents and admittedly his charm were genuine—and they weren't fading with age. They'd worked on her. Look how much shit she'd put up with for the past nineteen years. He'd literally charmed the pants off her. If only he'd learned how to save his passion for her.

Desi let loose on those drums, and the crowd responded. Their dancing reached a fevered pitch, with shouting, whooping, and whistling. Couples practically made love in the street. Lucy had never been so great at letting her hair down, even when it had been long enough to literally do so. In the early days, Desi had thought he could loosen her up with a little booze and sweet talk, but the more she drank, the sleepier she became. Inevitably, she'd ended up with a headache and he'd ended up disappointed. When he'd turned elsewhere, she'd punished him by barricading behind her resentment. Together, they'd dug a wide moat.

PARTY CRASH

One of the women hovering close to Desi brought him a drink. He waved it off, but she argued playfully with him until he accepted the glass. He glanced in Lucy's direction but avoided eye contact. He hadn't taken a drink.

Fidel returned to stand at her side as Benny made a show of coaxing Desi into singing and Desi made a show of giving in. No need to remind Fidel of her prediction. Desi saluted them with the glass, then drowned his cigarette in it.

"There," Fidel said, "I see strength."

Lucy said nothing, although she did feel relieved. She knew better than anyone how difficult it was for Desi to refuse a drink. He'd had to spoil it to put himself off.

Still. "Yeah, strength. Tell that to his pecker."

"You believe he would be tempted by all this female attention. Not one of those women can match your beauty or intelligence."

"Flattery aside, you assume he has standards." She took out her compact mirror and fussed with her hair, trying to look nonchalant as she continued to profess her husband's sins to a perfect stranger—and a rising dictator, no less.

"He thrives on attention."

Desi was really hamming it up, singing his signature "Babalu" while making the rounds of the crowd. He patted a couple of kids on the head and kissed a grandma on the cheek, which made the younger girls swoon even more.

"When a man has everything, he cannot be satisfied. The male nature is as conqueror. Without it, civilization would never have come into existence."

"Civilization? You make him out to be Alexander the Great. He has built us a nice little empire, though. Back in the day, I was hungry for fame and fortune. Then all I wanted was a family. We have a couple of kids. A nice home. Our friends are all right, even if they are rich, spoiled movie stars."

Fidel flicked the ashes from his cigar and peered down out of the corner of his eyes. "I am certain you had your own ambitions."

"You got me. Of course I did. Still do. No one in show business gets there accidentally. But no matter what we have, Desi is unsatisfied. When he's sober, he's restless, like a thoroughbred locked up in a stable. He paws at the ground. And when he gets out, he turns into a rutting stallion."

"Do you love him, or do you need him?"

Leaning on Fidel for balance, she took a seat on a couple of stacked crates. "You don't mince words, do you?" She removed a shoe and massaged her foot. "Of course I love him. Do you think I'd have put up with his crap for so many years if I didn't?"

Desi finished a duet with Moré and excused himself from the bandstand, despite the protests of the crowd. She thought he might come make an excuse for them to exit, but instead he gestured for one more minute and made a beeline for an older couple sitting at a small, candlelit table off to one side.

The couple rose to greet him, and the woman hugged him. It had taken Desi a couple of numbers to loosen up, but now he was in full social swing. He waved and called Lucy over, so she excused herself from Fidel's company. The couple looked at her as though they were Desi's parents and she were meeting them for the first time.

After that, Desi dragged her from table to table, translating some but not all of what was said, and she was forced to utter basic niceties and smile pretty. As it turned out, Desi did know a few of the people at the party. Some had been friends of his father the mayor. Others he'd known in grade school.

She and Desi were worlds apart. To her, it felt odd to return to Jamestown or Celoron, New York, even though she'd spent her childhood there. Celebrity turned you into something like a mannequin. You became nothing but what people thought they knew about you. It hollowed you out. Most people thought celebrities were detached out of ego or snobbery. They seemed to believe fame was some kind of commitment to make yourself available to every Tom, Dick, and Harriet. So you clung to the people around you who knew what it was like to be gawked at and pigeonholed, and you hoped that at least some of them were genuine enough to let you be yourself. The public sure didn't sympathize with a rich and famous TV star complaining about how difficult her life was.

Desi was carrying on a lengthy conversation with a woman who looked maybe ten years older than Lucy, late fifties or early sixties. After the usual greetings, he'd stopped translating, and Lucy waited politely behind him like a debutante. When the woman began weeping, Lucy became even more hesitant to interrupt.

When they finally broke away, Desi offered no explanation.

"Little old for you, isn't she?" Lucy jabbed.

"Look who's talking."

She'd thrown the first punch, but he'd gone for her jugular. She tried to resist wiping the tears welling up in her eyes but finally had to catch them with the heel of her thumb before they ran down her cheeks. She found her handkerchief in her handbag and dabbed up the rest.

Desi ignored her stunned silence without awaiting or offering an apology. "She worked for my father. She was his secretary. My father treated her like one of his own children. When we left the country, he kept trying to find out if she was safe, but we couldn't get in touch with anyone. This country was still too backward."

For all his flaws, Desi was one of the most compassionate men she'd ever known—for those he thought needed it most. Maybe she'd done too good a job playing tough, from her rough talk to the flaming orange hair. "At least you know she made it. You can tell your father."

"Her parents were murdered," he said. "She and her little sister fled into the mountains and hid. She was afraid to trust anyone, so they lived in the forest for months until they nearly starved to death. A coffee farmer found them trying to steal food from his house and took them in."

"You knew her family then? Before the last revolution?"

"Some revolution—a bunch of crazy Bolsheviks trying to take over the country, and all they did was burn down houses and murder innocent people. Even children." He accepted a cigar and a light from a passing well-wisher, hollowed out his cheeks with a big puff, and slowly released the smoke. "I knew her, but only because I would see her when I visited my father at his office."

She offered an olive branch. "I'm only wondering whether it's nice to see someone you knew back then."

He stared off into space. "Santiago was good place to grow up, but Cuba has gone from one disaster to another."

"Maybe this revolution is different. Don't you think he'll make a difference?"

"Castro?" He shook his head at her with a look of disbelief, as if she'd lost her mind. "He's just a kid. He thinks he owns the place already."

As Desi went off to pay his respects to the next table of guests, Lucy faded back into a wallflower's retreat off to one side of the street. She fidgeted with the little brass ring she'd always carried in her pocketbook as a good luck charm, a keepsake from a time in her life when everything seemed possible.

The more reminiscing Desi did, the more he seemed to assimilate, and the less relevant she felt. She was not accustomed to taking the role of silent wife. She couldn't blame him really. He was in his native land. She'd seen him wheel and deal in Hollywood, but no matter how much success they'd achieved with Desilu, Desi never fit in. He loved his adoptive country, but part of his persona was his difference, and it had worn on him.

Her watch said eight o'clock at home in LA, but she had adjusted to local time, 11 p.m. The party was still growing. It had practically become a festival. The street was packed with hundreds of people, maybe more than a thousand. Still more milled around at either end of the street, close enough to feel part of the festivities while taking a break from the blaring big band and laughter to enjoy a smoke and a quiet conversation. Two or three young couples had eloped to the shadows.

She couldn't guess what to expect if she were to leave Desi to his own devices, but she was his wife, not his mother. She was an outsider with nothing much to say or do, and to top it off, she was beat.

Parties had become tiresome in general. Hollywood social life was a professional necessity more often than not. There had been a time when they'd enjoyed the occasional get-together with friends, but they'd put off most of their friends by now with their constant bickering. She might have made more of an effort to hide their dirty laundry if she hadn't grown so tired of the pretense. As for the big Hollywood bashes, once you'd reached the top of the heap, you didn't need to waste so much time rubbing shoulders. For Desi, it was more a matter of ego and showmanship than a tool of the trade.

These folks here in Santiago de Cuba, however, weren't here to impress each other, except for a few pursuing romantic interests or superiority at dominos.

She spotted Fidel making his own rounds, playing politician. You'd have thought he was actually campaigning. Maybe he really was planning to hold elections. He sure seemed determined to get support. His revolution had started out here in the sticks, and it seemed like the last place he'd need to campaign.

Fidel noticed her and returned to take a seat at her side. He said nothing. For all his charisma—or bravado—he looked uncomfortable in close conversation. He was a bold orator, but one on one, he found it difficult to make eye contact. Unless he was preaching politics, he spoke softly and tentatively. Maybe he was simply exhausted by paranoia.

"I must apologize," he said.

"Whatever for?"

"I hadn't intended for you to be in any danger in Camagüey. You should have been perfectly safe in the home of Alfonso Lopez. I hope these events haven't furthered colored your impressions of the revolución."

He pulled up a second wrought iron chair, and she shifted against the hard seat of her own chair to get the blood in her backside circulating again.

"It all depends on how this works out," she said. "Once people at home get a load of this film, things could go very well or very badly for us—especially for me. They may forgive Desi for his optimism. They'll make mincemeat out of me."

"What makes you think it will go badly?"

"I think, Dr. Castro, that you'll do what you need to do and whatever happens will happen. I'm afraid we've put our fate in your hands."

"And you're displeased."

She tucked her dress in snugly around her thighs and kept her hands beneath her, arms pressed against her sides. If he didn't know of Dr. Lopez's involvement with the resistance movement, he wasn't going to trick her into spilling the beans. "I think you are well aware of what it means to be at the mercy of someone else's whims or choices. What happened to Dr. Lopez's son was shocking."

He leaned toward her and placed his hand on the arm of her chair. "I hope you believe that I expected your visit to be peaceful and informative. There is a positive side to these events, however."

"How's that?"

"Until the Batista sympathizers engage in treacherous acts, they are hidden like rats in the sewers. It's only when they emerge from their putrid holes that we can capture them."

"And you found the man who stabbed Marco?"

"Among others."

The little brass wedding ring fell from her fingers.

He rushed to retrieve it, missing it a couple of times as it rolled away before finally spinning to a rest.

He held it up near the tip of his nose. "A humble treasure."

She explained how she and Desi had eloped without purchasing rings, so they'd picked up this little brass band at Woolworth's. "We had very little back then. That ring reminds me to be patient. Things will get better."

"Does it work?"

"For some things. You give and take." She slipped the ring on the ring finger of her right hand and held them up to compare memories.

She resisted the impulse to ask Fidel whom exactly they'd captured and what would happen to them. She couldn't tip her hand by asking him about Dr. Lopez. Instead, before her silence could betray either her fears or regrets, she changed the subject.

"It's a lovely party."

He waved his arm at the crowd as if he were the master of ceremonies. "Desiderio Alberto Arnaz y de Acha III is an admired son of this city."

"I should think that would bother you. Aren't they celebrating all the things you detest? Yankee excess, celebrity, wealth, pretense?"

"It's true I wish for the Cuban people to be less concerned with fame and money. You've seen with your own eyes what the pursuit of individual wealth has done to this country."

"You would like them to choose noble poverty over greed."

"Not poverty. Poverty for all is no better than poverty for some. I only wish for every man, every woman, every child to have the same opportunity. Every person's fortune should rise together on the tide of freedom."

Another poetic flourish. "That's very expensive. How would you do that in a country that's so impoverished?"

"This is ordinary economic science. Wealth is not a pile of gold that is divided until its value is so small it cannot buy a sack of rice. Prosperity is created. It arises from the work of the people. The land and its riches are abundant to all who willingly earn its gifts. It's only when a few seize power that others suffer."

"Funny how a young man like you can remind me of my grandfather."

"I'm told I'm old for my age."

She narrowed her face and stroked her chin. "That might just be the beard."

He acknowledged the comparison with no humor. "I feel sometimes I have already lived two lifetimes. Cubans are strong people. They only lack education. They need teachers. Also, good doctors and hospitals to cure their illnesses and heal their injuries. With strong bodies and minds, they will attain the same comforts enjoyed by the citizens of your country. And they will do this without bringing harm to others."

The band teased the crowd with a stop beat, answered unexpectedly by several sharp cracks that reverberated down the street. The band tumbled out of tune and dropped to their knees or stomachs.

More shots. She couldn't tell where they were coming from. They jumped to their feet and she spun around, trying to figure out which way to run.

A popping sound came again from beyond the end of the street.

"Fireworks?" she asked, hoping for the best.

He shook his head curtly. "Gunfire." He placed a hand on Lucy's shoulder, as if to protect her by mere contact, and cocked his head. "It is beginning."

Was this really the start of an invasion? Here, so close to safety?

More out of hope than challenge, she asked, "Why do you think it's not just a local group of troublemakers?"

"The sum of all signs suggests a greater danger."

The crack of more gunshots caromed through the narrow streets. To Lucy's ears, they could have been miles away or right in front of her, ten shots or a hundred.

"You must wait here," he said. "You'll be protected. I will send guards to escort you and Mr. Arnaz to safety."

A fresh wave of terror overtook her as the gunfire was followed by shouting and screaming. A few musicians knocked over their music stands, holding their horns in one hand, snatching up their instrument cases with the other. The partygoers scattered.

Half a dozen Fidelistas rushed into the street from either end, their rifles at the ready. There was plenty of shouting in Spanish. The street had become either a refuge or a trap.

Desi looked across the street at her with equal shock. Fidel took Lucy's hand and led her through the panicked crowd to Desi's care, then ran off, shouting orders to his men.

They were on their own.

"We'll go," Desi said.

But could they? They really had no choice but to trust Fidel's judgment. She didn't see how Desi could get them past the half dozen soldiers at each end of the block.

More shots rang out, still at a distance. The party guests flinched with each crack. Several of them hunched over, then scurried away in the direction indicated by two of the men who'd posted themselves as sentries at the far end, behind the band.

Desi rushed the two of them into the shelter of a recessed doorway. As another shot cracked somewhere behind them, he covered her body with his, pressing her against the locked apartment door.

She laid her head against his shoulder. "You protected me."

He put one hand between her shoulders but said nothing. She felt his heart pounding against her breast and his chest rising and falling with each short breath.

Then he grabbed her hand and pulled her along, trying doors on every building. The first three were unlocked, but he looked inside and moved on to the next. Finally, he rushed her inside one, and they climbed a narrow staircase up four flights to the roof.

They'd be trapped. "Where are we going?"

"At least you don't see nobody shooting at us up here, do you?"

The buildings abutted each other side to side and back to back. He helped her over each parapet separating rooftop from rooftop, stopping on each building to check for an open stairwell door. They finally found an open doorway atop the last building facing the adjacent street. He flicked on his cigarette lighter and guided them down the unlit passage to the street.

Almost eighty pictures under her belt, and Lucy had never experienced action like this.

Desi jumped into the street to flag down a passing car. Two or three passed before one finally pulled over.

"Sí, Ricky Ricardo—'Oh, Lucy…'" called the driver, apparently delighted to make their acquaintance in the middle of a gunfight. He reached over and popped open the passenger door, urging them in.

Desi let Lucy into the back and then jumped into the passenger seat, banging his forehead on the door frame. She winced in sympathy. He rubbed the bump as he explained to the driver where they wanted to go. The driver must have known more about what was happening out there than they did, because he offered another suggestion, pointing this way and that. Desi accepted their driver's plan, and they pulled away.

Lucy could hardly breathe—in fact, she was beginning to hyperventilate. The driver, who introduced himself through Desi as Miguel Segura, peeked at her in his rearview mirror.

"Poco, poco," he said, nodding his head like a conductor to set the tempo of her breaths. Once she demonstrated she understood his instructions, he shook his head and chuckled to himself as though he couldn't believe his good fortune at meeting them.

"He says the señora will never believe this story," Desi said, still nursing his injury.

Lucy smiled grimly. The entire country had just been through a civil war, and this fella was still excited to meet a couple of movie stars. Oh well, why should it be any different here than at home? If they couldn't be useful, at least they could take people's minds off their troubles.

A group of boys ran shouting down the street, carrying a flag and a tinny AM radio. Desi had that vacant look in his eyes that meant he was fighting the urge to drink. She touched his face, hoping to distract him from his demons.

If only someone could do the same for her.

BETRAYAL

Desi directed Señor Segura down dark streets and a couple of alleyways, obviously with some destination in mind. Lucy was pretty sure she knew where he was headed—or rather, who he was hoping to find.

They stopped across the street from a lighted ground floor apartment. Through the curtainless window, sparse furnishings carved hollow shadows under a bare overhead bulb.

Desi talked to Lucy over his shoulder. "Maybe you should go first."

Her intuition had been correct. That flat didn't belong to just anyone from Desi's past; it belonged to someone who'd deliberately skipped the party in his honor. Now he was expecting Lucy to be the one to shield him from the heat a jilted woman's anger. He must have been hoping that her celebrity would keep Camille from slamming the door in their—in her—face.

Lucy checked her makeup with her compact mirror. She crossed the street.

The door opened before she could knock. Camille looked at Lucy and then past her toward the car across the street.

Lucy began to introduce herself.

"I know who you are." Camille nodded in the direction of the car.

"Why does he stand so far away?" She held the door open wide. "Come—quickly."

Lucy squeezed past her. "He—we—were afraid you would be too angry with him, and he wanted to respect your feelings."

"I am not a child." She waited at the door for Desi.

"Camille," Lucy said, "we're here to ask for your help."

Camille kept her eyes on Desi as he approached. He leaned toward her for the traditional cheek kiss, but she backed away.

"Buenas noches, Camille," he said.

She said nothing but let them in. He kept his distance from both women, lingering just inside the door.

The tiny flat was cramped. At the back was a kitchenette. The only furniture was a chrome table with a Formica top and four matching chairs, and against the side wall, one small sofa. The floor was covered in well-worn terra cotta, broken here and there. The bulb dangling over the table on its wire was topped with a funnel-shaped shade, which halved the room top to bottom into shade and light. The aroma of cooked fish lingered in the air, strong but not objectionable.

Camille didn't offer them a seat. She tapped a cigarette free from a pack of Winstons, and Desi leaned in her direction to light it for her at arm's length. Taking the cue that it was fine to smoke, he lit a couple of cigarettes for himself and Lucy. Smoke began to fill the small room.

"You choose a crazy time to come home," Camille said.

"It's been a little more than we bargained for," Lucy said.

"Bargained?"

"An expression," Desi explained. "She means we didn't know what we were getting ourselves into by coming here."

"So why did you?"

"We didn't have a choice. We owed a favor."

"It doesn't matter anymore," Lucy said. "We need to get out of the country."

"You and everybody else." She nodded toward Desi, who had stationed himself at the window. "You are American. You can go whenever you wish. It's you who should be helping me escape."

"It's not that easy," Lucy said. "We're stuck here. Castro's shut down the airports, and he's dragging us all over the country."

She widened her eyes. "You are prisoners—this is what you are trying to convince me."

Lucy put her handbag on the nearest chair. "Not exactly. We think he's using us for protection. He's playing a shell game with us. He thinks the Americans won't risk an attack if they think we're in the way."

Camille turned to Desi. "You have nothing more to dress up this story? You're the one with the golden tongue." She looked them both over and shook her head. "I think your friends sent you here as a decoy." She turned again to Lucy. "They want Fidel to think he can hide behind your skirt."

"We've got company," Desi said from the window. "Across the street. Two of them."

Lucy tensed. If they'd been followed, Camille might have just become the next local they'd put in danger. "Until we know who these fellas are, the best thing you can do is act like we're all good old friends. You and Desi have a nice reunion. Talk about old times. Anyone who's watching right now will think we just stopped by for a visit and you're just as happy we're here as Castro is. It's less suspicious."

Desi kept an eye on the street outside the window. Lucy took a long drag on her cigarette and blew the smoke up toward the bare light bulb hanging over the table.

"All right," Camille said. "Let's chat."

Camille must have been just as nervous as she was. Without objection, she put a pot of coffee on the stove. She again sat at her kitchen table, crushed out her cigarette in a well-worn ashtray, and lit another.

They needed to look to the outsiders as if they were invited guests. Lucy removed her coat, draped it over the arm of the sofa, and invited herself to sit at the table opposite Camille. Once seated, she nervously tapped her fingers on the marbled Formica table surface.

"You need to sit down," she said to Desi. "You look like you're standing guard."

"I am standing guard," he said.

"And the goons outside can see you. It means you're hiding something."

He waved at the men through the window.

"What the hell are you doing?"

"I'm gonna talk to these jokers," he said.

Over her whisper-shouted protest, he stuck an unlit cigarette on his lip, walked out the door, and headed directly for the men. She resisted the temptation to jump up and call him back inside. It was too late, anyway. She stood and watched from the window now, making no effort now to avoid detection.

Before he had reached the opposite curb, he was already greeting them, although she couldn't hear what he was saying. At first, the men looked confused, exchanging glances but no words. He accepted a light and offered them smokes, which they declined, and he struck up some kind of conversation, as if it were just another quiet night in Santiago. The men nodded as Desi poured on the charm. As he spoke with animated gestures, the glowing end of his cigarette darted around like a firefly.

Camille had been oddly silent since the men outside had shown up. "He loved me, you know," she said finally.

It was a strange time to pick a jealous quarrel. "I'm sure he did." She wasn't actually sure. "But you were kids. Once he went to the States, he had plenty of choices."

"And you think he chose you from all the others? A Latin man could never love a skinny white thing."

Not that she minded being skinny or white. Cuban women, including Camille might have been exotic and beautiful, but Lucy's looks had launched her career. But maybe Camille was right in one way. Maybe she was too white and skinny to fulfill Desi's desires. "That would explain some things."

Camille paused. Lucy's reaction had exceeded her insult. "He treats you badly?"

Lucy covered the sting by tossing in a pinch of humor. "He hasn't been the most devoted husband a gal could wish for."

"He's a bastard."

"He's not good at keeping promises."

It was surprising how easily the romantic triangle collapsed when two women began to commiserate over the man who had caused them pain. Maybe the revolutionary ladies would figure out how to break this particular brand of emotional bondage, the power men had over a woman's emotional vulnerabilities. If anyone could do it, it would be a tough cookie like Celia, Haydée, Vilma, or Melba.

"He left us here to die," Camille said.

"Us?"

"My son and me."

Lucy lost all interest in what was happening outside. She should have been shocked by the revelation that Desi had fathered a child as a teenager, but based on what she knew of his adolescent behavior—or for that matter, his adult behavior—it wasn't much of a surprise. Predictable.

"It wasn't his." Camille retrieved the coffee pot from the stove and poured them each a cup. "It was another boy. I was pregnant. Desi and I knew each other since grade school. He felt bad for me. Promised to take care of us. He said he loved me. But he never answered my letters."

She'd always known Desi had had a sweetheart as a boy. It never bothered her. She'd had her own youthful romances. Camille had been nothing more than the love interest in Desi's coming-of-age story—until she became flesh and blood. "Maybe he didn't get them."

"Are you saying you took them?"

For the benefit of their unwelcome audience, Lucy recommitted herself to holding the appearance of a friendly conversation, relaxing her forehead and jaw and raising the hint of a smile. "That was before my time. God knows I'm not above jealousy. If I'd known him then, I'd have probably thrown them in his face." She offered Camille the next round of cigarettes, leaving the gold case open on the table.

"So how do you know... What did he say? Do?" Camille asked.

"He tried to pretend that you meant nothing to him, said it was just an adolescent infatuation, but I saw right through him. I'd go to bed wondering what you were like and whether he still thought about you."

"All that?"

"Storytelling is my business. If you ask me, I'll paint you a picture. Besides, it's not all an invention. Neither one of us was the last woman to catch his attention."

Camille looked Lucy deep in the eyes. "This isn't just some story, is it?"

She found her words sticking in her throat. "Not all stories are made up. I'm not saying you and I are the same. We're probably not even similar. We just had Desi in common."

"He was just a boy when I knew him."

"He's still just a boy. He just has more expensive toys now."

"But you want to save him," Camille said. "Me? I'd like him stuck here in Cuba like the rest of us. Maybe I'll go with you, and we'll leave him here."

"I've half a mind to take you up on that offer."

A small truck rounded the corner and pulled up in front of Desi and the two men. The side of the truck was painted dull white with Spanish writing Lucy couldn't read—some kind of business name, from the look of it. It blocked all three men from view.

She leaped to her feet, spilling coffee and nearly tipping the table, but before she made it to the door, the truck pulled away, grinding its gears and trailing black exhaust.

Desi was gone, along with the men who'd tailed them to Camille's house.

"They took him!" she cried. "They took him."

Camille joined her at the window, but there was nothing to see but a cloud of smoke spiraling up through the light of the single streetlamp.

Lucy pulled on her coat. "Who should we call?"

"There is no one to call."

She felt light-headed. She was hyperventilating. She tried to slow her breathing the way she did whenever she had stage fright. "What are you talking about? What about the police?"

"There's no need," Camille said. "The police can do nothing."

"Do you think those were Fidel's men?"

Camille had turned cold, as if she had ice water in her veins. "No. They were not."

Lucy whirled to face her. She knew. She'd been expecting this. They had walked into a trap.

"Who were they? Where are they taking him?"

"He's safe," Camille said. "He is with friends."

"Whose friends? Yours? No friends of ours would kidnap us."

Camille tucked her chin and wrinkled her brow. "You really don't know, do you?"

And then she did. What dumb-ass plot had Desi signed them up for? "What's going to happen to him?"

Camille finally took Lucy up on her offer of a cigarette, and then handed the case back to her. "Nothing. He will be taken to a safe place. Fidel will go looking for him, and that will be the end."

She just said he would be taken to a safe place. She twisted to tuck her cigarette case back into her purse, and it popped open and spilled its contents on the floor. "End of what?"

"La gloriosa revolución."

She threw her purse down on the table and knelt to collect the cigarettes. "You're telling me my husband signed up as bait for an ambush?"

Camille knelt, too, and helped her. "Maybe he had no choice. I have been told you were suspected of communism. Isn't that why you were forced to come here and spy on Fidel?"

She wasn't about to defend herself against Camille. Camille had purposely distracted her. She'd been played for a fool by both Camille and Desi, the CIA, and God knows who else. She was a goddam living legend, for God's sake. They were living legends. And that was it. It was the perfect setup for those God. Damned. Bastards.

"There is nothing you can do," Camille said. "You must go to the Americanos."

"At Guantánamo?"

"You will wait for him there," she said, as if she was issuing an order.

She was right, if for the wrong reasons. Desi would get himself killed, and she had to stop him. The CIA hadn't vanished; they'd purposely left them on their own. She needed to get help at the naval station, but she also needed to warn Castro without putting herself back in the Fidelistas' hands. No more cat-and-mouse game.

Asking for help getting to Guantánamo might put Camille in danger. She didn't enjoy the same protections that Lucy and Desi supposedly had—that is, if either the CIA or Castro lived up to their promises. Anything Camille might do to help would put her on someone's list.

"Is there a bus to Guantánamo?" Lucy asked.

"Sí."

"When?"

"Next one? Hmm. Morning. Five o'clock."

It sounded like a guess, but the point was that she wasn't getting on a bus before morning. She couldn't return to the Hotel Casa Grande, or she'd have to explain what had happened to Desi and what they'd been doing wandering around town in the middle of an armed uprising. Come to think of it, she could've asked herself the same question. No surprise they'd ended up in more trouble.

Now she had to figure out where to wait three more hours for the first bus. For all she knew, she was still being watched.

"Don't be stupid," Camille said.

Lucille didn't blame Camille for her belligerence. She hadn't cooked up this foolish scheme, and yet here she was, an accomplice. If she had a better idea, Lucy was all ears. "Pardon?"

"You'll stick out like a cow in a henhouse."

"I have to get to Guantánamo. Preferably tonight."

"You can ride with *un granjero*." She responded to Lucy's puzzlement by miming a hoe.

"A farmer?"

"Sí, a farmer truck. No one will recognize you if you take off all that paint from your face and cover your head."

"That's a great idea, but I don't know any farmers here."

"My Uncle Ricardo will take you." Camille rose to make a phone call.

Twenty-three long minutes later, another truck rumbled into the narrow street, its open cargo bin piled high with cabbages. Its brakes squealed as it lurched to a halt, engine chugging, noisy and dilapidated. Lucy supposed she'd blend right in with the locals.

Camille made no ceremony of goodbyes. She showed Lucy to the door and closed it behind her.

Uncle Ricardo waved to Lucy but remained in his seat, nursing the tired engine when it threatened to stall. She climbed into the grimy cab and made herself as comfortable as she could on the lumpy, torn seat. As soon as she closed the door, which took a couple of tries, Uncle Ricardo shoved it into gear and rolled away.

He was a weathered man with a couple of missing teeth. He smiled and nodded pleasantly, but he spoke no English. For the first half hour, they occasionally passed back and forth a smattering of words they could recognize in each other's languages, but Lucy was beyond tired. Despite the noisy, rough ride and the terrifying scenes playing in her head of Desi being beaten and tortured in Castro's prison, she dozed off.

HOME FAR FROM HOME

"Señora," said Uncle Ricardo, waking her. It was still dark—according to her watch, 4:30 a.m. He'd pulled up beside a bench sitting alone at the intersection of two dusty roads.

"I'm going to the American base." Lucy resisted the temptation to speak loudly, as if that would help her communicate. The man wasn't deaf, although the truck's engine wasn't exactly purring. "Guantánamo."

"Sí, Guantánamo." He pointed down the crossroad.

"Can you take me there?" She pantomimed a steering wheel.

"No, señora. *Esto es sólo para los norteamericanos.*"

"You're sure this is it?" She pointed in the direction he had indicated.

"Sí, Americanos."

There wasn't much else to do. She couldn't go back, not without making contact with someone from the navy. And God knew where this man was headed next. If she was close, maybe someone from the base would come along and pick her up.

Gripping the wooden dowel handles of her canvas bag, she slid rather ungracefully from the truck cab, feeling for the ground with her toes. As soon as she shut the door, Uncle Ricardo again pointed her in the right direction, tipped his straw fedora, and drove off, gears grinding.

Most of the surrounding area was cleared land, but the road to the base cut through a sparse forest of spindly trees. In some ways, this part of the island reminded her of LA, with scrubby brush and a mixture of palm and leafy trees, including some magnolias. Someone was bound to come along eventually.

With no one in sight at the moment, she made herself comfortable on the hard, wooden bench and lit herself a cigarette. She would have killed for a cup of coffee, but there was not so much as a dinette or even a service station in sight.

Before little Lucie was born, when Desi was in the army or when he was in New York with the band, she'd spent many lonely nights on her own. That had been in the comfort of her home. She felt small in the wide, empty space that stretched out around her. Hills rose gently on all sides, and she assumed she was alone in this valley until she noticed a few twinkling lights below the northern horizon on the slopes to the east and west. Others were nearby, even if too distant to know of her predicament.

This trip might have been a mistake. She'd half a mind to take Camille's advice. Desi had gotten himself into this situation, and he could figure a way out for himself. Except she didn't know whether that was possible. For all she knew, something terrible had already happened to him. He might have been a bastard to her, but it was her job to dish out the misery. He didn't deserve to be permanently maimed—or worse—by getting himself between a bunch of squabbling political zealots.

By half past five o'clock, clouds of gnats or mosquitoes were swarming around her. She had to swat at them constantly to keep them from eating her alive. It was time to take a chance on foot, although she had not the slightest idea how far she was from civilization. She set out in the direction Uncle Ricardo had pointed. Thankfully, Cuba had no man-eating beasts. The last thing she needed now were lions and tigers and bears.

She knew she wasn't really in the wilderness here—no more than a couple of miles from some kind of civilization, including the large American base that lay somewhere down that dark road—but from her current vantage point, she might as well have been lost in the woods. Yet strangely, her anxiety had subsided. She inhaled deeply, enjoying the fragrance of the damp morning air, perfumed by dewy grass and leaves. She hadn't experienced this kind of peace and solitude for many years. What mother ever did? Least of all a showbiz mom. She hadn't realized how exhausting all that attention was until this moment. Work, children, friends, Desi's antics, parties, benefits, and talk shows had consumed every moment of every day for more than a decade. She loved it. Lucy was who she wanted to be. But she still needed time with herself.

From beneath the sounds of chirping crickets and pests buzzing her ears, a low mechanical drone arose in the distance. She stepped into the middle road to check for the glimmer of headlights. If a vehicle was approaching, she couldn't see it, but the engine noise continued to grow louder, eventually turning into steady a beating she could feel in her chest.

Over the tops of the trees, two helicopters appeared, low and loud, blowing up the dust on the road. She pulled her wrap up over her mouth and covered her ears with her hands. The two helicopters circled in opposite directions and then positioned themselves facing her, spotlighting her with brilliant searchlights that made it impossible for her to see the hovering aircraft.

A loudspeaker crackled. "Please identify yourself."

She wondered how she was supposed to answer this question with all the racket from the helicopters, but she shouted out her name anyway. "Lucille Ball!"

No response.

She removed the pashmina from her face and looked up in the direction of one of the beams, so they could get a better look at her.

"Are you Lucille Ball?" The speaker was louder than the engines, heavily distorted.

She exaggerated a nod.

Another pause.

"Do you need assistance?"

Of course not; she often strolled in the Cuban wilderness. Once again, she nodded.

"Do you need medical attention?"

Thankfully, the answer to that question was actually no, at least for the time being. She shook her head.

"Ma'am, we cannot land our aircraft. We are under strict orders not to set foot in Cuban territory." One of the helicopters disappeared over the trees. Someone in the remaining helicopter continued to speak through the tinny loudspeaker. "Please proceed to the station gate, about seven hundred yards from your current position."

She nodded and waved to let them know she understood. It was comforting to know she'd been found, but she really hoped they'd move off soon and stop sandblasting her. Good thing she wasn't wearing a wig; it would have been long gone. Regardless, her hair had taken a beating in the downdraft.

She coughed on the choking dust, and the helicopter backed away and gained altitude until she could hardly feel its prop wash. It hovered nearby where the pilot could keep track of her progress.

When she finally arrived at the guard house, the helicopter landed nearby.

"Aren't you Lucille Ball?" shouted a young MP who couldn't have been more than eighteen or nineteen.

"That's me," she shouted. Her ears rang from the noise of the helicopter.

Another young man exited the helicopter and jogged up to her. "It's another five miles to HQ. We'll give you a lift."

"Can't someone drive me?"

The MP explained that they'd have to call for a ride. It could be an hour before someone showed up, and then she'd have the drive back, another fifteen minutes. She was welcome to wait.

She didn't.

The helicopter crewman led her to the waiting aircraft, holding his hand over her head as a reminder to keep her head down—more for show than safety, given that even on her tiptoes, the whirling blades still would have been several feet above her. Once inside, he handed her a bulky helmet and a headset, the final insult to her coiffure. It was a heavy contraption, but thankfully the earphones deadened some of the noise.

Once the young man had plugged the coiled cable into a panel behind the cockpit, she could hear the crewmen speaking to her through their microphones.

"Would you mind, ma'am, if we asked you what you are doing out in the middle of the Cuban backcountry?"

"It's a pretty good story," she said.

Unfortunately, the bone-rattling vibration of the helicopter, not to mention the smell of fuel and exhaust, made her reluctant to carry on much of a conversation. She gave them the Reader's Digest version of their adventures in Cuba and explained she'd come for help finding Desi.

The crewman handed her some coveralls. She wondered how on earth they expected her to get into them. "What's this?"

"Flight suit," he said. "For your protection. Regulations. Keeps loose-fitting clothing from catching in the machinery."

The men turned around so she could change. She tried to step into the suit with her dress still on, but finally conceded that it would be much easier to finish the job if she simply removed it. She zipped up the front of the navy blue coveralls, and the moment she strapped herself into the jump seat, the helicopter leaped into the air.

A couple of minutes later, it landed on an airfield outlined by red, yellow, and blue boundary lights and watched over by a tower topped with a revolving beacon. Dawn had begun to illuminate the scene. She rolled up her dress and stuffed it into her bag, then accepted the hand of the crewman offering to help her disembark. He again held his free hand between her head and the rotor, which was still winding down.

Inside a stark office lined with putty-colored steel filing cabinets sat a man at a steel desk adorned only by a desk blotter, a pen holder, a telephone, and a harsh fluorescent lamp that less than stylishly complemented the overhead fluorescents. She disliked the way office lighting turned her skin sallow. Thanks to her career choices, she'd managed mostly to stay out of such places.

The ensign behind the desk patiently listened to her story about how she'd ended up in Cuba and about Desi's disappearance. She started to explain what she suspected about the scheme to capture or kill Castro, but as soon as she mentioned the CIA, he asked her not to disclose anything that may be classified. Then he opened a drawer, pulled some papers from various files, and laid them in front of her, along with a pen.

"We'll need you to complete some forms."

Unable to break through the bureaucratic impasse, she quickly filled in half a dozen different forms, most of which asked for the same information—name, address, and social security number—and a US Customs form asking her to declare any Cuban goods she was bringing into the country.

"Can't I do this when I return to the States?"

"You are in the United States," he said.

"That was the shortest international flight I've ever taken."

"Yes, ma'am."

Not much different than the usual flat reaction to one of her attempts at extemporaneous humor. The ensign leafed through the forms, asked her to sign one spot she'd missed, and then squared them up, clipped them to the inside of a file folder, and asked her to wait before disappearing through a door. A few minutes later, he returned and showed her into another office.

She sat across from the man they referred to as the CO, the commanding officer. The nameplate on his desk said Rear Admiral Benjamin D. Mahoney. He also leafed through the completed forms, as if they contained any useful information.

"How may I help you, Mrs. Arnaz?" he asked bluntly.

Her celebrity was buying her no special cordiality. In her experience, government officials spooked easily. She tried a simple smile and folded her hands in her lap. "My husband and I are trying to get home."

"That should be simple," he said. "I'm sure you could book a flight from any airport on the island. There is one nearby in Santiago de Cuba."

"Castro has closed all the airports," she said. "He's expecting a US invasion at any moment."

"It's not our policy to discuss military matters with civilians."

She hadn't actually asked. "Can you at least help me locate my husband and provide us with transportation back to the States?"

"This is a civil matter. You should contact the US Embassy in Havana."

"But we were sent here by the CIA."

He grimaced, apparently not a fan of the agency. "Again, not a military matter."

Time for the damsel in distress angle. She scooted her chair closer and rested her fingertips on the edge of his desk. "My husband is missing. He might have been captured by the resistance."

"That's also a civilian issue. Have you contacted the Cuban authorities?"

"Well maybe you can help me with that. I need to contact Prime Minister Fidel Castro. He was our guide on the island."

He leaned forward on his elbows as if he intended to cross-examine her. "You're aware he's a suspected communist."

"Completely aware. We were sent by our own government."

"For what purpose?"

"I'm not entirely sure, but it's possible the president thought we could convince him to change his evil ways."

Mahoney smiled in that way humorless folks do when they want you to know they understand a joke had just been made. "We take communist incursions very seriously, ma'am."

"Then you must appreciate my predicament," she said. "Is there nothing you can do to help me find my husband?"

He wrote a note on one of the forms she'd filled in. "As I said, this is a civilian matter."

"But we're in a war zone."

He squared up her forms once again and secured them with a paper clip. "A civil war. At present, you are on US soil. The United

States is not at war with Cuba. This is not a military theater; therefore, our personnel have no jurisdiction in that country."

She could see that the conversation would continue in circles. It was so simple. The US government—their own government—had put them into this predicament. The navy belonged to the government. Therefore, it only made sense that the navy would help her rescue Desi, if not return home.

"May I call the embassy from here?"

Without commenting, Mahoney looked up a telephone number in his Rolodex and dialed, then passed her the receiver. She had to lean closer to prevent the short cord from dragging the phone across the broad desktop. After convincing the functionary on the other end of the line of her identity, she re-explained her situation.

"What is your current location?" the embassy official asked.

"I'm at Guantánamo Bay Naval Station."

"So you're in US territory."

"I suppose so."

"We can't provide assistance to you while you are in the US. Part of our mission is to provide assistance to American citizens abroad."

Talk about getting the runaround. "I am abroad. I'm in Cuba."

"You are not, in fact, in Cuba," he said. "You are well within the boundaries of US territory."

So the navy couldn't help her because they were the military and not responsible for civilians, and the embassy couldn't help her because she wasn't actually in Cuba. But Desi was.

"I understand," she said into the phone. "But my husband does need your assistance."

"He's in Cuba?"

"Yes."

"And what is the nature of his emergency?"

Finally getting somewhere. "He's missing."

"What was his last known location?"

"He was kidnapped in Santiago de Cuba."

"By whom?"

It was useless to explain the truth to another bureaucrat. Better to make it plain and simple. "I don't know. Anybody. Someone who didn't want us here, I suppose."

"Do you believe his life is in danger?"

"I haven't the slightest. Do you?"

"What did you say was your relationship to the missing person?"

Not wanting to sound too exasperated, she held the phone away for a moment and calmed herself, then continued. "He's the father of my children."

"And your spouse?"

"For the time being."

"We don't have anyone in your area. Cuba has been in a state of civil unrest for quite some time now."

"You don't say?" She was teetering on the edge of blowing her stack. She might not have been a real redhead, but this was one time she was pleased she'd cultivated a redhead's proverbial temperament.

She demanded to speak with Ambassador Bonsal. The official began to object, but she cut him off, recited her identity, and restated her demand, making it plain she would take no more of his bureaucratic nonsense. She was placed on hold for several minutes before the ambassador picked up.

"Mr. Bonsal," she said, "as you know, we came to Cuba at the request of our government. We were promised that we'd be safe."

"Mrs. Arnaz, I understand your frustration, but you are here under the auspices of another US agency with which the State Department has no affiliation."

What pigheaded bullshit. "No *official* affiliation."

"I cannot comment on such insinuations. I can only tell you that your best option is to contact a member of the appropriate agency and enlist their assistance."

"You are saying that my own government, our own government, is unwilling to come to the aid of Desi Arnaz, a well-known and popular US citizen who was sent here in service of that government? Is that what you mean to tell me?"

"I do not. What I did say is that the State Department does not have the resources to conduct a manhunt. We are a small mission of diplomats, not a military or law enforcement organization—and even if we were, we have no jurisdiction. I am happy to contact the Cuban government on your behalf. Prime Minister Castro expressed his willingness to do whatever was necessary to ensure a safe and productive visit. I'm sure he'll be distressed to hear that Mr. Arnaz is missing."

"I'm sure he already knows."

"Then I would assume he's doing everything in his power to locate him."

She hoped not, at least not until she could prevent a massacre. "What makes you so certain?" She looked at Mahoney as she was speaking to Bonsal, as if carrying on two separate conversations. "The last time I saw Prime Minister Castro, he was running around like Chicken Little, expecting the country to be overrun with GIs. Is that what's happening? Are we about to invade Cuba?"

Bonsal was silent.

"That is not an encouraging response from either of you."

"Either of whom?" Bonsal asked.

"You or the admiral here."

"Rear admiral," Mahoney corrected her.

"If our government were involved in any kind of activity in Cuba," Bonsal said, "neither I nor the military officers there at Guantánamo would be at liberty to comment."

"So yes?"

"I wouldn't jump to any conclusions," said the rear admiral.

Bonsal asked her to repeat Mahoney's words and then offered predictable advice. "I suggest you return to Cuban soil and seek help from the regime."

"Our own government sent us here. Why is no one willing to come to our rescue?" She widened her eyes at Mahoney to proclaim her frustration at both him and Bonsal as proxies for every bureaucrat responsible for their predicament. "What is wrong with you people?"

"I'm certain, Mrs. Arnaz, that the organization responsible for your safety and well-being has carefully planned your operation."

Things were really beginning to smell bad. "What do you mean, my operation?"

"I only know that you are here on a mission of cultural exchange."

It was pointless to continue. Bonsal was right: it would take a Cuban to find her Cuban. "And what if I'm next? I wonder what kind of statement our government is going to make when the two of us disappear in Cuba."

"That would be a matter for the president himself," Bonsal said.

"I don't suppose you could get him on the line?"

After a pause to let Bonsal wonder whether she was serious, she ended the call. She would need to track down either Fidel or someone from the CIA, and neither of those were about to happen while she was hiding out at the naval station.

She asked Mahoney whether it would be possible to get a ride to the nearest Cuban town. Predictably, he explained that US personnel were under strict orders not to enter Cuban territory. They would set not one foot past the border station gate.

"However," he said, "we do employ Cuban civilians on this base. We could ask one of them if they'd be willing to give you a lift."

"If that's the best you can offer, then I'd be grateful."

Mahoney offered her guest quarters as a place to shower and told her she was welcome to stay for as long as she wished. "It's not every day we enjoy the visit of a popular celebrity. The USO doesn't spend much time down here. I'm sure the men and their families would be excited to meet you, but this doesn't appear to be a good time for you."

No, not a good time.

* * *

SHE'D JUST SHOWERED when someone tapped on the door. She quickly pulled on the clean dress she'd purchased in Santiago.

A young Cuban maid entered with a tray of toast and tepid coffee.

"Gracias," Lucy said.

"Sí, señora."

"Do you understand English?"

"Sí, yes. That's how I was able to have this job."

"I'm Lucy. What is your name, dear?"

"I am called Angela." The girl curtsied. She was a stout girl with a cute, round face, no more than sixteen or seventeen years old. "If you wish more meal, Señor Mahoney said you are welcome to whatever you wish in the officer's mess hall. I can show you the way."

Lucy rolled up the dress she'd worn to last night's party and packed it in her bag, along with her other few belongings.

In the dining room, she surprised her hosts with her substantial and apparently not very feminine appetite. It occurred that she hadn't had much of a meal since leaving Santiago early the day before.

As Mahoney had offered, he'd arranged transportation for her.

"Where will he take me?" she asked.

"To Guantánamo."

"I thought this was Guantánamo."

"This is Guantánamo Naval Station, in Guantánamo Province," he explained. "The city of Guantánamo is about fifteen miles north of here. Most of the civilians who work on the base live there."

He was sending her off to Timbuktu. Alone. And with no Spanish. "Any suggestions about what I should do once I'm in town?"

"I'm sure Castro's people will be in touch shortly. Until then, I recommend you make yourself comfortable."

"Really. Maybe you can recommend a place to dine or some local attractions."

"Baseball is always popular…" It took a couple of seconds for Mahoney to catch her sarcasm. "I understand your frustration, and I wish I could be of more help. Exercise extreme caution. The people of Guantánamo Province are sympathetic to Castro, but there are pockets of resistance everywhere. Maybe keep your head down—try not to attract any unnecessary attention."

That advice certainly put her at ease. She'd blend right in with the locals.

* * *

THE YOUNG MAN who volunteered to drive Lucy to the town of Guantánamo explained how to take the bus back to Santiago, then dropped her off on the street where the bus would stop that afternoon. He was pretty sure the one bus that made the trip each day would show up around two o'clock that afternoon, but it could be later. She'd have had at least four hours to kill.

The feeling of helplessness was wearing her down. The town was tiny, and there wasn't anything to do but wait. She bought a pack of cigarettes and a deck of cards and found a sidewalk café with a table in the shade where she could pass the time playing solitaire while watching for the bus. Her spotty Spanish was useless, but fortunately, it was easy to pantomime a cup of coffee.

Caffeine had long since lost its punch. The moderate heat and long wait conspired to make her drowsy, and she was sure she'd nodded off at least once or twice, despite imagining every horrible thing that could happen to Desi.

She was startled from a twilight stupor by a man's voice.

"Señora Lucy?" The youngish man standing before her was unwashed, with oily black hair that glistened in the sun.

"Yes, that's me. Is it time to go?"

The man handed her a folded note. She found her glasses and read it to herself:

Dear Mrs. Arnaz,

These men will bring you to your husband. Please do not discuss this with any person other than those I have sent to assist you, including anyone in Santiago de Cuba who may be expecting your return.

IT WAS UNSIGNED.

She fired off all her questions in a single breath. "Who are you? How did you find me? Is my husband okay?"

The man whistled, and four other men appeared, all of them

carrying rifles slung over their shoulders. She thought about shouting, but that would be useless and might only make them angry. They wore street clothes, not uniforms, which meant they were almost certainly with the resistance.

The man offered his hand to help her up. "I am called Esteban. We will bring you to the place of your husband. You are protected by we."

Desi had managed to drag her into his goddam mess. When she got hold of him, she'd shoot him herself.

A WALK IN THE WOODS

After establishing, with difficulty, that she had no belongings other than what she was carrying in her bag—a concern that seemed atypical of kidnappers and therefore somewhat comforting—the men drove Lucy to the end of deeply rutted dirt road. After all passengers had exited and the men had collected rifles from the trunks, the drivers drove their vehicles off the road into thick brush. The men covered them with loose branches, hiding them as best they could.

Lucy had no idea where she was being led. For all she knew, they'd shoot her and leave her there in the jungle to rot. She'd placed herself in their hands. The ground was rough and although she wore flats, in the deepening shade she had to mind each step so as not to twist her ankle on a branch or rock. The concentration was as taxing as the physical effort of hiking. In several places, she needed a hand to climb up boulder steps or over fallen trees.

Her guides rarely spoke to her, and when they did, it was in Spanish. They weren't particularly interested in a direct exchange of ideas, and their messages were usually clear without translation. They wanted her to keep moving, and they didn't like being in this territory, where they were likely surrounded by Fidelistas. These mountains had been the revolution's sacred ground, and their only hope on a good day was to blend in. That might have been easy in a country where you couldn't identify friend from foe by appearance, unless you were traveling with a pale white woman with bright red hair and inappropriate clothing.

Exhaustion crept up and then knocked the wind out of her. She stopped dead in her tracks, breathing hard and coughing. She would have blamed three decades of smoking, but almost every one of her guides was smoking at one time or another, even as they huffed up the steepest slopes. She was, plain and simple, a lazy, pampered American, at least physically.

They crossed a creek, where two guides helped her negotiate waist-deep water over slick rocks. The swift current threatened to sweep her feet out from under her. Clearly disgusted with their mission, her guides held her by each arm and half carried her the fifty feet to the opposite bank. Another man reached down to tug her up the muddy slope.

They were emptying the water and stones from their shoes when the man in front, who'd been slashing their path through the brush with a machete, hushed them.

The two who had helped Lucy cross the creek tugged her down, insisting that she lie in the brush. She did so reluctantly, camouflaging herself among orchids, moss, and ferns. If not for the guns and who knew what kind of bugs and snakes, this would've been a gardener's paradise, full of flowers. Right in front of her nose, a snail about the size of a walnut, with a colorful shell banded in black, orange, and yellow, slowly glided the length of a large leaf, painting a glistening trail.

Although she couldn't see what was happening, she heard the thrashing sounds of branches parting and her guides greeting other travelers, possibly two or three. The newcomers seemed to be doing most of the talking, asking questions. She looked at the guide lying beside her for answers, but he waved her off and repeated the hush sign.

The men began to argue. She knew it was serious when she heard guns being cocked. The tone of the conversation couldn't have been any more clear in English than it was in Spanish. It was a standoff, thick with Latin machismo.

Her heart pounded. No one was supposed to die on this trip, especially not her or Desi. How could they have been so stupid as to walk into the middle of a civil war?

She pushed aside the snail on its leaf and sat up. Six men were leveling rifles at each other. Not wanting to startle them and get anyone shot, including herself, she raised her hand and waved until they spotted her.

"It's about time you showed up." She stood, disentangling herself from vines and branches caught on her clothes.

Her two guards remained prone, with weapons ready. At some point, she'd need to expose them or they'd set off a firefight. She tried to disguise her shaking by tapping her foot, as if admonishing the interlopers.

"My name is Lucille Ball." Her head was starting to spin. She forced herself to close her gaping mouth and breath slowly through her nose.

The men looked at each other like a bunch of nervous roosters. She couldn't tell whether it was because they didn't know who she was or because they didn't know what to do next. Probably a little of both.

Her guides shook their heads in disbelief.

"What are you doing?" one of them shouted at her. "Do you want to die?" He kept his gun leveled at one of the revolutionary army regulars, who in turn had his sight set on one of her guides.

"Maybe everyone should put the guns down before someone gets hurt," she said.

No one did.

"Can someone translate, please?"

One of her guides, a man named Javier, repeated her request to lower their weapons. Still no response. If anything, they seemed more nervous. Each time one man would shift the weight of his heavy rifle, nervous twitches rippled through the others.

"Keep interpreting for me, please," she asked Javier. "I am a visitor from the United States of America. My husband and I are television actors—"

"We know who you are," one of the revolutionary army regulars interrupted in Spanish. Javier continued to interpret. "We have come to rescue you."

"Dead or alive?"

It was one of the best lines she'd ever come up with on her own, and her audience couldn't follow. Maybe she'd get a few laughs when she told the story later—if she ever got the chance.

"You don't look like you need no rescuing," said the leader of the army regulars.

"If you mean these men haven't taken me prisoner, then you're correct," she said.

He pointed at her guides with his rifle's muzzle. "You are helping these *hijos de la gran puta*. We should shoot you now."

She caught herself taking a half-step back and then reminded herself to hold her ground. "I would prefer that you didn't."

"Then you should not have come here."

Confidence—at least the appearance of it—was the key to any good performance. She picked a dead leaf from her hair. "You think you know why we're here, but you really have no idea."

"You came to kill Fidel."

She crossed her arms. "I am certainly no killer, and neither is my husband. You must know my husband and I came here to make a film about the Cuban people and the triumph of the Cuban Revolution."

"So you're just on vacation. Making home movies." The soldier surprised her with his competent sarcasm, the first she'd either heard —or at least the first she'd comprehended—since they'd arrived in Cuba.

She substituted indignation for fear. "Maybe you should shut your goddam mouth and pay attention." And it appeared that shock was just the ticket. "Fidel invited us here."

"You're nothing but spies," shouted one of the army regulars.

"If you mean we came here to find out what was happening, then yes. And Fidel knew what was up all along. He's been leading us around by the noses since we landed, showing us the so-called achievements of the revolution."

Another of the army regulars, a woman, lowered her gun partway. "I do not understand. Are you for Fidel or against him?"

Cubans saw everything in black and white. At one time, Lucy might have done the same. It would have been easy to dismiss Castro as a communist dictator who'd seized power. But it wasn't so simple. "What we've seen looks like an improvement."

"You make no sense," another guide named Alvaro said from behind her. "Castro would never let you see how many people the revolución tortures and murders. He shows you only the vermin who feast on the spoils."

"Who do you mean by vermin, farmers and children?" she asked.

"They don't know enough to understand what Castro has done to this country," he said.

"You are the vermin," shouted one of the revolutionary army soldiers. He turned his gun on Alvaro, who pointed his weapon back in response. "Where do you come from?"

"My family has grown coffee for over one hundred years," Alvaro said.

"And uses slaves to pick it, so you can sell it to the North Americans for rich money."

Even in the middle of the jungle, Cubans couldn't resist a political argument. It was as common a pastime as dominos.

"We do drink a lot of coffee," Lucy said.

The woman soldier gave Lucy the evil eye. "You are so arrogant."

The longer this confrontation dragged on, the more difficult it became to maintain her composure. She swatted away a bug. "Because I admit we buy your coffee? I don't know about you, but when I need something, I buy it."

"You never consider the blood spilled for you to have those things."

She took a step forward, reclaiming ground. "You're right. I never do. I'm not proud of it. It just doesn't come up when I'm in the supermarket. There's the coffee on the shelf. I put it in my basket. I pay for it. I take it home. It doesn't come with a whole story."

The Cubans argued among themselves, both the revolutionary soldiers and her guides. Javier declined to translate, although it wasn't really necessary. The same tired debate.

"If you came to make a movie for your government, then you must be against Castro," said Esteban, the leader of her guides.

"I didn't say that, either. Our fellas in Washington don't know what to make of your Prime Minister Castro. They worry about things they don't understand. They figured we could get a look."

The woman soldier moved her sight off the guide she was covering and aimed her rifle squarely at Lucy.

"She is a spy," she said to her compañeros.

CALLING THE SHOTS

"Bullshit," Lucy said.

She had never liked looking into a gun barrel, even when it was a prop. Now she needed to pour it on. She lit up a cigarette. It calmed her nerves, with the handy side benefit of making her appear indifferent to her would-be captors' indignation. It was a Hollywood cliché, but these fellas already saw her as a character, so she was sure it would serve her purpose.

Just to add a little melodrama, she took a couple of drags and blew out the smoke while they hung on her expletive. "You should probably talk to Fidel—he's the one who brought us here." She pointed her thumb over her shoulder at her guides. "Maybe we came to get their story, too."

The woman soldier stepped up from behind the men and approached Lucy. "You either came to champion the revolution, or you came to spy on us. It can't be both ways." She lowered her rifle and held it across her chest at the ready, comically large against her petite frame.

"Why not?" Lucy said. "We're not on either side. It's the same for most Americans. We've got our own problems to deal with. Paying bills. Sick kids. Sick parents. Broken-down cars. Rent. Too much rain.

Too much drought. Too fat. Too skinny. Too many wrinkles. Cheating spouses. With so much crap to obsess about, how much time do you think we spend worrying about Cubans? Look at me. Do you know how much time I spend coloring my hair and doing my makeup so I can pretend to look ten years younger? It's a goddam waste of time, but it's how I make my living. Your fearless leader"—a swipe lost on the present company—"wants to convince Americans that he's some kind of savior, like the second coming of Jesus, expelling the demons from Cuba and creating a worker's paradise. For the most part, our people don't give a shit what you're doing down here. We're self-obsessed."

"This is what we've been saying," the woman said.

Now that she'd commanded everyone's attention, she was feeling more confident. Doing her best to ignore their weapons, she asked the woman her name.

"Carmen," said the woman soldier.

Next, she approached the leader of the army regulars.

"I am Hugo."

"Hugo is a nice name. Cuban names are beautiful, like music. I married a man named Desiderio Alberto Arnaz y de Acha. At home, everyone calls him Desi. Waste of a perfectly good name. We have a son, also Desiderio, and a daughter named Lucie. Non Lucille con mia, just Lucie."

"So you do speak Spanish."

"Not much, but I've been married to a Cuban for almost nineteen years. I had to learn to tell him off in his native tongue." She took another cigarette from her shoulder bag, and this time one of her guards lit it for her. This was enough to get the other men to follow suit, and soon they were all smoking while trying to hold their guns at the ready.

"Things can still go either way. Americans may suddenly become interested if your revolution affects their pocketbooks or the Russians decide to get in on the deal—or, frankly, if anything happens to me or my husband, in which case people will expect our government to do something about it, and you'll be right back where you started. I don't think Fidel will be so pleased with that." She put on her poker face. Inside, she was Jell-O. "I've seen enough of your revolution. Thank you for coming to my rescue, but I'm going with these men to collect my husband and go home."

"You are not giving orders," Hugo said.

Both her guides and Fidel's soldiers were becoming impatient. They shifted on their feet and looked at each other, perplexed.

"I cannot allow it," Hugo said. "We have orders from Fidel himself that we are to locate you and Señor Arnaz and return you to Santiago de Cuba."

She turned to Esteban. "And how does that fit with your plans?"

He responded by raising his rifle again. All the others followed his lead. They were back where they'd started.

She was old enough to be any of their mothers. Time to act like it. "If anyone starts shooting, most of you will be dead. Hell, I'll probably be dead. That will make for one really bad day for all of us. I'll tell you what. I want to get off this island and go back to my kids. After I'm gone, you can play soldier to your heart's content. Kill each other off, if that's what you want."

She stepped forward, going toe to toe with Esteban. "Do you have a plan to get us out of this mess alive?"

No answer.

She marched up to Hugo, maintaining the most assertive posture she could muster on soft ground and tangled brush. "How about you? What's your strategy?"

No answer.

"I didn't think so." She marched back into the middle of the gathering, ignoring the raised weapons, and pivoted to address them all. "This is my party. It's all about me, and I'm making the rules. Hugo, you're all heading back. Esteban, I'm going with you. Lead the way."

"We can't let them go," Esteban said, nodding toward the soldiers.

She threw up her hands. "Fine. Everyone shoot each other."

Esteban waved. "No. Not shoot."

They were as scared as she was, and starting to talk sense. She put her hands on her hips. "Then just what exactly do you plan to do with them?"

"We'll take them prisoner."

She whirled around, put her hands on her hips, and squared off with Hugo. "You heard them. Esteban says you need to surrender."

The revolutionary soldiers stood their ground.

"I don't think that's going to work," she said over her shoulder to Esteban. She turned to Hugo. "I don't think my friends here understand this situation. Give me a minute to set them straight."

Hugo nodded. She directed Esteban toward the brush. Esteban hacked a path for them into a spot several yards away from the standoff. One of the soldiers kept his rifle trained on Esteban.

"You want them to deliver the message," she said. "They are supposed to bring me back to Castro safe and sound. You need to make them believe you're happy to give the Americans an excuse to send in our troops. It's the perfect setup. He'll be distracted watching out for an invasion while your forces attack from the rear."

Esteban shook his head. "They will not go. They will follow and shoot us."

"Not if they don't have any weapons. Give them a reason to surrender."

She raised her voice so the others could hear. She stomped her foot and clenched her fists. "You can't beat Fidel. He's the hero of the revolution." With the language barrier, they'd never see through her melodrama.

She locked eyes with Esteban. He might not have understood every word, but he got the message.

They emerged from the brush. Right on cue, Esteban shouted an insult at her in Spanish and wrenched her arm behind her, waving his pistol with his other hand. She noticed he politely refrained from actually pointing the muzzle directly at her.

"This woman is a communist collaborator," he said. "We are taking her as our prisoner now."

The soldiers on both sides twitched, sweeping their rifles from one person to another.

"Do whatever he says," Lucy said. "He's serious."

"Hand over your weapons," Esteban ordered.

The Fidelistas hesitated to comply. Lucy remained silent and tried to look defiant so the Fidelistas would buy the story.

Esteban gestured again with his pistol. "You want her dead? You want to explain to Fidel?"

He had natural talent.

Hugo lowered his rifle and placed it on the ground. Esteban signaled one of the other guides to collect it. Once Hugo was disarmed, his other soldiers followed suit, handing over their rifles, sidearms, and knives.

Esteban issued another order. The regulars turned around and Esteban's men shoved them into a straight line, shoulder to shoulder.

"What are you doing?" she asked. "This wasn't part of the deal. You said you would let them go."

He tightened his grip on her arm. "It only takes one to deliver a message."

He was already going off script. The whole bunch of them, guides and soldiers alike, seemed determined to get themselves killed. "How many people need to die in this goddam country? You're all a bunch of shits."

He held the gun closer to her temple. A little too convincing. The only thing keeping her from hyperventilating was his tight grip around her waist.

"The woman will go." He waved the gun in Carmen's direction.

"Wait," Lucy said. "I want her to take a message to Fidel."

"What message?" he said.

She asked Javier to bring her bag. Esteban held her arms pinned to her sides, so she told Javier to find her pocketbook and open it and hold it within reach of her hand. She removed the brass wedding ring and gave it to Javier, indicating that he should give it to Carmen.

Esteban halted Javier. "What is this?"

She had never let that little brass ring far out of her sight. "A message from me to Fidel. He'll know what it means. He'll know I'm safe."

"Why not send the one you wear on your hand?"

She widened her eyes dramatically, exaggerating an expression of shock. "He'd see that as a threat from you, an act of defiance. You might as well cut off my whole finger and send it to him. He'd send in his whole goddam army."

"We are not barbarians." He spit on the leaves at her feet and waved Javier on, a little melodrama of his own.

The other guides releveled their sagging rifles to provide cover for Javier in case any of the soldiers decided to try to overpower him as he handed Carmen, the female soldier, the ring. Hugo shouted something in Spanish, and Javier poked her with the barrel of his rifle.

She stepped away a few paces, then turned and stood her ground.

"We will shoot one of your friends at a time until you start running," Esteban said.

She refused to move.

He fired his weapon. One of the revolutionary army soldiers fell to the ground, shouting. Esteban had shot him in the leg.

Lucy pressed her eyes closed. "I thought you said you weren't barbarians."

"There are many places to shoot a man," he said.

"Carmen," Lucy said, "you must go. You've done your duty." She counted on her tone to make her point. "Remember, give it to Fidel only."

Esteban ordered his men to each approach the soldiers and aim point blank.

Carmen took off running back the way they had come.

Esteban's grip on Lucy's arm relaxed.

"No one was supposed to die." She could no longer hold her composure. She was shaking.

"And yet thousands have," he said. "This man will not die. He will suffer, but he will not die."

He ordered Javier and Alvaro to keep their rifles trained on the revolutionary soldiers while the other resistance fighters, Pablo and Victor, tied their wrists behind their backs and then tied them to trees.

"What will happen to them?" she asked.

He shrugged. "The woman will send help."

"And what if she doesn't?"

"Then she is an idiot. They are all shit and deserve to die anyway. Do you think they would have not shot us if they'd had the chance?"

Lucy squatted down next to the wounded man. He was bleeding and obviously in severe pain. She demanded that Javier tie a tourniquet around the injured leg and tried to apologize to them all. But now they saw the woman they'd come to rescue as a traitor and only glared at her with twitching rage.

FOUND AND LOST

By the time they reached the resistance camp, Lucy's legs were wobbling. She had asked to rest many times along the way, and her guides had let her, but never more than a few minutes. They clearly wanted to put as much distance as possible between themselves and Castro's army, in case they'd be on their trail as soon as Carmen delivered her message. To make them harder to track, Esteban wouldn't let the men machete the brush. Lucy's shins were cut and bruised from banging into fallen branches hidden by the dense foliage.

They had tramped through the forest for most of a day, arriving after dark under a steady rain. Her soaked watch pendant had stopped. Lucy had lost track of time. She was on the verge of collapse. The only thing more painful than fatigue was her thirst. When they arrived at the camp, she was handed off to two soldiers who took her into a makeshift shelter, a lean-to made of canvas draped over a stick frame. She sat on the edge of the one and only rickety cot in the tent, and when one of the men offered her a canteen, she guzzled nearly its entire contents. There was still no sign of Desi.

When an American voice addressed her by name, all she registered at first was the sight of the khaki uniform and cap. The GIs had finally come to the rescue.

And then she recognized the face. "Comandante Morgan?"

"Yes, ma'am." He brought a blanket, which he unfolded and helped her drape over her shoulders.

She couldn't decide whether it was appropriate to say she was pleased to see him again. Unless Fidel had sent him to rescue them, his appearance didn't bode well.

"Is this your merry band?" she asked.

"We are far from Robin Hood's thieves. That appellation would be more appropriate for Castro and his Fidelistas, as they like to call themselves." He took a seat on a tree-stump stool and scrutinized her. "We don't have any fancy name."

That clarified his affiliation, then.

"I'm looking for my husband. You haven't seen him, have you? Good-looking guy. Cuban. Likes to sing for the ladies."

"I do know Mr. Arnaz's location, and I'm happy to report he's safe and well cared for. And he likes to sing for the fellas as much as for the ladies."

She took a long breath, in and out. "Who took him? What do they want?"

"Mr. Arnaz is at another camp a few miles from here."

She imagined him bound and gagged, tied to a tree like the Fidelistas they'd abandoned in the forest. "Is he all right?"

"He's well." Morgan paused. "In better condition than you are, ma'am. Sorry for the harsh journey, but we are doing our best to lay low."

She was desperate to see Desi, but another hike was out of the question, especially in the dark. She dribbled the last of the water from the canteen over her scratches, which burned from the salt of her own sweat. She could feel the heavy bags under her eyes. She set aside the empty canteen and crossed her arms in a self-embrace.

"Are you cold?"

She shook her head once. "Not cold. Tired as shit. Worried. Terrified. But not cold."

He offered her a cigarette lit from his own, which she gladly accepted. "I understand General Castro has been showing you all his glorious accomplishments."

"I thought it was Prime Minister Castro."

"Hero, prime minister, general, judge, executioner—it depends on where he's standing."

This fella needed to get his story straight. Fidel had made it plain what he thought about turncoats. "You were one of his loyal followers, a hero of la revolución. Or were you working for someone else all along?"

He got her drift. "I'm no mole. I'm a servant of the Cuban people. I came here to fight for them, to give them a shot at what we've got."

"And then you gave up the soldiering game and took up frog farming."

"Yes, ma'am, I did. A man's gotta feed his family. Fidel couldn't find a place in the government for a plain old Yankee like me. I can't complain. There's good money in frog's legs."

She was aching to lie down on the cot, but she wasn't about to show Morgan she was anything but irate with whatever game he and his accomplices were playing.

"I can't figure it," he continued. "Why did you agree to risk your necks to come spy on a bunch of cane and tobacco farmers? Your husband doesn't seem like the type to care much about this country."

"Can you blame him?"

"No, I can't." He ran his hand over his blond crew cut, as if he needed to shake loose a thought. "Not after the louses tore up his family. Which begs the question."

"Castro invited us. Uncle Sam gave us some personal reasons to take him up on it. And cameras have a way of catching things that aren't intended."

He gave her a hard look, and then framed her face with his fingers. "They also have a way of creating false impressions."

She returned his gaze with a wry smile. "Funny that most people think of photography as truth, isn't it? If it weren't for the deception, there'd be no picture business at all."

"You can make up the truth of your choice. Is that what you're doing?"

He still hadn't given her much of an idea what was happening with Desi. She wasn't even sure Morgan himself was in charge. So far, she'd seen only her guides, the two men who'd shown her to the tent, and Morgan. Only the sound of chatter outside suggested that there were many more.

She wasn't about to explain herself to a man who couldn't decide which side he was on. "To tell you the truth, I had no idea what we'd find down here."

"Imagine," he said. "Lucille Ball, big-time American spy."

"That's a little grand. There are plenty of spies. This island is teeming with them. I may be misinformed, but isn't espionage usually carried out in secrecy? Fidel guessed what we were up to right from the start. Without all the cloak-and-dagger, we're just a couple of observers."

Morgan held his cigarette vertically between his thumb and forefinger, studying it as it burned down. He'd hardly smoked the thing. He hummed his disappointment each time the column of ash toppled away. "You will tell the truth?"

"If you can tell me what the truth is. I'd be happy to share it with the folks at home."

He leaned forward on both his knees. While crushing out his cigarette on the dirt floor of the tent, he looked up at her. "You could make movies of what is really happening in our country."

"Your country?"

"I was stripped of my US citizenship. Apparently Ike himself was none too happy about an American joining the fight against their pal Batista, no matter what kind of bastard he was. Now Cuba's about all I have to call home." His jaw tightened. He ground the smoldering butt under his toe.

"I'm sorry to hear that." She was. It wasn't as if the man had taken up arms against his own country. He was no more a traitor than Hemingway, at least as far as she could gather.

"A lot of folks think you're here to help Castro—to beef up support for him in the States."

"I'm aware. We've run into a couple of angry mobs."

He nodded and put his feet flat on the ground and his hands on his knees, as if preparing to deliver some news. He'd already told her Desi was safe, but her heart started pounding anyway.

"Dr. Lopez has been arrested," he said.

It wasn't surprising. The doctor had known he was taking great risks. "What about his sons?"

"Fernando too." He started shaking his head before she'd choked out her next question.

"And Marco?"

"His injury was too severe."

Dr. Lopez's sons hadn't exactly been kind to them, but the thought of losing a child tore her to shreds. She'd been keeping up the hard-ass bit for days, stuffing her fear and pain down inside. All at once, what felt like a year's worth of tears flooded her eyes and cascaded down her cheeks.

She looked away from Morgan, blotting her face with a corner of the blanket. "I want to see my husband."

He refitted his hat and nodded, sympathetically pressing his lips together. "I'll escort you to Señor Arnaz myself."

She rubbed her feet. "I hope you're planning to drive."

"Yes, ma'am."

He poked his head outside and gave some instructions. A few minutes later, a man arrived with a bucket of warm water, some soap, and a reasonably clean cloth.

"I'll leave you to sooth your injuries and wash, if you wish," he said gently. "I'll ask the doctor for some salve for your cuts and scratches. We'll leave early, before the light."

He pulled the flap down over the entrance of the shelter as he left to give her privacy. She had the feeling she was safe, but it was still unnerving to think she was probably the only woman in a camp full of guerrillas, with at least three or four talking right outside. It didn't help that she could only make out bits and pieces of their Spanish.

"Señora?" A girl's voice spoke outside.

Lucy peeked around the tent flap and invited her in. The girl brought a change of clothes and a tube of ointment. She spoke no English and gave no indication that she recognized Lucy, which made sense. It was pretty unlikely this child had ever seen her on television. The girl waited patiently just outside the tent flap while Lucy applied the ointment and dressed in the fresh clothing, which thankfully was not another heavy khaki outfit. They had dug up a pair of dungarees and a white embroidered blouse in the Cuban style, along with a change of underwear. She could just imagine the cracks Desi would make if—or when—he saw her in these high-waisted underpants and oversized brassiere. At least it wasn't a pair of men's boxers. This was one advantage of being in a country that included women in combat, for better or worse.

OFF THE WAGON

The predawn ride to the other encampment was almost as unpleasant, if less strenuous, than the hike to the first. The jeep's laboring engine made it pointless to drive under the cover of darkness. The first time it backfired, Lucy nearly crapped her pants. The dirt road—more a trail—was deeply rutted, and the previous night's rain had reduced large stretches to thick mud that caught the jeep's wheels, causing it to lurch from side to side. At a couple of spots, Morgan asked her to take the wheel while he pushed and rocked the vehicle out of a deep rut, giving him a mud shower from the spinning wheels. By the time they arrived at their destination, he looked as if he'd crawled there on his belly.

This camp wasn't quite as makeshift as the first. Instead of improvised shelters, there were a few small buildings in various states of dilapidation, along with a better-maintained building that must have been the main house. Although it lacked a big red American barn and silo, Lucy guessed they were on a farm, or the remains of one. A few chickens roamed around, although that didn't mean much, since chickens were common yard animals all over Cuba, even in parts of Havana. Hills blanketed in green foliage rose on three sides, sheltering the place like a bandit's hideout.

Morgan led her to one of the shacks, where a group of men were engaged in the national pastimes: drinking, smoking cigars, and playing dominos. Lucy wasn't at all surprised to see who was telling a story. She didn't need to understand all the words to recognize a tale of sexual exploits.

Desi was facing away from the entrance, but the change in expression on the faces of the other men must have clued him in. He stood and faced her, hesitating to approach.

Lucy didn't disguise her disappointment.

"How did you find me?" he asked.

She found herself unable to step more than two paces into the room. "Try to control your enthusiasm."

He steadied himself on the back of his chair. "I bet you're happy to see me."

"You're drunk."

"It's not the first time."

The other men chuckled and hoisted their glasses. Desi didn't.

She waited for silence. "It's who you are." It was neither insult nor reprimand, only fact.

Desi's face went flat. Even the booze couldn't anesthetize him against that one.

No further words were necessary. Both were right. Both were wrong. Desi's hard work and skill had taken them to the peak of success, and his weakness had taken them to bottom of despair.

"I'd best wash up," Morgan said. He left.

"You are Lucy," one of the other men said, either oblivious to the confrontation unfolding before him or because he intended to break the tension.

Lucy paid no attention. "You can't help yourself. These people are using you, and you still have to entertain them."

"What else should—am I s'posed a do? Maybe I'm better off fish bait than for you to nag me alla time."

With no one else to lean on, she steadied herself against a whipsaw of sorrow and rage by pulling her arms in tight. "Maybe I shouldn't have come looking for you."

"To tell you the truth, I was expecting your friend Fidel." He balanced himself on his own two feet and lit up. As an afterthought, he offered her a cigarette, but she wasn't interested at that particular moment.

"And then what?" she asked.

"Who knows? Catch him. Throw him in prison, maybe. What difference does it make?"

She pierced him with a stiletto stare.

She'd been coerced into this trip. Lied to. She'd been told to take some pictures, meet Fidel and his cronies, shoot their film, and go home. No monkey business. No assassination attempts. No guns. No spooks. Get in. Get out.

Desi staggered and lurched into the table, scrambling the dominos. The other men snatched their glasses to save their rum. He fell to the floor, toppling his chair with him. Holding the chair legs for leverage, he sat himself up and remained on the floor like a dazed child.

All the cheating paled in comparison to this plot. "You goddam bastard. Were you planning to shoot him yourself? 'Cause you're in no shape to poke him in the eye, much less blow his brains out."

She turned and left, as if she had someplace to go.

He didn't follow her. And that made her both more angry and sad at the same time.

COURAGE OF FOOLS

*L*ucy found Morgan outside washing himself with water from a trough. He was soaked from head to toe. He removed his shirt and wrung it out.

"You mind?" he asked, pointing to a tree branch where he apparently intended to hang the shirt to dry in the sun.

She shrugged, and he hung the shirt by its sleeves to spread it as flat as he could. He was not a particularly impressive-looking man, pale, doughy in the middle, a little muscular around the arms.

He tugged on his gray combat jacket, complete with ammo pockets. The Cuban mountains weren't very high, but it only took a couple thousand feet to drop the temperature by ten or fifteen degrees. "Is that all the clothing you have?" he asked.

"Afraid so," he said. "We travel light."

She smelled meat and smoke. Someone was cooking breakfast nearby, maybe inside the main house. She looked for a place to sit. "That food for us?"

He stacked some crates for each of them and invited her to sit. "Yes, ma'am. Keeping the troops fed."

So far, she hadn't seen anyone she'd call a troop. Morgan and half dozen drunks weren't going to take on Castro's combat-seasoned fighters.

"You plan to lure him here," she said, "and we're the bait."

"You weren't part of the plan. We couldn't risk you spilling the beans. You're in no danger, though. You'll be long gone before the Fidelistas show up."

"The fact remains, you're using us to assassinate Castro."

"If he surrenders, he'll be captured and imprisoned."

Lucy had learned enough about Fidel to know he'd never surrender. It just wasn't part of his nature. He'd go out in a blaze of bullets, believing the whole time that he was invincible. "What if he doesn't?"

"We kill only to defend ourselves. This is war. We'll do whatever it takes to achieve our objective. The people supported the revolution because Batista threw out the constitution, stole an election, and murdered a bunch of kids just for telling him what's so. Fidel promised to put things right again. Instead, he's taking Batista's place."

A man wearing a straw hat stepped out of the house, holding a tin coffee pot and some wooden cups. Morgan exchanged some words with him. "This is Señor Luis Ruz. He is a farmer."

Luis removed his straw hat and held it over his heart. When Morgan explained who Lucy was, he gently squeezed Lucy's hand. His hands were small, wrinkled, dark, and rough, exactly as she would have expected from the hands of a farmer, but much bonier. His dark face was gaunt. He looked to be as fragile as his house, a little bent and skinny as a stick.

Luis called to someone inside the cabin and introduced the woman who emerged as his wife. She carried a large basket, which turned out to be loaded with a welcome meal of bread, scrambled eggs, and slices of reconstituted jerky. The couple looked to be around fifty or sixty years old, but it was difficult to be sure. Decades of laboring in the sun had desiccated their skin, etching wrinkles in their cheeks and deep crow's feet around their eyes. In the States, people called them laugh lines, a pleasant euphemism, but for these rural folks, they betrayed a lifetime of hard labor.

"Señor Ruz, how do you feel about the revolution?" Lucy asked.

Morgan interpreted.

"Sí, viva la revolución," Luis pronounced proudly.

She couldn't make heads nor tails of this situation. How could these people be both for and against the revolution?

She turned to Morgan. "From what I've seen, most of the people in this country support Castro."

"They did. Millions prayed for the triumph of the revolution. Fidel was their hero."

"Then aren't they—and you—just being impatient?"

"These people are poor, but they had food, shelter, bare necessities. Fidel gives speeches about education and medicine. Those are fine aspirations, but these folks are hungry. Kids are starving. Their parents are starving. Meanwhile, Castro continues to antagonize the Americans and make life more difficult for his own people, who he professes to love and care for."

Morgan asked Luis a question and then interpreted his response for Lucy. "It was okay for a little while. He said they used to have cows, but they ate them. For a while, the trucks brought tomatoes and oranges. They ran out of food in October. They eat what they can catch and grow some cabbages. I brought them this food." He sighed. "It's a miserable existence, but life was difficult before the revolution. Now it's worse."

Lucy blushed at eating the food this family had shared. "Maybe it's too soon to tell what Fidel will become."

"Better too soon than too late."

She took a nibble of scrambled egg. Considering the sacrifice these folks had made to feed her, and also that she couldn't be sure when she'd see her next meal, she wanted to savor every bite. "Do you know what's going on in your own country? Everywhere he goes, the crowds go crazy for him. This isn't like Batista. They're not afraid of him. They think Che is Jesus and Castro is his father."

Morgan threw a stone at a nearby tree. "Cubans sacrificed their kids' lives, their own lives, and just about everything else to win their freedom. He promised elections."

"Is that what you're using for ammo?" asked Lucy.

He slapped the crate under his ass.

"Maybe you need to have a little patience."

"He will never give up power."

"You don't know that."

"Begging your pardon, ma'am, but you're not a politician."

She snorted. "You mean I'm nothing but a redheaded clown. I know. I've heard it. The red isn't even real, which maybe makes me more of a clown. But I'm also a mother, and I wouldn't want my children to be harmed or worse unless I knew they were fighting for their lives. I think you Cubans are so accustomed to fighting you don't know when to stop. You're like a bunch of punch-drunk prize fighters. Everyone you meet is out to knock your block off, so you walk around with your fists clenched."

"Our people at home hate the communists," he said.

"We're not big fans."

"Then it shouldn't be surprising that these folks feel the same. We should welcome their resistance."

It was a fair point. If the Soviets got hold of the place, God only knew what kind of mess that would start. The hawks would have a field day and end up reducing the planet to ashes.

"You're right," she said. "I'm not a politician or a general. So don't you think we should have a say in whether we participate in your coup d'etat?"

"I was under the impression that you did."

She looked away. She'd thought Castro had been dragging them around by the ears. This was the real setup, and Desi had been in on this bullshit from day one. The CIA had put him up to it, and for some reason he'd kowtowed. She resented the manipulation. The bastards had made a monkey out of the both of them, and these jokers were doing a fine job of doing the same to themselves.

"You're a bunch of fools," she said. "Just how many soldiers do you think Castro is going to show up with?"

"I'd imagine he'll send a column after us. Maybe two, three hundred."

"Against how many of you?"

"I'd rather not disclose that information, especially not out in the open. As they say, 'Loose lips sink ships.'"

Her queries were cut short by the arrival of a Chevy Bel Air that had seen better days. The bumper, which had been tied on at the right end with thick wire, possibly old coat hangers, squeaked and scraped. Several men jumped out and approached Morgan, chattering in Cuban speed-Spanish. They nodded politely to Lucy.

Lucy couldn't make out a single word. Morgan asked them a couple of questions, to which they together answered only, "No."

Morgan sat back. "We'd planned to get you out of here before Fidel shows up."

A chill ran down her spine. "Planned to?"

"The rains in the mountains have been mighty heavy. A bridge washed out a couple of days ago."

"So how do you plan on getting us out of here? I don't suppose your little outfit has its own helicopter?"

"Nothing so fancy," Morgan said.

"We'll have to go back the way we came."

"And run smack into the Fidelistas?" He shook his head.

"How about we make a deal with Castro? That way, no one gets shot."

"You mean maybe no one gets shot today. It'll take a couple of days to run us all through his kangaroo court." He stood and leaned on the edge of the water trough. "No, ma'am. These men would rather die fighting than volunteer to face a firing squad."

Castro wasn't about to charge in, guns blazing while America's Sweethearts were in the line of fire. His greatest fear was an American invasion, and he was smart enough to know the limits of provocation. There had to be a way to get out of this fiasco and possibly save the lives of these misguided misfits along the way.

"What scheme is she hatching now?" Desi was shambling up behind her.

Lucy fidgeted, sorting through the contents of her bag. Besides a damp change of clothes, she had only a few personal items with her: a lipstick and her compact, a few cigarettes, and a pack of paper matches. The matches and cigarettes were too waterlogged to salvage. She thought about hanging the clothes out to dry, but she wanted to believe she wouldn't be there long enough for it to make a difference.

"I can't believe you got us into this shit," she said to Desi. "When you make a bad decision, it's a big one."

He heel-kicked one of the unoccupied crates. "How is this my fault? This is because of you. I never joined no communist party."

"And it had nothing to do with you being Cuban."

"I was born here. I didn't choose."

"You can't choose your family, either."

"Maybe you should learn to think for yourself."

"You're a communist?" Morgan asked, apparently oblivious of Lucy's earlier troubles. Not surprising, considering his young age.

"She ain't no communist. She's a dictator." Desi invited himself to share Morgan's makeshift bench, then leaned back toward Lucy. "For someone who claims she's no soldier, you sure look like one."

"Just like the army days," he said.

She grimaced. "Is that what you wore while you were cleaning bedpans at the VA hospital, combat fatigues?"

"Listen, I went through basic training just like all them other guys."

"So now that you're suited up, what's your plan?"

He helped himself to the food. Just as well. The black coffee might sober him up. "This is my plan." He pulled a flask from his pocket and poured a slug into the coffee. "I'm finished with this business."

She didn't even bother to show her disgust.

"William," she said to Morgan, once again adopting a maternal tone, "we're just a couple of showbiz folk. We aren't politicians, much less soldiers. If you're asking us to join your fight, you're wasting your breath. Even if we could understand who's right and who's wrong, we're not mercenaries. We have our own lives, our children, our work. We didn't come here to fight your battles."

"And we wouldn't ask you to," Morgan said.

"Then we need to leave."

"Too dangerous now. I'll get you to Guantánamo as soon as it becomes safe to travel."

"You mean, as soon as you know Fidel's men won't find us before he runs into your ambush."

"As soon as it's safe," he repeated grimly. "You'll have to trust me."

She was speechless.

Desi was not. "You must be joking. Trust you? I don't trust nobody in this shithole country. Let me tell you something. When I was a kid, this was a nice place to live. One revolution after another, and nothing gets better. You can all go fuck yourselves and your revolutions."

When Desi was drunk, he seemed free to speak both their minds. Lucy was happy to let him. She didn't have the energy, and she needed to think.

In Hollywood, everyone wanted to be your friend, hoping your celebrity would somehow rub off on them. But here, their celebrity took on a nefarious purpose, used by one side against the other. Enough. She would not carry on her conscience the death of any human being—least of all an idealist who seemed determined to make things better for his people, a man whose intentions were noble, even if his actions were misguided. Fidel had served his purpose, but that didn't mean he needed to die.

Oh God, Fidel was too smart to fall for such an obvious trap. If anyone was going to die, it was the resistance fighters. Fidel would undoubtedly march in himself, leader of the rescue mission, while his men surrounded the camp and killed every last one of them. The thought nauseated her.

There had to be a way for her and Desi to get out of this mess. A bloodbath would be a terrible way to end a vacation. She'd have to make Morgan understand that he and his ragtag militia were on a fool's errand.

"Castro's got a trump card," she said. "The Russians. They're his insurance. It's like he's booby-trapped the entire country. He's opened the door to the Soviets just enough that his disappearance will result in a Soviet takeover. If your objective is to stop the communists from overrunning the country, then you want Castro to stand in their way."

"We're prepared for the consequences," Morgan said.

"How heroic of you," she said. "Do you speak for all Cubans? I hate to tell you, but you don't look or sound like any of them."

"This is true," Desi said.

She stood and leaned against a tree. A good femme fatale needed to look detached. "You're never going to get your democracy by murdering your political opponents. You want to be civilized? Then act like it. It's time to stop killing each other."

"I appreciate your concern," Morgan said, "but it's too late."

"Make Fidel put his money where his mouth is," she said. "He says he'll hold elections as soon as legitimate political parties establish themselves."

"And he defines legitimacy. It's a masquerade he puts on for the Yankees."

Morgan had adopted Fidel's language. In the war against Hitler, "Yankee" was a moniker of gratitude and pride. Fidel had turned it into a slur.

"What he means is your new pal Fidel is full of shit," Desi said.

Morgan hadn't shown himself to be a sophisticated man, but he was courteous. He couldn't know what kind of everyday language she and Desi were accustomed to, no matter whether they were angry or elated. For her, it was a habit she'd developed to throw off the instincts of Hollywood's alpha males.

"You know damned well what he means by legitimate," she said. "No guns."

Either tired of sharing a meager perch with Desi or disgusted by Desi's volatile breath, Morgan went to check his shirt. "He'll never accept any opposition."

"He made the promise in front of millions," she said. "And despite his chest-thumping, he's afraid the Americans will end his revolution. He invited us here to show our own people that there was no reason to worry that Fidel would turn Cuba into a Soviet outpost. Let's put him on the spot."

"This is why you aren't the writer," Desi said. "Nobody would believe your cockamamie stories. He's not going to come up here looking to make his picture."

"I wouldn't bet on it. He'd love to document a rescue. But that's not going to happen."

"How do you plan to stop his army from showing up?" said Morgan. "For all we know, they're already halfway here."

She put her hands on her knees. "We'll go to him first."

Morgan crossed his arms, shaking his head.

"What if we can strike a bargain? Get Dr. Lopez and Fernando out of prison and back Castro into a corner, to boot?"

He stopped shaking his head and waited for her to explain herself. Meanwhile, Desi continued shaking his head, pretending to only half listen—so talented at silent disparagement.

"As far as Castro knows, we're captives," she said. "You've got us, or at least Desi. He's got Lopez. Let's get his attention by offering him a prisoner swap."

He rubbed his forehead in disbelief. "You seen too many spy pictures."

She mocked his tone. "I don't watch no spy pictures." She had Morgan's attention, and that's what counted. Desi had made himself a pawn, and she'd let him play the part. "I'll go to Santiago. I'll tell Castro I was sent to offer a deal. You'll swap Desi for the Lopezes, and your people will declare yourselves a political party."

"I don't see him buying that story," Morgan said.

"He will if you aren't armed."

"You want us to march into Santiago de Cuba," Morgan said, pointing somewhere into the distance, "surrounded by Fidel Castro's army, totally defenseless? It's a suicide mission."

"We'll make an event out of it. He's counting on me and Desi to take some of the heat off him from the States."

Lucy could see that Desi, despite his drunken fog, was watching the story unfold as if he were directing a scene. He knew damned well that whatever happened afterward, they needed to give Fidel a good reason not to come in guns blazing.

Morgan paced.

"Why are all of you so determined to get yourselves killed?" she burst out. "This is a fight you can't win. You know it. If Castro could outmaneuver Batista at a ten-to-one disadvantage, you and your farm boys don't stand a chance. Your movement will die with you. No martyrdom to set off another revolution—and there might never be another election in Cuba. In fact, you're just proving his point. Political parties don't campaign with bullets."

It was a foregone conclusion. They had no fallback position. Castro knew this terrain better than anyone. It had been his base of operations for two years. For all they know, they were already surrounded.

Morgan must have known that.

"How will you get to Santiago?" he asked.

"You'll take me there," she said, "and not on foot. I've got enough blisters. He's never going to expect us to show up like we're stopping by for coffee and strudel. You're now officially my hero. You found me and smuggled me back out of danger, but Desi is still in captivity."

Desi held up his flask. "I'll tough it out."

She didn't even glance at him. "Once Fidel agrees to the swap, we'll need a messenger. You'll need to get some of your boys down there. No guns. They'll have to blend in but stay close. We'll meet in the main plaza, in front of the church."

"Plaza Carlos Manuel de Céspedes," Morgan said approvingly. "We can relay a message back to the camp in a couple of hours."

Lucy nodded. It could work. If Carmen had delivered the ring to Fidel, he would trust her—and he'd be patiently waiting in Santiago de Cuba.

WINNERS AND LOSERS

Castro wasn't present when they pulled into the plaza. Morgan, who was well known throughout the country as El Americano, the famous Yankee Fidelista, had no trouble assigning a soldier to send word. The concierge from the Hotel Casa Grande implored them to take seats on the hotel's veranda, where they were served more than ample refreshments.

When Castro arrived, he demonstrated great concern for Lucy's well-being, questioning every aspect of her physical condition and the treatment she'd received during her captivity. She assured him that other than a few scratches, bruises, and bug bites acquired on the trail, she was well and had been treated with complete respect.

Castro congratulated Morgan on his rescue effort and then proceeded to ask for every detail. Morgan demonstrated great story crafting skills as he detailed how he had stalked her captors back to their camp, easily overpowered a drunken sentry, and guided Lucy to safety. Castro asked Morgan whether he'd been harmed, and he explained that although he'd been held at gunpoint for several hours, he had not been physically injured in any way.

When he finally asked how they escaped, Lucy took over the account.

"As you can see," she said, "they're still holding Desi."

"That will be resolved soon," Castro said. "Now that you know the location of their encampment, we will carry out a mission to recover him. We shall destroy his captors."

"Prime Minister Castro," she said, "I'm terrified of what could happen to Desi. He's a bastard, but he's my bastard, and the father of my children. I'd prefer that you not take any drastic action that could get him killed. In fact, that's why I was sent back with Comandante Morgan."

Castro narrowed his eyes. He had obviously already been anticipating a proposal.

She carefully avoided any military language. "Those people up in the mountains are just like the folks we met in Sancti Spíritus. They're impatient. Hunger and illness are wearing them down."

"You sound like a sympathizer."

"I'm not taking sides," she said. "They've ask me to convey a message. They'd like to take you up on your offer."

"I never made an offer."

"You did—to establish legitimate political parties in preparation for open elections." She paraphrased his own words for leverage. "They wish to declare themselves the Reform Democratic Party."

He dismissed the suggestion with a sweep of his arms, knocking a glass to the floor. "A political party does not arm themselves against the recognized government of the country."

"They know this. They carry weapons out of fear, and they're willing to surrender them and accept a charter from you yourself recognizing them as a peaceful political organization." She was improvising, reading Fidel and prying at the openings he himself had been establishing. If it hadn't been a life-and-death situation, she might have paused to delight in her negotiating tactics.

He asked Morgan's opinion, but the rescue cover story gave Morgan an alibi to declare ignorance.

"They are kidnappers," Castro said. "Even in your country, this is a crime punishable by death."

He might have started the revolution with noble intentions, but the long, bloody fight had warped his sense of justice. It was time he realized death could not solve every problem.

"It was a foolish action," she said. "However, I believe it was done out of fear and not for extortion. They were hoping to get their voices heard, and like you, they thought that Desi and I could be messengers. What I learned is that they are just as loyal to the revolución as you are, just as determined to maintain Cuban independence."

"By overthrowing the government?"

"A democracy has detractors. By adding their voices to what you'd call the political discourse. Isn't this what you love most, the open and free debate? On the steps of the university, you told us how Batista silenced his political rivals. These may not be students, but just like those young people, they have hopes and dreams. What they want is to participate." She was rubbing his nose in his own words.

He laid his hand on the table, tapping out his words like Morse code. "I will not discuss any proposal to recognize them until they release your husband. I don't understand why you would come to me on their behalf as long as they are holding Desiderio prisoner."

"Because they offer an easy solution. As a symbolic gesture, they're asking to swap Desi for Dr. Lopez." She placed her hand on top of his. "You know that Dr. Lopez and his son are not soldiers. Dr. Lopez, like you, is an intellectual. He doesn't deserve to be locked in that horrible prison to rot. He's already suffered a terrible loss while trying to protect me and Desi. Aside from the exchange that these people are requesting, I'm personally asking you to be lenient."

"If I don't punish conspirators, Cuba will degenerate again into a haven for criminals."

"He was no more conspiring against you than any politician conspires against another. You promised elections. Wouldn't you then expect people of differing opinions to organize and support candidates? Violence begets violence. You're the victor, which means only you have the power to break the cycle."

He was running out of arguments. Unless he was planning to keep her and Desi from reporting back to their sponsors in Washington by throwing them in prison, too, he had little choice but to demonstrate that he fully intended to live up to his promises. It wasn't a matter of political convenience or promises made to be broken. It was defense against the threat of annihilation.

He turned again to Morgan. "Comandante, what do you think?"

"I cannot be certain," Morgan said. "It could be a ploy. I recommend extreme caution."

Castro's posture softened. He blew out a long breath before announcing his decision. "I will accept the exchange." He leaned back and lit a cigar—his tell, his habitual way of declaring himself in charge. "My soldiers will bring Dr. Lopez and will await the arrival of the captive. They will be armed. The captors themselves will come unarmed. At the slightest sign of deception, we will open fire. I'm afraid that could put your husband in grave danger. Are you and he willing to accept that risk?"

"I'm confident." She wished she was.

"Tomorrow, in the plaza. We'll meet at noon when there are few shadows." He had a flair for drama. He knew it and enjoyed it. "Comandante Morgan will see to your care. I assume you have an agent lurking who will relay your message."

She nodded. "Please allow me to communicate with that individual in complete privacy and with no fear for his safety."

"I give you my word."

She hoped he took his word seriously. The entire plan hinged on it.

Castro excused Morgan, sending him to the hotel to wash up. She would have to stick to her story.

"You and Señor Arnaz were not abducted together."

He was going to try to poke holes in her story. She tried to anticipate where he was heading. "I tried to find you, but you were busy, so I went to Guantánamo for help."

"Yet they were unsuccessful."

"They didn't try. The base commander, a fella by the name of Rear Admiral Mahoney, he said it was a civilian matter. I tried contacting Bonsal, too, but he said the embassy wasn't equipped for a rescue mission. He said I should speak with you."

"And here you are," Fidel said. "You evaluated your options. You assessed your resources. You made your plan."

He hadn't bought her story. "Plan?"

"You see, Señora Arnaz?" he said.

She looked up at him questioningly.

"You are indeed a skilled negotiator after all."

FAIR EXCHANGE

The next morning, the resistance fighters were to arrive in Santiago de Cuba. Rather than making themselves a potential target by rolling into town as a unit, they were supposed to trickle in, gradually gathering in the plaza for a peaceful rally. Morgan hadn't told her how many to expect. It could have been dozens or hundreds, for all Lucy knew.

She planned to encourage Fidel to speak, knowing full well he could ramble on for hours. She hoped he wouldn't take advantage of her clever plan to organize his own ambush. This spy stuff made her head spin, with all this "one knew that the other knew that the first one knew…" It was enough to give her a migraine. There was no way to know for certain who might make a wrong move, although if she were laying odds, she'd give the win to Fidel. He'd already beaten impossible odds and come through without so much as a scratch. If he hadn't won the loyalty of so many who followed him into battle, she'd have guessed his reputation as a military leader was more myth than fact.

Still, if anyone faltered today, bloodshed was inevitable. That wasn't part of the bargain. She wasn't about to spend the rest of her life lamenting her part in a massacre. She had no Shakespearean ambitions, especially not when real lives were at stake.

The protestors they'd met in Sancti Spíritus had confronted Fidel in the open, and he'd charmed them into capitulation. This was different. She didn't trust the resistance fighters to show up unarmed. One shot would set off a firestorm that wouldn't cease until one side or both had been reduced to a heap of corpses. Castro would continue his campaign against the counterrevolutionaries, no doubt, but on that day, she wasn't going to play a role in a massacre.

This situation had to be more complicated than it looked. It was too obvious a trap. Fidel obviously knew from experience that a small band of determined rebels could start a movement, and he clearly didn't plan to let that happen. For all she knew, the revolutionary army had already surrounded them and were waiting for the right moment.

But Fidel Castro wouldn't risk her life or Desi's. He was determined and obsessed but not a psychopath, and he knew their deaths would unleash a wave of resentment that could tip Eisenhower into launching a full-scale invasion. To Americans, killing her would be as serious a crime as killing the queen would be to a Brit—prima donna logic, perhaps, but she needed to pin her hopes on something to keep terror from reducing her to a sobbing wreck.

Whatever was happening, it was sure scaring the shit out of the locals. It wasn't doing much for her own peace of mind, either. Everywhere she turned, Fidel's rifle-wielding soldiers clustered on street corners. Overnight, Santiago de Cuba had transformed from an oversized, sun-washed Caribbean village into a militarized encampment.

At the Hotel Casa Grande, Lucy had enjoyed a warm bath, a lovely dinner, and clean, crisp linens to sleep on, while Desi had spent another night in a shack, most likely under a leaky roof. It wasn't full retribution for manipulating her, but it was a start.

After breakfast, she walked the short distance to the church and found a spot to stand in along the terrace railing, overlooking the plaza. It wasn't long before Fidel joined her. She'd expected he'd be watching for her.

"This is not what you expected." He looked worn. He clearly hadn't slept recently, and he could've used a bath.

"Predictability is death to comedy," she said.

"Is this situation funny?"

"There's some funny business going on."

He offered his puzzled expression, which had become an inside joke between them.

"It means someone is up to no good."

"Yes, I see. I already know."

"About the setup?"

"Of course. Nothing happens in politics that is not some kind of gamesmanship."

"You took a big risk by coming here," she said.

"Not so much."

She shrugged. "Of course, you have many soldiers with you."

"However, this must not turn into a gunfight. Once shots are fired, we'll be at war again. It's time to put combat behind us. Cubans must no longer shoot Cubans. It makes us weak and vulnerable."

"I can't tell you for sure who's on the welcoming committee. I didn't want any part of it."

"You are a good person," he said, "a friend of the revolution."

"Don't broadcast that too widely," she said. "Let's call me a friend of the Cuban people. Although it doesn't much matter anymore. I'm already in hot water at home. Just by being here, the press will paint me as a Red sympathizer. It's a damned good thing Desi and I have already had our success. I wouldn't be surprised if they run us out of the country."

"You're always welcome here. This is your husband's homeland."

She wrinkled her nose. "I wouldn't be so sure of that."

"Because he is a collaborator?"

"Let's just say he's not an innocent bystander."

"He is a man of contradictions. First he saves my life, then he would watch someone else take it."

"Desi may be a selfish bastard, but he's not an assassin. He's thinks you'll be exiled."

"It's possible."

"You're not convinced," she said. "Neither am I. Does it help to tell you I've had nothing to do with it?"

"It helps you. And that is my wish. No matter what the outcome, I believe you're not responsible."

"What if we were sent here to give you a false sense of security? For all you know, the invasion's already underway."

"I know that it is," he said. "Traitors are everywhere, and they are funded by your government. This is the game of the so-called Cold War. The North Americans and I agree on one thing—I disapprove of them and they disapprove of me."

"You know perfectly well why you didn't get a warm welcome in Washington."

"As you say." He held up his hands like claws and opened his eyes wide. "Red scare."

With that hairy face, he pulled off a reasonably good bear impression, but he looked more comical than threatening. If he pulled that shit on TV—maybe on their variety show, if it ever happened—John Q. might actually warm up to him. "You have your values, and you're free, even in the eyes of North Americans, to hold whatever opinions you wish. But don't expect to be loved up there."

"We believe everyone is entitled to his own opinion, as long as it's the same ours." He chuckled at his own quip.

She smiled. "So you do have a sense of humor."

"I am getting one. How else should I cope with so much fear and hatred?"

Physical fatigue was catching up with her. That long walk in the jungle had probably done wonders for her legs, but at the moment, she was all aches and pains. She leaned over to rest her forearms on the wrought iron railing.

Fidel's face and demeanor had become familiar. He'd cultivated a predictable persona. Politics didn't differ that much from show business. Politicians might have had access to guns and tanks, but celebrities could shape popular opinion and behavior in ways they didn't recognize themselves. Ozzie and Harriet, Ricky and Lucy, Ralph and Alice—typical American families.

"Do you really think the Russians are planning to protect you out of the goodness of their hearts?" she asked. "They've taken over one country after another. Cuba will be easy picking."

Fidel began to pace, and she followed.

"I don't think so," he said, with a surprising whiff of uncertainty in his voice. "Eisenhower and Khrushchev are too smart to start World War III over Cuba. We don't have oil. We only grow sugar, tobacco, and coffee."

"What you have is a great location, and as they say, location is everything."

He pounded his fists together. "Cubans won't have patience for the Soviets and the Yankees to fight out their differences at our expense. They must all go." He shooed away the imaginary adversaries with all ten fingers.

She raised an eyebrow. "I hate to tell you this, but the French, the Italians, and just about everyone else in Europe felt the same way, and we still turned their countries into battlefields."

"We'll see," he said. "I can only speculate. Cubans stand with the revolución. We have re-established a legitimate government, already recognized by your president. Armed opposition will be treated as criminal activity, whether from within or without."

"From without? I hope you're not planning to throw the entire US Army into prison."

"We are a little short of space." She'd come to notice that whenever Fidel paused to think, he took three quick successive puffs on his cigar, like smoke signals from his brain. "We have few defenses against the US other than the collective indignation of global leaders."

"If you seize more American property, they may not care much about what anybody else thinks. Our country has sacrificed thousands of lives and millions of dollars protecting the rest of the world. It makes us a little indifferent to international opinion. Americans like to win. Give us a reason to think we've got the upper hand, and we'll back down. Just make sure you don't overdo it."

"Our friendships will protect us."

"You said you don't want the Yankees and the Soviets fighting on your soil. There won't be anything left."

He raised his palm. "You misunderstand. I mean our friendships, not our friends. We would not ask our Soviet comrades to fight on our behalf, but perhaps our solidarity will deter your government. As you say, the North American people would not support a devastating war so close to home."

"So what's it gonna be? Is there going to be an invasion?" she asked.

"Whether real or imagined, a crisis is the best time to separate allies and enemies."

They paused and enjoyed a gentle breeze. She cleared her lungs with a deep draft of marine air. Political intrigue had proven surprisingly invigorating.

"What now?" she asked.

"Patience."

Dozens of people on foot were assembling in the square—men, women, entire families. Some were passing through, while others found places to congregate. One man might be a Fidelista, and the next could be a communist or a Batista sympathizer. The invisible enemy was the modern soldier's dilemma.

"You are nervous," Fidel said.

She sidestepped away playfully. "I'm standing beside a marked man."

"You have extraordinary courage."

"I'm making a bet, and I don't know whether it'll pay off. Maybe I'm just a stupid broad."

"Whoever might have told you such a thing has no respect for human dignity."

"Hollywood isn't known for humanitarian values."

The activities unfolding in the square before them were coalescing into an event. Some quickened their pace and left the square. Numbers increased. Either there were far more fighters hiding in the mountains than Lucy had imagined, or they'd managed to find locals to join the assembly. At least a thousand people had shown up, including the soldiers. Their numbers were oddly reassuring. She'd only known Fidel for a week, but she was certain he wouldn't order a slaughter.

She kept an eye out until she finally spotted Desi toward the center. His hands were bound, and he was being escorted by two men. He'd always wanted to try his hand at a dramatic role, albeit without live ammunition. This would have been a good show if Fidel hadn't already figured out their idiotic ruse.

Fidel stood with his back to the railing. He removed his cap briefly to scratch his scalp. Neither he nor Lucy smoked. Movement ceased. Soldiers stationed themselves around the perimeter of the plaza, redirecting traffic away from the square.

Fidel reassured Lucy by patting her hand, which she'd unconsciously placed on his upper arm. She let go and took her stage stance —arms loosely at her side, feet together, slowed breathing.

Fidel turned to the crowd and raised his arms. In just seconds, everyone hushed and turned in his direction.

"Compañeros," he said, commanding the attention already settling upon him. "Today we will begin the next step in the revolución, the restoration of political power to the Cuban people."

The crowd interrupted with applause.

Four soldiers escorted Dr. Lopez and his son out through the great wooden door of the church behind Fidel and Lucy. Fidel silently instructed the soldiers to leave the Lopezes. They took up posts at either end of the terrace.

Lucy embraced Dr. Lopez and whispered her regrets. He nodded and patted her on the shoulder. She held his hand as he stood close and interpreted for her.

Castro continued his oration. "Why did we fight in the revolución? Because tyranny is blind and deaf and must be removed by force. Now, however, we must settle our differences in the forum of ideas, not on the battlefield. When dialogue ceases, so does society, for society exists only in the conversation of a people free to speak their own minds. This is the essence of freedom."

"Fidel," someone shouted. "It is time for you to go."

"I cannot abandon the revolution," he said.

"The revolution is over."

"The revolution has just begun," shouted a second man.

Fidel pointed out the man in the crowd and explained privately to Lucy. "This man is Dr. Emilio Ochoa. He was a leader of the Partido Ortodoxo before the revolución."

"He's not with you?" she asked.

"No. Different party. We don't see eye to eye."

"You are a traitor to socialism," Ochoa shouted.

"He is a traitor to democracy," shouted the first man.

"You see my dilemma," Fidel said to Lucy. "I can please no one."

The great wooden door swung open again, and Morgan joined them on the terrace.

"There is the real traitor," called another man. "Comandante Morgan has led us into Castro's trap."

Castro waved his arms, attempting to calm the crowd.

Desi stepped forward, but it soon became clear he'd been pushed. One of the men from the encampment with whom he'd been carousing the day before now held a gun to his head. Desi was white as a ghost.

Castro's soldiers raised their weapons. The crowd was corralled in the plaza. If the soldiers opened fire, it didn't matter who else had smuggled in weapons. It would be a slaughter.

Lucy rushed down into the plaza. Castro sent guards after her, but she was already in the street in front of the church by the time they caught up with her.

Desi looked at her with eyes that showed more regret than terror. Many of the resistance fighters now held handguns. They'd broken the bargain.

"No one is going to die here today," she shouted.

Behind her, Castro himself interpreted.

She raised her hands in a calming gesture. "Prime Minister Castro has proclaimed publicly that he and the government of Cuba will resume democratic elections as soon as legitimate political parties have been established."

The crowd moaned and grumbled.

"You've all been struggling for so long you've forgotten that it's possible to settle your differences without bullets. Dr. Lopez, whom many of you know, is dedicated to the restoration of democracy in Cuba. Recently Dr. Lopez's son, Marco Lopez, was murdered when a frustrated countryman of yours mistook him for my husband. The man thought we were here to support the prime minister, to recognize him as the next Cuban dictator."

"I don't find this helpful," Castro called down to her.

She held up a finger indicating he should give her a minute to explain. "We didn't know what we'd find here. My husband, who was forced out of Cuba by the Bolsheviks, has been opposed to the revolución. Like many of you, he's been suspicious of Prime Minister Castro."

"Also not helpful," Desi called.

"I can't vouch for Prime Minister Castro or his government," she continued. "I can only take him at his word. He promised to end the corrupt Batista government and throw out the American gangsters who controlled them with blood and money. Did he do it?"

The crowd murmured with agreement.

"He promised to open schools. Did he do that?"

Again, they agreed.

"He promised to send doctors and medicine to all parts of the country."

"Sí," said a smattering of voices.

She looked back at Fidel, who spoke privately to Dr. Lopez, and then the doctor and his son Fernando left the terrace through the church. No one spoke until they emerged from the street-level entrance.

Castro called upon everyone's attention. "So long as there is no threat to our sovereignty from within or abroad, Cubans will re-establish our democratic processes as defined by the Constitution of 1940, beginning in September 1961."

Lucy held out her hand. The man threatening Desi glared at her. He clearly wasn't convinced by Fidel's words, but she persisted. Castro's soldiers were all around them. The man didn't even bother to look again. If the soldiers opened fire, it would be like shooting fish in a barrel.

She couldn't vouch for Castro, but she looked this man in his eyes and laid it out for him, plain and simple. "Do you really prefer to die today, right now, when there's even a possibility he means what he says?"

The man handed her his pistol and released his grip on Desi. Whether he was motivated by resignation in the face of overwhelming force or by sudden enlightenment, she couldn't guess. And she didn't much care.

Desi and Dr. Lopez approached each other. They clasped hands, and Lucy embraced them both. Fernando walked past without acknowledgment. She could hardly blame him. He was entitled to his disdain.

Desi joined Lucy at her side.

She stepped to the next man and accepted his gun, and the next. Then the resistance fighters began coming to her. She couldn't hold all those weapons and frankly didn't want to, so they began laying them at her feet.

Her breath returned.

Desi whispered in her ear. "That was a pretty good speech. I think that bastard was really going to blow my brains out."

"I didn't do it for you—entirely."

LIFTING OFF

*L*ucy took the left seat, behind the driver of the Lincoln limo. Fidel had ducked in first, oddly taking the center position. He kept his hands on his knees, and the top of his head touched the headliner. The middle position was not a good place for a tall man to sit.

Desi sat to his right.

"We're ready to go home now," Lucy said.

"I assumed," he said.

She wiped a tear from her eye, and Castro politely fixed his gaze forward. Desi's face was fully obscured by Castro's robust figure and beard.

She shut her eyes and tucked her chin, once more replaying the afternoon's events. Calm began seeping into her like the warmth of the sun. Desi had dragged her into an impossible situation, and she'd managed to bring them through it. Outside of her success as a performer, she'd won victories now and then managing her career, but none had given her the sensation of triumph she was experiencing at that moment—nor the mental and emotional exhaustion.

She turned to Fidel, feeling no need to beat around the bush. "Did you use us?"

"I assure you I did not," he said.

Desi shrank away, pressing himself against the right passenger door.

"Do you have anything to say to me?" Castro asked him.

"I have nothing," Desi said.

"It's not kind to plan the capture or assassination of your host."

"Look," Desi said, "I don't know who you are or why you took over this country. This was a good place to live before it became a game for politicians and dictators."

"It was always a dictatorship. I will change that."

"Why should I believe you?"

"Whether you believe it is of no consequence," Castro said. "The truth belongs to the Cuban people who have stayed and kept their homes here. You are a Yankee now. I speak to you only as if you represent the rest of your countrymen, although I understand you do not. Ask your government to not act hastily. You've seen with your own eyes what Cubans have endured. They deserve the opportunity to determine their own future without interference from your government."

Desi rolled down his window. "And that's what you think you're giving them, self-determination? It looks like a prison to me. No one should live in a prison, with or without bars."

"A man—or woman," he said, turning his head to Lucille while continuing to address Desi, "who cannot live by her own principles is a prisoner—or worse, a slave."

She nodded, but Fidel had the advantage. He had the footage. What would come next was easy to predict. Sentiment in the US was running against these communists or socialists, or whatever they wanted to call themselves. When the film appeared, she would be dragged through the mud, and Desi alongside her. Despite everything she and Desi had endured for the past nineteen years, she wasn't out to destroy him. But here they were. How had they believed they could shoot all this film, that she could appear in it and yet suffer no ill consequences? They were ruined.

At least they'd had a good run. If there was a good time to call it quits, this was it.

They pulled into Antonio Maceo Airport outside Santiago de Cuba.

"You do not like me. You do not trust me. You owe me nothing," Castro said to Desi. "But I thank you for your courage. You saved my life."

"That was nothing but a show you put on," Desi said. "It must be somewhere in that fat script of yours."

"It was no trick. That man intended to take my life."

The woman in the front passenger seat, who Lucy had mistaken for another male soldier, opened the door for Desi, while the driver opened her door. Fidel walked them into the terminal. The other passengers waved and called greetings as they passed through the building and out onto the tarmac.

Although their plane was waiting, Castro led them toward a large crate that was about to be sealed and loaded into the plane's cargo hold.

"For you."

"What's in there?" Lucy asked.

"Your luggage." Castro took a steel film canister from one of his aides and showed it to her ceremoniously before placing it in the crate atop dozens of others. "This belongs to you. Use it, or do not, as you see fit. Your government will scrutinize it. We have no secrets. They wish to paint us as devils to protect the masters who have enslaved our people. This is their choice, but they will take nothing from these reels to support their propaganda. You may say whatever you wish, both of you. I, of course, have no power over you. I only ask you to speak the truth."

"And you," she said, "remember what I told you."

He raised his hand as in a pledge. "So long as the empire chooses to respect our sovereignty and the rights of the free Cuban people, I vow to take no action and forge no alliance that threatens the United States and its sovereignty or the rights of its citizens."

"The vote is a trust more delicate than any other," she said, "for it involves not just the interests of the voter but his life, honor, and future as well."

"You quote Martí." He choked up and swallowed hard.

With or without God, this man devoted himself to his beliefs. Whether he'd back them up with righteous deeds, as her preacher used to say, remained to be seen. She pressed his hand between hers. "I think I'm quoting you quoting Martí. Is it any less true?"

"More so when spoken by a friend of the Cuban people."

Desi was already boarding the plane. He never looked back. He ducked through the door and disappeared. Lucy turned and waved to the other Santiagans assembled to see them off before following him up the stairs.

Desi sat in a row at the rear of the otherwise empty cabin. Once they were airborne, he'd order a couple of drinks and then doze off.

Just as well.

She took a seat in a row near the front on the opposite side of the aisle. As the engines roared to life, she asked the flight attendant for paper and a pen. Cuba fell away behind her as she began tabulating their assets.

AFTERWORD

This is a work of fiction. To the best of my knowledge, Lucille Ball and Desiderio (Desi) Arnaz, iconic celebrities in the United States and around the world, never met Fidel Castro or traveled to Cuba after he and his revolutionary twenty-sixth of July Movement seized power in January 1959.

What is true is that the Arnaz marriage was stormy and by the end of that same year, Lucille and Desi had already agreed to divorce. This story takes place in January 1960, two months before they filed papers. Their business partnership complicated their marriage and dissolution, and not just materially. They'd built their careers and identities together. By the late 1950s, they owned and operated the most successful television production studio in Hollywood. Desi had been a shrewd businessman, more confident than his peers in TV's potential, and thanks to their combined artistic sensibilities, Lucy and Desi had become a power couple, moguls and superstars.

Although to my knowledge Lucille never openly confessed to fearing what would become of her career without Desi, I've speculated that these anxieties contributed to her almost superhuman tolerance of Desi's relentless infidelity and acute alcoholism, which began almost from the start of their nineteen-year marriage. It's said that it

AFTERWORD

takes two to tango, and Lucille's culpability in their marital friction is difficult to guess, as Desi politely limited his public criticism of Lucille both during and after their separation. However, according to countless eyewitness accounts, in their vicious arguments they both flashed sharp fangs.

I wrote this story as a tribute to Lucille, a late coming-of-age story in which she proves to herself, under the tutelage of an unlikely mentor, that she, a woman among the cigar- and bourbon-fueled tycoons of the screen industry, had the strength and intellect—or as she might have put it, the balls—to assume control of a major studio. She did. It's no longer widely known that as president of Desilu, Lucille Ball approved the production of blockbuster shows such as *Mission Impossible* and Gene Roddenberry's *Star Trek*, which was filmed in the soundstage formerly occupied by *I Love Lucy*, all the while continuing her onscreen career as one of America's favorite and independent funny ladies.

For fun and effect, I've staged the final throes of the Arnaz marriage against the metaphorically rich background of the nascent Cuban social revolution. Frankly, the idea of sending them into Castro's inner circle tickled me. It all started with a whimsical thought that popped into my head more than thirty-five years ago, a silly idea that periodically prairie-dogged out of my subconscious until I finally had to pay attention.

While America's Sweethearts found it impossible to live with each other and they each remarried not long after their divorce, they adored each other until their dying days. In fact, as lung cancer was stealing Desi's final breaths, Lucy sat at his bedside and comforted him, and likely herself, by repeating to him three times that she still loved him. It's a show business irony that often the unhappiest people delight us with their warmth, charm, and humor. I grew up in a culture partly shaped by the public personas of these brilliantly talented people, and I apologize to them both if I've made any grave errors while borrowing their souls to explore the nuances of both a tangled history and a creative yet tortuous relationship.

ABOUT THE AUTHOR

At age five, while on a family vacation from Chicago to Los Angeles, Scott Jarol swam in the pool at the home of Lucille Ball, his first tenuous brush with celebrity. And thus began a lifelong fascination with this cultural icon. Scott lives outside Seattle, Washington with his wife Nancy, one remaining teenager in a series of six great kids, and a lazy Staffordshire Bull Terrier named Pumpkin Pie.

To learn more about me and my interests in some of the most fascinating things happening in the world, both real and imaginary, visit my Web site at:

http://www.scottjarol.com

If you like, leave me your email address there, and I'll let you know when I have fun stuff to share, including new books, giveaways, and reading recommendations. I promise never to share your email address with anyone, and you can unsubscribe whenever you wish.

facebook.com/AuthorScottJarol

Made in the USA
Columbia, SC
17 February 2023

12269705R00243